PARAGON OF LIGHT

SPECTRUM LEGACY BOOK FOUR

BETH ALVAREZ

The Allied Kingdoms of Amroch
DESHENI
CHITHAL
BESHNAI
YITHEL
The Scar
AMROCHAN
Lake Sian
GANEDE
The Ellean Sea
SAST
ESTKEL
JADORA
KOLMAR
TINITH
ADDARE
IRAGE
NIMULTIS
PARRAL

CHAPTER ONE

THE WIND WHIPPED across Lark's face with such force, she could not bring herself to open her eyes. The few times she had, she wished she hadn't.

Peace, Your Highness, Vorkaris whispered into her thoughts. *We'll be stopping soon.*

The savage sound of the dragon's wings ripping through the air had left her all but deafened, and the cold bit so harshly she'd begun to wonder if she still had ears at all.

Two of them, the dragon said. *You haven't frozen the points off yet.*

She would have preferred the winged Magister stay out of her thoughts. Ironically, she supposed he'd hear that, too, a notion confirmed by the low rumble of a draconic chuckle she felt through her legs. She squeezed her knees tighter against his neck, willing him to stay focused.

A shift at her back let her know the movement hadn't been subtle enough. "You all right?" Zaide asked, the words little more than a breath beside her ear, though she knew he had to have shouted to make himself heard.

Lark set her jaw and nodded, but still did not open her eyes.

In response, his arms tightened around her. It should have

been reassuring, a gentle reminder they were in this together. Yet they weren't. They couldn't be. She was Dasienna Amroch, Crown Princess and future queen, and her father wanted her dead. How could a refugee peasant boy from a secluded forest ever understand?

A peasant boy and your Bladebearer, the dragon beneath her said.

She didn't appreciate the reminder. *Keep to your own thoughts, Magister, and I'll keep to mine.*

As you wish, he replied, though once again, she felt the distinct rumble of his amusement.

A shift in their altitude came before she could return to her sulking. By reflex, she gripped the crest on the dragon's neck and the rest of her went stiff.

Zaide leaned against her back, reaching around her to hold tight to the dragon, too. Lark dared crack one eye as he found a handhold and dug his fingers into the ridge. The dragon's crest wasn't quite a fringe, nor was it spikes, but a bony protrusion that reminded her of a mountain range. Or the jagged molars of a dog. The hard ridge bore a soft glow, like heated metal, just like the rest of the beast. Against the backdrop of his scales, Zaide's hands were a shadow, as were hers. Their hands were close, and a tiny, weak part of her wished he would touch hers, desperate for comfort and yet hating that she wanted it at all.

It had grown darker since the last time she dared to open her eyes, and she wasn't sure if that was better or worse. Where she had seen rolling landscapes below them before, now there was only a black void.

Vorkaris tilted farther downward and she found herself leaning back against Zaide, pulling on the dragon's crest as if it might slow his descent, but the air only came faster. Her insides lurched, and for a moment she didn't know if the pressure in her throat was her thundering pulse or her stomach threatening to revisit her last meal.

Hold tight, all of you, the dragon warned, as if she wasn't already doing just that.

A trio of responses went up behind her, Tula's excited whoop mingled with Zaide's uncertainty and Andriun's exclamation in his own tongue, its cadence that of profanity. She screwed her eyes more tightly shut than before and clamped her jaw, lest she scream.

She was Dasienna, princess and future queen, and she hated herself for fearing something so trivial as heights.

A sharp snap sounded and a sudden shift threw all of them forward. Lark gasped as her chest hit the dragon's solid crest, but Zaide's arms went rigid to either side of her and he kept her from falling off. He grunted as the weight of the others pitched against his back, but she scarcely felt it through him.

Lark dared not ask what that lurch had been.

That did not go as planned, the dragon said, somewhat sheepishly. His wings still stirred the air, but the air had slowed, and a second later, the way his forelegs flexed told her they'd landed.

"Yeah, no kidding," Zaide said.

Vorkaris ignored him. *We will rest here for the night.*

"Why? Are you tired?" Tula pushed herself from the dragon's back without regard for the drop, though she squeaked when she hit the ground and fell on her backside. Lark could scarcely make out the girl beside the dragon's glowing hind leg.

I could carry us to the other side of the world without tiring, but it is dark, and I am easy to see in the night sky. It is imperative that our movements remain hidden. Vorkaris lowered his belly to the earth for the rest of them to dismount.

"If you say so," Tula replied in a sing-song voice. She dusted herself off as Andriun slid down beside her to land with considerably more grace.

Zaide was slower to dismount, but the moment his boots touched the ground, he turned to offer his arms.

Lark contemplated letting him help. It would be easier, faster, but it showed weakness. Instead of accepting, she turned her back to him and ignored the offer in favor of clambering down on her own.

She would be queen. She could rely on no one.

For a moment, everyone stood silent. There was little to see, the soft glow of the dragon's hide not bright enough to illuminate wherever it was they'd stopped, yet it made everything around them appear darker. Everything had been brighter when the dragon's wings still shed embers. For the sake of his passengers, he had subdued the magic that made his wings smolder.

"We have passed the edge of the desert?" Andriun asked after a time.

That much should have been obvious. It was earth beneath their feet, not sand, though the grasses were dry and crunched when Lark stepped away. As her eyes adjusted, shadows she assumed were trees began to stand out in the dark of night. One pale mark near the top of one explained the crunch and lurch at landing. The clearing was small. The dragon had struck a tree.

No, but we have reached the coast. Addare is near. The cliffs here are low. Seawater feeds the trees, so the forests may flourish. Vorkaris turned his head. *That is the direction from which we have come. Another day's flight will take us to Nimultis.*

"That's amazing." Zaide hefted his bag up his shoulder. They all carried supplies, but most of their things had been tied into slings and tossed over the dragon's back. "It took us weeks to get through the Jadoran desert by wagon."

Roads meander and beasts of burden tire, was all the dragon said. He flexed his wings, then squatted his hindquarters low to shimmy out from under the rest of their luggage.

"Is there a reason we cannot stop near the city itself?" Andriun asked as he retrieved his trident from the pile. "I do not smell the water from here."

It is best we avoid all eyes. Including those of people. Vorkaris turned one snakelike eye toward Zaide, where it hung for too long to be comfortable.

Undaunted, Zaide stared back. "No campfire, then?"

It would be best. Despite his role as Magister—one he shared with Tula in a nuanced relationship Lark did not yet understand—the dragon sometimes struck her as meek.

Was that the right word? She frowned as she took one of the bedrolls from the pile of abandoned luggage and looked for a place to settle. He was ancient, as old as the role of Magister itself, yet he shied away from giving orders in her presence. His deference was appreciated, but she couldn't help but feel it was misplaced.

For as often as you remind yourself of your rank, you are quick to forget what it entails, Your Highness.

Lark twitched and turned her frown toward the dragon, but he wasn't looking at her. Instead, he trudged in a slow circle, trampling grasses and twigs. Then he settled, creating a wide ring of flat, open space encircled by his neck and tail. The action reminded her of a dog, she thought somewhat uncharitably.

Vorkaris gave a soft snort and coils of smoke rose from his nostrils. *Likewise, your rank affords you a certain level of leeway, but you should not push your luck.*

She bit the inside of her lip and carried her bedroll to the circle. The sooner they parted ways from the dragon and she had her thoughts to herself again, the better. "We shall rise early. The sky grows light before dawn. We will take flight then."

Tula made a fist and pumped her arm in victory. Beside her, Andriun groaned. Zaide said nothing at all, just fetched his things and made his way to join her. He meant to position himself at her side, she realized, putting himself nearby in case she needed defense.

Before he could take the spot beside her, she stuck out her leg to claim the space. "Tula, come roll out your bedding beside me. The boys can sleep on the other side."

Zaide paused, but his expression didn't change. He'd take it in stride, like he took so much. Lark reassured herself it was the best decision. Girls on one side, boys on the other. As if there was any need for defense when a dragon lay curled around them.

Without a word, Zaide moved to the far side of the modest camp and unrolled his bedding.

Tula hopped over the tip of the dragon's tail and unfurled her bedroll in midair. It fell slowly, stalled by the air beneath it. "I can't wait to set out in the morning. What could be better than flying into the sunrise?"

"Flying in the opposite direction of the sunrise, because we are supposed to be heading west?" Andriun suggested. The only gap that remained was between Tula's bedroll and Zaide's, so he took it without comment on the arrangement.

Tula pursed her lips and tilted her eyes skyward.

"Nimultis is southwest from here," Lark said as she settled. The others would want to eat, but her stomach was still so uneasy after the flight that she doubted anything would stay down.

"Oh." Either the Magister girl's cheeks reddened, or the soft, warm light of the dragon's hide lent her the look of embarrassment.

Lark chose to assume the latter.

Feeling more charitable now that you've banished your protector to the teeth end of me?

Ignoring the dragon proved harder and harder. *I don't need him to protect me,* she thought back at him. Perhaps meek was not the right word for the beast, after all.

It isn't always about what you need, Vorkaris said, his tone uncharacteristically soft. *Sometimes we must decide based on what we want.*

Her shoulders tightened. She forced them to remain down, unwilling to allow herself the shrug of discomfort her body craved. *Do you speak to the others that way?*

I have scarcely spoken to them at all. But as you say to yourself, you will be queen, and the two of us shall have to work together, Dasienna.

He'd never addressed her so informally. Her skin crawled with goosebumps. *Don't call me that.* The order rolled through her head before she could stop it. Not that it made a difference; the dragon would have heard even if she'd only meant to think it to herself.

And why had she thought it? Was it the need for secrecy, or something else? The visceral negativity the sound of her name sent through her warred with the desperate need to remind herself of who she was. She braced for some sort of lecture or criticism from the great horned beast beside her, but none came.

Instead, her mind grew uncomfortably silent, devoid of both his voice and her own.

At last, he gave a soft rumble. *Yes, avoiding use of your true name is wise. We hide now for the same purpose: to remain unnoticed. Forgive me, Your Highness.*

Lark felt no need to forgive anything, but the conversation had lodged an uncomfortable notion in the front of her mind. She rubbed her arms as if to ward off a nonexistent chill, her palms doing nothing to smooth away the goosebumps.

She didn't notice Zaide's approach until he crouched before her and held out a small paper envelope.

"Mint," he explained before she asked. "Chew it. It'll help."

"Help with what?" Lark squinted at the envelope, its end open in a wide diamond. Its contents were dark, but so was everything else. The envelope itself was only visible because it was pale.

"Your stomach." He flashed her a smile, inadvertently revealing the leaf he held between his own teeth.

Lark straightened where she sat. He'd given no indication the flight bothered him. After how long they'd spent on the ship that carried them from Amrochan to Jadora, she would have thought him immune to motion sickness. Then again, she wasn't.

Slowly, she dipped two fingers into the envelope and removed a few of the dried leaves.

He sat at the foot of her bedroll and folded the envelope, tucking its top flap into a slit to ensure nothing would escape. "Are you sure you're all right? Aside from that? I know I asked earlier, but—"

"You don't know anything," Lark muttered. The leaves were dry and crunched when she crushed them between her teeth, but they were sweeter than she'd anticipated, making the whole experience a little more pleasant.

"Exactly," Zaide said. "Not until you tell me, anyway."

She considered giving him an honest answer. That no, she wasn't all right; her own father had likely arranged for her demise, her kingdom was at war, and the weapon that could have changed their fates had been rendered powerless. Her eyes slipped to the Spectrum Blade sheathed at his side.

He moved in response, letting his hand hover over the hilt for a moment before he curled his fingers into his palm and exhaled.

"Anything?" Lark asked, already knowing the answer.

"More quiet than the moment we first saw it." He was calm, but there was no mistaking his resignation.

Her throat grew tight. Swallowing didn't help. "The Oracle will know what to do."

"I hope so," Zaide murmured. They'd spoken little of what he'd done. Lark wasn't sure he even knew. The sword's power had been remarkable, but the price of such power had put them further behind than ever before.

"She will," she said, hoping her determination helped. He wore his regret plain on his face, but she did not blame him for what happened. They'd had no way of knowing what might come of it, yet even if they had, she was not sure she would have made a different choice. Ganede had been under attack, and even Vorkaris could not have taken down all those warships on his own.

Debatable, the dragon grumbled into her thoughts, but she chose to ignore him.

Zaide did not appear comforted by her conviction. He searched her face, but said nothing more. It didn't matter whether or not she blamed him; he blamed himself. No amount of reassurance would undo that the action has been his, and whatever warning the Spectrum Blade had given, he'd ignored it.

Eventually, he put away the paper envelope and stood. "Hope the mint helps you sleep."

Lark didn't know what else to do, so she merely nodded and chewed. The dry herb was not unpleasant, but she didn't like the texture. The gesture of offering it, however, had been kind. "Zaide?" she said as he turned to leave. He didn't look at her, but he paused to await her question, all the same. "How did you know to bring mint?" She assumed he'd bought it in Ganede, during those frenzied hours of preparation after the destruction of the warships and before they'd mounted the dragon to take flight.

Zaide glanced at the dragon's horned head, then offered a wry smile. "Tula warned me." He nodded to the red-haired girl on the next bedroll over before he returned to his own. Tula, however, was oblivious. Despite her bedding being right next to Lark's, she'd given her attention to Andriun, and the two of them huddled with the Magister's notebook and whispered over what was written inside.

"What are you doing?" Lark asked.

They both startled, but Andriun drew back with a distinct look of guilt.

"Just going over some of my notes," Tula said. She waved her little book with a cheery smile, then gestured at the silver trident on the ground. "Working out some details of Desheni culture."

Lark stared at her, unimpressed. "There's time for that later. Rest. Tomorrow, we fly."

Instead of putting away her notebook, Tula turned to a fresh page and scribbled something. "And then?"

"Answers," Lark replied. At least, that was what she hoped came next.

Vorkaris rumbled and shifted, though he never opened his eyes. *We shall see.*

As their princess and future queen, Lark was supposed to be the expedition's leader. Yet, as she nestled into her bedroll and shut her eyes, she'd never felt so lost or unsure of where to go.

Unsettled, she turned onto her side so she faced away from the rest of the group, shielding herself from the responsibility that already lay too heavy on her heart.

CHAPTER TWO

Dragon flight was exhilarating. Zaide leaned sideways to watch the coast shrink away. They'd ventured southwest before sunrise, breaking away from the shoreline to cross over the sea. The speed with which the world vanished behind them was astounding, but the farther he leaned over to watch, the more rigid Lark became. Unwilling to frighten her, he righted himself and returned his arms to the position they'd held before, braced to either side of her rib cage.

Even two days ago, touching the princess with such familiarity would have filled him with dread. He was her Bladebearer, her guardian, but it was too easy to mistake intentions from the outside. Until now, he'd feared what King Sendassian might do if he misstepped. Now, he prepared to defend her against the king, too.

Zaide had tried to let her know, though she seemed unwilling to speak with him. She seemed unwilling to speak with anyone, for that matter. Ever since Magister Vorkaris had arrived with the news, she'd been frosty and distant.

Or, more so than usual, anyway. Zaide wasn't sure he'd ever call her friendly. The princess was prickly and difficult, uncooperative and unwelcoming, but he'd seen glimmers of something else. There was humor underneath the unpleasant exterior that reminded him of the tall, thorny cacti they'd seen in the desert. A certain tenderness, too, and a steadfast determination that any soldier would have envied.

Now, the walls she kept around her personality had grown taller and thicker, shutting out any hope someone might see the pieces that were Lark buried within the hard shell of Princess Dasienna. He understood, given all they'd heard, yet it left him frustrated. It hadn't been easy to get close enough to consider her a friend.

You would benefit from learning patience, the dragon's voice growled into his head.

Zaide twitched. He knew the dragon could hear their thoughts—he suspected the number of teeth Vorkaris sported in his maw limited his ability to communicate otherwise—but having someone else in his mind was uncomfortable. Still, he had to admit having an alternative method of speaking was useful. He shifted on the dragon's back and tried to think back at him. *Can you ask her if she's all right? For me?*

You already know the answer to that question.

It's still polite to ask, Zaide replied, though he admitted he knew. How could she be all right? She'd given up so much to help her father protect the Allied Kingdoms, and he'd thanked her by proving himself a threat. Even if Sendassian hadn't meant for the false Magister in Jadora to harm his daughter, he'd arranged for the previous Magister's demise, deliberately stalling their efforts. Why, Zaide couldn't fathom.

For a moment, the dragon was quiet. Then Vorkaris projected a sound of annoyance into his head. *She doesn't wish to speak with you.*

Zaide considered trying again, but no other questions came to mind. There were other things they could discuss, and things they probably should, but those were better left to when they could use their own voices to do it. Fewer chances for miscommunication, that way. He fought back a sigh. *Thanks for trying, anyway.*

The dragon-Magister said nothing else, and in the distance, the last glimpse of the shore they'd left slipped away.

At first, as the sun rose over the glittering sea, Zaide was content to watch in silence and marvel at the waves so far beneath them. But as the sea stretched on and nothing else came into view, even that breathtaking sight became wearisome. The rushing winds stole their voices, and so he was left alone with his thoughts—the last company he wanted to keep.

More than once, his hand drifted to the Spectrum Blade at his hip. He'd checked a hundred times over, let his fingers play across the hilt and hoped for a response. He'd grown so used to the tingle of its presence, an awareness he couldn't explain. Every time he touched it now and felt nothing, it made his insides ache with growing uneasiness.

But the Oracle would know what to do. He reminded himself of that as he returned his hand to the dragon's neck ridge, letting his arms encircle the princess once more. He'd check the sword another thousand times before they landed, he was sure, but every time he moved, Lark grew tense before him and he suffered a pang of guilt.

Behind him, Andriun and Tula fidgeted and shifted, the sound of laughter occasionally rising above the noise of the wind. He couldn't see what they were up to, but he was the buffer between their horseplay and the princess's comfort, so he tried to ignore them. That left only stillness, staring into the sky and sea with the noisy and worrisome thoughts in his head.

At some point, Lark shifted and leaned back into him, her eyes closed, and he suspected she'd fallen asleep. Worry traced deep lines between her brows even then, and all at once she struck him as small and fragile, a frightened and helpless girl trapped in a world that refused to give her peace. The impression was even more unsettling than his own thoughts and he tightened his arms around her. If she knew rest and safety nowhere else, he'd do what he could to give it to her in that moment. He fixed his mind on that —the sole act of protecting his charge—and let the hours slip by.

Eventually, when his legs and back ached miserably and he'd begun to wonder the logistics and wisdom of an hours-long trip over the sea, Zaide spotted a glimmer of something outlined against the afternoon sun. He squinted, then shaded his eyes. Lark shifted against him and he responded by wrapping his other arm around her, lest she feel she might slip.

Is that Nimultis? He thought at the dragon.

Vorkaris rumbled. *That is the island that hosts Nimultis. It is a city, not the entire land form. Nimultis is on the eastern coast, near the center. To the north is Irage.*

Zaide tried to recall the island from the few maps he'd ever seen. *We'll stop there, right? In Irage?*

For a moment, the dragon did not respond. From the way Lark moved, Zaide assumed he was speaking with her. That was fair; Lark was the one in charge of the expedition.

When the dragon finally replied, his tone was flat. *We will go as far as we are able.*

Somehow, Zaide didn't find that promising. *I definitely suggest a short stop on land. We need to stretch. And get something to eat.*

We will reach Nimultis tonight.

You can reach Nimultis after taking a short break in Irage, he argued.

This time, the dragon's response came as a growl that vibrated through Zaide's legs and up his entire body. Wisely, he chose not to press further.

Despite the dragon's disagreement, they banked downward as soon as the island's pale beaches were in view.

Zaide saw no sign of the northern city, but supposed it wouldn't be hard to land where they wouldn't be seen. Dense forest covered the island, starting at the edge of the sandy shore and sweeping up over the mountains at the island's heart. The vibrant greens put an odd longing in the pit of his stomach, an uneasy yearning for a version of home he knew no longer existed.

All four passengers scrambled off the dragon's back the moment they touched down. There were a number of problems with long flights, Zaide concluded as he stomped feeling back into his legs and watched the others scuttle in different directions, but at least the island bore plenty of trees.

That's enough, Vorkaris announced as soon as he deemed his passengers properly refreshed.

"I haven't even gotten to eat yet," Tula protested, though she shuffled across the sand to rejoin the dragon. They hadn't been allowed much freedom to stretch their legs, so none of them had gone far.

Lark crossed her arms and looked doubtfully toward the sky as the others gathered near. "I don't see how you can possibly think of food now."

"It is not so bad. It is much like riding waves of water," Andriun said. After a pause, he added, "I think."

"You think?" Zaide stepped forward to assist the princess in climbing back onto the dragon, but she ignored him and ascended to her seat on her own.

Andriun grinned. "To be honest, I have not spent much time in the sea. The waves in the lake were not impressive."

"Quit chattering and help me up." Tula prodded him in the ribs, then pantomimed lifting.

"You have legs. Hands, too, that do not seem to know any manners." Andriun batted her hand away, but despite his protests, he inched closer to the dragon's side and offered a boost.

Zaide watched with the slightest tingle of envy as the Paragon of Water lifted Tula until she could reach the dragon's back and pull herself up to take her place. It wasn't that he wanted Lark to need him, exactly, and more that the smile Tula offered when she sat astride Vorkaris was appreciative in a way he'd never gotten from Lark. He'd sacrificed so much to help the princess. His eyes drifted to the thick forests that sloped up the island and again, he thought of Kolmar.

Mount, Vorkaris growled into his thoughts.

Startled, Zaide turned back. The others had already settled in. The gap between Lark and Tula was small, but they held that space for him, and all three of his companions looked down at him with expectant faces. Four companions, he corrected himself; the dragon stared at him, too, though he suspected that was with disdain.

I would gladly leave you behind, but I fear the princess has forbidden it, Vorkaris said as Zaide dragged himself onto the dragon's back.

"Of course." He squeezed in between the girls and tried not to sulk.

Lark wiggled about, adjusting herself until they were nestled together as comfortably as they could be. "I hate this part," she muttered as the dragon rose to his feet and spread his wings.

Zaide reached around her to let his fingers find the now-familiar shapes in the dragon's crest. "I've got you."

"I know," she said. "You always do."

The acknowledgment wasn't a thank-you, but it was the closest to appreciation he thought he'd get.

Vorkaris launched himself into the air without preamble, as he had that morning.

Lark groaned and tucked in her chin, a sentiment Zaide felt to his bones. Every inch of him ached after sitting astride the dragon for hours on end, two days running, gripping with his legs and trying to keep from being crushed between the other passengers. He couldn't offer verbal reassurance, what with the noise of liftoff, but he patted her arm and hoped it conveyed sympathy.

Before the day was over, they'd reach their destination and receive the guidance they so desperately needed.

With hope, Vorkaris said, and the doubtful note in the dragon's tone conveyed none.

~

When the first glimmers came into view, Zaide thought it a trick of the light against the sea. He tried to focus, but the harder he stared at them, the fainter each speck of light became.

They'd followed the island's coast south. Tula had claimed a trade route ran between Nimultis and Irage, citing maps she'd studied in the Grand Library of Jadora, but he'd seen no sign of anything but endless trees. Even those faded into nothing but shadows as the sun fell below the edge of the sea, and some time after that, the first twinkles appeared.

The lights were sparse, a faint line that traced a path along the beach, leading toward something he couldn't see. Then, all of a sudden, the coastline fell away to reveal an inlet, and he put a hand on the princess's shoulder.

"Hey," he half-shouted beside Lark's ear. "Open your eyes. You'll want to see this."

Her shoulders tensed, but he knew the moment she looked, for he felt his awe mirrored in the gasp that moved her whole body.

The city of Nimultis lay below, a sprawling series of stairways and tiers carved into the side of a cliff and surrounded by jungle. Lights glittered everywhere in the night, soft shades of yellow and gold, like warm stars fallen to the earth. Fire pits sat in open spaces, ringed by figures in white, their bodies little more than pale flecks against the backdrop of dark stone. Most people in the city carried lanterns, judging by the way the lights flowed down staircases and through narrow avenues, but the moment they noticed Vorkaris in the sky, their behavior shifted.

"Look!" Tula shouted, as if Zaide wasn't already. She pointed toward the city as people flowed toward one of the open spaces, assembling themselves near one of the fire pits and holding their lanterns aloft. They moved around the flames in a spiral, spreading farther and farther, then collapsing inward until their lights created the symbol of a sun.

Zaide leaned back and turned his head, hoping the human Magister would hear his shout. "What does that mean?"

"The mark of the Paragon of Light," Tula yelled back. She wiggled about with such energy that he put a hand back to stop her, lest she fall. His hand bumped someone else's, and he caught Andriun's laugh over the roar of the wind.

"So they know why we're here," Zaide said as he straightened, though he knew his voice was too low for anyone to catch the words. He'd trust Andriun to keep the Magister in place. He needed to focus on Lark.

Hold tight, children, Vorkaris rumbled into his thoughts. *It's time to land.*

They spiraled downward, slowing with each ring of their descent, until the crowd of people expanded to a wide circle and the gusting winds churned by the dragon's wings extinguished the fire in the center of the plaza. Vorkaris landed atop its smoldering remains.

"I am not a child," Andriun protested the moment the dragon's wings grew still.

"Don't tell him that," Tula said. "He'll give you more responsibilities."

Hush.

A cluster of people approached from the cliff side of the plaza, where doors and windows were cut into the stone. They walked in a V formation, with the people in either wing holding large lanterns. The dark-skinned man in the lead held nothing, and he spread his hands in greeting. "Welcome, Your Highness. We are honored by your arrival."

"How did they know it was us?" Zaide asked in a whisper.

"Don't be stupid," Lark murmured back. "This place is home to the Oracle."

"Yeah, but I didn't think she'd be anticipating everything we did. Is she watching us?"

The Oracle sees everything, whether she wishes to or not, Vorkaris said.

Lark pushed herself free of her seat at the base of the dragon's neck, though she winced. After staying in one place for so long, all of them would hurt. "I am honored by your welcome," she called as she climbed down unaided. "But I fear you have me at a disadvantage, for I don't know your name."

"You will learn what you need in time," the man reassured her. He glanced up and studied the rest of them with interest. "You are welcome here. All of you."

Zaide didn't like the way the man's dark eyes weighed on him as he said the last part, but he put his head down and focused on getting his feet on the ground.

"Thank you for your hospitality. It will be treasured after our voyage." The princess touched her chest to mirror her gratitude.

"Indeed. You have come far." The man smiled wide, his teeth as white as the clothing he wore, both stark against the deep tones of his complexion.

Zaide took his position at Lark's back as the others climbed down from the dragon. His hand twitched toward the hilt of the Spectrum Blade out of instinct, but he made himself curl his fingers into his palm. Touching it no longer brought comfort.

As Tula and Andriun stepped forward to flank them, the man moved aside and his followers split, forming two columns. One by one, they raised their lanterns high, and a hush fell as a figure appeared in the arched doorway they framed.

"Welcome, Dasienna," the woman said as she stepped from the shadows and light cascaded over her. A soft smile graced her weathered features and deepened the crinkles at the corners of her eyes. She wore white, like the rest, but her dress was embroidered with golden thread and a wide belt of gold encircled her waist. Patterns like the swirl and sun the lantern bearers had created on the plaza scrolled up her arms, painted on her dark skin with something that shimmered in the light. A diadem glittered on her brow, accentuating the aged gray-white of her hair. She turned her smile toward the others. "Welcome, Paragons."

Vorkaris gave a low, pleased croon. *Ah, Oroduna. You've grown even more divine than the last time I laid eyes on you.*

She gave a soft snort of a laugh. "That forked tongue of yours is still silver, I see." Her eyes twinkled as she smiled up at the dragon, but then her gaze fell to Zaide.

The moment their eyes locked, a surge of *something* washed over him, powerful enough to be crushing, chasing the air from his lungs. Confusion and instinct warred; the latter won. He sank to one knee and bowed deep.

The Oracle stopped before them and tilted her head. "Why do you kneel before me, broken-born?" Her voice was soft, tender and touched with curiosity.

It took strength just to find air. Power still bore down on him, weighing him down. His chest ached and he lowered his head, unable to make himself look her in the eye. "I don't know," he admitted, the soul-deep compulsion beyond anything he understood.

Inexplicably, Oroduna stepped forward and rested a hand atop his head. Her touch was warm, comforting. "Much of your life has been darkened by the shadow. No one so young should know so much loss. But shadow is ruled by the light, and it will not darken your fate forever. Rise, child. You are among friends."

The sensation of burden did not abate, but Zaide gathered his strength and made himself stand.

A soft, warm smile touched the Oracle's face when he managed to look at her again. She was tall; Zaide himself was not short, but they stood eye to eye, and again, meeting her gaze gave him a stroke of compulsion. "How do we fix the sword?"

"Zaide," Lark almost snapped.

Oroduna remained unruffled. "You already know the answer."

"I know we need the Paragons," he said, though part of him wished he could shut his mouth and wondered why he could not. "But how do we find them? How do we get them to help?"

"Fear not, Bladebearer. Your answers are here." Her smile

faded and she turned to Lark. "Many answers, for you have many questions."

The princess grew solemn.

"Your arrival was foreseen," the Oracle said, "and so we have prepared a meal and private quarters for each of you. You will be given time to refresh yourselves, then food will be served. Please, come with me." She turned with her hands clasped before her stomach and glided back toward the doorway.

"Do you think she has foreseen that we will follow?" Andriun asked in a conspicuous whisper.

Tula elbowed him in the ribs and trotted ahead, her notebook already in her hand. He grumbled something, but followed, rubbing his side all the while.

Zaide started after them, but Lark hesitated, so he turned back. "What's wrong?"

Her face grew wistful as she gazed after the Oracle. "Answers change things, sometimes."

That, he understood. "You're worried you'll hear something you don't like?"

"I'm worried what everyone will hear."

"Well, don't be." Zaide flashed her a grin and found it came a little easier; whatever the crushing pressure over him had been, it had faded, leaving him feeling more like himself. "We all knew what we were getting into when we decided to come along." He offered a hand.

Lark stared at it for a long moment, then strode past without touching him.

He fell in step behind her, electing not to take it as a snub. She'd always been independent. Now was no different. Part of him wondered if his words had offered any comfort, though, and his thoughts drifted from there. He didn't understand what could worry her. They'd already learned of King Sendassian's betrayal, the Spectrum Blade's weakness, and that they would need to turn to their enemy to restore its power. How much worse could the Oracle's visions be?

CHAPTER THREE

THE DOORWAY through which the Oracle had disappeared led into the face of the cliff. It took them to a series of hallways, but it also led up. Zaide caught sight of Andriun's back as they scaled the stairs. Lark had seen, too, for she moved in that direction.

The lantern bearers filed in after them, but instead of following them up the stairs, most of them turned to disappear down the halls. Only four trailed after them. One for each member of their party, he noted. Or, that was how many members of their party were inside.

Zaide glanced over his shoulder. "Is it rude of us to leave Vorkaris out there alone?"

It's rude of you to assume you have the authority to leave a dragon anywhere, the beast growled into his thoughts.

Embarrassment sent heat rushing to his ears. "Sorry," he muttered.

Lark gave him a thoughtful frown. "I was going to say no, but it sounds as if he's chastised you already."

"Chastised," Zaide repeated. "Right."

At the top of the stairs, they emerged onto a narrow walkway from which the plaza they'd landed in was visible. The dragon was no longer there.

"Magister Vorkaris has accommodations of his own," the Oracle said, as if she anticipated Zaide's question. A moment later, he decided that was precisely what had happened. They'd come to seek her wisdom, to take advantage of her ability to see through time. Why wouldn't she know what he was thinking?

"He addressed you by name before," Zaide said. "You know each other?"

The Oracle nodded. "That should come as no surprise. We have been friends for a long time."

"How does that work?" Tula asked. "Vorkaris was asleep for ages. As in, entire Ages. And you're kind of, um... Alive?"

A soft, lilting laugh came with the Oracle's response. "How is it my longevity surprises you, but my ability to see your destiny does not?"

Tula tilted her head, considered that a moment, and simply turned her attention to her notebook.

The Oracle did not stop walking, but led them into a new doorway and up another flight of stairs. "Magister Tula, your room is first. Shaman Andriun, yours is beside hers." She gestured as they reached the top of the stairs and emerged onto another walkway. This time, two of the lantern bearers that trailed behind them moved forward. "These two shall escort you and aid you with whatever you need. They will deliver your belongings to your quarters, as well as notify you when it is time to convene for the evening meal."

Andriun pressed one webbed hand flat against his chest, his fingers spread. "Thank you, Oracle Oroduna. You do us great honor, but I am only the Paragon of Water. I am not Shaman."

"That is not what I have seen," she intoned softly.

The Desheni hunter blinked twice. "You have seen this? My future? My people?"

"Of course, and I will be more than happy to answer your questions later."

A broad grin split his features and he gave a stiff but formal bow. "Then I thank you, Oracle. You are most gracious."

She smiled and waved him away, then turned as he departed with his new escort. "This way, please, Your Highness."

Zaide hadn't been addressed, but the two remaining lantern bearers continued up the next flight of stairs with the princess and the Oracle, so he followed, too. This time, instead of leading to a terrace on the face of the cliff, it led to a deeper hallway and a third stairway. They continued upward until they emerged onto a plaza, much like the one where they made their landing, but this one was framed with flowers and trees and the dense canopy sheltered it from the sky.

"Your Highness, your quarters are that way." The Oracle pointed and a lantern bearer stepped forward to escort Lark.

Zaide looked after her, a hint of uneasiness in his heart. She did not so much as glance his way as she turned to follow her new guide.

"Zaide," the Oracle said softly.

He startled at the sound of his name. It made sense that she would know it, yet he hadn't expected to hear it used.

Deep, mirthful creases deepened around her jet black eyes. "Walk with me."

Despite the invitation, he hesitated. "Am I going to my room?"

"Of course you are." She tilted her head toward the far end of the plaza, where the jungle grew dense and small stone lanterns lit the way.

"Oh. Lead the way, then, Miss Oracle. Uh, Missus. Are you married?" Zaide stumbled over the question and then averted his eyes. What a stupid thing to ask. There he was, walking with an ancient who could see through time itself, and the first question out of his mouth was about her marital status.

She giggled, the sound sweet and girlish. "Yes, I am married. Or I was, long ago. But you may call me Oroduna. We are friends, Zaide, though you do not know it yet."

He felt he ought to argue, or at least offer some sort of polite resistance, but all that came out was a murmur of thanks.

They continued past the edge of the plaza and into the sheltered path that cut through the jungle trees. The ground was hard-packed dirt, perfectly smooth and free of pebbles and weeds. It muffled the sound of his boots, and all around them, night insects sang. They'd gone some distance before he realized the lantern bearer had not followed.

"He will be along," Oroduna said when he looked back. "Don't worry."

The path was sinuous, winding around the dense growth and blocking what lay ahead. Belatedly, he realized she had not confirmed his room was their destination, only that he would end up there. "Where are we going right now?"

"There is a garden this way. It's peaceful. Quiet. I have seen the tumult of your mind. If anyone needs quiet, it is you."

Zaide wasn't sure he agreed, but he wasn't going to argue with the Oracle.

Eventually, the path ended in a round clearing that held nothing but a solitary stone bench. Lanterns ringed the area, their flames soft and welcoming. Oroduna strode to the bench, sat down, and patted the space beside her.

Unable to think of a reason to refuse, he crept forward and sat, then leaned forward until his elbows rested against his knees. His back and backside ached, as did his thighs. The long ride across the sea had not been difficult, but it hadn't been comfortable, either.

"I will speak with each of you, while you are here," the Oracle said without preamble. "I know you would ask. You are selfless that way, putting the others before yourself. They will have their turns."

His pulse sped. "What are we supposed to speak about?" Something she knew? Some warning she had to give? A reprimand for his mistakes? His fingers twitched, but he made his hand be still. The Spectrum Blade wasn't going anywhere, and its powerless touch offered no reassurance.

"Whatever you wish. A thousand questions burn within you. More than your friends. I sensed them within you from the moment you set foot on this island. So, whatever it is you wish to know, you may now ask."

Whatever he wished to know. Zaide's heart went from racing to pounding. Questions *had* burned in him, ever since the Spring Choosing when the Elder had pulled him aside. "Before we start, are there rules? Do I only get a certain number of questions?" Her estimate of a thousand probably hadn't been far off.

"No rules," she replied with a small laugh. "I cannot answer everything. I cannot see everything. Questions of the past come more easily. Questions of the future... sometimes those are murky, or beyond my sight altogether. We will continue until my sight grows dim and answers come to me no more."

His fingers twitched again, and this time, he allowed himself to touch the sword. "Will I be able to fix it? What I've done?"

Oroduna laid a hand atop his, squeezing his fingers to the blade's hilt. "You will know what you must do when the time comes. It will not be easy, but restoring its strength is within your power."

Relief poured over him, washing away aches he hadn't known rested in his shoulders. A moment later, sense caught up. "That wasn't a yes."

"The future is rarely a yes or no. What I see is only a collection of potential outcomes based on what has already occurred. Things that have yet to take place can alter the path of what is to come. A single person's path is not predestined the way you may like to think. It is not a single road the Maker has laid before you, but something that branches endlessly, like the limbs of a tree. I can see the tip of every branch, every potential path from where you stand now. Even if I could see the exact path you will take, the branches before you have yet to grow. The end is rarely the end."

So he should temper his expectations. He nodded slowly.

"Ask," Oroduna said simply.

Zaide considered his next question with more care. If her answers were vague, he'd be better served by being as tight and specific with his wording as possible. If his questions had answers at all. "I guess you can't tell me if we'll win this." It was the next most pressing issue, yet her explanation of what she could and couldn't see had already told him a clear answer was unlikely.

Oroduna shrugged. "Any outcome is possible. I see many ways for which this may unfold. I can give no immutable answer, but I can tell you that no matter who wins in the end, the battle will be costly."

"Wars always are," Zaide murmured. "All right, what about Lark? How can I help her?"

"You already are. No one could ask for any more. Stay your course. You help more than you know."

He shook his head, unsatisfied. "There has to be something else. She's been through so much. I can't just... What about Sendassian? What do we do if—"

"Zaide," the Oracle interrupted, gently scolding. "Your friends will have time to ask after their own problems. Do you mean to ask nothing for yourself?"

Of course he did. He shut his mouth and gave a single nod.

"Then why don't you?"

"It's just... all I've ever wanted to know just seems trivial in the face of..." He waved a hand. "Everything."

"Nothing that weighs on you is trivial." She patted his shoulder. "But I know you are nervous. We will speak when you are ready. We have time."

Until the others started to wonder what was taking so long. Would they be served a meal without him? Would they know he'd wandered off with the Oracle? Lark might have seen them go. Or maybe she'd never bothered to look back. Zaide laced his hands together and hung his head.

He doubted she'd looked. She'd remained cold with him after their landing, and though he couldn't blame her, it stung.

Much in his life had stung.

Zaide exhaled through his nose and made himself rake his fingers through his hair. It shouldn't have been so difficult to push questions to the tip of his tongue, but now that he tried, he moved them as easily as he might have moved one of the dragon's legs. He mustered what strength he could to get the first real question beyond his lips. "Is this why the Elder kept me in Kolmar?" He didn't need to indicate the sword at his side; surely the Oracle already knew what he meant.

"He knew the enormity of the task that lay before you, yes."

His nose crinkled. "Do you mean enormity like size, or like how bad everything is?"

"Can it not be both?" She raised a brow in challenge.

"I guess it can."

A hint of mischief sparked in her eyes. "Would you have learned both meanings of that word if you had not been the Elder's apprentice for a full year?"

Zaide gave her a dirty look.

"He knew you were needed for greater things than the battlefield. You have been there. You have seen the struggle and the waste. Yours would have been another life thrown at the flames, unable to quell them. You were needed here." Oroduna pressed a finger to the bench, grounding him in the moment.

"Then why do I feel like I'm ruining everything by being here? Like I ruined the only chance my friends had to end this?"

The Oracle shook her head. "Was it not the blade that told you to wield her power that way? To swing and let her might free?"

His brows drew together. "Her?"

"You have heard its voice, have you not?" A soft smile graced her lips. Her whole face warmed when she did that, the wrinkles of age making her look more friendly than she might have otherwise. "I have never been sure how to refer to the sword's spirit, to speak the truth. But I like to think of her as a sister. We are family, in a way. The sword. Myself. Vorkaris. Gadranus."

The last name sent a chill up his spine. "I wouldn't want him as family."

"We are all connected, no matter what you desire," Oroduna said.

Zaide supposed that was true. The Paragons were linked to the sword's power, and the Bladebearer was linked to Gadranus and his ultimate fate. Those connections held all of them together, but they were nothing like family. He stared at the earth under his feet. "I have another question."

"I know."

"How come you don't just give me the answers, then? If you know everything I'm going to ask?" That came out sharp enough that he winced, but there was no taking it back now.

To his relief, Oroduna was not offended. "As I said, I know a thousand questions plague your heart. But like the branching of the trees, I do not know which twig shall be our final perch." She motioned toward the trees above them as she spoke.

He glanced up. "I'm pretty sure palm trees don't have branches."

"Ask your question," she laughed, "before I send you to bed with no dinner in your belly as penance for that tongue."

Zaide suspected he'd deserve it. "My father," he said in a rush, not quite a question, yet the one that had plagued him the most.

The Oracle sobered. "Yes."

For a time, silence hung between them, burdened and thick. It made an itch crawl along Zaide's spine. "Yes what?"

"Yes, it is natural you would wish to know more about him. He was a good man. He would be proud of what you have achieved."

His heart sank. "Was."

"You have long known this to be true, Zaide. You hoped for news, but you never truly hoped to learn he was alive."

He hadn't. And yet some tiny part of him had longed for the impossible, and that part of him recoiled in pain now. "I did. A little. I just... I have nothing, you know? Nothing. I've never even known his name."

"Your mother called him Dharran."

"My mother never spoke of him at all," he fired back, knowing his frustration was misplaced.

Oroduna touched his shoulder, her hand warm and soothing. "He fell with great honor."

"To an enemy who has none. The shadow wasted his valor."

She shook her head firmly. "The shadow and the darkness are not the same, Zaide. Light and darkness are locked in an eternal battle, but light and shadow must coexist. One cannot be without the other. Where there is light, there can be no darkness, but there will always be shadow. You cannot compare them, and you cannot forget that."

His jaw tightened until a muscle in his cheek twitched, but he made himself nod.

The Oracle sat in silence for a while, stroking his shoulder the way a grandmother might. Fitting, he supposed, given her age, and yet that too was a harsh reminder of everything that had been stolen from him.

"How did he die?" he asked at last.

Pity touched her dark eyes. "At the hand of Gadranus."

Somehow, he had known.

"But you must not let this consume you," she added. "Your task does not change."

It couldn't. Gadranus would die by his hand. What had become of his father made no difference. All he could do was move on. He forced himself to nod, then swallowed hard. "I have one more."

"You may ask."

"Does Lark hate me?"

Oroduna's brows climbed. "I believe you already know the answer to that. And I believe your friends will be ready, and all of you will be hungry. Our time for conversation must draw to an end. There is just one last thing to discuss." She rose.

Zaide shifted to the edge of the bench. "What?"

Her eyes narrowed and took the empty, distant look of someone lost in thought. "The time will come for your actions to shape the way forward. Are you prepared?"

Wasn't that what he'd been doing? What he'd already done? "I think so?" he stammered out.

Oroduna raised her chin and her gaze focused on him again, though all its warmth was gone. "I suppose we shall see, won't we?"

The lantern bearer they'd left behind appeared on the path.

Slowly, Zaide stood. "What if I have more questions?"

"We will speak again," the Oracle said. "If the Maker wills it, you will have the chance to ask." She gave a nod of farewell and turned without waiting for his response.

"Come, Bladebearer," the man with the lantern said. "Your quarters are ready. You will have a few minutes to prepare."

Zaide lingered, watching as Oroduna slipped away, back the way they'd come. "Right." He'd asked the questions that were heaviest on his heart. He should have felt lighter.

Instead, the question she'd asked of him left him more burdened than ever before.

CHAPTER FOUR

LARK DID NOT FEEL ready when her escort returned. She'd scarcely been afforded a chance to wash her face and remove the tangles from her hair before the woman came knocking. Lark resolved not to be cross with her; a full night's sleep would not have made her any more prepared for the conversations to come.

"Are you refreshed, Your Highness?" the lantern bearer asked cheerily.

Lark refrained from telling the truth. "I suppose. It took forever to brush out my hair." She dreaded to think of the trip back to the mainland. Would Vorkaris carry them again? Or could they afford the time needed to travel by ship? Belatedly, she realized that her hair should have been her last worry. What was vanity in the face of war?

The woman at the door offered the sweetest of smiles. "Tomorrow, you shall have a dozen attendants to see to your needs. Fear not, the Oracle has spent much time preparing for your visit. She will not be concerned by the state of your hair." The faintest hint of a teasing sparkle touched the woman's eyes, and despite herself, Lark smiled back.

They walked together, not retracing the path they'd taken, but instead making their way to a large stone plaza atop the cliff.

Tantalizing scents rose with the smoke from fires that illuminated the obvious feast.

"We began cooking your welcome dinner this morning," the lantern bearer told Lark as they approached. Dozens of people in the same white robes sat around low tables that already hosted trays of food.

"Because you knew we would come," Lark murmured. It was no surprise, but having so many people prepare for their arrival before they'd even decided to come left her unsettled. She suspected the lantern bearer anticipated such thoughts, for she cast an uncomfortably knowing smile over her shoulder.

The tranquility of these people made her uneasy, Lark decided as she let herself be led to what she assumed was a place of honor. Tula and Andriun were already there, and Tula's notebook was peculiarly absent.

"Oh, wow, your hair." The Magister clapped her hands to her mouth too late to hide her smile.

Tula's delight at her appearance was a small reassurance; Lark did not often wear her hair down.

She averted her eyes and offered a thank-you to her escort before she sat. There were cushions on the flagstones in place of chairs, and while there were lanterns everywhere, the golden light they cast made her feel sleepy. A stiff chair would have been welcome to keep her awake.

As she folded her legs and sat back on her heels, she studied the food. Plates heaped with dishes both familiar and strange waited for them, covered with domes of glass. Some were fogged with rising steam and kept her from identifying them, but she recognized several plates as traditional foods from Amrochan.

"They have taken great care in making us feel welcome," Andriun said. The Shaman—as the Oracle had named him— inspected the food the same way she did, and his appreciative smile when he examined some made it clear which dishes were Desheni cuisine.

"They have had a long time to prepare." Lark gathered her loose hair over one shoulder and hoped it wouldn't get in her way. She'd grown so used to wearing it back in a ponytail or braid that having it tumble loose about her shoulders now struck her as inconvenient.

"Did you see the desserts?" Tula asked in a conspiratorial whisper. "I passed the table as my escort brought me over here. I've never seen so many treats in my life!"

Lark hadn't looked and didn't care to, not with the lump of dread that sat in her stomach. They were greeted with a celebration, but the reason for their visit was hardly worth celebrating. Did the apparent comfort of their hosts bode well for the trials ahead? Or was this meant to be a farewell?

Across the plaza, a group of men and women with lanterns escorted the Oracle toward the center of the feast. More people appeared, carrying a smaller table, and they settled it in the center of the flagstones, atop the heart of a spiral pattern Lark hadn't noticed before. The Oracle looked her way before she sat, a soft but saddened smile on her lips.

The lump in Lark's stomach grew heavier.

She will speak with you after we eat.

Lark startled, though the dragon's voice in her thoughts had grown familiar during their flight. She hadn't seen Vorkaris at first, but he lay at the edge of the plaza with a whole roast pig before him and a smug look on his draconic face.

Do you know what she has to say? She squinted as she thought back at him. She'd never quite determined how he knew when she meant to speak with him in her mind, but part of her preferred if it stayed a mystery. Her head was full of bitter thoughts, and the notion of someone else seeing everything that passed through her mind was disconcerting, to say the least.

I am not the Oracle, or we would not be here, Vorkaris replied with an odd touch of humor. He had not struck her as a light-hearted spirit. The pig must have put him in a good mood.

He must have heard that thought, too, for when he spoke

again, his tone was flat. *You think me terribly shallow. Whatever joviality I feel, it is due to the company we keep. Oroduna is a dear friend, and I have few left.*

Lark kept from wincing, though barely. She would have to do a better job of guarding her thoughts if she meant to remain diplomatic. *You had been asleep for centuries before we met you in Jadora. How can you know the Oracle?*

Her story is hers to tell, was all the dragon said.

"There's Zaide," Tula said. "Oh, he looks unhappy."

Lark blinked as if that could clear the dragon's voice from her head, then trained her eyes on the last pair to enter the dinner space. The lantern bearer moved at a brisk pace and Zaide lagged behind, his expression so bland it sent pangs of anxiety through her chest. He joined them at their table without a word and sat with crossed legs. Lark didn't know enough about Kolmari food to be sure of what was meant for him and she searched the table again, unsure if the distraction of a meal was welcome.

"Did they stick you in a room in the jungle?" Tula pointed toward the forest with a fork as she asked.

Zaide only shook his head and settled. He glanced at the food, his face revealing nothing.

Andriun leaned closer. "Something has happened?"

"Answers," Zaide replied.

All across the plaza, those gathered for the dinner had begun to join hands. Tula was the first to follow their lead, lacing her fingers with Lark's and then reaching for Andriun on her other side. She made a face when he slipped his hand into her grasp. "Oh, I forgot you're all webby. That feels weird."

"The Desheni do not hold hands," Andriun said, somewhat defensively.

Tula squinted at his fingers. "Is that so? How do you take walks with your sweetheart, then?"

"I do not have a sweetheart. But if I did, how would us not holding hands prevent us from walking?"

Lark hushed them both. The Oracle had raised her arms and everyone else had fallen to silence. Zaide watched Oroduna, his hands resting on his thighs. Lark stared for a long time before concluding he wasn't going to move on his own. Reluctantly, she reached to lay her hand atop his. He shifted it to grasp her fingers, the touch half-hearted.

"We are honored today," Oroduna declared, "seeing what the Maker has set in motion. The darkness rises. May we provide a light to push it back."

"May we provide a light to push it back," repeated dozens of voices.

The Oracle nodded toward their table and raised a cup, her smile warm. "Blessed is the Forest. Blessed is the Fire. Blessed is the Water. Blessed are the Shadow and Light. May we rise to answer the need of the Paragons."

"Blessed are the Paragons," people called, raising their own drinks in salute.

Uncertain what was expected of them, Lark awkwardly let go of Zaide and Tula's hands so she could lift her cup, too. Her companions joined her in the gesture. The Oracle seemed satisfied, and everyone drank. Lark had expected some sort of juice or wine. Instead, it was water.

"First, we feast," the Oracle announced. "Then, we speak. We shall need our strength for what is to come, so relish what the Maker has granted."

Applause followed. Tula rose to her knees and clapped hard, while Lark did so more sedately. Andriun only grimaced, and Zaide did nothing at all.

Eventually, the noise settled, and Tula was the first to pull a glass cover from a dish. "I'm ravenous after all that flying. Who knew it would be so hard to eat while you're up in the air?"

"An oversight none of us will commit again," Lark murmured. She admitted she was hungry, too, but the thought of the conversations to come left her uncertain she'd be able to eat.

"Yeah, maybe I'll get whoever's in charge of cooking here to make us something for the trip back." The Magister beamed as she shoveled a portion of every dish onto her plate. "So, Zaide, you already talked to the Oracle? That's good, maybe we're already done here. What did you ask?"

The look he gave her was the most awkward expression Lark had ever seen on his face.

She tried to be a little more gentle, though part of her hoped his bland demeanor had nothing to do with the purpose of their visit. He was the Bladebearer; his need was most urgent. What if the Oracle had already given him bad news? "You did speak with her?" Lark asked softly.

"I asked about our goal and the sword," Zaide said, squaring his attention on the food in front of them. He made no move to serve himself. "She told me to ask personal questions instead."

Lark raised both brows. "What did you ask?"

"About my father. I thought she might know what became of him after he left Kolmar." His voice grew softer, flatter, as he spoke.

"What did she say?"

"He's dead."

Her heart lurched in her chest, a strange ache that made her sick to her stomach.

Tula leaned forward to peer around her. "Oh, well that's a relief, right?"

Zaide's brows drew together. "What?"

"How could that be a relief?" Lark knew her voice teetered on the edge of demanding and she felt little remorse.

The Magister shrugged and speared something on her plate with her fork. She gestured with it as she spoke. "Well, if he's gone, you can't learn anything bad. What if you'd come back and told us your father was Gadranus?"

Lark gaped. "Tula!"

Beside her, Zaide grew dreadfully still. "You thought my father was Gadranus?"

"Nobody thinks that," Lark replied, perhaps a shade faster than she should have.

At the far end of the table, Andriun shrugged. "It could have been a possibility. He is said to be broken-born, is he not?"

This time, the hurt was clear on Zaide's face. "Does nothing I've done mean anything to you? Any of you?"

"Ignore her, Zaide. Nobody thinks that." Lark touched his arm, hoping to offer comfort.

He gleaned none, for he made a soft sound of disgust and pulled away as he stood.

"You are leaving?" Andriun asked between bites. "You have not eaten."

"Not hungry," Zaide muttered as he slipped away.

Lark shifted toward the cushion he'd just abandoned and hesitated. Part of her wanted to go after him, to offer some sort of reassurance, the way he'd so often done for her. But she recognized the anger in every step he took, and that made her sink back into her seat. She felt some of that, herself, though she suspected she did a better job of hiding it. Zaide wore his heart on his sleeve, proudly displayed for everyone to see. Hers was locked away and barricaded, instead.

Tula stuffed a morsel of something into her mouth and craned her neck as she watched him leave. "I thought it a little," she admitted between bites.

For an instant, Lark thought she might throttle the girl. "Now is not the time, Tula."

The Magister frowned back at her. "But what if he had been? Zaide didn't know, right? We're going to have to deal with more broken-born eventually, and if he asks the wrong questions—"

"The Maker spared no tact in making you," Lark snapped.

Andriun clapped a webbed hand over his mouth. At first, she thought it was in response to her words. Then a shadow moved over her.

"My apologies for the interruption," the Oracle said.

"No need for apologies," Andriun said.

"No interruption," Lark said at the same time. She shot him a frown. "We thank you for this gracious meal. Have you come to speak about why we are here?"

"In time, when all of you are gathered." Oroduna raised a brow and glanced the way Zaide had gone. Had she known he would leave?

Lark bit her tongue to keep it still, then drew a deep breath. "Andriun, would you take a turn?"

The Shaman stopped with a spoonful of something halfway to his mouth. "A turn for what?"

"Zaide duty," Tula almost sang.

His face fell. "Now?"

The protest made Lark bristle. "Would you just go?"

Andriun's mouth tightened, but he pushed himself up. "Excuse me, Oracle. I will return."

"See that you do," the Oracle said with a nod. "When you have eaten, and when all of you have rested and are gathered again, you may seek me in the Hall of Vision."

Lark didn't know where the Hall of Vision was, but its name told her enough to make her heart leap. "We've rested already. Can't we join you now?"

"All of you will rest, for what I must ask of you will be draining for you all. When the time is right, you will be led to me." Oroduna held up a finger, but instead of shaking it in reprimand, she reached out and tapped Lark on the nose. "Rest."

Lark blinked, but sank back onto her heels and stared at the food as the Oracle slipped away. She would bide her time and take something to eat, but rest was the furthest thing from her mind.

CHAPTER FIVE

THE FOREST PATH was dark when Zaide found it again, but the earth beneath his boots was firm and he followed it anyway. The farther he got from the feast, the easier it was to see, but the stone bench where he'd sat with the Oracle not even an hour before was haunting in the dark. He stared at it, yet could not make himself sit. Instead, he paced circles around it, raking his fingers through his hair. It fell before his eyes again after every pass. Snowy white, bright even in the shadow, a painful reminder of more than just the unwelcome conversation he'd left behind. He could hardly recall a time he *hadn't* noticed it. It was always there, just at the edge of his vision, ensuring he never forgot. He'd requested his foster mother cut it short, once, but that had only made it worse. What he saw, he had to accept. What he didn't felt like a dirty secret he could only hide from himself.

A whisper of movement on the path made him freeze. Willpower let him turn.

The shadowy figure of the Shaman was not unwelcome, yet Zaide still felt a twinge of disappointment.

"Dasienna?" he asked half-heartedly.

Andriun stopped at the edge of the clearing. "She is speaking with the Oracle."

That was what they were there for. It should have made him happy. Instead, Zaide had to force himself to nod.

For a time, neither of them said anything.

Eventually, Andriun padded forward to sit down. He said nothing, did nothing, but it still rubbed Zaide the wrong way.

"Did they send you to handle me?" Zaide asked sardonically, recalling the time they'd sent Tula after him when he was angry.

Andriun tilted his head and considered that for a long time before he spoke. "I do not think you need to be handled, but you may benefit from a listening ear."

Would he? Zaide hardly knew. Something about seeing his friend sitting so placidly on the bench struck him as wrong, given the tumult of everything inside him, but he couldn't fault Andriun for that. The Shaman was calm and steady as a person. A reliable leader and a perfect example of what Zaide hoped to be. That he could be a sympathetic ear made sense, yet Zaide was unsure. He kept pacing.

After a time, Andriun slid his hands down his thighs and sighed. "Do you want advice, or do you want to let frustration spill out of your mouth like a meal of bad fish?"

"That's... the most disgusting analogy I've ever heard," Zaide said.

"Perhaps your frustration is also disgusting. Perhaps it is like the fish, and you will feel better when it is out."

"Is that a Desheni saying or something?"

Andriun cast a thoughtful look toward the sky. "I am Desheni and I have said it, so I suppose it is close enough?"

Zaide stared at him for a minute, then returned to his agitated pacing. It didn't help his frustration, as Andriun called it, but after such a long flight atop the dragon's back, it felt good to move his legs. He circled the clearing for a long time before he let out an agitated sigh. "I should have dyed my hair dark when

Resia offered to help me. I should have done it then and never looked back. Kept doing it afterward."

"Changing the color of your hair would not change who you are," Andriun said.

"But no one even knows who I am," Zaide fired back. "From the first time we met, Lark questioned me. She constantly accused me of being on the other side. I've spent my whole life having to prove myself, over and over, for something that's outside my control."

The Shaman frowned. "But is that true? Or is that what you feel? The two are not often the same."

Zaide scoffed. "How can I not feel that way? Every time I turn around, someone else is accusing me of—of—"

"Walking in someone else's shadow?"

"Someone I've never met," Zaide said. "Someone I didn't even think was real until a few months ago." His shoulders sagged and he exhaled hard.

Andriun shifted to the far end of the bench, an invitation to sit down. "How does a soldier who sought to fight Gadranus think the man is not real?"

"I mean, I thought *he* was. I just didn't think all the stories... all *this* was real." Zaide motioned to the sword sheathed at his hip, and a hint of bitterness rose in his throat. It had been real, and he'd wasted it. He shut his eyes and called the Oracle's reassurances to mind. They'd fix things. Restore the blade. They had to.

"So is it that your doubts were proven wrong that bothers you now? You fear some other belief will be proven wrong?"

"No," Zaide said, a shade more defensively than he meant. He swiped a hand down his face and drew a deep breath before he spoke again. "I don't care if I'm wrong. I'm willing to learn. I'm just... tired."

Andriun gave a slow, thoughtful nod. "I understand."

"How can you?" Zaide murmured as he circled the bench one last time and then finally sat down.

"Have you forgotten? I am an outcast, too." The Shaman gave him a wry smile as he reached for something at his neck. He snagged it—a fine silver chain—and gave just enough of a tug to pull it out from underneath his shirt. The Captured Spring glowed a soft blue in the night.

How could Zaide forget? He'd been there the moment his friend made the decision that cast him out from his people. He tried to smile back, but couldn't. "Nobody seems to dislike the Desheni."

"Instead, I am disliked by my own people. Believe me, it is not a better fate."

Zaide frowned.

For a time, Andriun turned the glowing vial between his fingers, the movement sending light across his chest in waves that resembled water. "Zaide. I have not known you long, but we are friends, yes?"

"I think we are?" Zaide said, unsure if he should be concerned about what was coming.

"Then you will trust that when I say this, I mean it with no unkindness?"

Uneasiness bubbled in Zaide's middle in a way that made him reconsider that metaphor about bad fish. "What?"

Andriun pursed his lips oddly, then tucked the Captured Spring underneath his shirt and spread his hands wide. "Ah... Is it possible you simply care too much what other people think?"

Oh. Zaide snorted softly. He'd expected something far worse. "How can I not? From the very beginning, all the way back when I first set out with Lark, it's felt like everyone's dying for a chance to question whose side I'm on. Like they expect me to apologize for all these things I haven't done."

"There. See?" The Shaman ticked a finger. "Felt like. It has felt like. You do not know what others are thinking, only what you believe they are thinking."

"But it's not just thinking." Zaide protested. At least, it wasn't always. The princess had never hesitated to make her thoughts clear.

Andriun shook his head. "You can only know what they tell you. What have they told you?"

"You were right next to Tula. Don't pretend you didn't hear her."

"Yes, I heard. But I think that maybe you are overreacting to her concerns."

"How else am I supposed to take it? She literally said she thought I was the son of the man who's trying to destroy civilization and conquer the world." Zaide's fingertips brushed the hilt of the sword he kept at his side. He started to jerk it back, then touched it again, wishing he'd feel some sort of spark instead of cold steel. How long would he curse himself for the silence? Until it was restored? The thought of what was needed for that made his stomach that much worse.

Andriun turned his eyes toward the sky and contemplated his answer for a while before he gave it. "Perhaps it is just that she worries for you. You must remember what this task before us demands. We are all needed."

"Then explain Lark's questioning." Part of him knew he was being unfair to ask. She hadn't brought up her doubts in some time, but they still itched just below his skin, like a splinter he couldn't dig out.

"I cannot explain her reasons. I do not know them. But if I must make a guess, I would say everything she does is born out of concern, too. Perhaps for you. Perhaps for what we must do. It is a terrifying task, and I suspect she fears that she cannot do it alone." The Shaman paused, still gazing at the sky. "I believe that is why she wished for me to speak to you. Why she sent Tula to speak to you on the mountain."

Zaide snorted. "So she did send you."

Andriun raised his hands defensively. "I did not say that she did not. I only said that I do not think you need to be handled. I believe it is good for people to have space when they are angry or upset, for those are the times when things come from our mouths that we do not mean. But she wished for someone to speak to you, and she is the princess."

"So you're here," Zaide muttered.

"So I am."

The sword in his hand only fueled Zaide's frustration, so he pried his fingers from its hilt. "Did she pick you because you're diplomatic, or because she didn't want to do it herself?"

"I think she is used to delegating, and asking Tula to come would have made things worse." Andriun shrugged. "And also I think she has an unhealthy need to feel that things are always under control. She cannot bring herself to let things be if they are imperfect. She wishes everything to be fixed at once."

"Which is why we're here." Zaide waved a hand back toward the plaza they'd left behind.

The Shaman hesitated. "Do you mean here as in this grove where we sit and complain, or here as in this island? Or is it a more metaphorical here?"

Zaide blinked twice and then shook his head. "Never mind." He rubbed the back of his neck and stared up past the palm fronds, to the glittering sparks of stars beyond. It was strange, the way the constellations never changed. The summer stars here were the same as the ones he'd known in Kolmar. He could have found his way by them, traced a path back to a home that no longer existed. He ached for that home worse than usual, tonight.

At last, Andriun sighed and gave a single nod. "You do not need to be handled. You need to be trusted. I have not been part of your group long, but I see that the princess fears she will lose your skill. She believes you are the most important part of this group. And I know it is hard to see, but the princess trusts you like no other. That is why she has this need to ensure you are not given time to brood."

"I don't brood," Zaide protested.

Andriun raised a brow.

"I don't," he repeated, a little more insistently than he probably should have.

"If you say so," Andriun murmured. "Now, do we go back and find food in hopes the meeting with the Oracle has not already begun?"

Zaide shook his head. "Not hungry."

"Then do we go back and gather a hoard of food to spirit away to our rooms where we can eat in peace and not be fussed at?"

"That sounds better." Zaide pushed himself up from the bench.

"Good." Andriun stood with a grin. "There will be time for a moment to yourself when all is said and done."

Zaide shoved his hands into his pockets as they walked. "Yeah? And what if I die before that?"

"Then it will be a very long moment to yourself." The Desheni shrugged, and together, they made their way back to the plaza.

They had not been gone long enough for the meal to finish without them, but the table where they'd been before now had no occupants. Zaide scanned the area for the girls, then decided it didn't matter. Wherever they'd gone, they'd come after the two of them soon enough.

Andriun appeared pleased by the absence of the women, for he returned to his seat and the now-cold food on his plate with renewed fervor. He pointed at a particular dish. "Try this. It is made with fruits and nuts. It will remind you of home."

"Your home or mine?" Zaide asked as he sat. Without Lark or Tula there, his stomach settled, and the food looked more appealing. Most of the dishes set before them were unfamiliar, but he thought one looked like a traditional Kolmari stew. The pot was still warm, so he gave himself a serving of that while he sampled the one his friend suggested.

"Can it not be both? We are at opposite ends of the Allied

Kingdoms, but there are some commonalities found everywhere in Amroch."

Zaide didn't know how to reply, so he ate. The recommendation was not far off. The berries used were unfamiliar, but the sweet and rich flavor of them mixed with more common nuts reminded him of the spring tarts his foster mother often made as a treat.

"Good?" Andriun asked.

"Good." Zaide motioned toward the stew as his own suggestion, and his friend took a portion.

"Good," Andriun agreed after the first taste.

They finished half of what they heaped on their plates before the Oracle's grandson stopped in front of their table. "Your presence is requested in the Hall of Vision," the man said with a halting smile. "I am here to escort you."

"Requested or required?" Zaide asked.

The question took the man off guard. "I'm sorry," he said as he raised his hands. "I don't mean to impose."

"Which means required," Andriun sighed. He dusted his hands together and rose.

Zaide gave his stew a longing look.

"We will arrange for more food to be brought to your quarters. I am sorry, this appears to be urgent." The man stepped back, giving them space to follow.

When was anything they faced not urgent? Zaide hardly remembered the sleepy days of his apprenticeship with the Kolmari Elder. He would have given almost anything to be back in that life now, sitting up late among the books and daydreaming about what life might be like with a sword at his belt. The reality of those daydreams had turned out to be nightmares.

"I want to go home," he said without thinking, earning a startled look from the Shaman beside him.

"Yes," Andriun said. "So do I."

While most of the city appeared to be built into and against the cliff faces, the Oracle's grandson led them into a set of hallways that pushed deep underground. There was no light but what came from the lantern in the hands of the man who led the way. The dark stone walls loomed, close and oppressive, and it gave Zaide such a sense of dread that he said nothing.

At last, they reached an opening covered by a dark curtain. Their guide swept it aside with one arm and motioned for them to pass. Andriun went first, walking with more confidence than Zaide possessed.

The room beyond glowed with the light of dozens of candles. They sat in a ring around an unremarkable space, a bare circle of stone where the Oracle sat with Tula and Lark.

"Good," the Oracle said when she saw them, a broad smile brightening her face. "Sit with us. It's time to begin."

Zaide stepped past the candles, his movement making their flames ripple in a pattern that reminded him of waves. "Begin what?" he asked as he settled on the floor.

The Oracle smiled wider, but her eyes darkened. "The end."

CHAPTER SIX

LARK HADN'T BEEN sure Zaide would come.

He always came around eventually, able to move past arguments or disagreements in a way she found truly admirable, but reaching that point took time. Something they had in precious little supply, she feared.

He glanced her way as he sat cross-legged and settled with his hands on his knees. "The end? What does that mean?" he asked, and she suspected the question was not meant for the Oracle.

Lark tried to draw herself up and appear regal. "We've told the Oracle about everything we've learned from Vorkaris regarding the false Magister and my father," she explained. "Coupled with everything that's happened with the former Shaman, she believes there is a chance this may be the last Rise."

Both Zaide and Andriun looked to Oroduna so fast, they could have made themselves dizzy.

The Oracle merely nodded. "Upon all that followed the death of Shaman Athradan, my visions of the future have grown stark. It may yet change further, but right now, I see nothing beyond the demise of this incarnation of our foe."

Andriun leaned forward and laid a hand on the floor, his

webbed fingers spread. The way he hunched made him look like a frog, Lark thought, which was less kind than the Desheni deserved. "What does this mean? When you say you see nothing, do you mean a lack of visions? Or a lack of clarity?"

"It means precisely what I have said," Oroduna replied patiently. "When I look to the future beyond these looming battles, I see nothing. Nothing but black. This can mean one of two things. The end of my power, or the end of me. Both are tied to Gadranus. One way or another, it is the end."

Everyone sat in silence for a long time.

Eventually, Zaide shook his head. "I'm sorry, can someone explain what that means like you're explaining to a kid who missed the lesson?"

Of course. Lark exhaled. She knew of the gaps in his education, but hadn't stopped to consider how a lack of knowledge would affect his understanding of the Oracle's visions or role. "Her power is tied to the Rise." It was the best place she knew to start. "When Gadranus is gone, when he is truly defeated, her ability to perceive the future will be gone, too."

"Something I welcome, and pray for every day," Oroduna added.

"Power always comes with a price," Andriun said. "And it is more steep than I had imagined. My people have misunderstood your existence. We believed your gift of foresight was passed down through the Ages, a mistake I will struggle to correct in our oral histories. Your life has been long. It has cost you more than most. Family. Loved ones."

The Oracle gave a single nod, though she let her eyes settle on Zaide. "But I do not regret my choice, for the sacrifice I made has kept my family safe for Ages. When the world knows peace, I sleep. And with each new Rise, I awaken so that my gift may aid the Paragons once more."

"Like the dragon," Zaide concluded.

Again, the Oracle nodded. "Now, only the three of us persist from when the first Rise took place. Myself, Vorkaris, and Gadranus."

"And your family? Your children?" Zaide's brow furrowed with hurt and Lark felt a twinge of sympathy pluck at her heart. He'd grown up alone, the other end of a similar story, and the fact that loneliness was the first thing that sprang forward in him left her fighting back guilt.

She'd never considered what the Oracle had given up. All that had mattered to her was responsibility, the same way that was all that had ever mattered in her own life.

"My descendants live here still. All of them, out there. And some here." A twinkle of amusement glittered in the Oracle's eye as she looked Lark's way.

A flush crawled up her neck.

"What?" Tula gasped. She leaned forward to squint hard at Lark, then looked back and forth between the two of them. "The princess is related to you? You don't look anything alike!"

"Of course they do not," Andriun said, tone both dismissive and disinterested. "If the Oracle before us is truly the first Oracle, then they are separated by thousands of years. With that many generations between ancestor and descendant, the Oracle's bloodline has spread all across Amroch. It is likely that you are descended from her, too."

The Magister gaped. "Really?"

"You're a librarian, Tula, you should know this," Lark muttered, though she averted her eyes and rubbed her arms. The Hall of Vision was chilly, and the candles did nothing to stave off the sensation of ice that crept through her legs.

"Her lineage makes little difference in what shall be seen," Oroduna said, redirecting them all back to the task at hand. "It does not change what must be done, but if this is truly the last Rise, I will confess I shall be glad to know my descendants shall see it."

Zaide rubbed his hands against his knees as if to wipe them dry. Lark hardly recalled seeing him nervous before. He rarely got worked up about things related to their task; either he acted, or he didn't. Nerves rarely factored in. When he spoke, though, he struck her as calm. "The Rise is a cycle. Each time Gadranus is slain, he's later reborn and returns to power. He's been killed before, over and over again. If there's a chance this Rise could be the last, you're saying there's a chance to keep him from being reborn?"

The Oracle spread her hands and gave a helpless shrug. "I cannot say. The cause for the end remains murky in my sight. But this possibility is an outcome I have never seen before, which is why I summoned you with such haste."

A troubled shadow crossed Andriun's face. "You have not seen it? That makes no sense. My father said something similar. That this was the end of things. The last Rise. How could he know such a thing if you were not the one who told him?"

Both Tula and Zaide looked doubtful.

"Perhaps that's not what he meant." Lark saw no other possibilities, but if the other side had an Oracle, wouldn't they have known? "But it doesn't matter. Either way, something changed after we got here, if the Oracle's visions have changed. Our arrival here set a possibility in stone, allowing this potential outcome to be revealed." She tried to remain calm, though she curled her hands to fists and pressed them hard against the tops of her thighs. What they'd done to make it so was beyond her. Before the meal, the Oracle had wished for them to rest. What had happened that could cement such a powerful possibility? Only one thing had been out of the ordinary. Her eyes traveled to Zaide and then Andriun, a desperate curiosity over what words had been shared pressing to the front of her mind.

"But it has also outlined a path you must take, one that cannot be avoided. There is great urgency in a task that must be fulfilled, and I fear time is not on our side." Oroduna sat straighter. "Show me the blade."

Zaide rolled up onto one knee, giving himself enough space to draw the Spectrum Blade from its ordinary leather sheath. It gleamed in the candlelight, but it was only a reflection of their flames. Gone was the light, and with it, the glowing swirls that had once illuminated the sword's steel. He held it out atop flat palms.

Oroduna made no movement to touch it, or even to gain a closer look. "You understand what has happened?"

"Its power is depleted," Lark said. "It bears no light."

The Oracle nodded. "Its light has been depleted, but so too has its shadow, as they are two sides of the same force. One springs from the other."

"What do you mean?" Tula asked. Any other time, she would have had her notebook in her hand, but she must have left it in her room, for her fingers twitched against her knees with a clear desire to write.

"They are opposite sides of the same power, if you will." Oroduna took a candle from the ring around them and raised it for everyone to see. Her other hand passed from one side of it to the other, alternating which part of her hand was illuminated. "The light casts a shadow wherever it goes, and the presence of other lights does little to stop this from happening. The shadow is a counterbalance, one that can be manipulated, but never fully destroyed."

"But in light's absence, the shadow is gone, too," Andriun concluded.

"Leaving darkness in power," the Oracle agreed.

Zaide lowered the Spectrum Blade until it lay in his lap. "And what does that mean for the sword?"

"That the two missing forces must be restored in tandem." Lark's heart sank even as she spoke. It was bad enough they would have to confront an enemy for aid, but the opposing power—the power of light—remained unaccounted for. A sense of sorrow and hopelessness twisted up inside her like choking vines around her spirit.

Again, Oroduna nodded in confirmation. "Balance must exist

between those two powers. Shadow as a reminder of what you fight against, a step between light and darkness."

Tula leaned forward, drumming her fingertips against her knees. "Wait a moment. Doesn't that mean there should be a Paragon of Darkness, too? If shadow and darkness aren't the same thing?"

"There is no need. Darkness is the natural state of things, and the state of people." Andriun flattened one webbed hand against his chest. "When there is nothing, there is only dark. Everything else, every element represented by a Paragon, is something that exists only by chance. They represent change, while darkness is a constant."

"Very good." The Oracle's smile grew broad with approval. "Each element also exists as part of a spectrum. A range with two ends. Some can coincide with darkness. Others cannot." She motioned to Andriun first, then Tula. Water and fire, opposing forces.

The Magister gasped and clapped a hand to her mouth. "Is that why the Shaman was pulled over to the other side? Because his power is closer to the dark end?"

Lark shook her head. "Whatever the reason for Athradan's betrayal, it doesn't matter anymore. We have a new Shaman and we need to look ahead. We need the remaining two Paragons."

"The power of shadow will be found in the Shattered Lands," Oroduna said.

They'd already determined that part, but Lark still felt her throat grow tight. She swallowed hard and struggled to ask the question that frightened her more. "But how do we awaken the light?"

To her surprise, the Oracle chuckled. "My dear girl, is that not why you are here?"

Uncertainty tumbled through her and she rubbed her arms to stave off a chill that had nothing to do with the cold room. How did she answer? What was the right thing to say?

Andriun spoke before she could sort out her thoughts. "You know where we may reach the Paragon of Light?"

"I was under the impression you knew." Oroduna lowered the candle but did not put it down. Instead, she cradled it with both hands and held it in her lap while the flame burrowed deeper into the wax pillar. "Why else would you sit in the Paragon's presence?"

No one spoke.

Lark clenched her hands tighter and bowed her head.

"Wait." Tula held up both hands. "Wait, you mean you? That's why the people with all the lights made the swirly sun patterns?"

The Oracle raised her eyebrows.

"That is half the puzzle already, then. You will travel with us to the Shattered Lands?" Andriun brightened as he asked.

"I am not going anywhere," Oroduna replied.

"What? Why? You can't expect us to bring Gadranus all the way here to get it done." Tula pantomimed walking with two fingers.

"Please don't antagonize the Oracle, Tula. We're here to seek help." Lark's voice strained in her throat. She didn't want to speak any longer, not with the others around them, but there was no way to ask them to leave.

You will have your time to speak with Oroduna. All of you will. The dragon had been quiet for so long, Lark had almost forgotten he was there, waiting somewhere outside.

Zaide returned the Spectrum Blade to its sheath without a word, though he slid his fingers along the edge of the cross guard with a thoughtful frown. He cast Lark a look, though it was so uncharacteristically unreadable that she didn't know how to respond.

Oroduna grew solemn as she watched him. "I know you have come for guidance, and I will provide it. I will help to the best of my ability, but know before we begin that the coming days may prove trying."

This time, Lark didn't hesitate to speak. "We're willing to work hard, Oracle. If you can help, we'll do whatever is necessary."

"Working hard is not the problem, child, which is why I say it will be trying. I am not asking you to push. I am asking for patience."

Hard work made more sense. It was what Lark expected, what she'd braced and prepared for ahead of their expedition. How could the Oracle ask for patience when they lacked time? "I'm sorry, I don't understand. Patience for what?"

"I can give you what you need. A way to restore the blade's power after you reach the Shattered Lands." The Oracle's dark eyes bored into her, so intense that Lark almost couldn't bear to hold her gaze. "But it will take time."

"Yes, of course. I know that, and I'm ready—"

Oroduna raised a hand to stop her. "What you are ready for now matters little. What we need cannot happen on our timeline, and you have missed the full moon. It shall rise again in just over three weeks. Then, the power you seek may be ready."

Lark's heart plummeted like a stone.

"*May* be ready?" Zaide barked a laugh. "Every minute we're sitting here, Gadranus is—"

"Moving closer? Coming nearer, making himself easier to reach?" The Oracle tilted her head. "Is that such a bad thing, broken-born?"

He scowled back. "We can't afford to wait that long."

The Oracle shrugged. "You don't have a choice."

Andriun rubbed his mouth and stared at the floor. "The full moon is when light pierces even the night. It is when the power of light is its strongest."

"Which is why that is when the power of light has the greatest chance to manifest in the fashion you need. Right now, the night sky inches toward its darkest. Such strength cannot be awakened now." Oroduna raised her candle again and blew out its flame.

Tula shuddered at the sight.

"And what are we supposed to do until then?" Lark asked cautiously, mindful that her words didn't quaver like the anxiety that now trembled in her belly.

"You will train. All of you. Learn what you can, prepare for what is to come, and stand ready for the next fight."

Zaide turned away, his mouth drawn with frustration.

Lark sympathized, but part of her balked at his annoyance. He didn't know frustration yet. Not like she did.

He will learn, Vorkaris whispered into her thoughts, the quiet statement so foreboding that it sent a shiver down her spine.

CHAPTER SEVEN

ZAIDE STARED at the glass prism in the ceiling of his room. It was a strange thing, and he couldn't quite figure out how it worked, but the fragmented morning sunlight it let into his assigned sleeping quarters was welcome.

He'd expected the room to be stuffy, buried in rock as it was, but the bed beneath his back was plush and the down in his thick pillow poked the back of his neck in the mildly agitating way only feathers could. He didn't think he'd experienced such a luxury since leaving Kolmar. Who could have known a good pillow might bring such comfort?

His room was not far from those set aside for Andriun and Tula. He was unsure about being stuck so far from Lark, whose room was on a whole separate tier of the city, but the Oracle had appointed guards to watch over the princess and he forced himself to be content with that. He could not be there to protect her all the time, nor did he need to be. Lark was capable and independent, and he suspected his insistence on playing the role of bodyguard would have earned her ire. She was in a foul enough mood without his intervention, and the last thing he wanted to do was make it worse.

As soon as their meeting with the Oracle had ended, Lark

had demanded a record of moon phases. They'd missed the full moon by less than a week. Now they were twenty-three days from the next one, and there was little to do but wait.

Somehow, that struck him as the most insurmountable challenge yet.

Zaide rolled over and pushed himself upright. The prism in the ceiling provided plenty of light by which he could see, but it did not tell him how long he'd slept. Sleeping like that—in a luxurious bed, for as long as he wanted, without anyone or anything that demanded his attention the following morning—struck him as foreign. There had been lazy mornings in Kolmar, of course, but they were few and far between. Since his departure from the forest, only the boat ride from Amrochan to Jadora had been so idle. It left him with a curious sense of guilt and, as he pulled himself out of bed and fetched the clothing that had been laid out for him the night before, he wondered if he should have risen sooner.

It was not his own clothing. After weeks of travel and combat, to say his wardrobe had grown sullied was an understatement. The moment he'd made it clear he meant to turn in for the night, one of the white-robed people who escorted him to his room had spirited away every scrap of fabric packed into his bags. They'd provided nightclothes, a concept so bizarre that he still hardly knew what to think of the robe-like garment. Clothes meant specifically for sleeping might make sense for someone like Dasienna, who'd been raised in luxury, but the Kolmari were too practical to waste resources that way.

Only after the thought completed did he realize he'd thought of her as Dasienna and not Lark. It was strange how her identity had split in his mind. She was the princess, no matter what, but the version of her he knew as Lark was so much more practical, he couldn't picture her tolerating such frivolities.

He ran his thumbs over the brightly-colored tunic he was meant to wear for the day. The wool was smooth and soft, and the bold sky blue reminded him of what he'd worn when he'd first left home. A good color, though the brightly-colored pattern that bordered the short sleeves and the lower hem was unfamiliar. It resembled flowers with braided stems, and while he liked the yellow and white, he suspected his foster mother Sarma would have said the bold red and green clashed with the rest.

The tunic fit, and that was what mattered most, he decided. The plain black pants that came with it were a little loose, but he cinched them in with his belt and declared it good enough.

Beneath the folded clothing, he found unfamiliar boots and a wide woven belt in stripes of color that matched the tunic. The boots were too big, so he left them where they were. The belt was easy enough to figure out, but it came with a coil of narrow rope fastened to it and try as he might, he couldn't discern how to take it off. Eventually, he gave up and let the looped rope hang at his left side, leaving space for the Spectrum Blade on the right.

Satisfied, he padded across the room barefoot. They'd even taken his travel-worn boots, with a promise to have them cleaned and repaired before it was time to set off. With fortune, he'd have them back within a few days. He smoothed a hand down his front and opened the door.

"Good morning!" Andriun exclaimed.

Zaide all but screamed.

"Oh, sorry. I was coming to get you. It is time to break your fast. Just wait until you see what they have prepared." The Shaman grinned and stepped back. "I see they have dressed you, too."

His heart still pounded, but Zaide forced himself to be calm as he stepped into the hall. "Yeah, it's, ah... a little loose."

Andriun was dressed differently, too. The flight had required heavy winter gear to stave off the chill, and the cool weather in Desheni meant Zaide had never seen his friend in anything but leather and long sleeves. Now he wore close-fitting dark trousers and a sleeveless linen shirt, covered by what appeared to be knotted rope.

"Is that a fisherman's net?" Zaide asked.

"Hmm? Oh, yes. I am told this is the fashion of the Desheni who live in waters near here. Normally, they would leave space for a tail, but, ah..." Andriun offered a sheepish grin as he flexed and turned, showing off how nicely the clothing fit. "Well, there are obvious problems with that. Do not worry. After we eat, I will take you to see the tailor so your clothing can be adjusted. That was my first stop this morning."

"Fashion's more important to you than food, huh?"

"Well, no, it is just that I did not think a gaping window to my bottom side would be an appetizing sight."

Zaide was inclined to agree.

"Come," Andriun said, beckoning with webbed fingers as he started down the hall. "The others are already awake."

They worked their way back to the plaza where the feast had been held the night before. Though it was still decorated, it held only one table now, where Lark and Tula waited with the Oracle. Or, Zaide supposed they weren't waiting; their plates were already full and they'd clearly been eating. Both girls glanced up as they approached and Lark offered a small wave of greeting. It was so uncharacteristically friendly that Zaide almost tripped over his own feet.

Tula, on the other hand, took one look at him and let her shoulders slump as she fell into a pout.

"What's wrong with you?" Zaide took a place at the empty side of the table, where a plate waited for him to fill it.

"It's not fair," the Magister whined. "All of you get these fancy new outfits, and I look the same as I ever do." She spread her loose coat and scowled down at her clothing, the billowy pants and stomach-baring shirt the same fashion she'd worn when they first met. Even the jewel in her navel had not changed.

"That's because you've spent your whole life in the same

place you're from," Lark said, with all the annoyance of having repeated herself. "Why would they put you in anything other than Jadoran clothes?"

Zaide gave a small laugh and pinched the fabric of his tunic between his fingers to lift it away from his chest. "All right, but this isn't Kolmari. I don't even know what this is supposed to be." He plucked at the coils of rope by his side, separated one of the loops from the rest and stared at it in puzzlement.

"It's for your reindeer," Oroduna said.

He blinked at her. "My what?"

"Reindeer." The Oracle chuckled softly. "Your spirit is Kolmari, without a doubt, but you were born much farther east. Your clothing is the traditional garb of the people who birthed you, something all but lost to the Rise of Gadranus and his conquering ways."

Zaide dropped the rope. "And we have..."

"Rain-deer," Tula said, drawing out the vowels far longer than necessary. "I've never even heard of those, do they still exist? Why are they called that, are they wet?"

"No, no, it is reindeer. Deer that are led with reins, like horses." Andriun pointed. "The rope is to be used as a rein, is it not?"

"Are the Desheni familiar with reindeer, Andriun?" Lark leaned forward over her plate as she put some sort of pastry in her mouth.

He shrugged. "I have heard of them. I have not seen them. But I believe I would recognize one if I did."

"That's better than me, then." Zaide didn't know what half the things on the table were, but he added them to his plate anyway. The fruits, pastries, and tarts he did recognize were tantalizing enough. "What about you, though, Lark? That dress doesn't look like it's from Amrochan. That pink thing you were wearing when I first made it to the palace looked like some kind of mushroom."

She touched the bright fabric with one hand and a hint of color rose in her cheeks.

"Her Highness wears the traditional garb of her mother's family," Oroduna said. "Sendassian is only half of her lineage, and I suspected she would appreciate a chance to try something new."

"My mother was from Irage, just north of here." Lark rose to her knees and swished the patchwork orange and brown ruffles to the side with one hand. "Well, sort of. There is another island, farther north, where her people lived and built ships. They migrated to Irage and Addare when storms made the region inhospitable."

Tula straightened one of Lark's ruffles. "How'd she meet your father, then? Irage is so far from Amrochan."

Orodona rested her elbows against the edge of the table. "Because he came to see me."

There was a softness to Lark's smile as she sat down and picked up her food again. "His ship moored in Irage, as it's closer to the port in Addare. My mother's family presided over Irage at the time. It was their responsibility to welcome him."

"Sounds like they made him very welcome," the Magister teased.

Zaide ignored her, though Lark reddened more. "Well, the dress is nice. Why would Sendassian come here, though?" He turned toward the Oracle as he asked.

"What other reason is there? He had need of knowledge, and that's something I possess in great amounts." Oroduna gestured toward his plate. "Please, eat."

"It is a good question, though. Are we allowed to ask what knowledge he sought?" Andriun asked between mouthfuls of food.

"You should ask when your mouth's not full," Tula said.

He snorted. "The Desheni do not consider that rude."

The Oracle motioned for them to settle. "It is not as exciting as you may think. Early signs of the Rise had begun to show. He sought me because he knew if I was awake, it would be the clearest sign one could ask for. That he could ask me for guidance was merely an added benefit."

"And he needed to make contact with all of the Paragons anyway, right?" Tula crammed a piece of fruit into her mouth and made a show of chewing it, glaring at Andriun all the while.

Zaide shifted his attention from the Oracle to Lark, hoping for some reaction to that. He'd been surprised by the Oracle's assessment they'd come to Nimultis to seek the Paragon of Light, a suggestion that brought up even more questions than he'd held before. He was not surprised to know Lark was aware of the Paragon's location, but at the same time, something about the way Oroduna had presented the information the night before pricked at the back of his mind. Lark had looked troubled then, almost guilty. Had she hidden that knowledge on purpose? Her face now told him nothing.

"Precisely." Oroduna plucked a single berry from the trays at the center of the table. She didn't have a plate; Zaide hadn't noticed until now. "His task was much like the one set before all of you now, but you have one advantage he did not."

Reflexively, Zaide's hand went to the Spectrum Blade's hilt.

The Oracle grinned at him.

It didn't feel like an advantage, not with its power drained. It was possible it would present no added benefit at all. The thought stole part of his appetite and he stared at his plate. "The blade was stronger against monsters. Goborrins, and the thing that came out of the lake in Desheni. Has it lost that strength, too?"

"Oh, goodness, no." She almost laughed. "That power remains, no matter what magic blesses the blade. The Spectrum Blade was an answer to a plea for help, forged with the Maker's blessing. It will triumph against anything corrupted by darkness, even if the power of the Paragons fails."

He exhaled in relief. "And Gadranus?"

That dampened her demeanor. "I fear that is not possible.

The darkness within him is different. It's one that was chosen, embraced with intention."

"But the Maker's power is supposed to be infinite," Tula said. Her notebook had made a reappearance and it balanced against the edge of the table, a stick of graphite ready in her hand. "If the Spectrum Blade is blessed by the Maker, that should be enough to kill him, or else you're—what you're saying—"

"Would be blasphemy," Andriun finished for her.

Lark shook her head with conviction, her golden hair bouncing around her shoulders. It was pretty that way, left down out of her usual ponytail, and it shimmered in the morning sun. "Certainly not. The Spectrum Blade can still kill him, there's no doubt about that. But without the power of the Paragons to seal him away, the Rise would just begin again immediately."

Zaide thought of the temple outside of Kolmar, where they'd found the blade. "That's why the sword persists, but the seal eventually fails? Because the sword itself is a greater power than what the Paragons wield?"

"Yes," Oroduna said.

A quiet moment passed before Tula heaved a sigh and jotted something down in her book. "I don't know why the Maker doesn't just smite Gadranus himself."

"There are reasons, but that is a story for another time." The Oracle pushed herself up from the table, but motioned for all of them to remain seated. "I have enjoyed speaking with you, but the time has come for me to seek visions. Please enjoy your meal and use the days as you please. All of Nimultis is open to you."

"Thank you, Oracle," Lark said, shielding her full mouth with the back of one hand as she spoke.

Oroduna inclined her head in a gesture that was not a nod, but not quite a bow. "You are welcome. When you are finished, Your Highness, seek me in the Hall of Vision."

"Thank you for your company, Oracle Oroduna," Andriun said with a seated bow that was so deep, he almost put his forehead in his food.

The princess lowered her eyes and ate more quietly than before.

Zaide watched her as the Oracle departed. She'd sobered so quickly at that order. "Are you not supposed to rest and use the days as you please?"

"I am to assist the Oracle in preparation to restore the Spectrum Blade." Lark's response came fast, wiping away any traces of the friendliness she'd had to offer upon his arrival. "Someone has to know how things must go, and it's my responsibility."

"Not everything has to be carried on your shoulders, Lark."

Her deep blue eyes searched his face as her brows drew together, furrowed by some frustration he didn't understand. "This does."

"You can let us help," he protested.

Whatever openness he thought he'd found evaporated, leaving the prickly exterior she always used to guard her feelings. She pushed herself up from the table, as cold and regal as ever. "You've done enough."

Zaide fought not to wince, but he had no argument. He'd said the same thing to himself a dozen times over after the depletion of the Spectrum Blade.

"Oh." Tula covered her mouth with her fingertips and turned on her cushion as Lark stormed off to who-knew-where. "That didn't go very good."

It hadn't, and the princess's exit made him grit his teeth. He thrust himself to his feet and started after her.

"Zaide," Andriun called, halfway between reprimand and warning.

He ignored it and walked after her, his bare feet quiet on the sun-hot stone.

Lark glanced back twice before she realized he followed. "Leave me alone."

"No," Zaide snapped back. "If I'm not allowed to storm off and find somewhere to sulk, then you aren't, either."

Her face twisted with offense. "That's different."

"Different how? Because you're the princess?" The stones burned underfoot; he walked faster.

"Because I have to meet with the Oracle."

"Which you don't have to do alone. Let us help, Lark. Let me help."

"You help enough!" she snapped, and when she spun to face him, the tears in her eyes made him stop short. "Don't you understand? *You* retrieved the artifacts. *You* keep fighting all these monsters and saving cities. The Spectrum Blade chose *you,* Zaide. Not me."

All the reprimands for overreaction he'd come up with escaped without leaving his tongue, leaving him struggling for words. "Lark—"

"Leave it to me," she said before he could continue. Her hands curled to fists in her patchwork skirt and its patterned apron, though it did not stop their shaking. "Just this once, leave something to me."

Zaide stopped, dumbfounded, as she spun on her sandaled toes and hurried through a dark stone hallway, leaving him alone at the edge of the plaza.

CHAPTER EIGHT

"All right. So here's what I've got." Tula swept an arm down her back to keep her coat in place as she dropped to sit on the sand at Zaide's side. Her notebook was in her other hand, filled with scribbled lines of text that went in every direction.

Zaide nodded toward it. "Couldn't you just turn the page instead of trying to cram more words on there like that?"

"Hmm? Oh. I could, but that would waste paper. I'm going to need a new notebook before long, so I'm trying to save it." She held the notebook upright, then tilted it onto its side. "It's not hard to read, see? You write one direction, then turn it the other direction, and it's like having the space of two separate pages."

"I see." He doubted the Elder would have allowed that sort of note-taking, but he wasn't in the mood for an argument. Lark's abrupt departure had soured the day enough. The ocean offered some respite, though its lapping waves almost reached his bare feet. He'd have to find a new place to sit before long. When the tide rose, he suspected the firm sand he sat on would be underwater. He stared out at the waves for a while, then went back to what he was doing. The chunk of wood in his hand was warm from his grip and still smelled green despite the work he'd already done, providing a link to the forest he so achingly missed. His knife rasped up the side, shaving off a slim curl.

Tula grinned and turned her notes right side up again, evidently not noticing he was busy. "So, anyway. I couldn't talk to the Oracle or Lark directly, but the Oracle's grandson seems to be in charge of Nimultis, and he was happy to talk. I already discussed a lot of this with Vorkaris. He confirmed I understood correctly, but he wouldn't give me any further information."

"Maybe he doesn't have any." Zaide couldn't imagine the dragon would hide knowledge on purpose, not after he'd flown to find them the moment he'd learned something new.

"I think you're right, but he can be a little prideful, so I didn't want to offend him by saying it." Her voice dropped to a conspiratorial whisper.

He snorted. The dragon was eavesdropping on their thoughts half the time; whispering wouldn't keep him from knowing what was said. "What did he tell you, then? The Oracle's grandson, I mean. Sorry. I don't know his name."

"Me either. I probably should have asked who I was talking to, huh?" She tilted her eyes skyward and tapped the end of her stick of graphite against her chin in thought, leaving a gray smudge. "Well, it's too awkward to ask now. I'll just have to not know his name forever, unless someone else is brave enough to ask."

"Undolas," Andriun put in.

Tula squeaked and shot him a glare. "Don't sneak up on us like that!"

"I am not sneaking," the Shaman protested as he sat on Zaide's other side. "It is not my fault you try to listen with your mouth."

Zaide bit his lip to hold in a laugh. He wasn't about to put himself in the middle of one of their spats. One deep breath later, he'd regained his composure. "Undolas, you said?"

Andriun nodded. "The Oracle's grandson and the leader of Nimultis. His name is Undolas."

"Were you eavesdropping on us?" Tula's eyes narrowed with suspicion until they were almost closed.

"There are no eaves out here." He waved one webbed hand toward the sky, its broad expanse just as blue as he was. "Besides, I did not know this was a private beach. I thought I would come for a swim."

"You shouldn't swim alone. That's one of the first rules of water," she replied with a sniff.

Zaide's nose scrunched. "You know he can breathe underwater, right? I don't think it matters if he goes swimming by himself."

The Magister huffed. "Never mind. You two just want to pick on me. Do you want to hear what I learned, or not?"

"Yes," Zaide said quickly. "Sorry. Go ahead. You spoke to Undolas, and he said...?"

"That the Paragon of Light's power must be wielded at the same time as the Paragon of Shadow's power to restore the shades of magic to the Spectrum Blade, so the Oracle is just going to make sure we can take the Paragon's power with us!" She held her notebook out at arm's length and beamed at her notes.

Zaide exchanged bland looks with Andriun. That was nothing new at all. "And... how are we going to do that?"

"I have absolutely no idea." Tula lowered her book. "That's where he stopped answering questions, and Vorkaris acted a little nervous about the lack of information he had, so I couldn't push him very far, either."

"Perhaps..." Andriun's hand went to the silver chain at his neck, then slid down to clasp the Captured Spring through his shirt. "The three artifacts were made by harnessing the unique power of each Paragon, back in the First Age when their power first emerged. Perhaps they seek to do something similar."

"Make a new artifact?" Zaide asked.

The Magister took a long, drawn out gasp. "That could be

why they need the Oracle's power to be at its zenith, right? She's going to make a new one?"

Her reasoning was sound, but Zaide found himself shaking his head. "That doesn't make sense, though. We needed the Paragons themselves to restore power to the blade before, not just the artifacts. The artifacts were only the keys for letting us get *to* the blade."

"Perhaps. Perhaps not." Andriun shrugged. "We do not know everything that power can do, and the Oracle has lived since the First Age. As has Magister Vorkaris. They must know more than we do about how such things may work."

"Maybe," Zaide murmured. If Vorkaris knew and wasn't sharing answers with the girl who shared his power, that was a problem on its own. He frowned, then returned his attention to the piece of wood in his hand.

For a while, both Paragons watched him work. The rough shape he'd started during their travels had begun to emerge on one side, but it was crude enough to look like a child's work.

"You are still working on this? What exactly are you making?" Andriun asked after a time. Tula had gone back to writing and did not seem to notice.

Zaide held it out at arm's length, examining the shape. "It's just... that tradition I mentioned while we were on the way to Ganede."

The Shaman's brow furrowed. "You are carving a tradition out of wood?"

"No," he almost laughed. "The carving is the tradition, I mean. I told you about how it's part of the Kolmari rites of passage, right? I wish I'd gotten more done since I started it on the road, but..." He didn't have to finish that thought. To say they'd been busy would have been a ridiculous understatement. The world was falling apart around them, and it seemed like they alone were responsible for propping it up.

Andriun tilted his head to one side. "No one will blame you if you do not have it done by the traditional time. You face extenuating circumstances. It is not a good time for artistic pursuits."

"It's not just about the art, though," Zaide protested. "This kind of carving is always the first thing a man makes on his own. Do you know how many Kolmari fail to reach that milestone by their eighteenth birthday? I'd be the first. I've left enough of a bad legacy already."

"Ah. So it is a matter of pride, then." Andriun stroked his chin. "I would have thought a tool or something would be more practical to make."

Zaide shrugged. "The Kolmari think someone's first creation should be something that captures happiness. So you make something that means something to you, something to sit in your home and make you smile. Then when you find a woman you want to have sit in your home and make you smile, you give her the carving and see if she accepts."

Tula's head snapped up. "Like a proposal gift?" Her eyes sparkled with delight at the notion.

"Uh, I suppose so." He scraped a thicker curl of wood from one side, coaxing a new shape to the surface.

"That is so sweet," she sighed. "What's it going to be? Is that a sparrow?"

He paused with his knife against the block, suddenly self-conscious. "Something like that."

"Pearls," Andriun said.

They both looked his way.

"The Desheni proposal gift," he explained. "You dive for pearls and use them to craft jewelry. The jewelry should be to the taste of your intended. Color, texture, size, and quality are all important."

"I thought you said the Desheni had arranged marriages," Zaide said.

"We do, but that does not mean you should not woo the wife who is chosen for you." He seemed offended by the suggestion.

Tula clasped her notebook to her chest and gave a dreamy

sigh. "That sounds so romantic. Pearls aren't common in Jadora, I've hardly seen real ones. I guess the bay isn't a good place to find them. In Jadora, the proposal gift is a knife."

A sound halfway between a laugh and a choke escaped Andriun's throat. "A *knife?*"

"Yeah. And then if your sweetheart does something to make you angry, you've got something to get them with." She pantomimed stabbing.

"All right," Zaide said, waving both hands to call a cease to the subject. "That's enough. Don't you two have anything better to be doing?"

"Yes. I am going to swim." Andriun stood, but he was in no rush to depart. "What about you? Is carving how you will spend your weeks?"

Zaide raised his shoulders, not quite a shrug, but closer to a gesture of helplessness. He doubted rest would come easy, no matter what the Oracle encouraged them to do. Kolmar was safe as long as Resia was there to support the barrier of magic that sheltered the forest, but as far as he knew, the Kolmari were still trapped in Amrochan. They were still at risk, and the advancement of enemy forces continued every moment they spent sitting on the beach.

"There are guards here," he said after a moment. It was better if he didn't think about his loved ones trapped on the mainland. If he spent too much time letting those worries bounce around in his head, he'd never sleep again. "I saw they fight with a sword and shield. I was thinking about asking them to spar with me, see if I could continue the training I started with your uncle. He showed me a lot of forms I never learned in Kolmar, and I should spend more time practicing them."

Andriun nodded. "I believe that would be wise. I mean to train, too. And study."

"I mean to set stuff on fire," Tula said.

"I guess that's training, too, when you're a mage." Zaide turned his carving in his palm, letting his thumb explore the shapes he'd made. The little bird was supposed to be round, with a prominent beak. He'd work on chipping away wood underneath the beak next. "Three weeks, though. What do you think can happen in that much time?"

The Shaman spread his hands and shrugged. "A great deal, and yet not enough. But we are here, and we await direction for our next step. For now, that will have to do."

Zaide nodded in agreement.

The silence that followed was a perfect opportunity for Andriun to step away. He strode into the shallow surf and jerked his head toward the waves. "Tula, come swim?"

"Not on your life," the Magister scoffed.

Andriun grinned. "Your loss."

"I'll swim." Zaide tucked his knife into its sheath and stood to unfasten the colorful belt over his tunic, leaving the knife and his unfinished carving on the sand.

Tula made a face of disgust and scooted backwards, putting herself farther away from the water.

"She dislikes it now that she shares magic with Vorkaris," Andriun said. "It is uncomfortable to be faced with an opposing element."

"Weren't you always a fire mage, though?" Zaide peeled off his tunic and folded it neatly over his other things.

"Yeah, but it's different now."

The Shaman strode backwards until he was ankle-deep in water. "Because she is Paragon. I find I do not like fire, either."

"You seemed fine at the camp." The black pants Zaide found in his room were loose enough that they'd be a hindrance in the water. He considered them for a moment before he unfastened his belt and slid them off, too.

"Hey, hey!" Tula covered her eyes with her arm and held out one hand as if to shield herself. "I don't want to see anybody's undergarments!"

"Then don't look," he laughed as he folded the pants and

dropped them atop the rest. He strode out into the water until the waves pushed against his knees and slowed his movement.

Andriun had already waded out waist-deep. "I have decided that first of all, we should take the Oracle's suggestion of rest. Our burden is heavy, but it will be lighter in the water, no?"

"I don't know if all burdens float, Andriun." The water wasn't as cold as he'd expected, but it was still cooler than the sand and sun and goosebumps rose across Zaide's skin. He fought back a shudder as he went deeper.

His friend dropped all the way into the sea as soon as it was deep enough. "Then we will find out. As soon as we face Gadranus, we will throw him into the water and see if he sinks."

The notion of pitching a man whose face was still a mystery into the depths of Lake Sian earned a chuckle, but Zaide tempered it. "He floats. Right across the top of the water, like he's made of smoke." He smacked the surface of a wave, scattering droplets.

Andriun's brows rose. "I do not think I have heard this story. At least, not this part of it."

"When we went to restore the Kolmari Elder's power to the Spectrum Blade, he was there. Kind of." Zaide still didn't know what to make of that experience; looking back at it now, it felt more like a dream than reality. It had been more like a ghost than anything, but how could a man's ghost be anywhere when he walked the earth as flesh and blood?

The Shaman grew serious. "And you threw him into water then?"

"No. There's a pool under the temple, it's the source of Resia's power or something. I'm not a mage, I don't know how it works." That came out more defensively than Zaide intended, and he frowned at himself.

"Ah. He put himself in the water. Or, on the water." Andriun made a thoughtful face, then shrugged. "Well, I suppose that is good news, either way. Gadranus floats, so let go for a while."

He grinned and then kicked back, flowing backwards through the water with a practiced ease.

"Right," Zaide breathed. He lunged into a forward stroke and held his breath as he broke through the swell of a small wave. As the water deepened beneath him, it grew easier to glide, and he closed his eyes and let himself float for all of a moment. He was light, buoyant, and letting go should have been easy.

Why, then, did part of him still sink?

CHAPTER NINE

THE WARM SUN and cool ocean breeze was a welcome combination after all the places Lark had been. She shut her eyes and turned her face skyward, savoring the way the light cascaded over her skin. She couldn't stay there for long, leaning against the wall alongside a walkway and taking in the sights, but she enjoyed the moment of peace she'd caught.

From where she stood, near the top of the terraced stone city, most of Nimultis lay within her view. People bustled about the walkways and staircases, carrying baskets of laundry or freshly harvested fruits, armfuls of firewood, or buckets of fish destined to become an evening meal.

Vorkaris lounged on the beach often, and Tula spent most of her time right beside him. Andriun meandered through the city but spent a great deal of time in the water, and the proximity of sand and sea meant Lark often saw the two of them together when she looked outside. Zaide joined them sometimes, but now —and more often—he was in the plaza with members of the guard, practicing his swordplay.

"There are no rules saying you must stay up here with me, you know," Oroduna said from the doorway behind her.

Lark turned her head enough to acknowledge the Oracle's presence, but did not look away from the sights below.

The old woman chuckled at the lack of response. "I mean you can go spend time with your friends, if you wish."

"They're not my friends," Lark murmured.

Oroduna padded forward, her sandals all but silent on the stone. "Aren't they?" She leaned forward to rest her elbows against the wall, mimicking the way Lark stood. Her dark eyes swept the city below, a soft, fond smile curving her lips.

"They are here because they have duties to fulfill. They take their responsibilities seriously. That doesn't make us friends." Even as the statement left her mouth, Lark found herself dropping her gaze to her hands. She'd laced her fingers together, and now her hands squeezed so tight that her joints all grew pale.

"Do you believe they would say the same of you?"

The question was unwelcome, for she didn't know the answer and didn't know what she wanted it to be. Lark raised her shoulders in the tiniest shrug.

"But they are your allies," the Oracle added. "Surely that means something."

"It does." Lark appreciated them for it, though she did not know how to express it. In the wake of new discoveries, her list of allies had shrunk. The Paragons were on her side, but what did it matter when her own father wasn't?

"Hmm." Oroduna watched her face, studied every hint of emotion that made it to the surface.

Lark stared at the guards training below so she wouldn't have to meet the Oracle's eyes. There was too much peace there, a serenity that had grown unwelcoming in the tumult of feelings that tumbled through her every day.

At last, the Oracle sighed. "I know the questions that burn within you, dear child. I see the way they bubble to the surface each time we meditate together, but still, you do not ask."

Because she didn't want to know. Because the moment she

asked, she'd learn the truth, and she wasn't sure she was ready. Lark gave a bitter smile. "If I don't, it's easier to assume it's all a mistake."

"Do you believe it's just a mistake?"

"No." She wished she could, but she had no reason to mistrust Vorkaris. The dragon had been there when the first Paragons were named, when the Spectrum Blade was forged, and when the Shattered Lands were still whole. History and legend told her Vorkaris was trustworthy, and her history books had proven a more valuable resource than her father.

"Well, you are right," Oroduna said. "Though it is a more complicated situation than you think."

Lark almost snorted. Complexity mattered little; her own father had obstructed her quest, and the false Magister he'd put in her path had wanted her dead. "So you mean to tell me, whether I want to hear it or not?"

"I think there is value in knowledge. You know this, and no matter how wounded your heart, you cannot avoid it forever." The Oracle inclined her head toward the plaza below, where Zaide sparred with a man who appeared to be some sort of officer, judging by his more ornate armor. "Your father was meant to be the Bladebearer."

"I know. That was why I went to retrieve the Spectrum Blade. I thought it might accept me, since he refused to believe it was real. He rejected the call of his fate." That the sword refused her had hurt, but she had long since come to terms with it and no longer faulted Zaide for his role, no matter what she'd said to him. She had been sharp the last time they spoke, and he had not sought her out since. Regret would not take back her words, but she felt it, all the same.

Oroduna nodded and rubbed her hands together in thought. "Your part to play is different. Your father knew this. He came to fear it. He knew of possibilities, but his choices have been made based on beliefs, not knowledge. He came to see me before you were born. He has never come to see me since."

"So, what, you're saying he wanted me to fail because of a misunderstanding? Because of some assumption he's made?" Lark pressed a hand to her chest. "That doesn't make me feel better."

"Truth rarely makes us feel better. That's why we hide it, isn't it?" In spite of the weighty words she shared, the Oracle smiled at her, as sweet and genuine as could be.

Part of her wanted to ask for more, now that a sliver of the truth was out, but Lark restrained herself. Hurt feelings mattered less than the challenges ahead, and whatever she asked, it needed to be fruitful for more than just her. "You know all about my father's dealings with the false Magister in Jadora, then? We had assumed he might be an agent of Gadranus, sent to destabilize things in the desert." It certainly seemed like that had been the intention, what with the goborrins beneath the city. But then again, the goborrins had been as eager to slaughter the false Magister's guards as they were to face the guardswomen.

"Your father was forced to face his failings when you arrived with the blade he did not believe existed. It forced him to grapple with many mistakes and many truths he had denied. He believed replacing the true Magister with a man under his control would prevent Vorkaris from awakening, and prevent the sword's power from being unleashed."

"But why? He knew the sword was real, so he knew what must be done to end the Rise. Everything he's done has revolved around combating the rise, and Jadora was one of the strongest, best-defended cities in the Allied Kingdoms. Why would he undermine that? Destroy his own defenses? I don't know how to help Jadora recover now."

Oroduna spread her hands in semblance of a shrug. "Jadora's recovery will happen with or without you, so long as the Rise comes to an end. Things will grow worse for the Watcher before the end, but Vorkaris will rebuild the city with the Magister's help."

Lark opened her mouth, then paused. That response was simple, matter-of-fact. "You have seen this?"

"Yes. And no. I have seen that Vorkaris will preside over the city of Jadora until the end of my vision. If that end is my death or the death of Gadranus, does it matter? All that matters is the dragon will not abandon his city, no matter how grim things may become. Jadora will stand for as long as it can, regardless of what happens to you."

That planted another question in Lark's mind, along with putting a worm of fear in her belly. "Have you seen... what happens to me?"

"I have seen many things. Many possibilities. I see what you shall do while you are here clearly, and there are few ways for things to fork, yet all end with the completion of the same task. But there are many branches in your path after you depart. I do not know which path holds your ultimate fate. Some are kind. Others..." This time, the Oracle shrugged broadly. "But this was your father's failing. He did not see the branches. He did not see the paths or possibilities. He saw but one outcome, and the choices he makes seek to avoid it."

Fear wiggled deeper, burrowing into her spine. "What outcome?"

Oroduna lifted her head to gaze out at the sea, an expression like but not quite sorrow drawing her brows together. "Understand that this task was not meant to be yours, child. This fight was for the generation before you. Fate did not desire children as its heralds, but your father's choice meant there was little other choice."

"Answer me," Lark demanded. "What did he see? What did *you* see?"

The Oracle's eyes grew glazed. "If he took the Spectrum Blade and confronted Gadranus, he would die."

Slowly, Lark drew her arms back until she could lace her hands together against her stomach. She'd expected it to turn somersaults in her middle, but instead, she felt cold. "And if he didn't?"

"That his daughter would seek the blade, and then he would die. Either way, he saw that the Spectrum Blade would be his end."

Her heart thudded against the wall of her chest and her stomach sank. Lark held her clasped hands tighter to her middle. Her eyes swept to the plaza where Zaide trained.

They'd discussed this possibility long ago, on the day of their first meeting, when the eclipse had darkened the sky. The portent of death, the scholars had called it. Something that foretold the death of a king. For so long, she had prayed the one to die would not be her father.

Because of her, because she had sought the blade, it *would* be her father.

Tears brimmed on her eyelashes. "I've done this, haven't I?"

"Yes," Oroduna said, a touch of pity in her tone. "And no. This fate was always foretold, child. Sendassian was warned, given the chance for valor. He chose to hide instead of facing his enemy head on, and when you forced his hand, he sought to have you stopped by any means necessary. All of you."

"But Zaide didn't do anything," Lark protested. "He didn't know—"

"Neither did you," the Oracle interrupted, "but it doesn't matter. Your father's actions are still folly, for nothing has changed. King Sendassian will die, but this is not a failure, or a bad thing. All men must die. It's better for them if they don't know when."

"And... what about me?" Lark wrung her hands. The churning in her stomach had finally arrived, threatening to dispose of everything she'd eaten that morning.

Oroduna raised a brow. "What about you? You will die eventually, too. As will I, and everyone out there. Even Vorkaris will die. None of us are immortal."

"Except Gadranus?" The depth of injustice had never seemed

so deep, and bitterness flooded Lark's words. She couldn't have restrained it if she wanted. How was it fair that their enemy was born into the world over and over again when the rest of them died? How was it fair that he fought the light and shattered peace, and never faced penance for his actions?

Unexpectedly, the Oracle laughed. "Gadranus is far from immortal, make no mistake about that. He's flesh and blood, just like the rest of us, and he will die a bloody death, as he has over and over again for Ages. In that respect, his fate is worse than yours or mine, child. Death brings him no peace. But, if everything goes well... perhaps this time, it might."

"He doesn't deserve peace," Lark growled through her teeth.

"No, but when do we get what we deserve? And how do we know what we deserve? We are not judge of that, child. The Paragons least of all." Oroduna swept a hand toward the beach, to where Tula and Andriun stood at the edge of the waves, bright specks of red and blue against the white-gold sand. "We are not here to determine who should have what. We are the defenders of peace, Dasienna. We seek it for everyone. Not only those we love, but also those who have not earned it. Be better than your anger. You do your own strength no justice."

A humorless bark of a laugh snagged in her throat. What strength? It was her lack that had driven them here. Every step she took seemed to falter, every action landing them in deeper trouble instead of helping to set them free. Lark shut her eyes and inhaled. She could sulk, or she could try to collect herself and move on.

When she opened her eyes again, she had grown calm. "So my father seeks to save his own life now, by sacrificing mine. Will he succeed? Will he be able to kill me, or have me killed?"

Oroduna lifted her chin. "No."

The knowledge brought no relief. "And when he dies, will it be my fault?"

"No."

So in the end, their fates bore no impact on one another. That, too, brought no relief, but Lark would have been lying if she said it did not give her a sense of peace. Her father's fate was sealed; the blade had already been retrieved. "Then all we can do is move on."

"And enjoy the days you have," the Oracle agreed. "Now, go. Spend time with your friends. I will call for you when I need your assistance."

"I already told you, they're not—"

Oroduna clucked at her and ticked a finger to cut her short. "You may believe what you want, but my order remains. Go."

Lark tucked in her chin and held back any further protests. The Oracle smiled and touched her shoulder before she departed. It was a gentle, fond gesture, but deep inside, Lark felt a stubborn resentment rear its head. It had been the Oracle's visions that led to all this, and to Lark's refusal to entertain the friendships her companions had tried to offer.

They were too close to the end, and she would not surrender to the pangs of loneliness now.

CHAPTER TEN

"Break," the captain called.

Zaide lowered his shield and leaned forward to brace his hands against his knees. It was awkward, with his shield on one arm and his sword in his hand, but he didn't think he could stay standing much longer. Sweat dripped from his brow and he worked to level his breathing.

The drills were getting harder. They'd kept things easy the first day or two, while the officers learned his limits. Now, the goal seemed to be to push him to his breaking point as fast as they possibly could. He didn't blame them. He felt the same sense of urgency, a need to be better without a realistic timeline in which he could be. They'd already been in Nimultis for more than a week. The new moon had passed and a narrow sliver of a crescent now hung in the dusk sky. It would grow, and grow fast—faster than his competence with a sword.

His sparring partner slapped his back as he trudged past. "Good."

The praise was hard-earned, but it brought no satisfaction. Zaide trained against the best fighters Nimultis had to offer, and while he knew he was improving, he couldn't help but wish for more.

"That's enough for today. We'll pick up tomorrow morning, an hour after you break your fast." The captain refused to set hard times for training, allowing Zaide as much rest as necessary, but once they started, they worked to exhaustion. For the first few days, that had meant stopping just after midday.

That he'd reached nightfall should have made him proud. Instead, all he felt was a growing sense of anxiety, anticipation for something coming too soon. He tilted the Spectrum Blade until the slender moon reflected on its surface.

When it reached that phase again, they'd be on their way to the end, or maybe even have reached it.

He still didn't know what to expect.

Two more of the guards he'd sparred with shared words of praise and he made himself nod in appreciation as they left. He still hadn't caught his breath, but they didn't expect words, or that he would follow them to wherever they took their nightly meal. There had been no more feasts, but he and the Paragons were served at a table in the plaza every evening. Sometimes Lark joined them. Usually, she did not.

"You are improving," Andriun remarked from the side of what had become the training arena. He leaned against the stone wall at the edge, his bare arms crossed. Zaide had been surprised by his arrival, and it had come close to making him lose his match. It was the first time any of his companions had come to see what he was doing.

"Not as fast as I need to." Zaide sheathed his blade and ran his hand through his hair. It was damp with sweat and gritty with dust, and he suspected he'd be making a trip down to the shore before the night was over. The water was cool and comfortable even in the heat of midday. It would be more than welcome after a full day of training.

"But you are improving. You were already a good fighter. Now you will be great." The Desheni flashed him a grin as he pushed off the wall and straightened. "Will you join us for a meal?"

Zaide cast a wistful glance toward the ocean, but nodded. "Is Lark up there?"

"I do not know. I just came from speaking with the Oracle." Andriun's smile widened.

"I take it you got good news."

"I did." The Shaman nodded toward a walkway nearby, one that connected to their private rooms.

A chance to wash up and change into fresh clothing would be welcome and probably beneficial to everyone, so Zaide headed that way without any need for further suggestion. "What did she tell you?"

"That my future is promising. If we survive what is to come, I will reconcile with and be warmly accepted by my people, marry a beautiful Desheni woman, and raise many wonderful children."

Zaide blinked over his shoulder. "*If* we survive? What if we don't?"

Andriun shrugged, but a grin remained plastered on his face. "Then it will not matter and I will not care, because I will be dead."

"That's a weird thing to smile about, Andriun, I'm not going to lie." The threat of death was one Zaide preferred not to entertain. The Oracle still could not say if they would be successful, only that it was possible. Restricting victory to a mere possibility was no comfort at all.

The hall was wide enough for them to walk side by side, but Andriun trailed along a few paces behind instead, his stride long and relaxed. "I am not smiling because of it. I am smiling because there are great things ahead for me, and I have faith in our group and our cause. The Oracle said a world without Gadranus is one where my children can keep their tails. Is that not a reason to rejoice?"

Zaide supposed it was. "I'm glad you got a happy answer." His room was not far down the hall. He left the door open as he stepped inside and shucked off his tunic. A laundress would be along to scoop it up before he was done with his meal, and it would be back the following morning, ready for him to train again. His own clothes were more comfortable for training in, which left the traditional garb the Oracle had given him for dinner attire. It lay on the bed, not where he'd left it, but he'd already grown used to the city's staff moving his things. They left his unfinished carving alone, so he was content.

"Yes. Tula has not been so happy with the things she has been told. Apparently her fate will be to rule over Jadora, should we make it through the end of all things." Andriun lingered in the doorway as if unsure whether he should step inside or wait in the hall.

Zaide gave him no instructions as he leaned over his washbasin and dumped the water over his head. It was colder than he expected and he shuddered. "Is that a bad thing? She is the Magister, right?"

"Yes, but apparently she had hoped to live a life of adventure, or something like that. I do not think she enjoys the idea of settling down."

"I could see that. I can't picture her with a family or anything." Zaide scrubbed his face with his hands, then squeezed the water out of his hair. It was getting long enough to get in his eyes and would need to be cut soon. Something to do before they left, he supposed.

Andriun flicked his fingers and the water answered, drawing itself from Zaide's hair and splashing back into the basin. "What about you, though? What answers has the Oracle given you?"

"Ah, I haven't spoken to her again." To have his hair instantly dried was strange, to say the least, and Zaide smoothed it back with wet hands to ensure it would stay where it belonged. A cloth lay at the side of the basin's stand, and he dunked it into the cool water with one hand. A quick wipe of the rest of him would be enough to rid him of sweat. Not as refreshing as a dip in the sea, but good enough.

The Shaman finally made up his mind and stepped inside to

shut the door while Zaide finished changing. "Is there nothing else you wish to learn?"

Of course there was. Dozens of questions sprang to mind, but Zaide tried not to let them occupy his thoughts. Little mattered beyond training for what waited for them in the Shattered Lands. He remained silent as he finished washing and changed into his clean clothes. "Let's go eat. I'm starving."

Andriun took the change of subject in stride. "You need to consume more lean meat to keep up with the training you are doing. More eggs, nuts. It will help your strength grow."

"I feel like my foster mother would tell me the same thing." Zaide led the way to the stairs that led to the plaza where they ate.

"Then you know it is good advice."

"Sure." It sounded good, too. Sarma had always prepared hearty meals when he was focused on training. Now, those meals seemed an eternity ago. Had it truly been but a year and a half since the Spring Choosing when the Elder claimed him as apprentice?

They climbed the stairway without further conversation. On all previous nights, the plaza had been brightly lit and welcoming. This time, a lone lantern sat on the table between the trays of food, and the cushions on the ground beside it were empty.

Zaide's shoulders sank with his sigh.

"You were hoping for company," Andriun concluded.

"The girls must have eaten already." No matter how he tried to sound nonchalant, Zaide couldn't hide his disappointment. Their group had worked together so well in Desheni territory. How had that come apart so fast?

Andriun took a seat beside the table and opened the shutters on the lantern wider. A flame burned inside, instead of the bright stones in Desheni-made lanterns, and the warm light that spilled over the table flickered as if uneasy. "There will be time to speak with them. If not here, then after we depart, when we all must travel together again."

"Maybe. Maybe things will just stay quiet and awkward. Lark hasn't spoken to me in days." Not since he'd offended her, Zaide acknowledged. He hadn't meant to. He'd wanted to help. Instead, his efforts had driven a solid wedge between them.

"And you miss speaking with her?" Andriun asked.

Zaide didn't know how to answer. He puzzled over it for longer than it deserved, until movement at the far side of the plaza caught his eye and he turned toward it, hoping without reason that it might be a friend. Instead, he found the Oracle, her dark skin painted with new patterns of gold and her white gown all but glowing in the night.

He stared for too long, for Andriun cleared his throat and jerked his head in the old woman's direction.

Zaide shook his head.

"Go," Andriun whispered insistently. "Take your chance."

A joke about the Oracle not being who he wished for a chance with sprang to mind, but Zaide shut his mouth before it escaped. That was not the sort of joke that would help group relations. If anything, it would only serve to give the Shaman the wrong idea.

Rather than dealing with that awkward train of thought, Zaide swiped a dark brown bread roll on his way past the table and strode toward the Oracle.

She heard him coming, or else expected him, for she turned her head enough to offer a sweet smile as he approached. "Good evening."

He stopped a few paces away. "Andriun thinks I should talk to you."

"You must agree, since you're here." Oroduna glanced toward the table, but the Shaman sat with his back to them, eating contently on his own.

"It's more that I think his questions were about to get

uncomfortable." He'd received no invitation, but she didn't shoo him away, either. Zaide inched closer.

The Oracle continued along the path, one hand raised to brush the leaves of the plants they passed. Here and there, the lush flowers and vines spilled over the wall and narrowed the walkway, but she glided around them with a practiced ease. How much had the city changed in her lifetime? How different was it each time she woke?

She moved on and descended a narrow set of steps, to an outcropping Zaide could only describe as a balcony. There were fewer windows and doorways here, and the jungle hung close to one side of the space. They had a clear view of the sea, though, and the slender crescent moon cast a patch of glittering white against the waves. The Oracle did not signal for him to do anything, so he joined her at the low stone wall that enclosed the space.

"I thought of a question," Zaide said after a time.

"Only one?" She sounded amused.

"Well, no. I have a lot. But you told me I should ask something for myself." And he'd chosen to follow her, so he had to ask something.

"I see." It was neither invitation nor dismissal.

Zaide rested his elbows on the wall and laced his fingers together as he leaned against it. "What happened to my ear?"

The Oracle turned her head and gave him a look that was so neutral, it told him nothing at all. Surely she'd noticed it before. He'd always thought it hard to miss. But she stood to his right side and seemed to expect something, so he turned far enough to let her see.

A ghost of something unfamiliar crossed her face and she returned her gaze to the sea. "I fear you may think differently of me and my gift if I tell you the answer."

He stared. "What do you mean?"

"It was my fault."

It had happened before he could remember. That was all he

knew. But for the Oracle who stood before him to have any part of it seemed so unlikely that for a moment, he didn't know what to say.

He didn't have to say anything. Oroduna bowed her head and deep remorse twisted her mouth. "Understand that all power comes with a price, and to comprehend the choices I have made, you must know what I faced. The first Rise stood to take everything from me. The alliances that formed Amroch as a single country beneath one crown did not yet exist, and divided, we were doomed to fall. No one knew how to approach the evil we faced. No one could contest such power. And so I begged the Maker to give me something, anything, that would let me know how to keep my family safe. He gave me sight."

"And the price?" he asked softly.

"That knowledge could not be mine alone. My first vision made the consequences clear. I must share whatever I see with anyone who asks. To refuse would strip me of my power, and I would be condemned to the same fate as Gadranus. Then, in my desperation, the price was easy to pay. It has grown more difficult with time, but never have I hated the price that must be paid so much as I did when I was asked about you."

Something within him grew cold. "Who?" His voice rasped, barely a whisper, but part of him already knew.

Oroduna closed her eyes and tilted her face toward the sky. The soft, cool breeze stirred her silver hair. "Gadranus has not been this close to achieving his goals since the first Rise, when I chose to stand against him. I anticipated that he would someday risk life and limb to come to me, to ask for knowledge that might turn the tide in his favor. There was a moment, however brief, that I considered the punishment for refusal might be worth it. But I swore I would never fall to his level."

Zaide raised a hand to touch his ear. He explored the bumps and ridges of its blunted end with his fingertips. He rarely noticed the difference in day to day life. It affected the way strangers looked at him and impeded his hearing to an extent, but it was all he'd ever known. That the old injury had come from some sort of violence had always been obvious, but he knew his parents had been refugees. There were hundreds of ways a person could be injured while on the run.

He'd just never imagined he might have been targeted on purpose.

"Why did..." he started, though the answer to the question was already obvious. The fingers of his left hand remained against his cut ear as his right hand moved to the Spectrum Blade. It was cool and unresponsive beneath his touch, as it had been since their last battle, but now its presence brought a new and different sort of wonder. His throat tightened and he had to swallow before he could speak. "It's because of this, isn't it?"

The smile Oroduna offered was sad. "By the time Gadranus came to see me, Sendassian had already refused his fate, and a new path had formed. Killing you before you reached the height of your potential would have changed everything. So he came to me, in search of you. And I... I told him where you were."

Zaide didn't blame her, not with everything that had been on the line. He curled his hand around the sword's hilt and lowered his other hand. "Losing my ear wasn't so bad. It's not like I remember it."

"A small blessing," she laughed, though it was tinged with wistfulness and regret. "One I am grateful for every day. I saw a thousand possibilities for what he asked when he demanded I name you. Nearly all of them ended with death. There was only one path that presented differently. A path where the blade of the soldier sent to kill you missed. Where it was your ear the blade claimed, instead of your life. Every day that followed that monster's visit to me, I prayed that path would someday lead you here."

"So I could ask you this question?" And so he could learn how much of his life had been intentional, after all. His parents' flight from the Shattered Lands had always made sense, but he'd never imagined what could have been the final straw. He hardly knew how to grasp it. Gadranus had known. The Elder had known. His own parents, too, must have known. His brow furrowed. Had Verlin and Sarma known, too? "What about my parents?"

The Oracle tilted her head to one side. "Which set?"

"The living ones. Did they know all this?"

"No. I don't believe so."

Somehow, that was a relief. They'd never felt obligated to take him in for some greater cause, then; to them, he'd always been just a boy. Nothing greater than that. The thought of them seeing his life unfold without any shadow of fate or destiny brought comfort. Reflecting on everything he'd been through, it made sense; his foster family had been just as surprised as he when the Elder had pulled him from the ranks of the Choosing. If they had known, maybe they would have pushed him toward the library sooner.

Then again, he was the Bladebearer, and every hour he'd spent practicing against Aren and the others had helped prepare him for this task. He brushed his thumb over the sword's pommel. "How much of this is me, then? What I wanted, instead of what was picked for me?"

To his surprise, Oroduna reached out to lay her hand atop his and make his fingers be still against the Spectrum Blade's hilt. "All of it is you, Zaide. Nothing can force you to take one path over another. Sendassian's choice is proof of that. Everything is led by your choice, your desire. I merely know where those desires may lead."

He considered that for a moment, then nodded. "I think that's why I feel bad. About Lark, I mean. She wanted this. I didn't. I just touched the sword, I didn't think that meant it was mine. I was supposed to be finding it for her."

"And you did. You had no way of knowing you would be the sword's choice of bearer."

"Second choice," he corrected, though as the words left his mouth, he realized the weight of them had changed. He'd felt inadequate when he'd been told of Sendassian's role, that the king should have been Bladebearer and he had come second. Somehow, knowing he'd been chosen as long ago as his birth had softened the sting.

A soft sparkle lit Oroduna's eyes. "But you aren't the only one."

Zaide blinked. "The only Bladebearer?"

"The only second choice." The Oracle turned and nodded toward the upper levels of the city. "So few of you are in the roles you were meant to have. This Rise was meant to be faced by the older generation. By the Magister before Tula, by King Sendassian, by the Kolmari Elder, by Andriun's father."

Because if Sendassian had sought and accepted the blade, the fight would have come sooner. "So the only ones who were meant for this fight are you and Gadranus? What about Lark?"

"What about her?"

"Doesn't she have a role?"

She twisted back to look at the moon as it continued its steady trek into the sky. "She has a part to play, the same as any of you. A great and remarkable role in the battle to come. But that, too, is a choice, and it is hers alone to make. So leave it to her, Zaide. She knows what she must do, and while you wait for her decision to act, you know what you must do."

Train harder, he decided. Develop his skills and his battle sense, to become the Bladebearer Lark needed. "I do," he agreed.

"Then you know what you must choose." She touched his shoulder with a sweet smile and single nod, then drew away.

Zaide held fast to the Spectrum Blade as she ascended the stairs on her own, leaving him alone in the moonlight.

Taking the sword hadn't been his desire, but it had been his choice, and he didn't regret what he'd chosen.

CHAPTER ELEVEN

Time crawled by with all the tenacity of a snail hidden under a stone. Lark scrubbed her face with both hands and tried to focus, but the light from the candles had all begun to blur together and she could no longer get it to stop. Her frustration grew so thick, she thought she might choke.

Day after day, she'd planted herself in the Hall of Vision and tried everything she could to awaken the power that had always refused to answer. She had tried meditation, prayer, even just begging that her strength might awaken and grant her one single, solitary skill to aid the others in their quest against the darkness.

Still, nothing answered.

She set her jaw and squeezed her eyes closed.

How many times would she be rejected? How long could she stand to fight before her determination waned? Nothing she did made a difference, yet she couldn't help the disappointment that swelled in her chest as a white skirt swirled between her and all the candles she'd painstakingly lit.

She was out of time.

"Your Highness." The Oracle reached for her with both hands, offering to help her up.

Lark stood on her own, instead. "I'm trying," she said, so bitterly she thought she might make herself ill.

"No one has ever claimed that you aren't." Oroduna laced her hands together and held them before the wide belt of gold at her waist. Everything about her radiated grace, power, and authority.

Everything Lark should have, but lacked.

The Oracle did not offer her hand again, but her face grew somber. "It is time."

"I'm not ready," Lark protested, though her voice cracked. Would she ever be?

"What you are ready for does not matter. The moon is full. The magic we need is at its full potential. It is time, Dasienna. Bring the blade, and I will show you the way."

The candles flickered as if to taunt her. Lark set her jaw and made herself nod, then started for the exit. She expected Oroduna to follow, but the woman remained in the Hall of Vision. That was where they'd do their work, then. If they could. If *she* could.

The full moon still hung at the very edge of the horizon, naught but a glimpse of light between the trees. The city's bay faced the south, and the open sky over the broad sea glowed with the last light of the sunset. It was bright enough compared to the candles and dark hallway that she squinted when she emerged.

People walked the paths and staircases, milling about on everyday duties. Lark crept to the wall at the edge of the walkway and peered down, expecting to see Zaide training in the courtyard below. It was where he had been every day since their arrival. The space was empty now.

She caught her lower lip between her teeth. Had he known? They'd all been tracking the moon phases, but she didn't know how closely the others followed it. She'd gone out of her way to ensure she did not have to speak to him, giving him space to pursue whatever he felt necessary.

And so she didn't have to confront her failures.

Lark leaned forward to scan the rest of the city. She couldn't see well to the upper terraces, but every member of their group stood out against the traditional pale clothing the people of Nimultis wore. Only Andriun had been clothed in something drab, but the color of the man himself made him easy to see.

Eventually, she spotted a splash of red at the edge of the beach, far below. She drummed her fingertips against the stones in the wall and then headed for the stairs. When he wasn't training, Zaide had always been with the others. If Tula was on the beach, she might know where he'd gone.

To her relief, all three of the others were on the beach when she arrived. To her surprise, the red she'd seen had not been the Magister's coat.

"What in the world?" Lark couldn't help her exasperation. "What happened to you?"

Zaide couldn't muster a smile. The closest he got was baring his teeth. "Beach." He sat on the sand with his shirt off and his arms held precariously to the sides. Almost every inch of his exposed skin was as red as Tula's hair.

"Zaide doesn't tan," Tula explained as she spread some sort of clear salve up his arm, while Andriun did the same to his back.

"He looks like a boiled shellfish, does he not?" The Shaman flashed her a grin. He, on the other hand, had grown sun-kissed; every day they'd spent on the beach had turned him bluer, bringing a bold pattern of jagged stripes to prevalence across his arms and his bare back.

Lark frowned so hard, it hurt. "Why don't you just use the Captured Spring?"

"The medic said I might tan a little if this heals naturally. Right now, I don't even freckle." Zaide craned his neck to look at his shoulder. He was so red that freckling wouldn't have shown, either way.

"Besides, the spring is empty," Andriun said.

"Empty?" Lark almost sputtered.

Tula's face crumpled. "I said I was sorry!"

"She dropped it," Zaide explained. "That's why we went to the medic."

"But it will refill," Andriun added, almost before he finished. "It will just take a day or two, that is all. There will be very healthy creatures in the sand here for some time, though."

Lark squeezed her eyes shut and made herself exhale. It didn't matter. The rest of them were welcome to play; they didn't have the responsibilities or worries she had. "Fine. Do what you must. But I need to speak with Zaide." She touched his shoulder without thinking.

He sucked in a breath through his teeth.

She jerked back her hand. "Sorry," she muttered.

"Well, go ahead and speak with him, then. We will be done before long. And if it is a secret, I will hum quietly to myself and pretend that I do not hear anything." Andriun scooped another thick glob of salve from a jar.

"I won't," Tula said.

Lark ignored them both. "I need the Spectrum Blade. I need to... Oroduna said it's time." She winced even as she deflected the request to the Oracle. Who was she fooling? She wasn't going to do anything. She still didn't know what was supposed to happen or how, nor had she succeeded in touching the magic that should have been hers.

Zaide stood at once. The others both made chiding noises and followed him with salve on their hands, but he stepped past them to retrieve the sword from where it lay alongside his folded tunic on the sand. "Give me just a moment to get dressed."

"No," she said before he could do more than pick up his clothes. "Just the blade."

A silent moment passed.

Andriun turned away, humming softly.

Lark expected an argument, but Zaide merely studied her for a moment and then let his tunic fall back to the sand. The sword was sheathed in its leather scabbard, but when he extended it to her, she still hesitated to take it.

"Hold it by the scabbard and it won't bite." He smiled as he said it, though the expression was halting and unsure. He took her hand and drew it to the blade, pressing its sheath into her palm and curling her fingers around it.

His willingness to oblige made her heart twist, but when he squeezed her fingers into the leather, she did not resist. "You don't mind?"

"Why would I? I'm your Bladebearer, right? That means I'm just taking care of it for you." He held her there a moment longer, seeking her eyes with his.

Everything he did was so honest. So genuine. Guilt made her stomach churn. "I'll bring it back when I'm done."

"I know."

Shame heated her cheeks and she jerked her hands away from his. He let her go willingly, but Tula made a soft noise that sounded far too interested for Lark's liking. She tried to say something, but her tongue didn't cooperate. Instead, she pulled the sword close and ran for the stairs that led back into the city from the beach.

She'd held it that way before, hadn't she? With the buffer of a scabbard or cloth between them? She thought she had, but since the battle in Ganede, everything had become a haze. That, and she no longer trusted her own memory. She'd always thought her father was stern but caring, and now she found herself examining every recollection of her life to see if the truth stood out with what she now knew.

All of a sudden, she stood before the doorway to the Hall of Vision. She froze there, holding the sword with both arms, staring into the darkened hallway.

It was no longer a mystery why her father had refused to allow her to seek the sword. But if wielding it would bring his downfall, could leaving it powerless undo what she'd begun?

She squeezed the Spectrum Blade to her chest as the moon stole past the tops of the trees to continue its ascent.

If the blade was left unrestored, would it return her father's favor? She hadn't asked the Oracle. She didn't know if it was possible. Nor did she know if she *wanted* his favor. He'd sheltered and stifled her through her entire life. Shamed her for her lack of power.

The people she'd met since she made the decision to run away and seek the sword had been different. They respected her drive and her decisions, and had accepted her as their leader almost without question. The sword in her hands was a symbol of that. Zaide had handed it to her without hesitation, without doubt that she meant the best. That she knew what to do. That she could do it.

But they were followers. They weren't family. She'd worked hard to ensure they couldn't be, keeping all of them at arm's length so none of them could be hurt.

"But maybe they could be," she murmured to herself. When everything was over. When they'd done what they must. Then, maybe she could let them in. In the end, it took her back to her original question. A chance at regaining her father, or a chance to have a future?

A soft, strange sensation brushed her arms and hands, like the prickle of a sleeping limb.

Her brow furrowed as it passed and she made herself take a deep breath. That had been odd, but the body did strange things under stress. She rolled her shoulders back and tried to still her thoughts. The last thing she needed was a distraction.

Instead of relaxation, another prickle coursed through her, sharper this time. She shook her hands, one at a time, as if to wake them up. The moment she returned them to the sword, the sensation resumed.

A cold pang of mingled confusion, alarm, and something she couldn't yet identify dropped in her stomach. Excitement? No, that wasn't it. Hope? She dared not. The feeling in her hands and arms was odd and unpleasant. Was it trying to dissuade her from holding it? If so, it was the first sign of awareness it had shown since the battle in Ganede. If awareness was the right word. Zaide had never done a good job of explaining his connection with the blade.

She fixed her eyes on the sword's hilt. "Are you... are you awake?"

A pulse and tingle answered, making her palms itch, followed by an odd pressure in the front of her head. It struck her as similar to how it felt when Vorkaris spoke to her, and this time, her insides leaped with definite excitement. "You are! Can you hear me? Do you understand? Oh, I don't know how any of this works."

The pressure changed from an awareness to the impression of a question.

"I'm helping. I'm fixing this. Or, I'm trying to. I just need you to trust me. I'll take you back to Zaide soon, I promise." She had to look mad, standing at the doorway and talking to a sword.

The question faded, along with the pressure, and the tingling in her hands abated.

Her heart beat faster.

It understood. It understood and *accepted*. Lark clutched the blade to her chest and ran into the darkened corridor.

The candles were still burning when she reached the Hall of Vision. Oroduna stood in the center of the ring, though her back was turned and her head was tilted back, as if she gazed at something above. The dark dome of the ceiling overhead was bare.

"It spoke to me!" Lark exclaimed before she could help herself.

Oroduna turned to face her with a swirl of her white skirts. "What did you say?"

"It—well, it didn't speak, exactly." A hint of embarrassment crept through her and Lark winced as her cheeks warmed. "There wasn't a voice, but it communicated."

"That is better than I ever could have hoped for. Come, child. Bring it here. We must begin." The Oracle motioned her closer with both hands.

Lark picked up her ruffled skirt and tiptoed past the candles with the sword's scabbard resting against her shoulder. "What next? What do we have to do?"

"First, we sit and prepare ourselves for what is to come. Much will be revealed to us. A way forward, and a vision." Oroduna slid back a step and then sank to the floor in a kneeling position. Her movements were so graceful and fluid, one would never guess her age. Not that Lark could guess it; the long periods of sleep the Oracle experienced between each Rise had skewed her lifespan in more ways than one. The woman had lived for more years than Lark could easily comprehend, and had been awake for more than an average woman's lifetime.

But that was something to ruminate on later. Lark sank to the floor and arranged her skirt, then settled the Spectrum Blade atop her thighs. It was quiet now, no prickling or tingling in her arms to show it was aware, but she took the distinct notion it was observing. Waiting.

Lark waited, too. She expected the Oracle to explain things, to give her direction or instructions, but she sat silently with her eyes closed instead.

After a time, Lark shifted. "Oracle—"

"Patience," Oroduna said softly.

As if she had done anything other than wait. She bit her tongue to hold back her impatience as what seemed like an eternity dragged past.

Just when she began to think she couldn't bear the silence, something glittered directly overhead.

Lark looked up.

What began as a small glimmer in the dark swelled into brilliant light as the moon crept far enough overhead to illuminate the prism centered in the dome above. Pure white light zigzagged across the ceiling and down the walls, lighting up glyphs and patterns that had been invisible until that moment. It raced across the floor and twisted around them in strange spirals until it reached the candles. Then, all at once, the light poured in beneath them in a sunburst pattern, merging into a strange, narrow shape in the very center.

Her mouth fell open.

"Now." Oroduna's voice was just above a whisper, but a smile warmed her face. "Draw the sword. Put it in."

"In?" Lark repeated. She looked from the floor to the ceiling. Draw it? It seemed to have accepted her offer to help, but would it allow her to touch it directly?

The Oracle pointed at the narrow mark on the floor.

It appeared to be nothing but light. Lark slid a hand across it. The stone was just as flat and smooth as ever, cold beneath her fingers.

"Trust me," Oroduna said.

As if there was any other option. Fear and uncertainty twisted in the pit of her stomach, but Lark braced herself. She didn't want to touch the sword directly, didn't want to be shocked again and reminded of her failures. Her hand trembled, but she'd come here for a reason, and she would do her part.

Her hand closed around the hilt. It was cold and ordinary beneath her touch and the fear of pain that had gripped her before gave way to dread. It was wrong. She didn't know how or why, but there was no shaking the distinct sense that something was not as it should be.

Ever so slowly, she drew the blade from its sheath, the metal whisper-quiet against the leather. Hints of color marbled its surface, dominated by reflection of the light patterns on the walls and floor. Lark put the scabbard aside and wrapped both hands around the hilt. Uncertainty still made her shoulders tense, but she rose to her knees and lowered the blade's tip toward the floor.

Instead of striking the stone, it sank into the narrow band of light as if nothing were there at all. A gasp escaped her throat.

Oroduna spread her hands and drew them slowly downward, encouraging her to continue.

Lark pushed until it stopped with a clank, as if it had hit the bottom. The sword stood, halfway embedded in the floor.

"Now," the Oracle said, "turn the key."

The key. The words made her heart skip a beat. Was this what she'd been missing? If that was it, then it was a cruel joke. The sword had refused her at every opportunity. "Oracle—"

"Turn," Oroduna repeated.

Lark swallowed hard and twisted the blade.

It rotated slowly in the floor, taking the line of light with it. Whatever mechanism moved, it fought her, and she gripped the hilt hard to keep it from turning back.

The moment the sword had rotated ninety degrees, something clicked. It dropped into the ground an inch farther, and streaks of light shot outward from the blade, slicing the circle around it into eight sections. Another click. The sword dropped more, and the stone hissed as it split into segments and retracted into itself.

The Spectrum Blade tipped sideways as it was released. Lark drew it back and held the hilt against her chest as the glowing marks on the walls and floor extinguished, leaving only a mellow light in the hole that had opened up before her.

"There." The warmth had returned to the Oracle's voice, but she did not stir.

Lark hesitated, her hands trembling enough to make the sword's tip rattle against the floor.

Oroduna motioned to the hole and the light within it, a silent order to look.

Slowly, Lark leaned forward to look inside.

She expected... well, she didn't know what she expected. Something blinding, something unfathomable, maybe an entryway to some secret realm the blade had kept locked away.

Instead, the hole before her was nothing but a simple recess in the floor. At its bottom, a crystal glowed. Her breath caught.

She'd seen a similar crystal, years ago, in the pages of a book in the royal library. "A Sunshard? But..."

"Take it," Oroduna said.

Lark lowered the Spectrum Blade to the floor and leaned farther. The rich golden crystal was rough, longer than her hand and sharp on both ends. With how steadily it glowed, she expected it to be warm, but when her fingers brushed its surface, it was just as cool as the stone around it. She curled her hand around it and sat back to cradle it in both palms. "I don't understand. The Paragon of Light—she's been gone for years, how did...?"

"She left it here. For you." The Oracle rested her hands in her lap, her eyes distant and glazed.

"But how? She never came back to Nimultis, how did she know? How did she have time?"

"Because she asked before she left to marry your father, sweet girl. She knew she would not live long enough to aid you."

Lark's throat tightened. "And she went anyway?"

"Not all of the Paragons rejected their roles." Oroduna laced her fingers together with a sad smile. "She knew the risks and pursued what meant the most to her. Not everyone is so easily swayed by fear and the promise of self-preservation."

And yet Lark had hesitated at the door, wondering if a rejection of what she'd started might help her regain her father's favor. Her gaze fell to the Spectrum Blade at her side, still no brighter, no closer to regaining its power, but gleaming in the light of the crystal her mother had left behind.

"I don't know how to use this," she admitted, though the words threatened to choke her. "I don't have any power. You told my parents I would follow in my mother's footsteps, but nothing I've done indicates I'll ever be any more than I am."

"And what if what you are is enough, hmm? What if this is all you need? You may not know how to use it now, but that doesn't mean you'll lack that knowledge forever."

Lark clutched the Sunshard tight and squeezed her eyes closed. "Is that a vision? Can't you tell me? What do I have to do to find the power I need?"

The Oracle drew herself up straight as a solemn look took her face. "All power bears a price, dear child. To unlock it—"

"A price must be paid," Lark finished for her, frustration bubbling beyond what she could hold. "I know. My mother told me. She said when I reach my power—"

"That you will lose everyone you hold dear," Oroduna concluded.

"I already know that." Everything she'd done had been in a vain hope of changing that, of counteracting the prophecies that foretold her father's death. How foolish she'd been. Tears blurred the glow of the Sunshard and the candles around them. In the haze, she thought she saw a flutter of movement to the side. "I know I'll have to accept that."

"Can you, though?" The Oracle's tone dropped, her voice dangerously low. "Can you accept the consequences of the path you've begun?"

"I have to," Lark insisted. She'd spent her whole life preparing to pay. The cost of her mother had been steep enough, and she'd worked hard to wall herself off and ensure no one else grew close enough to risk themselves.

Again, something moved. She turned her head to catch it. A smudge of color reflected on the wall. As she stared at it, more traces of motion stirred. A flash of blue, higher up. A multicolored blur on the far side of the room. Lark snapped around to try and catch it, but it was already gone, and more images flickered just outside her clear field of vision. Faces, she realized.

Oroduna spread her hands. "You are prepared to lose them?"

Lark's stomach lurched and she held the Sunshard to her chest. "I—"

All around her, visions of faces flashed across the walls. She stared hard at a patch of dark stone, willing the visions to dissipate. Instead, they grew stronger, clearer.

Blue skin, red hair, warm smiles, and white.

White.

"Are you?" the Oracle challenged, and a low wind kicked up around them, snuffing the flames of the countless candles they'd lit and leaving them shrouded in shadow that even the Sunshard could not hope to pierce.

Everywhere in the dark, faster and faster, Lark saw flashes of white, of cold blue eyes, of cheerful smiles that had once warmed her heart. Now, they tore into her like the fangs of fear itself, plunging venom like ice into her veins.

She choked on a sob.

Zaide.

CHAPTER TWELVE

"Maker's mercy," Andriun breathed. He and Tula both stared into the sky beyond the plaza, his expression distressed, while the Magister's eyes widened with awe.

Zaide had apparently settled on the wrong side of the table. He twisted in his seat to see what the two of them gaped at.

His heart lurched.

A pillar of white light pierced the sky, reaching farther than he could discern. He leaped from his cushion the moment he saw it, upsetting dishes on the table. The Magister and Shaman both yelped as food spilled across them, but he didn't even have the presence of mind to apologize. Instead, he bolted across the plaza, toward the stairs he knew led to the Hall of Vision they'd all visited before. It had to be there. Nowhere else made sense.

The light quavered and narrowed, then flickered out, resembling a plume of smoke more than a beam of light.

Magic.

It had to be.

He almost tripped on the stairs in his haste to descend, but he dared not slow down. His sense was not as fast as his feet, and it caught up with him along the way.

Why was he running? The princess had ordered him to leave her be, and she was with the Oracle, doing whatever was necessary to restore the power of light to the Spectrum Blade. There were few places she would be safer. Yet whatever he'd just seen, it had been nothing like the blessings the other Paragons had bestowed upon the blade, and the difference put a knot of dread in his stomach.

Oroduna intercepted him at the mouth of the Hall of Vision.

"Lark?" he asked as he looked behind her. The corridor at her back was empty.

"She has done what she must," the Oracle said simply, her countenance like a cold mask. "Your work here is now complete. Meet me in the feast plaza in an hour's time. I shall order preparations for your next task."

That her work was done should have been inspiring. Instead, all it sparked in him was fear. "Where is she?"

Oroduna pointed back over her shoulder and then strode by, unbothered.

Zaide ran for the Hall of Vision without looking back.

He heard Lark before he saw her, her body silhouetted by a soft golden glow. She shook as she cried and he rushed toward her, all but kicking darkened candles out of his way.

"Lark," he breathed as he skidded to a stop beside her and knelt. He touched her shoulder before he realized it was a bad idea, but instead of snapping at him, she turned and lurched forward to bury her face in his tunic. It was not the first time she'd cried in his presence, but she wrapped her arms around his middle and did not let go.

The pain of his sunburn hurt less than the way those tears tore at his heart. Lark was so fierce, so stoic. What could have shattered her that way? Zaide wrapped his arms around her, unsure what else to do.

Footsteps echoed in the hall behind him, their harsh click magnified as they spilled into the domed room. Andriun was the first to speak. "What has happened?"

"What is *that*?" Tula asked before he could respond.

Zaide glanced down at the crystal on the floor. It was impossible not to notice it, given how it glowed, but the princess had been his first concern. Now that he looked, he saw the Spectrum Blade laying beside it, but its surface was no different than it had been. "I... I don't know." No matter who he was replying to, the answer would have been the same.

Andriun made a soft sound of confusion as he knelt and reached for the crystal. He tapped it with a finger, as if he expected it to retaliate, but nothing happened. He took it from the floor.

Tula gave a soft, awed gasp. "Did the Oracle make it? Is that why she needed the moonlight?"

"A new artifact?" Andriun guessed.

Lark's arms tightened around Zaide's ribs.

He hugged her harder in return. "What happened? Are you all right?"

She shook her head, almost imperceptibly, and said nothing.

Andriun tilted the crystal, examining it from end to end. "There is much power captured within this. But what of the Spectrum Blade? Does this mean its magic has been restored after all?"

Zaide glanced at the sword on the floor. It looked no different, its strange light still absent, leaving behind only a faint, oily sheen of color. He cradled Lark in one arm, reached for the hilt, and let his fingers slide around the grip. It was cold, lifeless. No different from before.

Maybe that was why Lark was crying.

"No," he said, careful to keep his tone level. They'd known it worked like this, that the power of light had to be restored alongside the power of shadow. There would be no change in its might until they confronted Gadranus. The impossibility of the situation bore down on him with such weight, he didn't know how he stayed upright. "I guess that's what that crystal is for."

"But how do we use it?" Tula leaned forward until she saw

herself reflected in its gleaming facets. She crinkled her nose and squinted.

Zaide rested his hand on Lark's back. "Did she tell you?"

"No," the princess murmured into the fabric of his tunic. "I can't do it."

"Then either she'll tell us when we see her in an hour, or we'll figure it out along the way." He tried to soothe her, hoping the gentle way he rubbed her back might reinforce his words. It didn't matter that she hadn't learned. It was still a step in the right direction, and it was everything they'd been promised. He drew the sword back as if to sheath it, then recalled Lark had taken the scabbard, too. He craned his neck to search before he found it discarded on the floor, but it was too far away to reach.

Andriun retrieved it for him. "I apologize. I did not mean to be overly eager. I just hoped the Paragon had found a way."

Lark flinched hard enough that Zaide frowned.

"So we just stick with the plan, then, right?" Tula straightened and stepped back with her hands on her hips, giving them space to rise. "The Oracle gave us an hour. That's not very long to pack up."

"Will Magister Vorkaris be aiding us again?" Andriun didn't know what to do with the crystal in his hand. He glanced at Lark, then caught Zaide's eye and held it out in offering.

Zaide took it without a second thought. The Shaman had said it felt powerful, but he felt nothing. It wasn't even warm against his skin. "I guess Tula had better go ask. Andriun, you go start getting things ready. Let me borrow the Captured Spring?"

"It has not yet recovered a whole drop," Andriun said, though he slid the chain off over his head and passed it over. "I do not think it will be much help for your sunburn right now."

"It's fine." Zaide wrapped his hand around it and nodded toward the door. "We'll be along in a few minutes."

No one argued, and the two Paragons were sober when they departed. Before long, only silence remained in the empty Hall of Vision, the soft golden glow of the strange crystal and the blue glow of the Captured Spring not enough to chase away the dark.

For a time, they sat, and Zaide waited patiently as the princess's tears tapered until she could lift her head. When she did, he offered the spring.

Lark shook her head. "I'm not hurt," she said, her voice changed by the stuffiness of her nose. "Not in body."

"Just the heart, huh?" He pressed the silver vial into her palm anyway.

She said nothing.

He hadn't yet sheathed the Spectrum Blade, but he was reluctant to pull away from the princess, so he sat, still and quiet, until she eventually pushed herself upright. She slid the Captured Spring's chain over her head and scrubbed her eyes with the back of her hand. Her face was red and puffy, but not as red as he'd managed to bake himself on the beach, so he pretended he saw nothing out of order as he put the golden crystal on the floor between them. Then, finally, he returned the sword to its sheath.

Lark stared at the crystal and wiped her nose. She didn't say anything, her shoulders slumped and her face forlorn.

Zaide had seen her struggle, had seen her disappointed, but he'd never seen her so defeated. He didn't know what to feel or how to help, and the hesitance that gave him made the distinct helplessness that welled within him that much stronger. He remained on the floor and busied himself with fastening the Spectrum Blade at his belt.

"I'm sorry," she said at last.

He frowned. "For what?"

"That I couldn't do it. I couldn't learn." She sniffed, long and hard, the sound most unbecoming and unflattering.

Zaide willed the thought of a goborrin's snorting and snuffling out of his head. Such a comparison wouldn't help in the best of times, and now was not them. "Nobody expected you to do anything. We already went over that. The Oracle said the power of light would have to be restored at the same time as shadow, so there's no point in trying anything before..." He trailed off, unwilling to devote more than a thought to the challenge ahead.

When Lark did not move or speak again, he took the crystal from the ground and held it out for her to take.

She didn't. If anything, she recoiled. "Why are you giving that to me?"

He weighed the crystal in his hand. It wasn't heavy, but it was a burden, all the same. One she'd fought hard to shoulder on her own. "Because it's you, right?" He raised a brow at her, then offered the glowing artifact again. "The Paragon of Light?"

Lark's face grew pinched with distress.

Slowly, he withdrew his hand. "Tula and Andriun assumed it was the Oracle, but she never said that. Just said we were in the Paragon's presence. If she doesn't give clear answers, then she's probably hiding something."

Grief twisted her face. "I'm not." Everything she left unsaid showed in the lines of pain that skirted her eyes.

"Because you haven't learned?"

"Because I failed. I told you ages ago. My power never manifested. I... I'm not the Paragon. I can't be." Tears returned to her eyes, but she dashed them away with her fingertips before they could spill free. "I couldn't do it. I couldn't awaken it, no matter how I tried."

"That shouldn't matter," Zaide protested. "Maybe it didn't awaken yet, but we have this thing, and we have you. That's all we need, isn't it?"

She scoffed. "The only reason we even have that Sunshard is because my mother left it here. Because the Oracle told her I'd need it. Everyone always knew I would fail. The Oracle foretold it." Her shoulders sank again. "I never had a chance."

"I don't believe that." He turned over the crystal in his hand.

A Sunshard, she called it. A fitting name, with how it glowed—
and how sharp its pointed ends were.

"Well, it doesn't matter what you believe. The simple fact is
we have it, but we have no idea how to use it. We have no
Paragon of Light, and without one, we have no hope of ending
this war." She started to push herself back, but he leaned
forward to catch her by the arm. She tried to resist, but he pulled
her hand forward and pressed the Sunshard into her grasp.

"I don't believe that," Zaide repeated firmly. "The Oracle said
there's a chance this is it. That we can make this the end.
Athradan said the same thing, and he wasn't even on our side.
I'm going to hold onto that hope for as long as possible."

A flicker of uncertainty crossed her expression, but her
fingers curled around the shard.

He stood and offered his hand.

Lark hesitated before she took it and let him pull her to her
feet. "Don't tell the others," she whispered. "Please."

"It's not mine to tell." His eyes flicked to the Sunshard she
cradled to her chest and he mustered a small smile. "Doesn't
matter much, anyway. We have what we need. Maybe we'll get
lucky and the next Paragon we have to visit will know how to
use it."

That was the wrong thing to say, for she grimaced and
withdrew from his touch.

"Sorry," he said.

"No. You're right. All we can do right now is move forward.
No matter where that path must take us." She sounded
determined, but a strange gleam of pain shone in the depths of
her eyes.

Zaide made himself nod. "Let's go, then. Do you want me to
walk you to your room?"

"No. I'd rather have a moment alone."

"As you wish, Your Highness." He motioned for her to go
first, and when she started down the hall, he fell in step behind

her with his hand on his sword. It had regained no power and still felt strange beneath his touch, but he still felt better with the Spectrum Blade at his side as they marched toward the unknown.

CHAPTER THIRTEEN

THE HOUR they had been given was not yet up before the four of them convened in the plaza. A number of people—advisors, soldiers, and others Zaide could not name—already populated the space. More came and went as supplies for their next journey were collected and deposited in a pile. Vorkaris sat at the edge of the plaza, overseeing that part of the preparations. He flicked his wings now and then, sending showers of embers to the stone.

Zaide did not see the Sunshard among Lark's things when she joined them, but he didn't see the other artifacts, either. All of them spent most of their time put away, hidden safely out of sight so they wouldn't draw attention. She didn't look at him. She didn't look at any of them, just took her place beside them and stared at the growing pile of bags the dragon would have to carry.

They hadn't stood for long before the Oracle appeared, flanked by her grandson and the others who had come to greet them when they first arrived.

"You will be leaving soon," she announced without preamble. "Everything you will need has been prepared."

"Vorkaris agreed to take us back to the mainland, then?"

Zaide glanced at the dragon first, then to Tula. He should have asked her first.

The Magister shrugged. "He has to. We don't really have time for boats, I think."

"You do not," Oroduna agreed.

The dragon rumbled, a note of displeasure in his deep voice. *I will take you to the mainland, and then take you to the road that runs between Addare and Parral. Then I must return to Jadora. My city still needs my protection. I fear things will only grow worse.*

"And from that road, we will travel to the Shattered Lands?" Andriun asked. He stood gripping the pole of his trident, as if he didn't trust the city's workers to pack it.

The Oracle inclined her head, a simple confirmation that offered no comfort. "To seek the strength of the Paragon of Shadow. You must be prepared for his might."

"Does that mean Gadranus hasn't yet reached Amrochan?" Lark laced her fingers together before her chest, almost as if she were pleading. Zaide sympathized; his family was in Amrochan, and he had shared the same fear.

"He remains in the Shattered Lands, but where, I cannot say." Oroduna's face retained all the equanimity Zaide had come to expect, but something about the set of her mouth was troubled. "My vision grows murky when I try to discern his location."

Andriun rubbed his chin. "What causes such uncertainty?"

"He could be on the move," Zaide said. "Maybe he hasn't decided where he's going. If he's having trouble making up his mind, that could make things muddy for the Oracle, right?"

"It is one possibility," she agreed.

Zaide nodded, then looked to Vorkaris. "Can you take us as far as Tinith?"

You are fortunate I'm willing to take you anywhere at all, the dragon snarled. He shook his wings as they extinguished, shedding ash and embers to the stone beneath his clawed feet.

"It shouldn't be that much farther," Tula said. "But what difference does it make if we go to Tinith? We shouldn't need to visit a market when we've got all that." She swept a hand toward the pile of bags, which had stopped growing, but the workers who had gathered them now stood, troubled, as they tried to determine how to fasten the bags on a dragon.

"Because it's a few hours more by flight, but shaves days off our expedition and lets us get news sooner," Zaide said. "We've got two options for getting to the Shattered Lands from there, and the sooner we can decide which way to go, the better."

Andriun muttered something to himself and slung the bag he'd packed for himself forward over his shoulder. "I do not know these places you speak of well enough to offer an opinion. I need a map to examine." Someone reached for his trident, intending to help, and he frowned as he let go so it could be packed with the rest of their things.

"Here." Tula bounded over to the pile of bags waiting to be strapped to the dragon's back and dug into them as if she knew where to find one. Evidently, she didn't, for a handful of workers joined her in the search. They produced a map eventually and when she returned with it spread wide between her hands, the four of them huddled around it while the Oracle watched in silence.

"So Tinith is down here, see it?" Tula tilted the map. She couldn't point, since it was suspended in her grasp. "If you follow that spot on the map to the east, that's where Kolmar is."

"I know of Kolmar," Andriun said, somewhat defensively.

Zaide touched a finger to the tiny dot he'd called home, then traced a line westward. "The garrison is over here. Kolmar is safe because of the Vale magic Resia restored, but last I knew, the garrison was overrun by goborrins and their armies had pushed all the way up to Amrochan."

The Shaman hummed thoughtfully. "I do not think we have the fortitude to face entire armies."

"I bet I could." Tula snapped her fingers and a small flame sparked above them, though it extinguished just as fast.

"While I'm sure your power has grown respectable, what

with all the flame I saw you spouting on the beaches," Lark said in what had to be the most diplomatic assessment of what the Magister had done, considering how many trees she'd burned down, "I suspect it would be wiser to conserve our strength. I assume you mean to hire a ship that will take us past the front lines?"

Zaide nodded. "It's the best chance we've got, unless—"

"Go north," Oroduna said abruptly.

Everyone paused. The Oracle's eyes had grown distant and glassy, her face as still as etched stone. A sense of tension rose among those gathered and no one spoke, waiting for the moment to pass, for her vision to be complete. Even the dragon lowered his head and waited, perfectly silent.

A shiver coursed through Oroduna's body and she sucked in a breath. "He has chosen. He goes north, into the mountains, where the snows persist. You will find him there, in the coldest regions of that which he has broken."

Zaide touched a hand to his bag. "Did everyone pack their cold weather gear?" It had been warmer in Desheni territory than the first time he'd ventured that way. What he'd worn had been suitable for the cold air they encountered during flight, but there was no way to know if it would be enough for their destination.

"Yes," Tula sighed.

The Oracle's grandson raised a hand to signal the workers, but Lark gave her head a firm shake. "I did not anticipate flight so soon, so our things are in our bags, not among what the rest of you prepared. We will dress ourselves before we take off. If we require heavier coats later, we'll buy what we need when we reach the north."

"All right, but how are we going to get to the north? We can't ask the Dragonster to take us that far," Zaide said.

"*Magister* Vorkaris can take us back to Ganede," the princess said with a frown of distinct disapproval for the nickname.

"It is a very long walk from Ganede to the Shattered Lands."

Andriun drew their attention back to the map and traced a finger along the winding road. "To get from Ganede to Yithel would take days or weeks, and we do not know how long it would take to traverse the wilds between there and where we mean to be. We have no way to know Gadranus will still be there when we arrive, and we will have no way to ask the Oracle for assistance finding him after we leave this island."

Tula tilted the map so the northern part was higher. "We could sail around the coast again. We took that route when we left Amrochan, so we wouldn't have to deal with the goborrins outside the city. It would be faster than walking, but..."

"It would still take weeks," Lark finished.

Zaide lifted his head and locked eyes with the dragon.

All he got in response was a snort. Bold puffs of smoke rose from the beast's nostrils.

"Come on," Zaide said. "You're part of this trip, too, and you know more about traveling to and from the sister cities than the rest of us. Are we better off traveling weeks by boat, or weeks by foot?"

The dragon gave a low rumble of annoyance and turned his gaze to the princess. *I can carry you to Yithel in seven days. It would be six, perhaps as fast as five, but I fear the air above the mountains is too thin for your fragile bodies and it would be unsafe to travel in a straight line.*

Tula bit her lip and studied the map. "We can't ask that of you. It keeps you from Jadora for too long."

Your sister Elsanna is a capable leader, and I have been gone for nearly a month. If the people left on my plateau cannot defend my city for another ten days in my absence, they do not deserve my protection.

Zaide drew a line across the map with one fingertip. Going straight from Nimultis to Yithel crossed the highest range of mountains in Amroch. "What about the Hymnflute? It has some power over the air, could we use it to ensure we can breathe?"

"There's the barrier the Captured Spring makes, too," Lark said. "Its purpose is safety, so there's a chance it could work."

Andriun made a cutting motion with both hands. "I am sorry. The *what* that the Captured Spring makes?"

That fight was so long ago, Zaide had almost forgotten. "We used it in Kolmar's temple. We'll tell you about it on the trip."

The Shaman's brow furrowed, but he didn't ask any more questions.

I would be glad to risk your life in order to find out, but I am less willing to sacrifice the princess or the Paragons, Vorkaris said dryly, his glare fixed squarely in Zaide's direction.

"Then we'll go around the mountains. Seven days, you said?" Lark's attention remained on the map before her. Skirting the mountains took them near Amrochan, but what she thought of that was impossible to tell from the cold way she examined their options. She struck Zaide as collected and confident, a natural leader planning yet another campaign. No one who looked at her now could have guessed the way she'd cried into his shirt.

As close to it as one can hope. I would suggest we pack lightly for this trip.

The princess gave a single stiff nod, left the map to Tula, and marched across the plaza to gesture at the pile of provisions that had been gathered for them. "Consolidate the barest necessities into as few bags as possible and get them loaded onto Magister Vorkaris for the trip. We shall need to leave immediately so we may make landfall before morning."

Tula trotted along beside her and knelt to open a bag as the workers busied themselves with reducing the number of supplies. "Didn't we camp overnight so we wouldn't be seen flying in the dark?"

"We're unlikely to encounter trouble over the sea. It will be morning by the time we reach the mainland, and we'll be arriving over the southernmost part of the Jadoran desert. There are no settlements there." Lark did not join the preparation efforts, but Zaide and Andriun did.

What was necessary for such a trip? Zaide hardly knew. He stared at the leaf-wrapped foodstuffs in the bag he claimed, unsure what to remove. He wasn't even sure what sort of food it was. Unsure how to help, he passed the bag to someone to his left and reached for another. That one was full of warm-weather clothing. "Won't be needing that where we're going," he muttered as he put it aside.

"We are indebted to you, Magister Vorkaris. Your assistance in reaching the Shattered Lands is most generous." Lark strode past the steadily shrinking pile of bags so she could bow before the dragon, but Vorkaris raised a forefoot before she did more than dip her head.

Your gratitude is appreciated, but not necessary, Your Highness. Do not forget, this is my battle, too.

"Load what is ready onto the dragon's back," Oroduna called.

Someone reached for the bag in Zaide's hands and he shook his head. It was the first one that required sorting, and he was determined to finish something.

A moment later, someone crouched by his side. The Oracle's grandson. "Come, Bladebearer," Undolas said with a smile that was both friendly and tired. "Mount and leave final preparations to us."

"You've already done a lot to help." Zaide stood anyway, shifting the bags he'd packed for himself and still carried. He was reluctant to let go of those, though Lark shifted to the dragon's side and passed her things to the first pair of waiting hands she encountered.

"It's the least we can do. Our guards will keep us safe for as long as they are able, but if Amroch falls, Nimultis will go not long after." Sadness touched his smile, but Undolas retained the same sense of calm as his grandmother, no matter how many generations separated them.

"Then thank you." Zaide didn't know what else to say. He strode toward the dragon and slid his bags from his shoulder to retrieve the heavy clothing that had protected him from the cold winds as they crossed the sea.

The others did the same, and before long, all four of them had pulled on their heavy leather gear over their clothing—or under it, in Lark's case. Her ruffled and layered skirts looked absurd with the thick leather pants underneath, but there was no longer a moment to spare.

"We thank you for your hospitality, Oracle Oroduna," Tula said as they lined up to climb onto the dragon's back. Lark went first, hoisted up by a man in white robes. Zaide stifled his annoyance that she was willing to accept help from anyone but him.

"You are always welcome here. I only pray my words have aided your path." Oroduna's brows drew together. "All of you."

Andriun tapped Zaide's shoulder and pointed up at the dragon's back. He nodded in response and climbed into his now-familiar place behind Lark. Tula followed, and Andriun took up the rear.

By the time they were settled, more than a dozen workers had slung bags over the ridges on the dragon's back and secured them with ropes and netting, and before anyone could say another word, Vorkaris lurched backwards and spread his wings.

Below, people scattered, but Oroduna stayed in place. The first powerful downstroke of the dragon's wings lashed her skirt around her legs, but she stood firm and raised an arm to wave goodbye.

"We're never going to see her again, are we," Tula said beside Zaide's blunted ear. It was not a question.

Zaide shook his head, not trusting his voice to carry over the sound of their takeoff, but he suspected they all already knew.

CHAPTER FOURTEEN

BY THE TIME they reached the mainland's coast, everyone was so tired that they all unrolled their bedding and fell into it to sleep without conversation. Morning was no better. An uneasy sense of urgency hung over the group, driving them to a silence that set Lark's nerves on end.

The Jadoran desert was empty below, nothing but the glitter of sand beneath them. The only road through the desert was to the north of their flight path, too far away to see, and there were no settlements between the coastal city of Addare and Parral, which sat several days to the south.

They stopped for a short meal on the sand with the dragon's wings sheltering them from the blistering heat of the sun, and aside from Tula's teasing remarks on the color of Zaide's sunburn, little was said.

Lark stopped him at the dragon's side when it came time to mount up. "Before we take off again, you should have some of this." She fished the Captured Spring from underneath her protective leather gear and uncapped the vial.

"We should save it for emergencies," he protested. "We don't know what waits ahead."

"Regardless of what's ahead, it'll be several days before we reach it." She leaned close enough to press the vial to his lips without removing its chain from her neck, robbing him of the chance to refuse.

He pulled back, but licked his lips out of reflex. The droplet of the blue liquid that he'd taste on his skin would be enough to mend something so minor. A hint of displeasure twisted his mouth, but he kept further objections to himself as she closed the spring and put it back.

As if to hurry them along, Vorkaris rumbled and gave his wing a flick.

Lark tucked in her chin and turned to the dragon's side. "Give me a boost?" She'd never asked for help and didn't need it, yet some part of her felt she owed Zaide a hint of cooperation after forcing him to taste the artifact's remedy.

The sound he made was half surprise and half confusion, but he laced his hands together against his knee and boosted her to the dragon's back without complaint. Good; she didn't think that would be enough to ease his frustration with her, but it was a start.

You owe him more than that, Your Highness, Vorkaris murmured into her thoughts.

Lark grimaced and was glad the others were at her back and would not see it.

She owed him a great deal more. For everything he'd sacrificed. For everything he had yet to face. The vision she'd seen in the Oracle's presence hung heavy in the forefront of her mind, but they could not discuss it during flight, nor did she wish to share it where others could overhear. Getting Zaide alone during the trip to Yithel would be impossible, which meant all she could do was bite her tongue and bide her time.

Both left her feeling ill.

The second night, they camped in the foothills of the mountains, not terribly far south of the pass she and Zaide had traveled on their first expedition together. The memory put a smile on her lips, though it was rueful.

How confident she'd been, then. So certain of her path. She'd been so sure they would locate the rest of the artifacts and end the war. How little she'd known of war then.

How little she'd known of *anything*.

She ate her share of the evening's provisions and tried not to stew in the shadow of such thoughts, but they would not leave her be.

We are faced with a decision, Vorkaris announced at dawn on the fifth day of their travels. They had settled early the evening before, their campsite perched higher in the mountains than either of the previous stops. The dragon never showed any sign of weariness, but he was hesitant, and Lark glanced to the jagged mountaintops that loomed above their heads.

Precisely. Vorkaris swung his head to the east. *We will pass the end of the range today.*

"As we agreed previously." Lark tried to hold on to her patience. The draconic Magister had shown himself to have a memory like a vise. There was no way he had forgotten their conversation.

Yes. That means Amrochan's fields will be visible, as will the ravages of war.

Ah. She pursed her lips. How did she address that without sounding flippant? "I am aware of the goborrin encampment outside of Amrochan." She and Zaide had passed straight through it, wielding the Hymnflute and the Spectrum Blade. She couldn't imagine it would be more frightening from the air.

Do you wish for us to intervene?

Lark blinked twice. That, she hadn't considered.

I cannot afford to spare the time for us to land and fight, the dragon cautioned. *But should you desire it, we can shift our flight path so we pass close by the capital and give Sendassian's soldiers a bit of assistance, if you understand my meaning.*

The goborrin hordes that tried to invade Jadora had been terrified of Vorkaris. Then again, she had been afraid of him, too. Everyone had. They hadn't known then that the dragon was on their side.

"Yes," Lark said without hesitation. "If it doesn't affect our journey, we should do anything possible to aid my people."

Very well, the dragon said, and the smugness in his voice made it clear he'd merely been waiting for approval. *We make good time. We will see the fields outside of Amrochan late in the day.*

She braced herself for the devastation they would find.

When they crossed the last ridge of the mountains and the marsh-ringed meadows of Amrochan came into view, Lark held her breath. Little was different from what they'd seen before, though she no longer knew if that was good or bad. The same seemingly endless goborrin army camped outside the city's walls, their oily fires filling the air with dark smoke.

"There are more of them," Zaide shouted beside her ear to make himself heard. He pointed beyond the rivers both north and south of the city. The goborrin hordes sprawled, spread thinner and spaced farther, but he was right. There were more, and they had swallowed the road in both directions.

Soldiers in gleaming armor defended the walls and fought to drive enemies from the gates, but how little the battle had changed since their departure from Amrochan left Lark feeling sick. How long could her father's armies hold out? How many of them *were* there?

Brace yourselves, children, Vorkaris announced as he shifted their flight path east, taking them closer to the city. *Sendassian's men won't be expecting this. I anticipate arrows.*

We'll have the Hymnflute's barrier ready, Lark thought back as she wiggled her hand into the small bag she still carried over her shoulder. She had been unwilling to let the artifacts out of her grasp. Now, she was glad for it.

All four of the dragon's passengers shifted and leaned in close as Vorkaris tilted his wings and began his descent. Lark gripped tight with her legs and held the Hymnflute ready. The first pass wouldn't take them close enough to the city walls for archers to reach them, but she didn't know what to expect from the goborrins. Lending aid to Amrochan would require a balance between holding a barrier and fighting for breath against rushing winds, and she prayed the monsters below wouldn't have projectiles.

Warning bugles went up all across the army. Amrochan's soldiers raised the alarm, too, and the archers Vorkaris predicted flooded to the tops of the city's walls.

Let's see how fast they determine whose side we're on, the draconic Magister remarked. His chest swelled with a great intake of breath, and as they dipped low enough to see the gleam in the beady black eyes of pig-faced brutes, he exhaled a howling torrent of fire. It struck the ground and rolled across a wide swath of goborrins, yielding squeals and howls of pain as it raked across the field.

Tula lurched sideways on the other side of Zaide. Andriun shouted a reprimand, but it was lost beneath her whoop as she flung fireballs of her own into the fray.

"Spears," Zaide called.

Lark had almost missed the row of goborrins that ran toward the flames, spears upraised and ready to launch. She sucked in as much air as she could and launched into the well-practiced song that would spin the Hymnflute's protective barrier around them. The goborrins threw, and the spears bounced off a sphere of air that surrounded the dragon's passengers.

That was a problem she hadn't considered. Vorkaris was too large for her to encompass him with the shield.

Worry about yourself, Your Highness. Dragon hide is far tougher than what these piddling excuses for weapons can pierce.

It wasn't his hide she was worried about. She couldn't bring herself to think back at him while she was playing, but her eyes swept down the length of his massive wings. Surely the membranes were at a greater risk.

The pass ended and he pulled upward with a few mighty flaps. *Worry about yourself,* Vorkaris repeated.

They banked and came back across the goborrin army the same way, but going the other direction, and Lark did her best to play loud and hard, enlarging the diameter of her shield. It would never be enough to protect his wings, but if she gained him even an inch of safety, it was enough. That was all she wanted, all she'd ever sought. Safety for her home. Her people. And for those she'd so desperately tried to keep from caring about as more.

The thought lanced through her with all the force one of the goborrin spears might, if her distraction made the barrier fall. She shook her head and made herself focus on one note at a time.

Pass by pass, they moved closer to the city walls, and over the high notes of the Hymnflute in her hands, something brushed Lark's ears. She tilted her head and tried to listen past the music she created each time they swung low, but the answer came by sight.

Cheers.

Soldiers leaped and waved atop the walls and in the space before the barricaded gates, cheering at each sweep of the dragon's flame across their enemies.

Vorkaris gave a low rumble of a smug laugh.

Lark smiled as they scaled beyond the reach of the goborrin spears, but her heart twisted. What a difference the dragon could make, if only he stayed in Amrochan.

I am sorry, Dasienna, Vorkaris said with real remorse. *But you know I cannot forsake my city. The best we can hope to do is show the soldiers here they are not alone. We can lift their spirits, but I must return to Jadora.*

I know. She couldn't blame him, but she still regretted it.

Bolstering the defenses in Jadora is the wisest use of my time. I could spend a hundred days pouring flame over these monsters, but their numbers would never truly thin. For each goborrin I destroy, another dozen are born to replace it. Their lives are not like ours.

That she knew little of the monsters they fought had never crossed her mind. Neither the royal library nor the Great Library in Jadora had much in the way of information on the goborrins. There were passages on what they looked like and what sort of battle tactics they used, and some on how they treated their dead in the wake of battle, but with countless beasts below them, the gaps in that knowledge struck her as stark.

Worries for another day, Vorkaris suggested. *We will make one more pass, then the field before Amrochan's gates will be clear enough to grant your people a moment of reprieve.*

Thank you, Magister. She positioned herself to watch the soldiers on the final pass. The heat from the dragon's flame put sweat on her brow and made her eyes water, but she could not keep from staring as they made a final sweep toward the north, and the direction her mind went left her uneasy.

Had they seen who aided them? Had she been recognized? If her father was alerted to her presence near the capital, it could affect the mission they now pursued. She swallowed hard as the last cycle of the barrier song ended and the shield fell. The sound of the soldiers' celebration had already faded, but she clung to the memory of the cheers as they scaled higher into the air and crossed the marshy lowlands where the many rivers around Amrochan lay.

Long after the sun set, Vorkaris made his landing in the middle of the northern road.

We are safely away from the armies of Gadranus, he announced as they touched down.

"For now," Zaide said. He was the first to climb off the dragon, and he grunted when he landed hard. "How long before they push farther to the north?"

"They are more likely to come from the north," Andriun said as he descended. He reached up to help Tula, but she launched herself from the dragon so hard that her landing took both of them to the ground.

Zaide turned as if he meant to do the same for her, but Lark had already gotten to the ground on her own. She straightened and smoothed her skirts. "A pincer, coming around Lake Sian from both sides?"

The Shaman nodded. "That would be my guess. My experience with these armies is limited, but we have our histories. To swarm and overwhelm has always been a favorite tactic of Gadranus and his followers."

Yes, Vorkaris agreed grimly. His head swung toward the west and for a time, he looked lost in thought.

Lark fought back her uneasiness. "What's over there?"

Nothing, now, the dragon said. He circled around to the south of his passengers.

Zaide turned as the dragon moved around them and settled his big, glowing body across the road. "I thought I saw something in that direction while we were in the air. The landscape looked strange. What was it?"

"The Scar," Tula whispered ominously.

The dragon snorted plumes of smoke into the air. *The final resting place of my kin.*

Lark's stomach sank, but she fought to keep her expression smooth. "The Last Battle of Dragons took place there. Have you read of it?"

Zaide shook his head.

"There's little information about it, even in the royal library," she said. "Jadora's library might hold more, but I don't think it's necessary. We've discussed before how we knew Gadranus had pushed toward Amrochan once previously?"

"Through Kolmar," he agreed.

Tula planted her hands on her hips and turned toward the west, as if to study the landscape they discussed but couldn't see. "The Last Battle of Dragons was before that, but the dates were not well recorded. It's been several Ages ago, but you know each Age is really just an estimate."

"And it has to do with enemy armies?" Zaide rested his hand on the Spectrum Blade as he followed the Magister's line of sight, but the lack of tension in his hand and shoulders made Lark think it was an action of habit, rather than seeking.

"Yes. They made it to Yithel once, coming from the north. They might have reached Amrochan then, but they were stopped in that field." Lark glanced to Vorkaris as she explained. Did he find her summary of events appropriate? He looked so distant and thoughtful that she twitched in surprise when he rumbled deep in his chest.

His armies were powerful during that Rise. He still had the full force of the Shattered Lands behind him then. Had my kin not intervened, Amrochan may well have fallen. But their numbers were great, and even a being as mighty as a dragon can be overwhelmed. The dragon's mental voice was abnormally subdued.

"Like when ants swarm over a larger insect," Andriun mused. "They are tiny, their bites little more than an annoyance, but danger comes in numbers."

Yes, Vorkaris agreed. He did not appear sorrowful, but the calm way he laid his forefeet atop each other and gazed at the ground showed his resignation. *Theirs was a great sacrifice. It ended that Rise and changed the landscape forever. Few dragons remained after that battle. One by one, his armies have ended them, until only I remain.*

"Which is why I don't ask you to help with this fight," Lark interjected. The dragon had done more than his share, aiding them in Jadora, granting Tula the power to bless the Spectrum Blade, carrying them to see the Oracle, razing the goborrin armies outside her father's walls.

Vorkaris scoffed. *Arrogant of you to believe my answer would be different if you asked me. We will reach Yithel tomorrow, at the end of our sixth day of travel. As promised, I have brought you across the country in less than a week.*

"For which we are infinitely grateful, Magister Vorkaris," Andriun said. He dropped an armful of sticks into the middle of the road. Lark had not even noticed him scouting for firewood, but Tula joined him beside it and knelt to ignite the wood.

The dragon only flicked his tail.

The fire crackled as Tula coaxed the flames up each branch, and Andriun rooted in his bag for provisions to heat. The moment was quiet and should have been peaceful, but Lark found herself looking at Zaide and an uneasy sense of dread rolled through her.

She needed to pull him aside, to find time to discuss what she feared might await them, but her tongue felt stuck when she opened her mouth and it took everything in her to loosen it. "Zaide?"

"Hmm?" He shrugged out of his coat and draped it over his arm. The night was warm, and the insulated gear that was perfect for flying was too much on the ground.

The two Paragons looked her way, and she quailed. "Be sure to take inventory of your things so we can make an appropriate list for what supplies we'll need when we stop tomorrow. I don't know how much we'll be able to find once we cross into the Shattered Lands." It was a lame excuse, and hardly important now.

Zaide nodded and settled cross-legged by the fire. "I'll look before I go to sleep. Maybe Tula can write it down in that notebook of hers."

The Magister grinned.

"Of course," Lark murmured as she, too, sank to sitting, a new weight dragging her heart down in her chest.

There would be time to speak. There had to be. What might happen if he didn't know?

CHAPTER FIFTEEN

YITHEL HAD NOT CHANGED since Zaide had been there last. He didn't know why he'd thought it might; it had only been a few months since he'd made the trek from Desheni.

Tula oohed and ahhed over the city with its pale plaster buildings and the riverside walkway with its gray stone balustrade, but Lark and Andriun were not impressed. Vorkaris had not joined them in the city, and Zaide suspected that had been a wise decision. The dragon had landed just south of the settlement and let them off on the road, where the trees had sheltered them from view.

Even so, it had been night when they landed, and there was no hiding the way his scales glowed. Townspeople had seen him. Now they scurried about in a panic, shouting about it to anyone who would listen.

"Didn't you see it, boy?" an old woman asked as she shuffled by. "Aren't you afraid?"

Zaide met her with a bland stare. "Why would I be? The dragon is on our side."

She blinked, taken aback, and hurried off to tell someone else.

"Should we be concerned that word about Jadora's new

Magister has yet to travel this far?" Lark twisted the strap of her bag with both hands.

"Probably wouldn't help if we were. The desert's been busy dealing with a lot of unwelcome surprises. Business is down, and that means travel is down, too." Still, Zaide found it odd. Cutting off communication between regions wasn't easy, and aside from the goborrins outside of Amrochan, they had not seen any sign of armies.

"They'll hear about what happened in Amrochan within a few days, right? They'll know that Vorkaris is one of the heroes after that." Tula walked with big steps, swinging her arms farther than necessary.

Andriun trailed along behind her with a more sedate pace. "Perhaps we could begin the spread of that information before we set out in the morning. I would think everyone in the Allied Kingdoms would benefit from good news."

"Especially once you get close to the border." Zaide stopped in front of a taller building with well-kept plaster and big windows. Lanterns glowed on the other side of the dark wooden frames. "Looks like an inn. Do we stop here?"

Lark headed for the door. "We borrow their light to look over the map and finalize our list of supplies, then we continue north."

"Don't you want to sleep in a real bed?" Tula didn't whine, but came painfully close to it.

"She's right. We need to hurry. And I don't know about you, but I could go for stretching my legs a bit after spending days riding." Zaide kicked his legs out, one after the other, to make a show of stretching. He didn't need an explanation for why the princess didn't want to stop. They were close to Amrochan, close enough for word of her presence to spread fast, and it was better to distance themselves from her father.

Lark mouthed a silent "thank you" at him before she slipped inside. The rest of them followed in silence. Everyone had removed their cold weather gear and donned their own clothing, but there was no helping that their group would stand out. Zaide entered last, and the pensive way he examined the others did not go unnoticed.

"Tell me if you have heard this one," Andriun said softly. "A Jadoran, a Desheni, an Amrochanite, and a broken-born walk into an inn."

Zaide snorted, but couldn't help his smile. "Amrochanite? Is that what you call them?"

"Is that not what you call them?"

"They're Amrochans, as far as I know." A few faces turned their way and Zaide pretended not to notice. Lark chose an empty table for them, and they all sat. The room was not crowded, but there were enough people there for a meal or a drink that their presence wasn't likely to be forgotten.

The Shaman frowned as he settled. "But that is a plural. Singular, it would be Amrochan. The capital city is called Amrochan, and the Allied Kingdoms are Amroch. Amrochan as a description of a person merely implies they are from the Allied Kingdoms, does it not?"

"Amrochanite is fine," Lark said as she laid their map on the table. She unrolled it before the conversation could continue and planted a finger on the road north of Yithel. "It looks as if the road follows the river until this point. There should be a bridge across the river, and the road continues to Chithal from there. Unless there are other bridges, that will be our crossing point."

"No other bridges, miss." A pleasant-looking woman with a flour-dusted apron stopped beside their table and rested her hands on her hips. There was flour in the creases of her knuckles, too. "Drinks? Food? Rooms?"

Lark nodded. "Yes, please. Whatever meal you have to offer is fine. A pitcher of water for drink, as well. No rooms, we shan't be staying that long."

"No water for me," Tula said. "I want one of those great big wood mugs like he's got, with all the frothy ale."

Andriun grinned. "Me, too."

"All right." The woman cast a thoughtful eye toward Zaide. "What about you?"

"Water is fine, thank you." Something about the way she examined him made his skin prickle, so Zaide did his best to smile.

She nodded. "I'll have it for you in just a moment, then. Make yourselves comfortable."

"Thank you." He'd already said that, but repeating it seemed proper. Zaide's smile faltered the moment her back was turned. "Is ale a good idea?"

Andriun shrugged. "I do not know the cultural norms of your people, but I am a grown man and may do as I please. A good drink now and then, when one does not have to swim, can be good for settling the nerves."

"And I've never had any," Tula chimed in excitedly. "In Jadora, it's against the law."

Everyone froze.

The Magister giggled. "It's fine, though, we're not in Jadora. The lady would have told me if it's not allowed, right?"

"You'd better hope you like the taste, then," Lark muttered before she tapped a finger on the map to draw their attention. "We're going to encounter a problem as soon as we're off the road, I believe. There don't seem to be any roads running in that direction, and there are no maps available anywhere these days that show what anything outside the Allied Kingdoms is like."

"I saw a few maps in the Elder's library when I served as his apprentice, but they were so old, they wouldn't be any use now." Zaide stared at the point where Amroch ended. At least returning would be easy; all they had to do was travel east.

The woman returned with mugs, cups, and a pitcher in her arms. She passed them out around the edges of the map. "Food will be along in a moment. Where are the lot of you off to, then?"

Tula wrapped both hands around her mug. "We're going to the Shattered Lands to kill Gadranus."

Mugs thumped and people fell silent at nearby tables.

Someone coughed.

"Well," the woman sighed, "far be it from me to try and keep you from a fool's errand. Drink up, I'll be right out with those plates."

Andriun sucked the foam off the top of his ale as the woman retreated to the kitchen. "Perhaps we should not so loudly announce our intentions from here on out?"

Zaide resisted the urge to make a face and poured himself water from the pitcher. "Definitely not. We can get away with that here, and people might even encourage us, but we don't know what sentiments are like on the other side of the border. We're going to be in enemy territory. We don't want to seem threatening."

"Although I am unsure how we can be anything but threatening, given the things we carry." Lark did not have to specify the Spectrum Blade for him to know she meant it. She rummaged in her bag for a minute to produce a pencil, then sketched a loose outline of mountain ranges at the edge of the map, where the Shattered Lands were left undefined.

"Doesn't look like there are many options for directions to go. We'll have to get around those mountains, and then from there, we head north, right?" He filled Lark's cup, too, though she ignored it.

"That was what Oroduna said. I don't suppose either of you know anything about the landscape there?" She glanced at the two Paragons on the other side of the table.

Both shook their heads.

The princess sighed. "Surprises for all of us, then."

"Ew."

Zaide lifted his head in time to catch the way Tula scrunched her nose and scraped her tongue against her teeth. She pushed her mug forward until it crinkled the edge of the map. He lifted the thin paper to keep it from tearing. "That good, huh?"

"It's illegal for people under twenty years of age to drink it in Jadora. With how bad it tastes, it should be illegal for everyone."

She shuddered and scrubbed her lips with her sleeve, then snatched Zaide's cup of water. She drained it in a few gulps.

All he did was roll his eyes.

"Well," Andriun said as he turned her mug so he could grasp the handle and pull it close. "Your displeasure is a treat for me, then!"

Lark shook her head, but said nothing and finished drawing her plans.

"I should have asked for a wineskin of that drink," Andriun announced several days later, when they had crossed the bridge and ventured off the road to see what lay beyond Lark's map.

Zaide climbed the rocky slope to join his friend, leaving the girls behind in the brush. They'd taken the lead for most of the way, following game trails through the dense woods and breaking new trails whenever it had grown too thick for them to pass with ease. The stony slope bore little but scrub, though, and he assumed they could get through that on their own.

The slope crested in a ridge of pale stone and fell away fast, to a deep, rocky and turbulent river below. Zaide stared down at it for a while, then scanned farther up the ridge. There were no lower points in either direction. "Drinking before climbing doesn't sound like a good idea to me."

"Climbing?" Andriun's brows rose. "I meant to make me foolish enough to dive. I can sense the water is deep enough to be safe, and there are open spaces without rocks, but I believe the drop is thirty feet. That is not a comfortable fall."

"Even if it were comfortable, that's fast water. Tula doesn't swim well enough to deal with that. Even with your help." Zaide rubbed his chin and let his gaze wander. "But we're going to have to climb down and swim across, I think. Can you tell if there's anywhere nearby with a slower current?"

The Shaman pursed his lips, then pointed south. "It is wider in that direction. More shallow. As the river grows narrow, it gains speed."

Lark broke through the brush first. "What's down there?"

"More water." Zaide pointed. "We're going to go that way."

Tula reached the ridge a moment later, huffing for breath. "Well, this would be a good time to have a dragon, wouldn't it?"

"Not helping," he said.

Lark turned to march south along the ridge without missing a beat. "I suppose there's one advantage of running into something like this."

"Which is?" Zaide shrugged his bags higher onto his shoulder. They snagged against the shield on his back and he righted them before he started after her. Andriun would likely take the lead before long, if he was the one who could tell where the shallow place was. The ability to sense water struck him as a remarkably useful gift for traveling the wilds, and he wondered how much easier his early trips would have been if he'd always known where to look for it.

"If there's a river here, it'll keep goborrins out."

It wasn't funny, but he still chuckled. At least there was that. He'd used rivers to separate him from enemies more than once.

As he predicted, Andriun trotted to the front of their procession. "The water slows about two miles in this direction."

Zaide blinked hard and gave his head a slight shake. "Two *miles*? Have you always been able to sense water that far out?"

"No. This is something that has grown stronger since I replaced my father as Paragon."

"You know, my power has grown a lot, too." Tula threw her arms wide and turned her hands toward the sky as if she meant to summon fire, but the princess cleared her throat and she dropped them back to her sides. "I mean, I didn't have much of any that I knew of before Vorkaris picked me as his new Magister, but I keep getting stronger as time goes on."

A faint crease formed between Lark's brows.

"A lot of skills are like that," Zaide said, and the weight of his gaze caught the princess's eye. "They get better a little bit at a time. Sometimes it feels like nothing for ages, then, suddenly, you can do it."

The way the corners of her mouth drew down made him wonder if that had been a mistake, but when she spoke, her voice was soft. "Is that so?"

"Of course. It just means you shouldn't quit." A hint of a smile tugged at his lips.

A moment later, the smallest flicker of a smile graced her features, too.

"Hmm," Andriun said.

Zaide turned, expecting some sort of problem or obstacle, but found his friend examining the two of them with a shrewd eye instead. For some reason, the scrutiny made him feel odd, and the heat of embarrassment crawled up beneath his collar.

The Shaman said nothing else and returned to the trek, but they hadn't gone far before an odd noise filled the air and echoed off the cliffs. He slowed to a stop and held up a hand to command silence.

Uneasiness made Zaide's shoulders itch. He chose his footing more carefully and moved as quietly as possible.

The ridge and the river below took a turn, and in the crook of land below, two dozen goborrins swung hammers.

They were building a bridge.

CHAPTER SIXTEEN

"Well," Lark said, mindful not to let her voice break a whisper. "We didn't have to go far to find them."

Beside her, Zaide wrung the hilt of the Spectrum Blade with his right hand. "Look at it this way. At least we know they still can't swim."

"But there will be armies behind them." Andriun squinted at the horizon, perhaps trying to locate a larger camp, but there was nothing to see among the trees.

Only Tula remained silent, though she drew her notebook from her pocket to scribble down notes. Lark made a mental note to ask to review the observations later. It was odd how seamlessly the Magister had replaced her as the note-taker of the group. In some ways, she missed it. With her lack of power, it still felt as if she had nothing to offer. She considered asking that Tula leave the note-taking to her, but a librarian was more fit to document their expedition than she was.

She wasn't fit for any task at all.

"How do we want to handle this?" Zaide glanced to her as he asked. For all that she'd demanded that he defer to her in decisions and matters of leadership, any time he did it made uncertainty and self-doubt flare within her.

"We could keep going and try to stay unnoticed," Andriun suggested. "There is no good way to get down the cliff to face them."

"Goborrins can't swim and they can't climb, but we don't know what sort of weaponry they have. If they have anything that can be thrown, we'd be putting ourselves in unnecessary danger." Lark tried to reassure herself that leaving was the best choice, but she found herself worrying her lower lip with her teeth. She didn't believe it, not really. If they allowed them to complete a bridge, it would make the invasion of the northern part of Amroch that much easier.

Zaide watched her face instead of studying the monsters below. Eventually, he nodded. "So we go down on the other side, where it's safe to climb down and we're out of their sight, then we come back and wipe them out."

Tula crinkled her nose. "Wouldn't it be smarter to just keep going?"

"Are you really going to pass up the opportunity to set their bridge on fire?" Zaide countered.

The Magister's head tipped to one side as she considered that option.

"We don't have a good way to send a warning back to Yithel at this point," Lark said. "It would be irresponsible of us to leave them. A few hours of our time now can buy the north at least a few more days."

Andriun frowned so deeply, she was sure he meant to disagree with her, but he nodded. "We must exercise extreme caution. We are vastly outnumbered and while I can use the river's water to aid us, I cannot hope to control so many. We must strike hard and fast, and we must have a plan for retreat if there are more than what we see below."

"If we need to retreat, we get Tula to make a fire wall to hold them back until we can get up the cliff. We'd have to find a new crossing point, but the cliff is our safety since goborrins can't climb." Zaide inched back from the edge and started off again, headed for their originally agreed-upon point of descent.

They tried to avoid the edge of the ridge, though Andriun crept closer now and then to see what waited below. There were no signs of other camps or waiting armies, so once they were clear of the bridge builders, they moved faster.

When they reached their intended point of descent, the Shaman slid over the edge of the cliff and was halfway down before Zaide produced a rope from his bags. He tied it to a sturdy sapling and motioned for Lark to go first.

She signaled to Tula instead. "Go. Have your fire ready when you get to the bottom. I'll cover you from up here." She hadn't needed her compact crossbow in some time, but it was tucked in the bag at her side with the artifacts, so it was close at hand.

"There better be somewhere dry to put my feet down there," the Magister grumbled as she seized the rope and began her cautious descent.

Zaide triple-checked the knots in the rope as she disappeared from sight. "You next, Princess."

Lark hesitated. He'd only ever addressed her that way when he was unhappy or offended, but she couldn't fathom what she'd done. "Excuse me?"

"I'll go down last," he explained with a gesture toward the rope. "I'll untie it and climb down the regular way. Probably won't be the last time we need this." The smile he gave her was halting and uncertain. He certainly didn't look unhappy with her. Nor did he sound it.

Belatedly, she realized what she'd done. He'd been stiff and formal with her since she'd snapped at him in Nimultis, when she'd demanded space. There had only been one moment after that in which he'd sought her out. The thought of him rushing to her aid because he thought she might be in distress should have been sweet. Instead, it was tainted by her failure and the vision the Oracle had shared.

She should have been glad that he distanced himself and tried to offer more respect. That vision was a perfect example, and proof that she'd done the right thing. Long had it been foretold the Rise would take all that was dear to her, but it was easy enough to fight. All she had to do was ensure no one got close enough to *be* dear.

Yet now that they stood with a gulf of formality between them, the distance made her heart ache. She stared at him until it grew awkward, her throat tightening as his smile faded. "Zaide, I..."

His brows rose.

"I'm afraid of heights."

"I know," he said. Of course he did. He'd been the one she clung to on the lift back at Jadora's docks. The one who held her steady on the dragon's back as Vorkaris flew them across the sea and back again. Compared to those, the cliff beside them was nothing, but he still took her complaint seriously. His attention drifted from her to the rope, then to the cliff's edge. He strode to its crest, trailing his fingers along the rope.

Lark watched, uneasy.

"It's sturdy enough to hold two. Come on." He extended an arm.

Just like that. So simply, he'd accepted the problem and offered a solution. Guilt churned within her and she almost refused, but sense won the tug-of-war inside her head with little effort. She was good enough at climbing, but going up was different from going down. She had no doubt she *could* work her way down the cliff's face on her own, but it would be faster and easier if she didn't try.

She strode forward and reached for his hand.

Zaide steered it over his shoulder. "This is going to be awkward, so try not to think about it, and don't look down, all right?"

Lark answered with a mute nod. It was easier to hold on to

him from the front; the shield he carried on his back would have made the reverse like trying to cling to a turtle.

"Put your arms around my neck and hold on. I'm going to go down backwards." He guided her arms to where they needed to be, then readied the rope. She couldn't see how he grasped it or why he positioned it the way he did, but she assumed it was to make the descent easier. He drew her close against him. "Ready?"

"No," she said.

"Yeah, me either." He pushed off and pulled her with him.

Lark squeezed her eyes shut tight and clung to him as her heart leaped into her throat and panic stirred her stomach until she thought she would be ill. His boots crunched against the stone and beneath hers, his body swayed. It was not the uneasy rock of some wind-battered descent, but the soft undulation of slow and deliberate movement.

"What is this?" Andriun asked. His voice was not far below, but Lark refused to check. "You are supposed to climb like a normal person, after you untie the rope."

"Yeah, yeah." Zaide grumbled. The complaint came out strained, and she cracked open one eye. Perspiration speckled his brow and his arms were taut with effort, but his face bore pure determination.

Again, guilt wrenched her.

Andriun muttered something on his way back up the wall and she craned her neck to watch him climb. The top of the cliff shrank away at a rapid pace, and they stopped.

"Hop down," Zaide said.

She made herself look. They hovered a scant few feet from the ground, low enough for her to look Tula straight in the eye.

"No fair." The Magister crossed her arms and pouted. "Nobody helped me down."

"Well, you aren't a princess." Lark tried to sound haughty, but it came out strained. She wiggled to the side and let herself slide until her feet touched the ground.

Zaide finished the descent on his own, then leaned against the cliff and worked to catch his breath. He hadn't before the unfastened rope dropped over the cliff and fell atop his head and shoulders, coiling around him like a snake.

"Catch," Andriun called.

"Funny," Zaide replied. "Now get down here and show us how we're getting across the water."

"The same way you cross any water. You get in it, and then you go across." The Desheni came back down the cliff a little slower than he'd descended the first time, but he was not winded when he reached the ground. "Come. It is only thigh deep."

"On who? You? That's going to be hip deep on Lark." Tula cast the water a disdainful look as she hefted her bags in her arms and checked to be sure none hung low enough to get wet. As an afterthought, she let them all hang and sat on the rocky outcropping to remove her boots.

Zaide followed her lead, and Lark sat to do the same.

Andriun waded in until the water reached his knees. "It is cold, but the bottom is solid. Rocky. It will be easy to walk across."

"Better than the rivers I've crossed before." Zaide rested his boots atop the rest of his belongings and moved to the water's edge. "Take Tula across with you? I think she'll have the most trouble."

"I think I've had enough of water for one adventure," Tula agreed as she tiptoed forward and let Andriun take her arm. He held her steady as they waded across the river, their path simple and straight.

Reassured, Lark hitched her bags up above her waist and moved forward.

"We're lucky there aren't any bugraks over here." Zaide followed her into the river, his step slow and sure. He never tried to pass her, nor did he attempt to offer help or walk by her side.

Bringing up the rear, she decided; there were no enemies to be seen, but he was leaving no chances.

Andriun helped Tula out of the river and stripped the water from her clothing with a flick of his webbed hand. He dried his own while she put on her boots again, and did the same for Lark the moment she stepped from the water. It was a strange sensation, the rapid wicking leaving her skin cold. Goosebumps rose across her thighs and up her back and she shuddered.

The Shaman looked north as he dried Zaide, too. "Now for those goborrins."

"We make it fast." Zaide hopped on one foot while he got his boot on the other, then repeated the process. His bags jostled and rattled as he did, earning a frown. "We're going to need to leave our things here, or we won't be able to fight."

The first thing that crossed Lark's mind was the night they'd encountered the broken-born men in Desheni territory. They'd been forced to run when the bugraks came after them. What hope did they have to escape goborrins if something went wrong? "I'm keeping the artifacts with me. Just in case." Her hand settled over the bag that hung beside her hip once more. The Vale Hymnflute had its sling, the Captured Spring had a chain, and the Molten Dagger was easy to tuck under her belt, but the Sunshard had nothing.

"The rest stays, then." He dropped his things and rolled his shoulders as they came free, then readied his shield and checked the Spectrum Blade and the Jadoran long knife at his belt. He'd scarcely used the knife, but now his hand lingered there.

Lark knew what he was thinking. After he'd destroyed the ships in Ganede's harbor, there had been no time to test the Spectrum Blade again. He'd used it when sparring, but this would be his first battle since the blade's light was extinguished.

His concern was justified.

She slid the rest of her bags to the ground and checked her silver knives. The longer they traveled, the less adept she felt, but she'd not had time to practice the way the others had. Instead of counting on the knives, she drew her crossbow from the bag where the artifacts hid. As an afterthought, she took out the Hymnflute, too. It would be more useful if she wore it in its sling, so she could summon its power at a moment's notice.

"Are we ready, then?" Andriun's hands flexed on the pole of his trident, betraying his lack of confidence wielding it as a weapon. Lark suspected he would have been happier with a spear, but there was no sense in carrying more than one weapon. The similarity between the trident and his usual stone-tipped spear made her suspect his reservations had more to do with what the silver trident stood for, rather than how it was used.

"Personally, I think you're all taking too long." Tula rolled up the voluminous sleeves of her robe and marched along the river's edge.

The rest of them rushed after her.

Zaide ran a few steps to put himself in the lead. "Andriun, you use the water to try to contain them. See if you can do that thing where you trap their legs in ice, that should slow them down long enough. Tula, you focus on the bridge. Destroying it is more important than killing all the goborrins. If we can wreck the bridge, it won't matter if we leave some alive, so torch it as fast as you can. Lark, you cover them, since you've got your crossbow out."

Lark had no complaint against providing cover. She had replenished her supply of bolts, but they wouldn't last long in combat, and she didn't know when—or if—she'd have a chance to purchase more. "What about you?"

He flashed her a nervous smile and drew the Spectrum Blade by an inch or two. "I guess we'll see."

There was no cover, no brush along the edge of the river to hide them, and the moment the goborrins came into view, one of them let out a bellow of alarm. The sound struck her as more cow-like than that of a pig, and she snorted at how easily her mind tried to wander. She readied a bolt on her crossbow as Zaide drew his sword.

A handful of goborrins fell into an inverted V formation and marched toward them with crude logging axes in their hands instead of battle axes, but Andriun swung his trident toward the river and drew water over its banks. It flowed around their ankles and crackled as it froze, but these goborrins were larger than those they'd fought outside his home, and they grunted and snarled as they tore their hooves free of the ice.

Andriun snapped something in his own tongue and seized the water again. A second squad of goborrins had already formed and marched toward them, close behind the first.

Zaide darted forward with the Spectrum Blade in hand. The lack of swirling colors on its surface left Lark sick, but his skill had grown. He intercepted a goborrin's axe with his shield and drove with his sword to strike the monster down.

There was no flash, no blaze of light like there once had been, but it sliced through the beast's flesh just as easily as ever. Lark leveled her crossbow with a monster's head and waited, though her heart hammered at the base of her throat as Zaide spun to take on the next goborrin.

Beside her, Tula spread her arms wide. Magic flared in her hands and raced up her arms, igniting the glowing dragon marks on her skin that only showed when she wielded her power. Flames licked her fingers and she took running steps to start her pitch, then lobbed her fireballs over Zaide's head and into the second formation of goborrins. The flames burst on contact, yielding bellows of pain.

Another wave of water surged up around the beasts. This time, it coiled up the legs of several before it froze and locked a handful of goborrins in place.

"Move forward," Zaide shouted as he dispatched one of the trapped monsters. His blows were fast, clean, and precise, and for the first time since their expedition began, Lark realized how dangerous he truly was.

Tula rushed ahead, skirting the icy ground and preparing another pair of fireballs. She squeaked and skidded to a halt as she rounded the trapped goborrins and almost collided with one that was free. It drew back its arm to swing its axe, and she flung a fireball directly into its face. It toppled backwards with a shriek like a frightened piglet.

"You're lucky I didn't shoot," Lark shouted. She'd had her crossbow pointed right at the monster's head when the Magister's hand shot up and blocked the way. Had she been even a second faster to fire, her friend would have been the one wounded.

All Tula did was grin over her shoulder.

"Forward, Your Highness," Andriun called. He intercepted an oncoming goborrin with his trident.

Lark hurried after them. The way they pressed forward was relentless.

"Six down," Zaide announced. The first formation was already dead.

"Seven!" Tula added.

Every time the crossbow found a target, someone else swung in and destroyed it. How many had they counted? Twenty-four? Anxiety ran cold through Lark's veins. The rest of the goborrins had abandoned their bridge and charged them with axes ready.

Two broke away from the group to charge Zaide from the side.

"Look out!" she shouted as she swung the crossbow toward them, but Andriun was faster. Twin lances of ice sprang from the ground to spear the goborrins as if they were charging boar.

Zaide spun to finish the job. "Save your bolts."

The order hurt. It *had* been an order, a terse command he had no time to soften. She could fight. He knew she could fight. After everything they'd been through, everything she'd done, why did he resist her help now? She swallowed hard and kept her crossbow up, all the same.

Andriun's water magic snared three more goborrins. Tula

darted past them and hurled fire at the half-built bridge with a whoop. Fireball after fireball struck the wood, while the Spectrum Blade carved through beasts like butter, and as the last of the monsters went down, Lark was left standing, as useless as she'd proven herself in the Hall of Vision.

CHAPTER SEVENTEEN

Snow crunched under Zaide's boots. By his estimation, it was nearly autumn, the equinox—his birthday—only a week or two away. In Kolmar, it had always felt like late summer. The days grew shorter, but the weather stayed warm, and the leaves on the forest's trees did not begin to change colors until a month later. The fond memories of sitting outside with his foster family, watching fireflies blink while they ate the berry tarts Sarma always made for his birthday, struck him as a distant memory instead of something they'd done only the year before.

The trek into the mountains had been slow, and the cold crept up on them as they climbed. Andriun had been the last to change into his cold weather gear, while Tula had been the first and the loudest to complain.

"It reminds me of home," Andriun remarked as he stomped the white crystals. They were icy, rather than powdery, the remnants of something that had melted and re-frozen in the cold of night.

Something about the statement made the hair on the back of Zaide's neck prickle. He smoothed it with one hand. The cold of his fingertips made him shudder. It hadn't been cold enough to justify getting his gloves out of his pockets, and as the sun rose into the morning sky, he expected the weather would warm enough to warrant keeping them put away. For now, he just jammed his hands into the pockets of his coat. "Where do you think we are?"

The Shaman studied the position of the sun and the angle of the shadows with a thoughtful frown. "Farther north than Chithal, I believe. Farther than my home territory."

"I would have thought we'd see the ocean by now." Tula's teeth chattered as she spoke and she kept her arms wrapped around herself, desperate to hold whatever heat she could. Not for the first time, Zaide wondered why she didn't figure out how to use her magic to keep herself warm. That she was Jadoran explained why the cold was uncomfortable, but she was the most powerful fire mage of all. If anyone could warm herself, it should be her.

He watched the ground as he walked, planting each foot on as much snow as he could. The crunch and squeak of it was pleasant in a way he couldn't explain. "The Elder's maps were all really old. I don't remember much, but I think I remember seeing something that showed the Shattered Lands reach to the top of the world."

"The top of the world?" Tula repeated in disbelief. "How could that be?"

"You're the librarian, Tula. Shouldn't you know? I'd expect the Great Library would have more robust collections of maps than the Kolmari Elder." Lark had spoken little since they'd demolished the goborrin bridge the week prior. Zaide wasn't surprised that the few times she'd opened her mouth, she'd been cross. She'd been unhappy since she accepted his help in descending the cliff, and her ability to sulk was unparalleled. He tried to ignore it, let her be sullen if that was her wish, but the attitude had begun to bother him. At first, he'd assumed the negativity grated on his nerves. The longer they traveled, the better he understood it.

He missed her. The version of her he'd grown to like, the

version that was open and vulnerable, unafraid to share thoughts and shed tears. The moment on the cliff had been a glimpse back into that—into Lark, instead of Princess Dasienna —and it was a sore reminder of everything she'd walled off.

But fixing it wasn't his place, and there were bigger things to worry about than the friendliness of Amroch's princess. The Spectrum Blade's power was only the start of their concerns.

He shook those worries loose with a shake of his head. "To be fair to Tula, Jadora's pretty far from the border. Most of the Elder's maps came from..." He trailed off as they crested a peak and a valley opened below them.

Snow lay thick in the long shadows cast by the mountains, the skeletal remains of charred buildings stark against the white.

The others approached in silence to join him. He said nothing, just took his time studying the husk of what had once been a village. He could still make out the frames of houses, barns and sheds, taller buildings that might have been inns or chapels devoted to the Maker. Scrubby trees surrounded the place and tall grasses lay weighted down by the snow.

Whoever lived here, they had been gone for a long time.

"We can't be surprised by what we see here," Lark said softly. "We call them the Shattered Lands for a reason."

"I know." Zaide knew that better than anyone, yet the sight was still sobering. Slowly, he turned to resume travel, and the party's mood grew solemn.

There were more villages in the hills and valleys that formed the mountain range. Waypoints that must have been rest stops or inns with stables sat at intersections in long-abandoned roadways, where the hard-packed earth beneath scraggly weeds was all that remained to give them away. Little remained of the buildings, either. Some were empty frames that stood upright, others lay in charred heaps, the ashes long since gone.

They stopped near one such point for their noon meal. Tula rooted around in the rotten remnants of a wall with a stick while she ate with one hand. "How long do you think it's been since these places were burned?"

Zaide would have preferred if that question had come from someone other than the Paragon of Fire. "A few years. Probably not more than that." He thought of the smithy in Kolmar and how fast the burned materials had been reclaimed by nature, but perhaps that was different. The forest was wet and warm, the scent of rot always heavy in the air. Who knew how long charred beams could stay standing somewhere like this?

No one else had anything to add. Tula turned over a piece of broken pottery with her stick and crouched beside it to make notes, but whatever it was she wrote in the little notebook that disappeared into one of her deep pockets, who knew.

More ruins littered the way after their meal. More villages, more houses, more farmsteads. Eventually, Zaide trudged off the old road they'd decided to follow and made his way to one of the ruined farmhouses.

Andriun checked the height of the sun with his hand before he joined him. "Do you wish to camp here?"

"Just looking." Zaide didn't know why. All the ruins were the same, pieces of some broken life that could never be restored. Some had shown signs of goborrin encampments, but this one did not. There were other signs of life, but they were the sort that were less offensive. Rub marks on charred wood. A strange antler shed by some sort of deer. Tula was fast to claim that, holding it to the side of her head and making thoughtful sounds while she examined its shape.

Zaide scuffed a boot through the dirt, earth mixed with ashes, dense after countless rains. "I wonder how many places there are like this, farther in."

"As many as you can imagine. And some you cannot." Andriun rested the end of his trident on the ground and leaned against it. They had not often stopped, but had traveled with all the haste they could muster. After days, it had begun to take its toll.

"I've heard there were once great cities, far to the east," Lark said. "Palaces as large as the one in Amrochan. After Ages of fighting, they've all fallen."

"But there have to be settlements somewhere. Gadranus mostly leads goborrins, but there are people, too. They have to live somewhere, right? Have cities?" Something clinked when Zaide moved his foot again. He crouched to turn over a shard of pottery. Bright colors peeked out from under a layer of dirt. He ran his thumb over the glazed surface to clear it and blinked at the pattern underneath. It pricked at the edge of his memory, making him squint.

"Well, of course there have to be cities, but..." Lark said something else, but he didn't hear it. He dug for the other pieces of pottery buried under the ashy soil.

Two pieces of broken ceramic fit together in his hands, providing more of the image. His heart fluttered uneasily in his chest. He knew this pattern, had seen it long ago. His head snapped up and he searched the rotting walls, but nothing else remained to tell him more.

"Zaide?" Andriun prompted, tone thick with worry.

He sat back on his heels. "I've seen this. I know this pattern, it..."

A shadow moved over the shards in his hands and Tula leaned close over his shoulder. "What do you mean, you've seen it? Where?"

"The hem of my mother's dress, when I was small. Before the fever took her. The colors... It's all the same." It didn't feel real, either. He gripped the broken pieces as if they might disappear.

"Even in Amrochan, It's common for certain folk patterns to become popular enough to be used on everything." Lark inched closer, her step cautious. "It's not as if seeing it on one broken vase means anything."

But it did mean something. If Zaide gripped the shards any harder, they would cut his hands. He made himself put them down, but his shoulders remained tight. "Folk patterns are regional. If I recognize this here, then..." The early snow, the pale mountains, the clear sky that matched his eyes. It made sense, and yet none at all.

They were farther north than any of them had ever been.

If this was his home, how had he ended up in Kolmar?

Something moved and he went rigid. A shadow on the other side of the wall, visible through the narrow cracks between the rotting boards. His hand went for the Spectrum Blade, then he thought twice and drew the Jadoran knife instead.

"Zaide?" Lark stepped backwards, but her hands went to her knives, too.

He hopped to his feet and raised a finger to his lips. There wasn't much left to the farmhouse, just one wall and enough of another to create a corner where dirt and snow collected. It wasn't enough cover for more than a solitary goborrin. *Or a family of bugraks*, he thought with a grimace.

He leaped the corner and spun to face the eavesdropper with his knife in hand.

The creature jerked backwards and tucked its tail between its hind legs.

A second later, Lark rounded the corner with her knives ready. Her hands dropped. "A dog?"

With its head lowered, ears pinned back, and its eyes gazing up at them from beneath deeply worried brows.

Zaide motioned for her to stay put at the same time Andriun and Tula appeared at her back. Nothing about it was frightening, aside from its size. Had it not looked so guilty, he might have mistaken it for a wolf. "A scared one. What are you doing out here, fella?" He still gripped his knife, but he sank to one knee and held out his right hand in invitation. There had not been many dogs in Kolmar, but the soldiers at the garrison kept a few. He'd heard them now and then in his youth, barking when the soldiers hunted in the woods.

"Maker's mercy," Andriun laughed. "It looks just like you."

"Shut up," Zaide muttered, though he had noticed. Its fluffy coat was pure white, its eyes the same sky blue. It was odd, the way their matching coloration gave him an immediate sense of kinship with the beast.

Slowly, the dog leaned forward to sniff his fingertips. The tension in its haunches eased and its tail gave a tentative, friendly swish.

"Oh, it's a *girl* dog," Tula intoned.

As if that had anything to do with anything at all. Zaide stayed still. "Do you think she belonged to whoever lived here?"

"Not likely. This house was burned years ago." Lark sheathed her knives and paced backwards. "We should keep going. We've dallied long enough."

"Dogs mean people," Zaide said. If there were people nearby, he wasn't certain it would bode well for them. The dog looked like him, but so had the broken-born men in Desheni territory. Those had been the last dogs they'd seen, and they meant he wouldn't make the mistake of trusting familiar strangers. "There might be trouble ahead."

"All the more reason to get moving." The princess gave the dog a disdainful look, then turned to head back to the road.

The Paragons followed and Zaide slowly drew back. Part of him wished he could stay, maybe camp the night in the remnants of the burned farmhouse, but he knew it made no sense. He'd recognized something; that didn't mean he had a connection to the place, and it wasn't as if it had been his home that burned.

Or, it had—it simply hadn't burned *here*. There was no denying that Gadranus's forces had destroyed his family's life, no matter where home had been. Still, he cast the abandoned shards of ceramic one last look before he trudged up the slope.

He'd uncovered something, there in the ash, and it wasn't just a shattered piece of pottery.

It was a piece of his life—a piece of himself—and the awareness that he still knew almost nothing of himself was a heavier burden than anything else he carried.

CHAPTER EIGHTEEN

"That dog is still following us." Tula stared over her shoulder, but never stopped walking. She almost walked into Lark's back before she caught herself.

Lark bit her lower lip. There was no explanation for why the creature made her uncomfortable. It was foolish to think a dog's presence meant anything; it wasn't as if it could be used to spy, though she supposed it was possible the animal could lead someone to them later. "Well, see if you can scare it off, then."

"Maybe she's hungry," Zaide suggested. That was the most likely guess. If it had smelled their rations, it made sense that it would follow them in hopes it could beg for a bite. He slowed to a stop in the middle of the overgrown roadway and opened one of his bags.

"Do not feed that thing," Lark snapped.

He froze with a piece of something in his fingers. "Why not?"

"We barely have enough rations to get us wherever we're going. We don't know if we're going to be able to replenish our supplies, and it's a dog. It can hunt for its own meal." It certainly looked like it could, anyway. It was tall enough that she likely could have touched its head if it stood by her side, but she wasn't eager to try.

"It's just a bite, it won't hurt anything." Zaide clicked his tongue and the dog trotted forward with its ears upright.

Lark bit back a scoff and turned back around so fast, her ponytail whipped all the way around and slapped her in the face.

Tula snorted a laugh, earning herself a glare that was so vicious that Andriun tilted his eyes skyward and trudged on ahead, humming to himself.

Frustrated, Lark peeled golden strands from her lips and flicked her hair back over her shoulder. Perhaps she'd grown too accustomed to Zaide following her directions. He'd always given in, at least when it mattered. Maybe that was the difference. Maybe this didn't matter. In the face of everything ahead—and everything she had not yet had a chance to tell him—it probably *shouldn't* matter. Yet the way he laughed behind her made her bristle with irritation, and she curled her hands to fists at her sides.

The dog was still following them when they stopped for the night, and it made itself comfortable at Zaide's side as soon as he settled. "I'm going to call her Daisy." His fingers sought the dog's white scruff and the beast looked straight at her, its tongue lolling as if to mock her.

"Don't name it," Lark protested. "First you name it, then you keep it."

"You sound like my foster mother," he teased.

She didn't think that was supposed to be an insult, but it still rankled. Lark bit her tongue to keep it still, then drew a long breath in through her nose. There were bigger issues to deal with. She had to remind herself of that. To her chagrin, those suddenly struck her as easier to address than the canine at his side. "May I speak with you for a moment? In private?"

His brows knit. "What? Why? She's not hurting anything."

Her mouth pressed to a thin line.

"I think they're going to fight," Tula whispered conspicuously as she started the evening's campfire.

That, too, hurt when Lark suspected it shouldn't have. "Please, Zaide."

Clear disappointment drew itself across his face, but he stood and motioned for her to lead the way.

Now her nerves surged. She crossed her arms to keep her hands from shaking and picked her way into the grass. Zaide followed, and the blasted dog stood as if to join them.

He held out a hand. "Stay."

Daisy stopped, then slowly let her haunches sink back to the ground.

Zaide's face lit up. "Did you see that? She knows stay!"

That the dog was already trained was almost as concerning as the fact Lark had already thought of her as *Daisy*. "Lovely." She shuffled along until they were some distance from the camp. The dog watched them, while Tula and Andriun pretended not to. She continued a bit farther, until the shadow of night swallowed them both.

Zaide spoke first. "I won't give her any more rations. If she needs something to eat, I'll hunt it."

"It's not about the dog, Zaide." A chill raced through her. "But her presence is useful for keeping the others from being too curious."

A flicker of uncertainty touched his eyes. "What do you mean?"

Maker's mercy, but she'd dreaded this. Her mouth was dry as Jadora's sand. "I... I've been trying to think of how to discuss this. We've not had a single moment alone since Nimultis, and..." Her voice caught and she swallowed hard, though it did nothing to loosen the constriction in her throat.

His uncertainty shifted to wariness. "Did I do something wrong?"

"No," she replied, so fast it took them both by surprise. "No, it's not you. It has nothing to do with—except it does, it..." Again, her voice caught. How was she supposed to do this? She couldn't even speak.

Zaide's brow crinkled, but he said nothing else, giving her space to speak. That quiet patience he'd developed with her was enough to put tears in her eyes.

When she found her words again, they quavered. "I saw something, in the Hall of Vision. The Oracle showed me something, and I... I'm scared."

That was it. The thing she hadn't been able to grapple with, that she didn't know how to voice. Fear constricted her chest until she almost couldn't breathe. It stung her eyes and sent hot tears over the edge of her eyelashes, and still her mouth was so dry that her tongue felt wooden. There was none of the royal grace to these words, nothing to make her sound like a leader or a practiced politician. It was only her. Lark. A frightened girl who'd made a terrible mistake.

He stepped forward, hands out as if he meant to embrace her, but she held a palm out to stall him.

"Please, just listen."

"All right," he said slowly, but he grew still and listened.

Had they not just met the Oracle in the flesh, she would have sounded mad. "If we do this, if we continue here, if we find Gadranus, people will be lost." She fought back a grimace. Of course they would. It was war. "It was a prophecy. A vision given to my parents, before I was born. Because of what was foretold about the eclipse, I always thought it meant my father. I thought if I claimed the Spectrum Blade and ended the war for him, he would be safe."

Zaide nodded slowly, but his brow furrowed. "And the blade didn't change anything."

"All I knew was what my parents told me. But then the Oracle gave me the Sunshard, and the vision wasn't him." Tears tightened her throat until she thought she might choke. "I saw you, Zaide. It's you. You're the one in danger."

The lines in his face softened. "I know."

Those two words struck like a blow to the chest and knocked her strangled tears free. They rolled down her face, their hot tracks rapidly cooling in the chilly night air. She sucked in a rattling breath. "You *know*?" All this time, all the torment of feeling she had to tell him, and he knew?

His shoulders rose in the smallest of shrugs. "I never thought this was going to be easy. You were the one who made me stop and think about it. Back in Kolmar, after we retrieved the Spectrum Blade from the temple. It was raining. Remember?"

It had been in the spring, what now seemed an eternity past. She made herself nod.

"You said this was a choice. The decision to put myself and my needs aside for the greater good. And I..." His fingers twitched toward the sword at his right hip, but he stopped himself and spread his hand toward it, instead. "I already made my choice. I know it's dangerous. I knew that when I picked this up and made the choice to follow you. I know I might not live through it. But I said we were going to do this, and I still mean that."

He was so confident, so determined, that it made her heart ache. Lark sniffed hard and squeezed her hands together before her chest, a feeble shield for the part of her she knew was most vulnerable. Her failing. "You don't understand," she whispered.

"Then give me time to try. We've made it this far, Lark."

Her shoulders ached with longing for the hug she'd already rejected. "The Oracle said—"

"She said a lot of things," he interrupted. "I didn't like everything I heard, either. But she made one thing clear, and it was that nothing is set in stone. Everything she sees is a possibility. Just a possibility. We might all die, or we might not. We don't know yet, so don't give up yet. We have to see signs of an army's passing at some point, and then it's time to meet Gadranus and finish things. How that goes, even the Oracle couldn't say, and she's the one who can see the future."

Lark squeezed her eyes closed, worry and fear twisting with her admiration and envy of his courage. All this time, he'd been walking with his head up and his eyes wide open, knowing death waited ahead. Yet he persisted. Never failing, never cowering, never showing doubt. Her hands tightened before her chest and she could not keep them from shaking. "And you're not afraid?"

"Of course I am." He almost laughed, but it was dry and without mirth. "Why wouldn't I be? Nobody's excited to go walking off into something that could kill them. But it's out there, whether or not I want it to be."

Her shoulders bunched and she wiggled to force them down. "I'll never know how you do that. How you face all this like it's nothing."

Zaide cracked a smile. "The same way you face anything else, Your Highness. One step at a time."

She wished she felt as confident.

When she said nothing more, he sobered. "Now I have to ask you something, though."

Lark wiped the drying tear trails from her cheeks with the back of her hand. "Ask, then." It was the least she could offer after he'd so calmly heard her out.

He shifted his weight and glanced back the way they'd come. "We can keep the dog, right?"

If she hadn't just bared her heart, she might have throttled him. "Fine," she said with a heave of a sigh. "You can keep the dog."

His smile almost made it worth it.

Two days passed without trouble before they found themselves at the mouth of another valley. Instead of the charred remains of a village, an army threaded through it, their march a steady rhythm that echoed in the still.

Lark squinted at the ranks for a long time without making out anything meaningful. Just when she thought her frown could not deepen any further, Tula presented a spyglass from her bags. Lark took it without a word. They'd all fallen silent as soon as the noise of footsteps reached their ears. Now they crouched at the very top of a slope and she prayed the four of them were not noticeable.

She knew what she would see before she put the spyglass to her eye, but she did it, all the same. "Goborrins, mostly," she whispered. "A few men." The latter were officers, based on their attire. They did not wear armor, but instead sported dark coats with reddish-brown capes drawn forward over one shoulder. Some sort of insignia decorated the exposed sleeves of their uniforms, but they meant nothing to her.

"Is Gadranus with them?" Tula whispered back.

Lark barely stifled her snort. How was she supposed to know? She had no idea what the man looked like. The apparition they'd fought beneath Kolmar's temple had never resolved into a wholly human form, and there were certainly no ominously swirling clouds of dark magic in the army below. But not all of the men were broken-born like Zaide, either. Men of every complexion walked alongside the pig-faced beasts. Somehow, she had never stopped to consider that possibility.

She held out the spyglass to one side to let Zaide have a turn.

Daisy tried to take it in her teeth.

"Aht," Zaide scolded softly. The dog settled, but her tail still swished and her tongue lolled. If only the rest of them could be so oblivious.

"I do not think he will be with them," Andriun said. "They are going south. The Oracle said he traveled with an army headed north. It is unlikely they would have reached their destination and immediately turned around."

Zaide gave a thoughtful hum. "More likely to be an occupying force. They've got supply wagons. Headed for the bridge we tore down, probably. Going to invade Chithal or Yithel."

Lark hated to think of the northern cities being overrun by the army below, but she saw no way they could stand against those numbers. Those ranks had to hold tens of thousands of goborrins. "Where do they all come from?"

"When we see Gadranus, I'll ask him," Zaide said dryly. He lowered the spyglass and passed it back.

"So what do we do now?" Tula fiddled with the cuff of her sleeve. Her billowy red and gold coat had been put away some time ago, and the dull brown of their leather gear let them blend into the hillside better, but she kept tugging at the tight-fitting sleeves as if they bothered her. After the loose Jadoran clothing she was used to, maybe they did.

"I hardly know," Lark admitted as she handed the spyglass back to the Magister.

Zaide bit his lower lip.

"What?" She didn't like that look in his eyes; that was the sort of face he made before too many terrible decisions.

"I have an idea, but I don't think anyone is going to like it."

Lark grimaced. How had she known?

"Don't make that face," he whispered. "You don't even know what it is yet."

"Knowing you, I will support the princess in her preemptive face-making." Andriun grinned to soften his teasing, but he grew serious as soon as the jest was clear. "What is your idea?"

Zaide scratched behind the dog's ears and stared at the army. "We sit down right here, eat something, and wait for them to reach us. Then we ask for directions."

Lark shook her head in disbelief. "I'm sorry, what?"

"Think about it. There are four of us, and none of us are dressed like soldiers. We're sitting in the middle of territory Gadranus has controlled for years. Even if the Spectrum Blade were at full strength, we wouldn't have a hope against an army like that." He nodded toward them. "They have no reason to think we're hostile, and plenty of people here will admire their leader. It won't be unusual for people to seek him, the same as people in the Allied Kingdoms seek audiences with Sendassian."

Her mouth fell open. "That's—"

"That is probably the best-reasoned plan you have ever presented," Andriun said before she could finish.

It was far kinder than what she'd thought, and she shut her mouth to let the Shaman speak.

Zaide nodded, as if he'd expected that. "You said I should work on impulsiveness. I'm working on that."

"Well, I am pleased to see improvement." Andriun gave the army one last appraising look, then nodded, too.

"So we just sit here and eat, then?" Tula lowered herself to the ground with a sigh. "I'm all right with that."

How could they simply sit back and accept it? Lark stared at the three of them in disbelief. "And what if they decide to flatten us? They're goborrins, Zaide. They won't have any qualms about killing us for fun."

"Some of them are people," he replied as he settled. "I'll just try to appeal to them."

Lunacy. She was half tempted to get up and leave right then, let the three of them be goborrin fodder on their own. But walking away wouldn't save her, either; if the army decided to kill them, they'd hunt her down with ease. Sullen, she dropped to the ground to sit cross-legged.

The marching monsters threaded their way through the valley a bit at a time, following the same overgrown roadway they'd been using until they'd spotted the horde. It had to lead somewhere, then; armies had to come from somewhere. Her heart hammered against her ribs until they ached, but there was no stopping the force that came toward them.

Nor did the army seem to care. They did not try to hide, but the goborrins did not react to their presence, and as they grew near, they showed no sign of stopping to interact.

"What do we do if they just walk by?" Tula asked in a whisper.

Zaide considered the question for a moment, then pushed himself to his feet. The dog leaped up beside him.

Standing, it seemed, was enough.

Someone shouted words Lark couldn't understand. Andriun's mouth tightened, but neither Tula nor Zaide reacted at all beyond exchanging glances.

A scowling man with a weathered face and age-grayed hair broke away from the ranks and strode toward them. He repeated the question as he walked.

Zaide raised his hands, palms out. "I'm sorry," he called back, though cautiously. "I don't speak Torec."

The man snorted. "Then how do you know it's Torec?" He spoke with a thick and unfamiliar accent, but his command of the Amrochan dialect was smooth.

Zaide's eyes traveled toward the goborrin army behind the stranger. "Ah... just guessing."

Lark winced and shrank back, but a hint of amusement twisted the older man's mouth.

"Fair." He rested his fists against his hips and examined the four of them. If he thought anything of the odd mix, he didn't show it. "What brought you out here?"

"We heard a rumor that armies were on the move. We thought we might—that is, we hoped we might be able to see—" Zaide faltered and looked to the others for help. They hadn't discussed *how* they would go about asking for directions.

The man seemed amused until Zaide turned his head. Then his eyes fixed on Zaide's blunted left ear, and such intensity filled his gaze that it made Lark's stomach turn. She stood, her hands itching for her daggers, though she knew drawing would be a mistake. If anything, she needed to draw the Hymnflute, to brace for the possibility they'd need its barrier to escape.

"You're looking for Gadranus," the stranger said.

Zaide turned back to him in surprise. "Yes."

Slowly, the enemy officer nodded. "Good."

"Why *good*?" Lark asked as her hand settled on the Hymnflute.

"Because," the man replied with a dry smile, "His Imperial Majesty is looking for you, too."

CHAPTER NINETEEN

ZAIDE SHOULD HAVE REALIZED the folly of his plan far sooner. The Oracle had explained his cut ear; she'd warned him that Gadranus knew what he looked like.

It was a miracle nobody had chastised him during the walk. Everyone had been grim, solemn, and silent—save Daisy, who still trotted along by his side with her tail curved over her back and her tongue hanging out of her broad smile. The dog looked to him now and then as she pranced, but she never went far from their group, even when they stopped at night.

"Here," the officer called as he stopped atop a hill. The road beneath his feet was sprinkled with gravel, making it as stark white as the snow that clung to the mountainsides. The tops of buildings peeked over the hilltop, and wood smoke scented the air as it curled into the gray sky. Zaide dreaded what they might see, but Daisy's ears perked and she loped ahead. The dog had not been at all put off by the presence of the old man or the small squad of goborrins that surrounded them, something that grated on Zaide's nerves far more than he would ever admit.

He tried to ignore the goborrins as he strode ahead to see what awaited them. His brows drew together as the peaks of buildings came into view, then stopped at the man's side to stare into the city below.

"Clean water in that river, makes it a good place to settle. Fed by springs up in the mountains there." The man—Zaide still didn't know his name—pointed across the valley to a tall range that looked to be more snow than stone.

Zaide had known there would be settlements in the Shattered Lands somewhere, but the sprawling city they stared at now brimmed with life. That life after destruction could be peaceful had never crossed his mind. It sent a strange prickle down the backs of his shoulders and he shrugged, since he couldn't scratch. "What is this place?"

"Toren, our current capital. Where else would we be?"

Toren. Their language was Torec. Zaide nodded slowly. It made sense. The place was certainly large enough to act as a capital, with hundreds of buildings spread across the slopes. They followed the river as it curved to the south, and small vessels floated on the water, departing for who-knew-where. "I didn't expect it would look like this."

"That's what happens when you're out of the Motherland for too long. You forget what home looks like." The officer clapped a hand to Zaide's shoulder, then looked back. "Come. We'll take you down, get you settled. Then you can head for the palace. His Imperial Majesty will be waiting for you." He started toward the city without waiting for a response and the goborrins followed, herding the rest of them forward like sheep.

Zaide waited for them to catch up, while Daisy trotted on down the hill.

"This is a trap, Zaide," Lark whispered as she drew close. "It has to be."

He didn't disagree. The dozen goborrins that formed their escort had never done anything threatening, or even interacted with them at all, but their presence alone made him uneasy. Now they marched down a hill on the heels of an enemy commander of some sort, toward a city brimming with more goborrins, more officers, and—

"Oh, look!" Tula rose on tiptoe and pointed toward what must have been a farmstead, where a handful of children ran circles around great, wooly cattle that sported curved horns atop broad heads. "Little Zaides!"

"You sound like a five-year-old," he muttered, though he stared, too. The white-haired children might have blended into the snow-flecked field without their clothing, the same bright blue with bold embroidery that had been presented to him in Nimultis.

Torec. He was Torec. The realization made him ill. He stared at the ground ahead of his feet and resisted the urge to shake his head.

Daisy took it as an offering of attention and trotted back to circle around his ankles. All of a sudden, the dog's presence struck him as painful, rather than novel, an unpleasant reminder of things that had never been pleasant to begin with. Her blue eyes were bright, cheerful, and did nothing to warm him.

No wonder she'd been so friendly. He was precisely what she was used to.

Strangers in the company of an officer meant little when one of them was broken-born, it seemed, for no one paid them any mind as they reached the city's main thoroughfare. Goborrins and the commanding officers leading them moved freely up and down streets, carrying on with everyday business. People came and went from shops and houses, the same as they had in Amrochan or any of the other cities they'd visited. Goborrins stopped at vendor stalls to sniff the fresh foods being offered, but they behaved with a discipline that left Zaide startled, moving on their way or stepping aside out of good manners to let people by. It felt wrong enough that it sent a shudder down his spine.

"Here we are. This will do." The officer stopped outside a tall building of whitewashed wood, its narrow angles and sharp peak reminding Zaide of a scrubby pine in winter. The man said something to his goborrins in Torec and one grunted in response before the whole squad moved to the side of the road to wait. Then he tilted his head, beckoning the four of them to step inside.

Zaide motioned for Lark to precede him, but she scowled and stayed rooted in place. Tula squeezed past both of them to follow the man to the innkeeper's desk.

Andriun waved for them to move. "Sulking in one place will do nothing," he said softly. "We have come this far. Let us see this to the end, eh?"

The princess huffed and stomped inside to join the Magister. The officer spoke with the woman at the innkeeper's counter in what Zaide still assumed was Torec. Her brows rose as he gestured and explained, but she nodded enthusiastically and pulled a tasseled key from a pocket in her apron. In return, the officer drew a folded paper from a pocket on the inside of his jacket and made a pinching gesture with his right hand that Zaide recognized as a universal request for a writing instrument.

"The emperor's treasuries will cover the expense of your stay, meals included," the man explained when the innkeeper turned away to fetch a pen.

"Is the emperor always so generous?" Lark's tone scraped like a dry razor.

The officer flashed her a grin. "You may ask when you meet him."

The innkeeper returned with a pen and he wrote something in an unfamiliar alphabet, then slid it across the counter in exchange for the key, which he presented to Zaide, tassel first. "May your visit be fruitful. Welcome home."

Zaide took it by the yellow tassel. The key was warm against his chilled skin and he curled his fingers around it.

The man nodded a goodbye and slipped out the front door without another word. He called for his goborrins and they snuffled as they moved into formation and departed with the nameless officer who had led them from the wilds to the heart of Toren without a single question having left his lips.

The moment the goborrins passed out of view through the large glass windows, the innkeeper cleared her throat. "No Torec?" she asked, the words thickly accented.

Tula shook her head first, then Lark. Zaide shook his head at the same time Andriun nodded, earning himself a double-take.

"Wait, what?" Zaide asked. "You speak it?"

The Shaman nodded again. "I know enough to get by."

Lark's glare could have melted ice. "And you don't think that would have been useful to share sooner?"

"I did not think it was relevant."

Zaide raised his hands to his head. "There is nothing more relevant! How long have you understood it? What was he saying to the goborrins while we traveled?" Hadn't he claimed he didn't speak it, when they'd run afoul of the broken-born in Desheni territory?

"Ordinary things? Basic commands? It was not important. I would have told you if I ever heard things I understood that were important." Andriun gave a broad shrug.

The innkeeper cleared her throat again. "No angry. Come."

"Yes angry," Lark grumbled as the woman beckoned them toward the stairs.

Zaide was of a mind to agree, but the woman was right. Their argument was best saved for when they had privacy. The innkeeper led the way upstairs and he followed, the key in one hand and the hilt of his Jadoran long knife in the other. Lark eyed that knife with a frown. She already knew what it meant; his primary concern was people.

The upper floor of the inn was quiet, and the innkeeper led them to a door at the very end of the hall. "Here, rest. Ah... Down, if want..." She pointed to the floor, then pantomimed eating.

Zaide nodded back. "Thank you. We'll come down if we want food."

She smiled with uncertainty, but curtsied and shuffled past them, leaving them to unlock the door on their own.

Lark snatched the key from Zaide's hand before he could fit it to the lock.

"How long have you spoken Torec? How did you learn?" She unlocked the door so forcefully, it sounded as if she might break it.

Zaide leaned through the doorway to peer into the room the moment she had the door open, but it was empty. Windows lined the far wall. At least they would have plenty of escape points.

Andriun tilted his head back as he sorted through memories. "I learned some because of the broken-born who passed through the lands of my people. I have told you this. I could identify the tongues then, but there was little to do in Nimultis, so I studied."

"And you learned enough to 'get by' in just a handful of weeks?" The princess planted her hands on her hips, clearly not believing a word of it.

The Shaman was unbothered. "When you speak five languages already, adding another is not difficult."

"*Five* languages?" Tula ticked off all her fingers on one hand, then held up one more. "*Six?* Maker's mercy, Andriun, what else do you speak?"

"Well, there is Torec now." Andriun raised one finger. "Two distinct Desheni tongues, the common Amrochan tongue, then—"

"Enough," Zaide cut in. He shut the door once all of them were inside. "Be glad he speaks enough Torec to help us while we're here, but we've got bigger things to deal with." Like the fact just seeing his blunted ear had been enough for a military officer to break away from his army to personally escort them to the capital.

Lark nodded in agreement. "First in the order of things is the fact we are not staying here. We'll wait until that man isn't likely to cross our path again, then we need to leave."

Tula dropped her hands, her counting forgotten. "Why would we leave? We just got here, and Gadranus—"

"Gadranus being here is precisely why we need to leave. For all we know, that officer went straight to report our presence, and an army will be arriving to kill us in the next twenty minutes." The princess crossed her arms and paced back and forth in the wide room, as restless as a forest wildcat caught on a snare.

The Magister stomped one foot. "But we came all this way to see him!"

"And we will," Zaide said. "But Lark is right. It's better if we stay somewhere nobody knows about. We'll keep the key to this place, just so it's not suspicious, but nobody will be surprised if we want to slip out and see some of the city."

Something scratched at the door and all four of them jumped. Zaide's hand was on his knife before he caught the soft whine and exhaled hard.

Lark grumbled something about the dog as he opened the door to let her in, but Daisy didn't seem offended by having been forgotten. She sniffed around his ankles and continued across the floor, in between the beds.

"Sorry." Zaide wasn't sure if he was apologizing to the dog or the princess, but it didn't matter. Both ignored him.

For a while after he closed the door again, Daisy's snuffling was all there was to be heard.

When Lark finally spoke again, she was more subdued. "I don't believe Gadranus will pass up the opportunity to harm us. The future queen of Amroch, two Paragons, and the Bladebearer all in one place? We're too tantalizing of a target."

Which made it foolish that they'd come together to begin with. Zaide exhaled slowly as he steeled his resolve. "You're right. I'll go alone."

"What?" Tula and Lark exclaimed at the same time.

He held up a hand to forestall any arguments. "Think about what you just said. If something happens to you, that's the end of your bloodline. If something happens to Tula or Andriun, someone has to be blessed by Vorkaris or the magic water place under the mountain in order to have a new Paragon." He grimaced at his own words. So eloquent. But his lack of verbal grace changed nothing, so he went on. "Out of all four of us, I'm the one who's easiest to replace. If something happens to me, the Spectrum Blade will pick a new bearer immediately, whoever is best fit to wield it in that moment. That could be any one of you. All three of you have touched it already, haven't you? It already knows you."

"I have not touched it," Andriun said. "My magic touched it. It was not the same."

Tula frowned. "I touched it with a fingertip, I think, when I restored my portion of its power. It didn't do anything to me."

"And it didn't do anything to me when I touched it in the Hall of Vision," Lark admitted.

Zaide almost asked what she meant, but it didn't matter. He hadn't seen her handle the blade, but he'd seen it on the floor without its sheath. Obviously, it had accepted her hand in that moment of need. "So it could accept you, if something happens to me."

Andriun shook his head. "I do not like this idea."

"I don't, either." Lark crossed her arms a little tighter. "If something happened to you, how would we get to the blade to claim it? What's stopping him from keeping it locked away, so no one has any hope of facing him?"

"What part of that changes if we all go?" Zaide dropped one of his bags on one of the beds. He hadn't noticed until that moment that there were only two. More reasons to move elsewhere, then; he didn't want to share a bed with Andriun, and the other options were out of the question. "He can kill all of us and keep the sword just as easily. We're in his territory. We'll be in his castle. The only thing that's going to keep us alive is... I don't know. Good will."

The princess scoffed. "What in the world makes you think you can earn good will from someone like that?"

He slid the rest of his bags from his shoulders and sat them down more thoughtfully. "Because we have something he might want. Where's that crystal? The one we found in the temple, after we fought that shadow?"

Alarm twisted her face. "The fragment of power? Why would you give that back to him? It could make him stronger than he is now."

"Like I said. Good will. I give him power he can use to kill me, he gives me power I can use to kill him. It's a fair trade." And quite possibly a terrible idea. Zaide peeled off his cold weather coat and dug in his bags for the embroidered Torec tunic he'd been given. If he dressed like he belonged, he'd be more likely to be left alone in the streets.

"And what if he just kills you and keeps it all?" she demanded.

He shrugged and turned his back to her to dress. "Like I said, I don't think that changes. No matter what we do."

No one said anything else. He tried to reassure himself that meant they agreed this was the best plan. He tied on his colorful belt with its rope meant for reindeer and smoothed his tunic with both hands.

When he turned, Lark held the deep purple prism. Her fingers tightened on it until her whole hand grew pale.

He closed the distance between them with a few steps and laid a hand atop the stone. "Wait ten minutes or so after I leave, then go. All three of you. Find somewhere else to hide and take Daisy with you. When I come back, I'll look for her in the city. Maybe she's smart enough to lead me back to you."

Lark held his gaze, her eyes glassy. "This could be what I saw. What I was warned about."

"I know." He drew the prism from her hand. She didn't fight him. He slid the room's key into her grasp instead.

Tula curled her hands to fists just below her chin. "Be careful, Zaide."

"You, too. All of you." He turned the odd purple stone over in his hand before he slid it into his pocket. It was so large, it almost didn't fit. With that as his final preparation, he turned toward the door.

The dog rose as if to follow him, but Andriun put a leg out to stop her. "Safe waters, my friend."

Zaide nodded back and slipped outside.

No one looked his way as he descended the stairs and crossed to the door; not even the innkeeper as she wrote in ledgers at her desk. He stepped out into the chilly air and wished his tunic had been made of thicker wool. He'd put on something long-sleeved underneath it, but the dark cloth was thinner than he'd hoped and it didn't take long for him to shiver.

He turned east, toward the large stone structure he assumed was the palace. None of the people or goborrins on the streets tried to stop him, and he tried to walk with confidence. The keep stood in the center of the city, built of such pale stone that it could have been made from snow. Odd, he thought, that a man as wicked as Gadranus would call a white palace home.

There were guards at the entrance, but they looked at him as if they'd expected his arrival and asked something Zaide didn't understand.

"I've come to see Gadranus," he replied, hoping the name might sound familiar.

They nodded as if they'd expected that, too. One replied, again in Torec, then motioned for him to follow.

Instead of steel portcullises, the way was barred by tall wooden doors carved with patterns reminiscent of the embroidery on the hem of his tunic. The guard knocked on one in a particular cadence, and someone on the other side opened the door.

Zaide forced his hands away from the hilts of his blades as he followed his new escort into the courtyard and the tall door closed behind them.

This was a terrible idea.

The walls loomed high overhead and the courtyard was filled with men instead of monsters, not a goborrin to be found, and their absence struck him as strangely uncomfortable. He swallowed hard as they made their way to the keep.

More guards stood beside the doors to the keep, the arched entryway smaller but no less intimidating. Just inside the door, another guard intercepted them, and the men exchanged words before the newcomer beckoned Zaide toward a hallway that branched from the grand entryway. Standards bearing a ram's skull cascaded down the walls, their black, orange, and gold colors a bold contrast to the pale walls. The colors were different from what he'd seen painted on the floor in the forest temple, but the symbol had not changed at all, and the familiarity gave him a chill.

They wound their way through the hallways and up two flights of stairs before the guard halted outside an unremarkable door.

Zaide stared at it until the guard jerked his head toward it. Puzzled, Zaide knocked.

The guard made a sound of annoyance and motioned for him to enter.

This would have been easier if he spoke their language.

Flustered, he reached for the knob, but the door opened before he did more than graze it with his fingertips. A servant held the door wide and bowed from the waist as Zaide stepped inside.

Across the room, a man in black stood beside the window, his hands clasped behind his back. "So we meet at last."

Zaide's mouth went dry. "Gadranus."

CHAPTER TWENTY

ZAIDE DID NOT KNOW what he had expected, but it was not the man on the far side of the parlor.

Gadranus turned to face him, his demeanor both calm and quiet. His face was serious, but serene, and he was not as old as Zaide pictured. He couldn't have had more than forty years behind him, his smooth face clean-shaven and his long black hair untouched by gray.

They regarded each other in silence for a long time. Then, at last, Gadranus motioned toward the chairs. "Please, sit. We have much to discuss."

"I'd rather stand." Zaide lingered beside the door. His left hand flexed, yearning for his sword, but he kept it by his side. This was the man who had destroyed his life. Who destroyed his home, who killed his family, who had shattered the world.

But the time to kill him was not now.

"Then you are welcome to stand." Gadranus bowed his head in acknowledgment, a gentle smile on his lips. "Esli, fetch us wine. No—wait. The Kolmari do not imbibe, is that correct? Forgive me, I did not think. No alcohol. Bring cider, and a service for tea."

The servant woman by the door bowed and scuttled out into the hall.

"I don't want your hospitality," Zaide said. It was all he could do to stay where he was, to keep his breathing level while his pulse thundered in his ears.

"Then I won't force it upon you, but it will be here, ready, should you decide to partake." Gadranus strode to one of the chairs and sat with his elbows propped on his thighs and his fingers laced together. He studied Zaide for a long time, his expression unreadable, then gave a long, soft sigh. "It really is you, isn't it?"

The question rankled. It was touched with awe and a strange note of respect, both of which grated against Zaide's sensibilities. "The ear gives it away, doesn't it?"

"A mark to find you by, when this day finally came."

"A mark caused by you trying to kill me," Zaide retorted.

Gadranus raised a hand, palm out. "Your anger with me is wholly justified, but please, do not let it interfere with the opportunity before us. You've come to me for a reason. You have many questions, I am sure. Believe me, I am eager to answer."

The first question out of his mouth should have been about the Spectrum Blade and whether or not the man before him would help restore its power. Instead, Zaide thought of half a dozen others before the sword came to mind. A twinge of guilt pinged inside his chest, but he stifled it. He'd come too far for something as simple as guilt to hold him back. Gadranus had hunted him, had murdered his father, or so the Oracle said. Zaide trusted Oroduna's word, but so many gaps remained in the story.

He stared at the man for what felt like an eternity before he finally drew breath and spoke. "Everyone told me you're broken-born."

"I am," Gadranus said simply.

Zaide didn't frown, but he lowered his chin. "Your hair..."

"Ah." The man chuckled and gave a single nod. "Your people are from the north. I am from the south."

"But you speak Torec."

"I do. It is the most widely spoken language in the Shattered Lands. Toren was once the seat of a great empire. It is my hope some of that glory will be restored when all this is over."

Zaide bit back a scoff. "You're the one who destroyed it."

"Never happily, Zaide." Gadranus shook his head, and the movement showed more differences between them.

"Your ears." Zaide's brow crinkled. It was a rude observation, he realized belatedly, but the man before him didn't seem to mind. In fact, he didn't respond at all, merely stood from his chair when the door opened and the servant woman reappeared with a wide tray in her hands.

Gadranus strode to meet her and take the tray from her hands. "Thank you, Esli. That will be all for now. Please, allow me some privacy with my guest."

The woman curtsied and scuttled away, leaving them alone once more. Gadranus carried the tray to the low table that sat between chairs and filled two tall crystal goblets with warm-colored cider. The appealing scent of spices touched the air, and he sat down again.

"They say the people of this world were given such long ears so they could hear the Maker's whispers throughout all creation. The Torec, the Jadorans, the Amrochans, even the Desheni bear them." He took one of the goblets from the tray and gave a soft, regretful sort of smile as he cradled it in his hand. "It was the first thing taken from me, when I was reborn. I had ignored the Maker's call too many times, and so I would never hear it again."

Zaide touched the scarred edges of his cut ear without thinking. "How did it happen?"

Gadranus raised his brows. "Your ear?"

"Your curse."

"Ah." The cider in the goblet swirled. Gadranus drank, then

leaned forward to take the other goblet, too. He locked eyes with Zaide as he sipped from it and swallowed, then returned it to the tray. Strange, how hard he worked to instill comfort. He leaned back in his chair and stared at his own drink after he'd proven both safe. "I've wondered that often, myself."

"You don't know?" Zaide's legs had begun to ache, standing still in one place. He shifted his weight between his feet and hoped he didn't look nervous.

"Oh, I know. And I have regretted the choices I made for Ages, but there is no undoing them. Only living with them, and moving forward. Sit, please. I have no secrets to keep from you or anyone else."

Against his better judgment, Zaide paced forward and perched on the edge of a chair, keeping enough distance between the two of them that he could rise and draw the Spectrum Blade before his enemy came close.

Gadranus leaned forward to rotate the tray of drinks, so the goblet of cider sat closer. "What do you know of goborrins?"

An odd question. "They're ugly and the big ones are hard to kill," Zaide said.

"And they exist in great numbers. They breed fast. They grow fast. And while they try to mimic our behaviors, they have no real skills. No ability to reason. They're hostile, aggressive, and they were killing my people."

Zaide blinked.

"When I look back on things now, I wonder why I didn't ask more questions. Where they came from, how they came to be. Folklore said they were birthed from darkness, but that story is so long lost that I am the only one who recalls it." Gadranus held up his goblet and turned it in the light, examining the way the amber liquid glowed. "It doesn't matter anymore. All I knew was that my people were struggling, were dying to these monsters. We lived a vagrant lifestyle, and they followed us. Hunted us, as if it were sport. Our numbers were not great enough to defend our clan, and so I begged the Maker for help."

The scent of the drink grew more appealing, the longer Zaide smelled it. He leaned forward to take the goblet from the tray, never taking his eyes off his foe. "It doesn't sound like you got it."

"Oh, but I did. A miracle—an incredible blessing. I was given the ability to speak with them, to communicate through means they understood. The power to touch their minds and turn them away from my people."

Zaide shifted back in his chair, making himself more comfortable, though he still sat poised and ready for combat. "Then why are they here?"

"The goborrins proved easy to dissuade. But they were also easy to command. It wasn't long after I turned them away from my clan that I realized they had other uses. Powerful fighters in their own right. Useful tools against my enemies. This was a misuse of the gift I'd been given."

"So you were punished?" Zaide guessed.

"Eventually. But that story is not why you are here." Gadranus drank from his goblet, still calm, but anticipation made his movements slow and cautious. "Tell me, Zaide. Why have you come?"

"How do you know my name?" The sound of it sent an unpleasant prickle down the length of his back. Had the Oracle told him? It was the first thing that came to mind, but the dark-haired man in the other chair shrugged.

"I've always known your name. Since the day you were born." A thoughtful look touched his chilly blue eyes. "You resemble Dharran so strongly."

Zaide cradled his cider with both hands. "The Oracle of Nimultis said you killed him."

Gadranus gave a slow exhale, then nodded. "Dharran's death is one of my greatest regrets, through all the Ages I have lived. He was a brilliant soldier, a cunning strategist, and a dear friend. Had I known it was you—Dharran's son—who was the child whose fate was so twined with mine, I would never have let such fear consume me, and we would not be meeting as we are." Genuine regret pinched the corners of his eyes. "But I did not know. You were with your mother in what the Oracle revealed to me, and I did not know Dharran's wife."

Thoughts of his mother filled Zaide's head. The patterns on her dress, the same as what was on the broken pottery in that old farmhouse. Her tender smile. The warm, sweet fragrance of her long white hair. He shut his eyes. "He was part of your army?"

"Commander of the North Armies," Gadranus said. "And for what I had done, he turned against me. I do not blame him. He knew he could not hope to stop me, but he hoped to buy you time. I... am grateful that he did. He was a man of great honor. He would be proud of what you have become."

Knowledge of his father was the one thing Zaide had hoped to find on his travels. Now that he had it, it planted pain like nothing he'd ever known deep inside his chest. A crack in his heart, driven wider by words he'd dreaded he might hear.

What if he didn't like what he heard? That possibility had plagued him since he departed from Kolmar. Now it had come to pass, and it was almost as bad as Tula's unkind assumptions.

Zaide swallowed hard. His chest was tight and his throat grew thick, but he would not allow himself to mourn the truth here. "This isn't how I thought this was going to go," he admitted.

"There were only two ways for it to go," Gadranus said as he raised his drink to his lips. "Either you came to kill me, or you came to learn something from me. You have yet to draw your sword, so which is it?" He arched one eyebrow as he drained the last of his cider, as if in challenge.

Now was the time for the question that would reshape everything. Gadranus could help him, or he could kill him. Zaide weighed both possibilities as he shifted to slide a hand into his pocket. "I came to give you something."

Not what Gadranus had expected. He leaned forward to put

his empty goblet on the tray between them, curiosity and surprise clear in the way he stared.

Zaide slid the prism from its hiding place and leaned forward to present it on his open palm. It gleamed in the cool light that poured through the tall windows, rippling purple shadows turning over in its depths, like plumes of smoke rising from a snuffed candle.

"Incredible," Gadranus breathed as he reached for it. He drew it from Zaide's hand with care and wonder, turning it over to examine it from all angles. "Do you know what this is?"

"We found it in Kolmar's temple," was all Zaide said. Beyond that, he admitted that he didn't.

Gadranus nodded slowly. "This was a piece of the seal used to hold my spirit there. I never anticipated I might see this again."

"We fought you there. In the temple. Or, some kind of you." A remnant of power, they'd concluded before. Zaide still did not understand, but how could he? He bore no magic; that half of the world was beyond what he could comprehend.

"Of course. This is what held it there." The prism glinted and for a moment, the strange purple light came from within it, rather than from the windows. "This is a Shadowsliver. It's a unique tool. It absorbs whatever power is fed to it and can retain it for a long time. Perhaps indefinitely. A fragment of my power must have been what was trapped there, caught in part of the seal."

And Zaide had brought that power back to him. Lark feared what that might mean. Now, as Gadranus rotated the prism between his fingers, he did, too.

"The strength of that seal was why I was reborn so late this time," Gadranus said. He lowered the Shadowsliver and met Zaide's eyes with a level gaze. "This is a precious gift."

Zaide's pulse had never settled, but now it roared, climbing until it made his hands shake. He leaned forward to return his cider to the table, untasted. "Now I need to ask a favor."

"Name it."

"The Spectrum Blade's power is unbalanced. If I'm going to fight you, if I'm going to win—" His voice cracked. Maker's mercy, what had given him the nerve to try this? His stomach turned over so hard, he thought he might be sick on his boots. "I need its power restored."

Gadranus leaned forward to rest one elbow on his knee. He stroked his chin in thought while his other hand rolled the Shadowsliver, over and over again.

Zaide steeled himself and tried to summon whatever strength—or idiocy—had made him set foot in this parlor. "We both know how this is going to end."

"Perhaps. Perhaps not." The dark-haired man grew still, but his gaze slid to the sword at Zaide's belt. "May I see it?"

Was this it? The moment that ended him, or ended everything? Zaide rose slowly, too aware of the stories of the man across from him. Gadranus was said to be an unparalleled swordsman.

Yet he had no sword. He sat in the parlor with no weapons at all, from what Zaide could see. There was only the Shadowsliver in his hand, a force Zaide could never hope to comprehend.

He curled his left hand around the Spectrum Blade's hilt and drew it from its sheath, one inch at a time, until he held the sword horizontally, flat side out.

Gadranus stared. His face revealed nothing as he examined its short length and lacking colors. "Remarkable."

"You've seen it before." Zaide didn't mean to sound defensive, but he gripped the sword tighter, nonetheless.

"More times than I can count," Gadranus said. "And when I see it next, it will be in your hand, the moment you take my life."

The sword dipped and Zaide shook his head. "How can you say that? Without any fear?"

Gadranus gave a small shrug. "I don't need to fear it. I've felt it countless times before. But this time... this time could be different." He gazed at the blade with longing—an expression so unexpected, it seemed wrong. "We could do it, couldn't we? We could end all this."

Understanding lit within Zaide like a spark and he lowered the Spectrum Blade to his side. "The last Rise."

"So it could be," Gadranus said.

Zaide would have given anything for a response from the sword. Some prickle of protest or a hum of confirmation. He'd never realized how much he'd begun to let the blade guide him.

A long, thick silence hung between them before Gadranus sat up straight. "I know this is difficult to understand, but please, hear me. I have no desire to be your enemy, Zaide. Not yours, not Sendassian's. The war, the bloodshed, it's not what I want."

"Did you decide that before or after you tried to have me killed as a baby?"

"A mistake I will atone for, eventually. I don't expect forgiveness. I know I won't receive it. But when I say it was not a personal slight against you or your family, I beg you to understand the difficulty of where I stand." And stand he did. Slowly, Gadranus rose from his chair. He was tall, up close—a towering man who would have been a devastating foe with a blade in his grasp. But he held none, just the strange dark prism of the Shadowsliver, which turned in his hand like a worry stone. He gave the sword in Zaide's hand one last, longing look, then turned to pace back to the windows. "Had Sendassian been willing to reason with me, this could have been over by now. You would have been spared this price. This fate."

"You can't blame your actions on another king." Zaide considered sheathing the blade, then thought better of it. Now they both stood, and the tension of hate that thrummed in his shoulders warned him of the risks that brought.

"No. I don't blame him for his decision." Gadranus sighed, and his shoulders sank beneath the weight of a great weariness. "I blame him for his pride. We could have ended things, and no one ever would have needed to know. Sendassian held the power to end this curse. To end me, and bring about the last Rise. He refused. And then he refused to accept the blade and face me. He could have stopped this, twice over. Either permanently, or at least for your time. He chose neither."

Zaide felt as if he should have understood what that meant, but uncertainty hung over him like a haze. "What are you talking about?"

"My gifts let me seize power," Gadranus stated simply. "And so they became my curse, and also the way free. 'When every knee does finally bend, so the pain of rebirth shall end.' Thousands of years of struggle. Burying family, friends, pushing ever closer to this freedom I so desperately desire. When the last piece of the world falls beneath my rule, when the last kingdom is finally conquered, then... then I will be free."

And the Allied Kingdoms beneath Sendassian were all that remained free. Zaide stared at his back as a warped sense of pity and disgust twisted up inside him. "You want to die."

"Yes."

All of a sudden, the Spectrum Blade's modest weight felt heavier. Zaide clung to it until his knuckles ached.

"I have lived far too many lifetimes," Gadranus continued. "I have known too much pain. You understand, then, why I am eager for this to end."

"I can't just stand back and let you kill Sendassian."

"I don't expect you to. But when I do, the crown will fall to his daughter. My hope for peace lies with her, and that is how you may help. I understand you travel with her." The look Gadranus cast over his shoulder was sharp enough to pierce.

"I can't make her bow to you," Zaide said.

"I don't expect that, either. But you are her Bladebearer, and if anyone has her ear, it's you. Speak with her. A peaceful surrender, that's all I ask. When Amroch's crown is in my hands, the world will be beneath my control. And when I am gone, I care not what comes after me." He smiled sadly down at the prism in his grasp, then turned to extend his hand.

Zaide drew back, his sword ready.

Gadranus gave his hand a small bounce, making the offering clear.

Slowly, Zaide eased his stance. He crept around the table to reach for it.

"You asked a favor," Gadranus said. "Take it, and you will have everything you need."

The prism was warm beneath Zaide's fingers as he drew it from his enemy's hand. The smoky magic trapped inside roiled. "How do I use it?"

"That's for you to learn. You already know I cannot touch the blade." The man's smile was gentle, sincere, the farthest thing from what Zaide had ever imagined.

Unsettled, he slid the Shadowsliver back into his pocket. "Thank you."

"You are most welcome. I am glad you sought me out. That you have been willing to speak. Truly." Gadranus touched his chest in a show of sincerity, then paused and raised a finger. "One moment. There's something else I'd like to give you."

Nervous warnings clanged in Zaide's head and he backed away with his body tense, ready to strike, but Gadranus ignored him and paced toward a large desk against the far wall. Until that moment, Zaide had not realized it was a study they sat in, rather than a receiving parlor.

Gadranus opened a drawer with one finger and drew a small box from inside, along with a small, timeworn leather book. "I recall the day you were born. To say your father was proud would be an understatement. You were born on the equinox, a date that represents harmony in Torec culture. An auspicious day for a firstborn son to enter the world, to say the least. That means your birthday is fast approaching."

"I don't want a gift from you," Zaide said. Nor did he like the idea of the man being prepared to offer one.

"Then consider it a gift from your father. They were among his things when your family's quarters were cleared, after... well." Gadranus handed him the box without finishing that thought. It was small, wooden, but hinged on the back. "I kept these, after your father's death. After I understood the mistake I had made. I realize it likely does not comfort you to know I considered him a dear friend, but I always hoped I would have a chance to offer you something that had been left behind. It does not make up for what was lost, but I hope it serves to strengthen some connection to what was wrongfully taken from you."

Zaide cracked open the box. The hinge creaked and resisted, but he managed to pry it open with one hand. Inside, two small hoops of a strange, bluish metal rested on a pad of black velvet. His brows knit. "Earrings?"

"A tradition of your people. Torec men wear them to symbolize that they have come of age. What you do with them is your choice."

The box snapped shut and Zaide lifted his head, unsure what to say.

Gadranus shook his head. "Please, do not look at me that way. I expect nothing of you right now. No feelings, no forgiveness. My only goal is to help you understand what we can achieve through peaceful means, and I don't expect an answer now. Nor do I expect one until the choice is Dasienna's to make. But consider my offer. We are on the same side, Zaide. We both desire the same thing." He offered the book next.

"Thank you," Zaide said as he took it. Strange as it was to thank their enemy, it was the only thing that felt right. He opened the book, but the words inside were foreign, so he shut it again and tucked it under his belt.

"You are welcome. And when we meet again, may it be in quiet council chambers instead of the battlefield."

There was nothing left to say. Nothing left to do. The box with the earrings clinked against the Shadowsliver as Zaide dropped it into his pocket, and he sheathed the Spectrum Blade on his way to the door.

Gadranus remained where he was, and the silence between them was strangely comfortable, despite all that lay ahead.

No matter how they met, whether in peace or in combat, the ending would be the same.

The Spectrum Blade would bring Gadranus's death, and the sword would be in Zaide's hand.

CHAPTER TWENTY-ONE

"Do you still see him?" Lark strained on tiptoe to see past her companions, but they were both taller than her, and she only succeeded in seeing the backs of their heads as they crowded by the window.

"No," Tula said. "He just passed out of sight."

"We will wait a few minutes, then it will be safe for us to go. Wherever it is we are going." Andriun leaned back, but checked over his shoulder to see where Lark had gone before he moved from his spot.

She inched backwards to give him more space, but the moment the window was clear, she posted herself there to scan what she could of the city. Where were they supposed to go? She hadn't determined that yet. "We should find something to eat."

"Downstairs?" Tula suggested. "They said it was paid for."

Lark could have shuddered at the thought. "No, not here. Not where someone knows who we are." They were leaving the inn for the same reason; anywhere someone knew they could be found, someone might know to harm them.

"Out in the city, then. It will be safest." Andriun crossed to the bed where Zaide had left his bags and picked them up, one by one. It doubled his load and he jostled it to try and make it settle. "This may be conspicuous."

"Good thing *somebody* knows Torec and can think of a way to explain it to anyone who asks." Tula stuck out her tongue.

He failed to be offended. "The structure of Torec sentences is very similar to that of your tongue. I believe they stem from the same root. All that is necessary is a few adjustments and the learning of the words."

"Be grateful he can speak for us," Lark said. "It was wise of him to learn." At least one of them had taken the time to think ahead. They'd all known they'd be headed for the Shattered Lands, yet only Andriun had taken the time to truly prepare. Lark tried to remind herself that she'd had her own duties in Nimultis. That she'd failed to fulfill them hardly mattered now.

She had not put down her own belongings, but she checked the straps before she made for the door. The dog sat there, gazing at the knob in anticipation. Eager to leave, or hopeful that Zaide would return? Both left her uncomfortable.

"Here we go, then," Tula sighed as Lark led the way into the hall.

It was a short trek back to the entrance, but the innkeeper was no longer busy. She looked at them in surprise and jerked a thumb toward the kitchen. "Food?"

Andriun slid to the front to answer. He spoke slowly and paused often as he chose his words, but the woman's face brightened and she asked something else. He reached for one of his bags and made a sound of frustration when he could not reach the fastenings, then caught one of Tula's bags and opened it, instead.

"Hey!" she protested as he lifted her red and gold coat with the dragon designs, spreading the fabric enough to be seen.

The innkeeper oohed in delight, then gestured vigorously as she explained something and Andriun stuffed the coat back into the bag.

He grinned and spread a hand over his heart in a Desheni gesture of sincerity, then strode out the door.

Lark followed, bewildered. It had been a fast exchange, but she hadn't understood a word. "What did you tell her?"

"I said we brought Jadoran silks to trade, and asked which merchants would offer the best prices." It was such a simple ruse, reinforced by the existence of Tula's clothing. He went in the direction the innkeeper had indicated, but they only made it two streets down before Lark took the lead. She cut down a smaller side street and inhaled. She was hungry, and a rich, savory fragrance hung thick in the air.

"We'll find something to eat first," she said. "Then we'll explore until we find someplace to hide."

"Yes, I understood that to be the plan." Andriun put out the end of his trident to steer the dog away from something she'd grown too interested in. "I am uncertain, however, of Zaide's plan to have this creature of his assist in finding his way to us."

Lark had her own concerns about that. "We'll worry about that issue when we come to it. Look there, that vendor stall. That should do." The carts and booths selling food reminded her a great deal of Ganede, the last place they'd had the luxury of buying meals for themselves. She'd never imagined they would find something so ordinary here, deep within the Shattered Lands, and part of her wondered why. Wars were expensive; one could not fuel endless battles without a strong financial backing and a wealth of resources. Those required at least some sort of stability within one's borders.

Judging by the bustle of the city around them, Toren had a healthy supply of both money and resources.

They'd reached the vendor's cart before Lark realized a problem with her plan.

How was she to pay for their meal when she only carried Amroch's currencies?

"You," someone snarled.

Lark spun in place and her eyes widened as a broken-born

man clawed his way through the crowds, his lip peeled back in a snarl.

Andriun spat a curse. He seized her by the arm and lit into a run. Tula leaped after them, and Daisy bounded along at their heels.

"Stop! Stop her!" the man shouted. The press of people opened before him and he raced after them.

"Is that—" Tula started.

"From the mountains," Andriun confirmed before she finished.

Lark grimaced. She knew she'd recognized him, and his presence here meant nothing good. "As if we had any doubts they were spies."

They ducked down another side street, their bags bouncing as they ran. Shouts rose behind them, followed by a harsh whistle.

"Is that an alarm? Are they calling an alarm on us? We're the emperor's guests!" Tula scowled, but didn't stop running.

"This just proves he meant us harm," Lark panted. Andriun had a long-legged stride, and she struggled to keep up.

The Magister harrumphed and started rolling up her sleeves.

Lark raised a finger in warning. "Don't you dare start throwing fireballs!"

Tula's lower lip jutted out, but she abandoned the effort.

The narrow roadway they followed spilled onto a larger street and Andriun hissed when they almost crashed into pedestrians. "We must get across the river."

"How?" Lark saw the gleaming water ahead, but there was no sign of a bridge in either direction.

"Then into a boat, I do not know," he snapped.

More whistles sounded behind them, harsh and grating, and when Lark turned, the sight of a squad of armored goborrins marching their way made her stomach flop.

"A boat!" Tula pointed with her whole arm.

Lark turned toward it and ran with all her might, darting and weaving between strangers on the street. Angry exclamations rose behind her, but she dared not look back. The boat Tula had seen was nothing but a narrow rowboat of some sort, tied to a dock nearby. The river was not wide; they would cross it fast. "And goborrins can't swim," she breathed to herself.

Tula reached the tiny vessel before she did, and Andriun skidded to a stop and seized the rope. The Magister all but leaped into the boat. The force of her landing sent it drifting from the docks, and Andriun grunted as he hauled back on the rope to keep it from floating away.

Lark wasted no time. She hopped the growing gap and landed hard, her knees cracking against a beam in the bottom. The boat rocked so far, she thought it might capsize, but Andriun was on it in the next second, shoving the boat's end away from its moorings with such force that he almost fell off. Lark and Tula both lunged after him to grab him by the coat and keep him from toppling into the water, but he was so laden with bags that neither managed to catch hold of anything but luggage. It was good enough; they steadied him, and he thrust a hand toward the water.

Magic surged in Lark's senses as his power propelled them across the river, ignoring the natural current. It was so fast, so effortless, and she fought back a rising wave of envy.

"I have discovered a flaw in our plan," Andriun said the moment he caught his breath.

"I think there's more than one," Tula replied, though she motioned for him to continue.

"We have continued to travel together. I believe our group is more noticeable and distinct than if we were to separate."

Lark squeezed her eyes shut and cursed herself for not considering that sooner. "We can't split up, though. We'll have no easy way to find—wait." Her stomach dropped. Where was the dog? She spun in her seat and scanned the docks with her tongue clamped between her teeth.

"Ah, fish guts," Andriun groaned. A blur of white darted

back and forth on the docks, yipping and whining as they drifted farther away.

"Don't leave her behind," Tula cried. "Zaide won't be able to find us without her."

He let out a sharp hiss of frustration and began to shed his bags.

Lark grabbed him by the shoulder. "Don't swim back there just for a dog. She'll find a way across."

"I suppose my trident will bring itself across, too, then?" Andriun stripped off his coat next, the blue of his bare skin stark against the muted colors of the city.

Before Lark could say anything, he leaped off the boat and into the water. She winced and raised her hands to guard her face from the splash.

He did not resurface before their boat skidded against the shallows of the far side.

Across the river, goborrins piled into a vessel of their own.

Tula snatched the discarded bags by the straps, stringing them up her arms. "He'll catch up."

"He'd better." Lark, too, grabbed as many as she could carry. They both stumbled on their first step out of the tiny boat, the sucking mud of the bank threatening to hold them until their pursuers could arrive. She gritted her teeth and worked hard to free her feet and climb to the roadway on the other side. They'd already drawn a crowd of spectators, and people gasped and shuffled out of the way as they tried to run. The extra bags were a burden Lark wasn't ready for. They bounced hard against her back and their weight made her body feel leaden. Her footsteps landed hard and uneven, and her breath had grown ragged by the time they reached the first row of buildings.

Something white streaked past her feet and she yelped in surprise. The dog ran to the next corner before she shook, water splattering in every direction.

"Daisy!" Lark had never imagined she might be so relieved to see that creature in her way.

A second later came heavy, sloshing boot steps. "I do not have the blubber for this," Andriun hissed through clenched teeth. He'd retrieved his abandoned coat from the boat they'd left behind, but he ran with it slung over his shoulder, his trident gripped tight in his hands.

"I'll make us a fire later," Tula called from half a dozen paces ahead.

Andriun snatched a handful of straps at Lark's shoulder and all but tore the bags from her back. With the load lightened, she ran a little faster. The sound of whistles had faded behind them, but she dared not look back to see where the goborrins were.

"Keep going," Andriun urged. That was enough of a warning; she gasped for air and struggled onward, and by the time they broke beyond the city's edge, the edges of her vision had darkened.

"I can't," Lark panted. She stumbled twice and almost fell, but hands caught her arms from both sides. She hadn't realized Tula was that close. The shadows began to recede as she sucked in air.

The Magister gave her a shake. "Don't stop yet. I can still see them, we have to keep going."

Maybe it would have been better to surrender. Lark struggled to lift her head. The moment she did, something stung her cheek and she flinched.

Tula's eyes drifted upward. "Snow?"

Perfect. Lark fought back a groan and made herself move. The snowflakes were small and scouring, biting at her exposed face and hands. Beside her, Andriun muttered something that had to be a curse. He drove his trident points-down into the earth and jerked on his coat over his still-wet skin.

Lark squinted against the wind that drove snowflakes into her eyes. "Over the hills. That way. There has to be some way we can lose them."

The others resumed movement, but instead of running, they kept to a steady trot. It was easier to maintain; Lark only hoped it was fast enough to keep the goborrins tailing them from catching up.

They crossed two hills before something gray came into view against the mostly-white landscape. Andriun singled it out with a finger. It looked awkward when he pointed, the webs in his hands pulling strangely, but it was friendlier than if he had pointed with the trident in his other hand. "There. We will camp there."

"What if it's occupied?" Tula spread her hands as if to shrug, but Lark suspected it was a suggestion, meant to imply fire magic.

He shook his head. "It won't be."

There was so much certainty in his words that Lark frowned. "How do you know?"

Andriun did not reply right away. Instead, he stared at the structure through narrowed eyes. "It is empty. I can feel it."

"*Feel* it?" she repeated.

"I have told you, my ability to sense water has increased. Living things contain much water. There, I feel nothing."

It was enough of an explanation for her. She nodded and gripped the straps of her bags with both hands.

They did not slow until they reached the foot of the old watchtower.

CHAPTER TWENTY-TWO

TULA TRIED THE DOOR, but it didn't budge. She grasped it by the iron ring beside its latch and thumped it against its fittings. "It's locked."

"Another way in, then." Lark glanced over her shoulder, but the snowfall had grown thicker, the fat flakes obscuring the landscape.

They circled the foot of the tower, but there was only one door. The windows were nothing more than slender arrow loops on the higher floors, and the smooth mortar that filled the gaps between stones prevented any decent handholds. Before long, they ended up back at the front door.

Lark stared for a moment and fought back a sigh. "Do we keep going?" She didn't want to; they needed to stop. It had never been warm, but the temperature was dropping fast. Daisy stood shivering beside her, and Andriun was wet, too. The Shaman needed a chance to dry them off, or they would both suffer.

Tula held out her hand. "Give me the Molten Dagger. I'll get us in."

The question of how sprang to Lark's lips before she thought better of it. If one of the artifacts was involved, it was better if she didn't know. She found the bag that held them and produced the dagger without a word.

The Magister plucked it from her grasp and shuffled to the door. She positioned herself so that neither of the others could see what she was doing, but the acrid smell of hot metal singed the air and gave it away.

Andriun coughed, and whether it was from manners or the odor, Lark wasn't sure.

The door swung open a moment later. "There we go!" Tula blew on the dagger as if to cool it. Oddly, or perhaps humorously, the glowing veins beneath its surface went dark.

"We should be able to barricade it from the inside," Lark said as she slid into the tower with the others. She shut the door and regretted it almost immediately when it shut out the light, too.

A moment later, a tiny flame sparked to life over Tula's fingertip. "There's a fireplace. Looks like wood, too. I'll get something started so we can warm up."

"Please do," Andriun said with an unhappy sniff. "I am too far land adapted for this weather."

The Magister made a face. It looked stranger in the odd, writhing shadows cast by her tiny light. "Don't you live in a frigid region?"

"Yes, and I have the sense to stay out of the water in cold weather, because I do not have blubber." He started with his hair, curling his webbed fingers beside it and pulling downward to strip it of water.

Lark watched as he dried himself and his clothing. He had not relied so heavily on gestures when she'd first met him, and she suspected he did not need them now, but she had not considered how they might help one focus. She almost asked him to explain, but changed her mind almost as soon as she thought of the question. Asking advice for how to awaken and use her magic meant discussing what her power was meant to be, a conversation for which she wasn't ready.

"Hmm." Tula dumped a few split logs into the fireplace and

spread her hands before them. Fire crawled across the surface and burrowed into the wood, but she did it without looking. Her eyes were fixed on Andriun as he shook out his coat and dried his bare skin. "I think you're fine without blubber. You didn't have any problems swimming in Nimultis."

"And I do not care what you think," he muttered. "Nimultis is on a tropical island, of course I did not have trouble. There is a reason my uncle took our people to find warm waters."

"Do you think the smoke will give away our location?" Lark doubted it would be easily visible through the falling snow, but asking would distract from such pointless bickering.

Tula sat back and looked toward the ceiling. "I don't think so. At least, I hope not. I haven't figured out how to manipulate smoke yet."

"You can manipulate smoke?" Lark hadn't realized that was something fire magic could govern.

The Magister crinkled her nose. "No, I just said I can't yet."

"But she will, eventually." Andriun funneled all the water he'd stripped from his clothes and hair into a barrel nearby, one likely meant for holding water rations. It was empty now, and when he released the water and let it drop, it hit the bottom with a strange crack. "Just as I am able to manipulate snow. When one is practiced in their element, they will find they have influence over things they had not considered. Water is not only water, but also ice. Steam. Humidity and fog, the clouds in the sky. It is the sweat on one's brow and the blood in their veins."

The thought of the Shaman having power over *blood* made Lark shudder unbidden.

He snapped his fingers and clicked at the dog, until the poor, shivering thing hobbled over to him. A gentle swing of his hand began to draw the water from her coat. He went on without noticing Lark's discomfort. "Likewise, fire is not only fire, but the destructive force of consumption and the power of heat. Her magic will bear power over the smoke because of the heat that rises from the flames. She will be able to alter winds, because they are affected by the temperature of the air. And I suspect she will be able to manipulate the temperature of her own body, allowing her to survive in places that are inhospitable to life."

Tula's eyes widened as he spoke. "Vorkaris only talked about smoke and magma, but he said I need to get better with flames, first. Are you sure I'll be able to do all that?"

"Other Paragons have." He shrugged. "If our oral histories say you can, then I have no reason to doubt." He finished drying the dog with a flick of his fingers, leaving her coat so fluffy, she resembled a sheep with pointed ears on top.

More than once, Lark had wondered if the practice of storing knowledge in books instead of using oral histories had hindered her people. The artifacts had become rare knowledge, the Spectrum Blade all but forgotten. How long would it be before knowledge of the Paragons fell by the wayside, too? "Do your histories say anything about the Paragon of Light? What that sort of power can do?"

Andriun moved his discarded bags to the corner beside the staircase that led to the upper floor. Once they were piled, he sat and reclined against them. "I know very little, to be honest. Other clans or tribes of Desheni may know more, especially those who are native to warmer waters, since they will have been closer to Nimultis, and so closer to her."

Lark almost asked who he meant before she recalled the assumption he and the others had made. She could not blame them; after the welcome they'd been given, it certainly appeared they had been welcomed into the Paragon of Light's home. She was reluctant to disabuse him of that notion, particularly after her involvement in retrieving the Sunshard her mother had left behind.

The Sunshard she still had no idea how to use.

"I don't suppose you know how to make use of the artifact the Oracle gave us, then." She'd stood in one place so long, she'd almost forgotten she still carried all her things. One by one, she added them to the pile Andriun had started.

"I do not," he said slowly, "but we already know it cannot be used alone. With hope, Zaide will bring us better news."

Lark made herself nod.

The fire snapped and crackled in the still.

"Well," Tula said with a huff, "I don't know about the two of you, but I'm hungry, since we never got anything to eat. Who wants me to warm up some rations?" She pulled a paper-wrapped packet from her things and raised it overhead when the dog nipped at its corner.

"I believe she does," Andriun laughed.

"So much for Zaide hunting to feed her." Lark dug out some of her own food, then motioned for Andriun move so she could retrieve something from Zaide's bags, too. He was the one who'd wanted to bring the dog along, so he was the one who could share his meals. She found something she thought was meat and carried her selections to the hearth.

Tula had produced a pan from somewhere. She considered how to position it for a moment before she reached into the fireplace to rearrange the burning logs with her bare hands.

Lark shuddered. "That's horrific. Please don't do that again."

"How come? It's not like it hurts. It's just fire." The Magister wiggled her fingers above the flames before she sat the pan atop the wood.

"Not like it hurts you," Lark corrected. "It hurt me just looking at it."

Tula grinned at her as if it were a joke, and she saw no need to correct it.

They ate in silence as night fell and the creeping cold sank deeper into her bones.

After everything was eaten, she climbed to the second floor of the tower to peer out the arrow slits. Cold air gusted through the holes, and she suspected she knew why the tower was not in regular use. The landscape outside was brighter than she expected, with a fresh coat of white powder, and a warm glow sat on the horizon in the direction of Toren. The hills bore no sign of anyone having followed them so far. Satisfied, she returned to the warmth of the fire on the floor below.

Instead of settling with the others, she crossed to the door. Aside from the bar that held it closed after the latch was melted, they had not barricaded it, and the single piece of wood was easy to lift free. "We should send the dog out now."

"I am not certain she is ready for that task," Andriun said.

Tula made kissing noises at the dog until Daisy went to greet her. "I don't think she's smart enough for it." Despite the criticism, she buried her hands in the dog's scruff and cooed as she tousled her white mane. "But you're gonna try, huh? You're gonna go find Zaide, right?"

Lark opened the door. The dog's ears perked and she abandoned the petting to trot out into the snow. "If she doesn't, I'll go out after her in a few hours. I don't look broken-born, but I'm closer than either of you, so I should be harder to notice."

Andriun frowned as she barred the door shut again, sealing Daisy outside. "Was it not you who was recognized by that broken-born soldier we ran from?"

Heat rose in her cheeks. "I'll wear a hood up, this time. I won't make myself easy to recognize. Besides, it's not like I'm going right now. You never know, that dog might come through."

Tula gave a long, doubtful hum. "I'll go upstairs and watch. If she never goes anywhere, we'll know we need a new plan. If she does go somewhere, well, I guess it would be good for someone to stand watch and make sure the right person follows her back."

"It's cold," Lark cautioned.

The Magister beamed. "Yeah, it'll be a perfect time for me to try that temperature manipulation thing blue boy was talking about."

Andriun sat bolt upright. "Blue boy?" The words oozed indignation.

Lark motioned for him to settle down. "It's not as if she's wrong."

"Right or wrong does not matter here," he protested. "That was terribly impolite."

She waved a hand in dismissal. It wasn't worth the fight. He grumbled, but settled as Tula trudged up the stairs. In her absence, things were quiet. After a time, the silence began to itch under her skin. Lark paced circles in front of the door. She stopped before the fire now and then to warm her hands, but uneasiness crept up on her if she stayed put.

As if to contrast her restlessness, Andriun stayed put and busied himself with examining the condition of his gear.

It was wise. Lark considered it. Instead, she paced.

By now, he had to have concluded his meeting. If he was an expected guest, they would have let him in right away. Taken him inside. Maker's mercy, she wished she knew what the palace was like.

They would have talked. Perhaps argued.

She pulled her hair down from its ponytail and ran her fingers against her scalp. The rake of her nails was grounding, but did not ease her stress.

He would have offered the gift. Given their enemy new power. Asked for help.

How long should it all take?

Her stomach knotted with anxiety and she shook her head as she walked. Her circles came faster as her pace grew more agitated.

Without warning, her foot came down wrong. The heel of her boot crunched and her ankle twisted, and she stumbled into the door to keep her balance.

"Mmm," Andriun intoned. "A restless deer is most likely to trip."

The urge to glare at him was strong, but she tempered her response and kept her head down. "I'm not a deer."

"It does not matter. You are restless, so it is the same." He shifted until he sat cross-legged, then patted the ground in front of him. "Sit. Check your gear."

Lark didn't want to. She wanted to keep pacing, to climb the stairs and see what Tula saw, to find a quiet moment where she could silently pray that Zaide might be cresting the horizon. Yet her nervous pacing helped nothing, and if she hurt herself, she'd be no help to anyone. She pushed herself off the door and hobbled over to join him.

"Your ankle?" Andriun asked without looking up. She'd hardly paid attention to what he was doing; he sat with a bag in his lap, mending a strap that had begun to pull apart.

"Fine. I think." It was uncomfortable, but not badly twisted enough that she would be unable to walk. Her boot, on the other hand, had popped a seam on the side of the heel, and her pale woolen sock peeked through. She stuck a finger into the hole.

He glanced up. "Take it off. I will mend it."

Something she should have been able to do, herself. She was competent with a needle and thread, considering handicrafts like sewing and embroidery were the only things her father had ever approved of her doing, but working with leather was different. She drew up her knee and began unlacing her boot. "You seem to have skill with a lot of domestic things. Sewing, cooking, herb lore. This." Her toes tilted up, indicating her damaged footwear.

"The Desheni consider these basic skills. You do not know where the tide may carry you, so one should be able to survive on their own." He finished the repairs to the bag and restrung his needle with a different thread, something heavier that he rubbed across a block of beeswax until it was stiff. "Zaide has many of these skills, too."

Lark tugged off her boot and sat it on the ground beside his knee. "I don't think any of those skills are going to help him right now."

"Fortunately, he has others that may. He is, for example, very good at befriending those others cannot." Andriun looked at her as he made that pointed observation.

The scrutiny was unpleasant. She pulled her knees to her chest and hugged her legs to herself.

If only he knew what that friendship could cost.

Andriun prodded at the edges of the ruptured seam for a while before he set to work. The webbing on his hands should have been an impediment, but he had admirable dexterity and it did not take long for the gap to begin to close. "You have walked many miles in these boots," he murmured as he worked. "I am not surprised at the wear. You have been through a lot together."

Lark started to nod, then pursed her lips. Somehow, she doubted he meant the boots. "I've done what I must."

"Hmm."

She didn't know what that was supposed to mean, so she stared at her shoeless foot and wiggled her toes. Even with her thick socks, she felt the cold, and it wouldn't be long before her toes went numb.

If only the rest of her lost feeling so easily.

Andriun turned the boot in his hands, adjusting the angle from which he worked. "Have you told him?"

Lark twitched at the question. She didn't know what he meant—who he meant—until he lifted his head and met her gaze. His dark eyes were hard, shrewd, and cut through her like a knife to leave her raw and exposed. Her heart gave a nervous flutter and her hands tightened against her shins.

He stared for a long moment, then shook his head and returned to his work. "If you have not told him, he does not know."

"I don't know what you're talking about." Her voice cracked partway through and she struggled to be calm.

Andriun gave her a pointed look from beneath his strong brows.

It was all she could do not to shrink. How dare he? She was princess of Amroch, and he addressed her as if she was... was... well, she didn't know, but she didn't like it. She drew herself up and glowered back at him, but the Shaman remained unbothered.

"There is worry, and then there is *worry*. I believe that you try to hide it, but I see. And he is brash, but he will assume nothing unless he is told." He knotted the thread and cut off the excess, then sat her boot in front of her. "That is all I will say."

And for being so few words, they cut straight to her heart and made her soul bleed. She bit her lower lip and jammed her foot back into her boot, as one hand went to her chest as if to cradle the hurt—or defend herself and the walls of unfriendliness she'd worked so hard to build.

Andriun tucked his tools back into his mending kit. He said nothing else, as he'd told her he would, but the silence was awkward and made her flustered.

"I'm going to go check on Tula," she muttered as she stomped to square up her boot on her foot, then hurried for the stairs. The laces dragged and she was in too much of a hurry to tie them, but the Shaman remained silent behind her.

He was right. She knew he was right. But the visions the Oracle had given her dangled threateningly in the forefront of her mind, and she steeled her resolve as she marched up the steps.

She would tell him nothing.

If she did not love, then she could not lose.

CHAPTER TWENTY-THREE

THE SUN HAD JUST FALLEN below the horizon by the time a guard escorted Zaide back to the castle gates. Snowflakes drifted on the air and the ice burned when they landed against his bare face. He caught himself holding his breath as they walked. There was no helping his tension; he wouldn't feel safe until he was out of the palace, out of the city, and back with his friends.

Work in the castle went on around him as if he weren't there. Hammers rang in forges, an apprentice loaded an ox-drawn wagon with pieces of finished armor, and pages ran errands from doorway to doorway. The rest of the city struck him as quiet, but he recognized the signs of preparation from his brief time in Amrochan.

Few things he'd seen had been more disheartening. Toren was a large city—almost as large as the capital of the Allied Kingdoms. It had been easier to imagine himself defeating Gadranus when he hadn't known what sort of resources the man had at his disposal. A failing on his part, he supposed. He was supposed to be a scholar. He should have stopped sooner to consider that the Shattered Lands hadn't just been broken, they'd been conquered, and all of that territory now served to feed his enemy's armies.

Amroch's peril had never seemed so great.

The guard motioned Zaide through the tall wooden doors that led back to the city without a word, his behavior as calm as if visitors like him came every day. For all Zaide knew, maybe they had, before the Allied Kingdoms were all that stood in Gadranus's way. How many times had the man tried diplomacy? He wasn't sure a request for the surrender of the crown was all that diplomatic, but he'd never been a king, and wasn't likely to become one. At this point, he wasn't certain he was likely to *survive.*

Zaide thanked the guard anyway.

Warm lights populated the city's streets, illuminating the fat snowflakes that floated on the wind. Business had not slowed, though, and for all that Zaide fit in with Toren's people better than he'd fit anywhere, he'd never felt like more of an outsider.

He found somewhere to sit in a small, park-like space beside the river, where flames burned steady in tall lamp posts and benches offered a view of the water that might have been charming at any other time. He made himself breathe deep as he sat. The air was sharp and metallic in his nose, but it roused his senses in a way he needed. His head was muzzy after everything he'd heard. He leaned forward to cradle it with both hands and rake his fingers through his hair.

The entire encounter had been odd. Amicable. The old stories called Gadranus many things, but *friendly* had never been one of them. Zaide had expected someone cold and harsh. How was he supposed to prepare himself to kill someone he'd liked?

The silent admission made him sick, but he had to decide if he wanted to hold his stomach or hold his head, and his head felt more appropriate.

He'd liked the man. Or would have, if he didn't know who he was. Every bit of their interaction had been cordial. Comfortable, even, though he'd done his best to stay alert the whole time. But speaking to him had been easy, his demeanor had been honest, and nothing he'd said or done had felt like any sort of threat.

Maker's mercy, Lark was going to kill him.

He made himself rise, unsure of where to begin, but they'd discussed sending Daisy to find him and he could only hope they'd figured out how to make it work. That the dog understood commands in his tongue and not Torec was an oddity, but they'd found her closer to the border. There was no telling how far she had wandered on her own, or who she had belonged to.

There was no sign of a white dog anywhere he looked, though. He saw several similar canines with black or gray patterning on their coats and considered asking their owners if they'd seen a white one, but that idea stalled the moment he remembered he spoke no Torec at all. Going back to the inn, similarly, struck him as pointless. They wouldn't have told the innkeeper where they were going, and he hadn't kept the key, so it wasn't as if he could let himself back into the room. So he walked the city streets, looking and listening, hoping for some sign of where he would find the others.

The first clue came when he ventured back to the river and the sound of complaints reached his ears.

A cluster of people stood at an unremarkable dock. A handful were guards, but more were bystanders, and a few were the ones who complained. They gestured toward the river with increasing agitation and the guards tried to settle them.

Zaide watched and listened until someone stepped close beside him and asked a question he didn't understand. He turned and was met with an armored guard's breastplate. He raised his hands, palms out, and took a step back. "I'm sorry, I don't... ah..."

"Borderlander?" the guard asked.

It took a moment for Zaide to do more than blink. "Yes." It was close to the truth, anyway; Kolmar was near the border, just on the other side.

The man nodded knowingly. "A lot working their way to the

capital these days. Preparing for the war to begin. When did you arrive?"

The idea the war hadn't already begun gave him a chill. He'd seen the armies outside Amrochan himself. If they didn't consider that a war, then what was? "This morning. I'm going to need to learn Torec."

"Soon," the guard agreed. "But find soldiers if you get lost. Those of us who have campaigned on the border speak both, but most of these people don't." He made a circle in the air with his finger, indicating the city.

"Thanks." Zaide glanced back toward the group at the docks. "What happened? I thought Toren was a peaceful city."

"Is, usually. The goborrins keep people in line, but with so many borderlanders reporting for duty, we get some trouble. Then you get crackpots like these." The man nodded toward the cluster. "Old man says a Desheni stole his boat. I don't know what he thinks he'll get from that story. What would a Desheni need a boat for?"

Zaide's brows shot up before he could catch himself.

"Exactly." The guard rolled his eyes.

"Good luck sorting it out." Zaide glanced across the river. If Andriun had taken a boat, they'd either gone downstream or crossed to the other side. If it was the former, it didn't matter which side of the river he followed. "Is there a footbridge? I didn't see one on my way in from the west."

"There is." The guard turned to point upstream. "If you go that way, there's a—" He stopped short when Zaide turned to look.

The sudden halt set Zaide's pulse to racing and he took a step back.

"Turn your head," the man said.

The last thing he wanted right now was a problem. Zaide turned, suspecting the guard had seen his ear. The way the man's face hardened confirmed it. Maker's mercy, had every soldier in the Shattered Lands been told to watch for him? "I've just come from meeting with him," he said, trusting he didn't need to explain who he meant. "He's told me what he expects me to do."

"And you're doing it?" the guard asked slowly, a chill in his words.

Zaide nodded. He could be truthful; all that had been asked of him was that he discuss the matter with Lark.

The tension dissipated and the man nodded back. He pointed up the river again. "A bridge, that way. Good fortune."

"You, too." Zaide assumed that was the right response, for the guard turned away and moved to join the others in their efforts to placate the man whose boat had been stolen.

There was no way to cover his ear without being conspicuous, so Zaide just tucked in his chin and walked as fast as he could without drawing attention. He kept his left side toward buildings, so people would be forced to pass him on the right.

He combed as much of the city as he could, looking for more hints, but there were no more clusters of guards along the river. There should have been, if they were looking for a boat. "Which means they must have gone across," he muttered to himself.

The city was longer than it was wide, and it didn't take long to find himself at the fringes, where wide fields spread beneath a deepening blanket of snow. He'd put so much energy into walking that the cold didn't start to bite through his tunic and shirt until he was beyond the last of the buildings and exposed to the wind. The first gust that hit him wracked his whole body with shivers.

Across the field, a pack of goborrins walked in single file. They were no threat here, not within their own territory, but their presence still put him on edge.

They were looking for something. They had to be.

Zaide stared at the snow and wished he'd brought less colorful clothing, so he could slip across the field unnoticed.

He'd barely left them alone for a few hours. Wasn't he the one who usually got into trouble when he was unsupervised?

He made it as far as what he assumed was a barn, based on the smell, then crouched behind it to wait for the goborrins to disappear over the next hill. He hadn't crouched there for long before something caught his ear. His head tilted out of reflex, turning his better ear toward the sound, a long habit he'd likely never break.

The crunch of snow and an odd snuffling, too small to be a goborrin.

Zaide leaned forward until he could peer around the corner.

There, a familiar white mass of fur wandered along the side of the barn.

"Daisy!" he shouted in a whisper.

The dog's head snapped around, her pointed ears standing straight up.

He motioned violently for her to come. She bounded forward and greeted him with a lick up the underside of his nose.

Zaide snorted and tried not to gag. "What was I thinking, bringing you along?" He wiped his face thrice over with his sleeve and exhaled hard through his nose several times, effectively purging the rest of her saliva. "Where are the others?"

Daisy sat and stared.

"Lark, Tula, Andriun. Where are they?"

The dog looked around and over her shoulder before she turned back to him, her head cocked at a curious angle.

He sighed. That was too much to ask, it seemed. He planted a hand on top of her head and made himself get up. "All right. Well, you had to come from somewhere." And by some miracle, there was snow on the ground. Finding her path couldn't be easier.

Zaide checked for goborrins before he stepped out from behind the barn and examined the tracks the dog had left in the snow. Her trail was loopy and meandering, but came from one general direction. He kept the tracks in sight as he trudged along that way, grateful that his nighttime vision had always been good. A snowy field was nothing compared to the dark of Kolmar's forests at night. He followed the dog's tracks as easily as if it had been broad daylight.

Eventually, an old stone tower came into view, a dark shadow behind the falling snow.

"Is that the place?" he asked, as if Daisy had some way of answering him. She trotted along at his side, just as happy as ever. Smoke rose from the chimney, he saw as he got closer, so he assumed it was.

Then, when he finally drew near, the door swung open and silhouetted a familiar figure with firelight.

"Heard you stole a boat," Zaide called.

Andriun's face crumpled into a scowl. "I do not steal things. I merely borrowed it without permission."

Zaide laughed and stepped forward to clap his friend on the shoulder. "And here I thought they were making it up."

Footsteps thundered down a flight of stairs inside and he clicked to get the dog's attention. She didn't need much coaxing, and Andriun stepped back to let both of them in.

Lark stood halfway down the flight of stairs, her eyes wide. "You made it."

"You're alive!" Tula shouted as she leaped off the bottom step.

"Should I be insulted you think that's a surprise?" Zaide helped bar the door behind him. He didn't think the goborrins had seen him cross the field, but he couldn't be sure. There was no hiding the tracks he and Daisy had left in the snow. They'd fade within a few hours, though, and he had to hope that would keep the monsters off their tail. Defending the watchtower wouldn't be easy, and starting a fight while they were within the Shattered Lands seemed unwise.

"We were worried," Lark said before Tula could answer the question. "I didn't know when to expect you. Was it... did you..."

He nodded, sparing her the search for words. "I met with him."

She descended another step, hope burning in her rich blue eyes.

Zaide lowered his gaze and crossed to the hearth, where he crouched to warm his hands. They prickled as the heat seeped into his skin.

"That doesn't look like it went well." Tula's whisper was just a shade too loud to stay private.

He bowed his head. "The sword's the same. We still have to figure that out."

Silence.

He dared not look back. He could already picture the way Lark's shoulders dropped. She'd be trying hard to hide her disappointment, but he'd know just from looking that she felt defeated. It was the last thing he wanted to see.

Andriun lingered by the door, a shadow that moved in Zaide's peripheral vision. He rocked from one foot to the other, then inched closer. "The way you say that is strange. The sword is the same, but he cannot restore its power without the other half, correct? He could not have done anything without the Sunshard. So when you say we must figure out something, do you mean he refused to help?"

"No. He was..." Zaide snorted softly and shook his head. How should he explain it? "He was very agreeable."

Again, silence.

He couldn't blame them. He'd never expected Gadranus to be cooperative. It had to be a shock to them, too.

"I gave him the prism we found in the temple," he explained. "He seemed happy to have it. Said it was a precious gift. He told me about the seal in Kolmar, and how what we fought there had to be a piece of his power that had been trapped. Then I told him I was there to ask for a favor."

"And told him about the sword?" Lark descended the rest of

the stairway slowly, the heels of her boots tapping with every step.

He gave a single nod. "He asked to see it. Then he gave it back." He still couldn't wrap his mind around that. How readily Gadranus accepted his fate. How eager he was to see it fulfilled. Zaide stood and pulled the prism from his pocket. "He called it a Shadowsliver. He said if we have this, we have everything we need to restore the blade's power."

The princess crept forward, staring at the prism all the while. Instead of wonder, dismay filled her expression and a misty sheen glassed her eyes. "You mean we had it? This whole time, the other half was already in our hands?"

Tula fumbled with her coat for a moment, then grumbled and went for the pile of bags beside the stairs. She produced her notebook from one of them and sat on the floor with her legs stuck out before her.

"It would have helped to know this when we were still in the presence of the Paragon of Light," Andriun sighed.

The Magister shook her head and scratched something out in her notes. "I don't get it. If we always had that Shadowsliver thing, and it was what we needed to be able to restore power to the Spectrum Blade, wouldn't the Oracle have known that? She knows everything that happened in the past, wouldn't she have seen that we had it?"

Zaide's eyes flicked toward Lark, just in time to catch her grimace. He hadn't expected her to tell them while he was gone, but he didn't know how to discuss the matter without giving it away. Instead, he'd sweep away the question and try to focus on the problem. "It doesn't matter now. Obviously the Oracle wanted us to learn something here, because this is where she sent us." What that meant was another concern, but he'd already decided he wouldn't mention the request Gadranus made until he had a chance to speak with Lark in private.

The princess nodded and blinked rapidly. Her eyes cleared. "Or maybe she knew this was where we needed to be, regardless. We know where Gadranus is now. If we're able to restore power to the sword here, then we'll be able to face him at once. We can end things now."

Yet if that happened, all they would achieve was sealing him again.

One hundred years of peace before the man was reborn to continue his quest. Zaide had been so sure it was enough, but what was one hundred years when they had the chance to change everything? To end things forever? The Shattered Lands —and everything beyond them—would be set free.

More things they couldn't address until he had a chance to speak with Lark alone.

"We're getting ahead of ourselves." It felt strange to be the voice of reason, but he curled his fingers around the Shadowsliver and let his hand drop to his side. "Right now, we need to focus on fixing the sword. We can't make plans for something that's not even possible yet."

To his surprise, Lark was the first to nod. He'd thought she would be most eager to push forward. "You're right. We start with the sword. And..." She stared at his hand, at the dark prism in his grip, and he thought he caught the faintest glimmer of worry in her eyes. "We'll begin tomorrow, after we've had time to rest. We don't know what will happen when we use the crystals, so we'd best make sure we're ready for any outcome."

"So this quest will be continued." Tula snapped shut her notebook and jammed it back into her bag. "When I get back to the Grand Library in Jadora, they'll have to make me a fully-fledged librarian with all *this* information to share."

Zaide slipped the Shadowsliver back into his pocket. "Can you still be a librarian if you're also the Magister and therefore ruler of the entire city?"

She tilted her head to one side. "Hmm. I suppose I could just order them to make me a full librarian, but that's less rewarding than earning it, right?"

Andriun shook his head and pulled their bedrolls from the

pile. "And that is a problem for you to solve when this war is over. It is night, most of us have eaten, and I think we should follow the dog's example." He jerked a thumb toward Daisy, who had curled up beside the hearth.

"I can agree with that." Zaide hadn't eaten, but in the wake of everything that had happened, he found he wasn't hungry. He caught his bedroll when Andriun tossed it his way, and tried to ignore the way the Shadowsliver poked at his leg while he unrolled it and settled. It could dig and jab all it wanted, but it would change nothing.

Morning would come, but they'd be no closer to knowing how the crystals worked.

CHAPTER TWENTY-FOUR

LARK JERKED UPRIGHT with a sharp gasp, the cold air hitting her sweating skin like a slap. She still saw them when she closed her eyes. Claws of shadow tore at her golden hair and her ruffled skirt. Formless hands seized her arms and wrapped around her throat, threatening to choke the light out of her.

It was a nightmare she'd had too many times, yet waking from it never grew easier.

She swallowed hard and wiped her face.

"Yeah," Zaide said softly. "Me, too."

She hadn't noticed him until he spoke. He crouched beside the hearth, prodding the fire with a stick to keep it alive. Lines of weariness etched his face, and they aged him. It was the first time she'd looked at him and seen the weight of his burden.

So much of that had been her fault. She was the one who'd demanded his help, who'd sent him into peril time and time again. Yet he never showed how it wore on him. Even now, when he glanced her way, a hint of a smile touched his lips.

"The spiders, for me. That hallway in Kolmar. They still wake me up at night." He prodded the fire some more, then rested his elbows on his knees and watched the flames.

Slowly, Lark let her eyes drift to the others. The Paragons still slept.

"It's almost morning," he murmured. "It won't hurt them to wake."

So she shouldn't feel guilty for wanting to talk. It was a simple statement, a gentle invitation, without making her feel obligated to say anything. She could have easily turned over and tried to go back to sleep, and she suspected he wouldn't have said a word.

She slid out of her bedding instead and inched over to sit on the edge of the hearth. The freshly-stoked fire was comfortably warm. She put out her hands to warm them. "How long have you been up?"

"Ah..." He looked toward the door, though it was tightly sealed and still barred, then glanced to the stairs. Neither place gave him the answers he was looking for, she assumed, for he shrugged and turned to sit like she did. "Didn't sleep much. I'll be all right, though."

Lark still pitied him. "Maybe you should try to get some sleep now. I'll keep watch. No spiders." She tried to smile, to let him know she was teasing, but she couldn't hold the false expression for long.

"I'll be fine," he insisted. "We should get things ready, anyway. Do you have any ideas? For what we should try?"

She wished she did. The Oracle had told her so little; she'd been left to her own devices, trying every trick she'd ever read in hopes it would cause her magic to awaken. In the end, it had been a waste of time. "I'm open to suggestions."

"I guess the first thing we do is just put them all together." Zaide stuck one leg out long, giving himself enough room to dig the strange, dark-colored prism out of his pocket again. Once he had it, he held it out to her as casually as if it were a rock instead of some powerful artifact containing the power of the man they meant to kill.

Lark took it, though it made her skin crawl.

"Is it time?" Andriun propped himself up on one elbow and rubbed his eyes.

"It may as well be." At this point, there was no reason to delay. Lark found the bag in which she'd kept the artifacts and rooted blindly until her fingers found the rough facets of the Sunshard. It always glowed, but when she pulled it free of the bag, its brightness struck her as amplified. She sat back on her heels and studied its surface until the prism in her other hand caught her eye. Its surface had grown darker, its purple core more intense.

"What's wrong?" Zaide asked behind her.

She wasn't sure anything was wrong, but she moved the two objects closer together and farther apart several times before she answered. "They appear to be reacting to each other." The closer together they came, the brighter the Sunshard glowed, while the Shadowsliver grew darker.

"That is what we want to happen, is it not? A sign that things are as they should be?" Andriun crawled from his bedroll and sat upright, rubbing his eyes more. His braided hair was a mess and stuck up strangely around his ears, but he watched the two stones with close attention. He was awake enough to be involved, at least; beside him, Tula merely groaned and rolled over to hide her face from the light.

"I'm going to guess it is." Zaide returned to where he'd slept. The Spectrum Blade rested atop his bedding. It was so ordinary in its plain leather scabbard. It certainly didn't look like the kind of weapon that could change the fate of the world. He took it, then returned to the hearth before he unsheathed the blade. It gleamed in the firelight, but the colored patterns on its surface remained still. The marbling reminded Lark of the sheen atop a soap bubble, iridescent, but lightless.

She moved closer, and he laid the sword on the stone hearth. The crystals she held looked no different for being nearer to the blade, and their lack of response to it made her uneasy.

Zaide moved back, giving her more room. "Just try." His

voice was so soft, so reassuring. It made no sense; he knew. He was the one person who had figured it out, had determined her role and all of her failings. Yet he smiled when she looked at him, nodded his affirmation and gave her space to work.

If only she could believe in herself the way he believed in her.

Lark swallowed hard and knelt beside the sword. She dared not touch the blade, even after it had allowed her to handle it once. Instead, she placed the stones atop it and balanced them on the steel.

All she had to do was determine how to move the power trapped in those gems into the blade. She held a hand above the Sunshard and willed herself to feel it. She was always aware of magic, could sense its presence and determine what it was supposed to do, but for all that she could touch it, she couldn't *move* it. The glowing yellow crystal pulsed in her senses, a tingling warmth that flooded her arm and made her fingertips itch.

Perhaps if she could touch the power in the Shadowsliver in the same way, something would happen.

Slowly, she spread the fingers of her other hand above the prism. Something tingled there, but where the Sunshard was warm, the prism's power was cold. It bit into her like ice and sent goosebumps up her arm until a shiver coursed down her back. Everything about it was repulsive and her stomach turned as she made herself hold that contact.

Now, move, she thought. She lowered her hands, tried to will the magic to seep from the crystals into the blade beneath them. She pictured it in her mind, as vividly detailed as she could. The way the light and shadow could bleed from the crystals, leaving them lifeless and dull as they imbued the blade with new power.

Nothing stirred.

Nothing moved.

Please move, she silently pleaded. She held her breath and tried to imagine herself pushing, wielding enough power to force the magic from the stones. She pushed harder, until the tendons in the backs of her hands stood out with her effort.

Her chest began to ache. She held for as long as she could, straining against the power until she cracked and the spent air in her lungs burst free.

Nothing.

Nothing.

All the countless hours of her life spent training, preparing for this one moment, and she was left sitting, gasping for breath, unable to coax the one thing she was meant to have power over to obey. Tears stung her eyes until she couldn't see.

Zaide's hand landed on her shoulder, strong and grounding, and she turned to slide her arms around his middle and hide her face in his shoulder.

He hugged her back. "We'll figure it out," he murmured. "We're just missing something, that's all."

Through everything, Andriun had sat in silence. Now, the Shaman's voice came touched with hesitance. "I did not realize that Her Highness was a mage."

Shame poured over her, thick as a mudslide, threatening to bury her and steal her air. She rubbed her face into Zaide's tunic and struggled not to make a sound.

"Sort of," he answered for her, his arms around her like a shield, sheltering her from criticism no one there had posed. "She can feel it, but it never really woke up. I thought you knew."

"You never told us," Tula almost whined, her voice still gritty with sleep.

"It doesn't matter," Zaide said. "Right now, we need to figure out what to do next. Tula, you're Paragon of Fire. Your power is closest to light. Andriun, the Oracle said you're closer to shadow. Come over here and see if you can do anything."

The scrape and rustle of movement reached Lark's ears, but she dared not lift her head. She didn't want to face them, didn't want to meet their eyes and see their disappointment. It was bad enough she couldn't help, but she'd hidden so much. How were they supposed to forgive her for everything she'd failed to be?

Power rose in the two Paragons as they tried to touch what filled the crystals. It hummed in Lark's senses, distant but *there* —something her own power had always failed to be.

It held steady for a long time, then Andriun made a sound of frustration. "I feel it, but I cannot connect with it. It does not resonate with me."

"So either there's a trick to using those things, or we need to figure out how to get the Paragons together so they can do it themselves," Zaide concluded. It was a suggestion; his fingertips moved against her back, tracing a shape she thought was a question mark.

The very notion of appearing before Gadranus as she was, powerless and weak, made Lark's stomach churn.

There had to be another way.

She made herself sit upright, wipe her tears and gather what little composure she could. All she could think of was the feeble hope her mother had left behind knowledge of the shard and how it was meant to work, but where would that be? She'd pored over as many books in the royal library as she could, and her mother had not spent enough time in Jadora to add anything to their collection.

But maybe it hadn't been added to the library. Her mother might have kept journals, or written letters, or entrusted scholars with the knowledge that would someday have to be passed down to the next Paragon. She'd had an advantage; she'd known who her successor would be.

"We'll return to Amrochan," she said, though her nose had grown stuffy and she feared her voice was not as strong as it could have been. "There has to be information on the Spectrum Blade buried somewhere in the palace."

The heavy silence that answered indicated no one liked that idea. She didn't like it, either, but what choice did they have? She'd touched the shards and failed to activate the power in either one, and daring to appear before Gadranus like this—lacking power, lacking knowledge—could only make things worse.

"What about your father?" Zaide asked.

Lark still didn't know. She sniffed hard and turned to take the Sunshard. She left the other crystal where it was. The murky feeling it sent through her was so unpleasant, she didn't even want to touch it. "I suppose he'll have to answer for his choices. Maybe he'll have a better explanation than anything we've found out here."

He frowned, but didn't protest. When she didn't take the Shadowsliver, he picked it up and followed her to add it to her bag.

"It is a long way to Amrochan," Andriun said slowly. "It would be best if we leave at once. It may take weeks to get there, and we do not know if that is time we have."

She thought of the army of goborrins they'd passed as the monsters marched west, toward the bridge they'd destroyed. With that many hands at work, they'd have it rebuilt within a day. What were the odds they would beat an army of that size to the capital? The situation was so hopeless, it was all she could do to keep from crying again.

"Well, we've gotten out of every scrape before. Maybe this will be the same." Tula wiggled out of her bedding and began to roll it, ready to pack and prepare.

Zaide, too, began to gather things. "Do we retrace our steps? It's a long way back to Yithel."

Andriun shook his head. "I am uncertain of our location, but I will have a better idea of where we are once the skies clear and I can see the stars."

"Same," Zaide agreed.

"We should plan to go southwest for now. We have to go that way, no matter what. It is only a question of whether we should aim farther west, or farther south." The Shaman shrugged as he sat atop his bedding and began to undo his braided hair.

"You should be packing," Tula said.

"I do not need to pack anything but my bed. I did not get out anything else that I did not put away. So, now I have time to be vain." He shrugged and continued, unbothered.

Lark tried to ignore their bickering. She wiped her eyes once more and retrieved her coat from where she'd left it, draped over half of her bags.

Zaide finished his preparations before she did. He returned to the hearth and returned the Spectrum Blade to its sheath. "We can keep trying with the shards while we travel. Maybe something will change."

She appreciated his optimism, but the likelihood of her power suddenly revealing itself, purely in their moment of need, was laughable. "Perhaps," she agreed, though she had no confidence in the notion at all.

One by one, they picked up their bags, and when they set out toward the southwest with Zaide's dog bounding along at their heels, the new sense of anxious urgency kept all of them silent.

CHAPTER TWENTY-FIVE

THE PATH they chose let them skirt Toren, sparing them the trouble of running into the goborrins or armored broken-born guards again. Zaide didn't think they'd be a problem, given that all of them apparently knew who he was and knew he had earned favor from Gadranus, but he had no plans to test his luck.

They set as hard of a pace as they could through the snow. The night was so bitterly cold that they soon switched to sleeping in the early evening, making the most use of the sun's warmth. Tula was the only one who was unbothered by the cold, which was odd, given the way she'd shivered and complained before. She was Jadoran, born of the desert, and had never left its heat until he and Lark had entered her life. Whatever caused the sudden shift in her ability to tolerate winter, he'd missed it.

Every time they stopped to rest, Lark retrieved the crystals from her bag and sat with the Spectrum Blade on the ground before her. She did not cry again, but her pain and frustration was clear each time she failed.

Zaide tried to make gentle suggestions for things she could try, and the list of things she attempted grew long.

She tried holding the Shadowsliver and focusing on its power, since its power supposedly bowed to her.

She tried placing the crystals at different points—beside the sword's cross guard, at its tip and its pommel, balanced on the blade and atop the hilt.

She tried holding the crystals on opposite sides of the blade.

She moved them. She switched their locations or positions. She tried to attune herself to them.

After three days of traveling and trying, still nothing had worked.

"We'll figure it out," he tried to reassure her at the end of her evening attempt, but her demeanor had grown cold and she did not respond. He took back the blade and returned it to its sheath.

Zaide had begun to wonder if they would. Nothing seemed to make any difference with Lark's power, and he dared not make suggestions that might reveal her. He had no idea why she was determined to hide her identity as Paragon of Light, but after his meeting with Gadranus, he understood. He had his own secrets now.

What would they think of him, if they knew the rest of his story?

If they knew about his father?

If they knew how agonizingly easy it had been for him to speak to their enemy?

The thoughts raced through his head and made his chest grow tight. He rubbed his sternum without thinking but he didn't have long to sit and stew, for Daisy nosed at his other hand to beg for attention and he knelt to give it while the others settled for the night.

Tula started a fire, as usual, but instead of sitting to cook, Andriun settled at the campfire's edge and cleared his throat. "Tula and I were speaking while the two of you worked on the sword. We have an idea we would like to propose."

"An idea for what?" Zaide buried his hands in the dog's scruff and rubbed aggressively, hoping the apparent distraction made him look casual. He did not want to worry any of them with his troubles, not until he had time to sort through all his thoughts on his own.

"How we are to get to Amrochan." The Shaman grinned and in the firelight, he looked almost as crazed as the Magister did whenever she was hurling her fireballs about.

Lark fastened her bags shut after the crystals were secure and sat primly, her legs tucked underneath her and her hands resting atop her thighs. "Let's hear it, then."

Andriun raised a hand in a gesture of sincerity. "I believe we will encounter a river if we head due south for another few days, then tilt to the southeast."

"Can you sense that from here?" Zaide knew his friend's power had grown, but that would have been a stretch.

"No, but I have observed the shape of the land. There are certain patterns one can expect, and the patterns I have seen indicate there will be a river of substantial size."

"A river will mean settlements." Lark's hands curled to fists; she didn't like the idea of running into more people in the Shattered Lands.

Tula nodded. "Yeah, that's exactly the idea. We go find one of these settlements, and we take a boat!"

The princess shook her head vigorously. "We can't just hire a boat, we haven't got any money in... whatever currency they use here. I don't even know. We haven't anything of particular value that could be traded, either."

The Magister blew a raspberry and waved a hand. "I didn't say hire a boat, I said *take* one. Who's going to stop us? We're Paragons, a princess, and the Bladebearer."

"Titles that might not mean anything in the Shattered Lands," Zaide said as Daisy tried to climb into his lap. He wrestled her paws to ensure she didn't step on anything painful, a practice he'd grown used to over their travels. Any time he sat on the ground, the dog tried to climb into his lap, as if she'd forgotten she was so large that her head reached his hip when he stood.

"They'll figure it out pretty quick, I think," Tula said with a shrug.

Lark didn't like it. She shook her head again. "I can't abide *stealing* boats, either."

"Then consider it borrowed," Andriun suggested. "Based on what I know about the lay of the land, any river we encounter will flow in the opposite direction of what we need. I can address this for a small vessel, enabling us to sail against the current, but when we reach our destination, there is nothing stopping us from merely letting the vessel drift back to where we first found it."

"That seems extremely unlikely to work." It was the most polite objection Zaide could think of.

"The sailing part would work for us, though," Tula said. "It's that or walking all the way back to Amrochan, and hoping we get there before that army we saw."

The princess crossed her arms. She was deeply troubled by the suggestion, but she no longer protested, either.

Zaide frowned. "You're considering this?"

"I don't like it," Lark replied hotly. "I just don't see what options we have. We know Gadranus intends to take Amrochan. If he wants to confront my father, it means he'll have to go, himself. It's not just a matter of getting there before him, Zaide. We need time to research. Time to try things. We just need more time." The desperation in the last word planted guilt in his chest.

"Then we'll give it a try," he said as the dog settled atop his legs. "Who knows how to sail?"

Tula and Andriun exchanged awkward looks.

"So none of us. Great." Zaide forced a smile and knew it came out strained.

"We will learn," Andriun said.

"You'd better." Lark shifted so she sat more comfortably, though her hands remained curled to fists. "Now, explain how you plan to find a boat. And how you intend to get it back to its owner when this is over."

The Shaman cleared his throat and launched into his explanation.

It was, perhaps, the worst plan Zaide had ever heard.

~

"There," Andriun whispered. "That one."

At least half a dozen boats lined the long wooden dock that framed the river's edge, and of course the Shaman had picked the largest one.

Zaide sucked on his teeth as he tried to think of a response. To be fair, the other boats were tiny, nothing more than open-topped rowboats one might use for fishing. The vessel Andriun picked was the only one with a cabin, and it was small enough that even four people might make for a crowded trip.

"Are you sure you can move that?" Lark asked. They lay on their bellies atop a hillside above the village, letting the tall grasses that poked above the crusted snow hide them. This was not the first settlement they'd seen outside of Toren, but if the plan went well, it would be the last.

Andriun's face twisted with both annoyance and offense. "I am more than capable of moving such a small watercraft."

"She's just saying that because you struggled in Ganede," Zaide murmured.

"With ships as long as that entire village, loaded down with enough goborrins to lay siege to both Ganede and Jadora," the Shaman protested.

Zaide waved a hand, dismissing what would have been a pointless argument. "Forget it. How long do you think moving it will take?" He already had doubts about his part in this scheme.

"I will need to go slowly at first. Ten minutes? Perhaps?"

Far more than he'd expected. Zaide grimaced. "Can you make it in five?"

"That is a very small amount of time for how much water will need to be displaced in order to—"

"Yes or no, Andriun, I don't need a whole lesson on the magic."

The Desheni snorted. "Fine. Yes. I can make it in five."

"Good. Let's go ahead and get started, then." Zaide had already shed all his bags, leaving him with just the Spectrum Blade and his Jadoran long knife. He rose to his knees and double-checked the belts.

"Be careful," Lark whispered.

He wasn't used to hearing such concern from her, and he held her eyes for a long moment before he offered a nervous smile and stood. "You, too." He clicked his tongue and held out one hand, beckoning Daisy to his side. He remained unconvinced this would end well, but they'd gone along with his last terrible plan and nobody had gotten killed, so he owed Andriun this much.

Tula and the princess shuffled back down the way they'd come and began their trek to the south, carrying all of their gear on their own. They looked like turtles, hunched over with the rounded mass of bags on their backs. Zaide cracked a smile at the sight, then began his descent toward the village.

For now, Andriun stayed put.

"Here's hoping this works," Zaide murmured to the dog as she trotted along beside him. He was still relatively certain that providing a distraction was the worst possible job for him, but they'd all agreed he was the best choice, as he most resembled the majority of the village's residents and would be less memorable. He disagreed. Sending him into the center of a village to cause a distraction when he didn't even speak the common tongue would make him noteworthy, and while he pulled up the hood of his coat to hide his blunted ear, it wouldn't take much of a misstep to reveal.

"Wouldn't that figure? Leave a clear trail all the way to Amrochan so Gadranus knows I turned tail and ran?" He tried not to sound bitter, but it was hard to reassure himself that he wasn't running. He wasn't a coward.

He was an idiot, though, for going along with this.

No one noticed him at first. They'd chosen this place on purpose, the town right in the middle between the size of Toren and the numerous farming villages they'd passed. A stranger wouldn't be conspicuous, but there wouldn't be more than a handful of guards stationed there to keep the peace.

Peace was an odd term to come to mind when thinking of places in the Shattered Lands, but Zaide figured he'd sort out those thoughts later. "Plenty to worry about already," he murmured.

They strode through the place as if they belonged there, casually examining storefronts and stepping out of the way of passersby. Or, Zaide did; the dog looked in every direction, but he suspected she didn't particularly care what she was looking at or why. She'd come along, though, as happy as could be, and he smiled ruefully as they made for the docks.

There was no good way to do what Andriun had asked. He was going to get caught, no matter what he did, and while he wished he had a smaller knife to use, the Jadoran long knife at his belt was it. He gripped the hilt with his left hand, thankful he kept it on that side, because at least drawing it wouldn't be so obvious.

"Now would be a good time to go steal some fish or something," he whispered with a jerk of his head toward the workers nearby. A few had noticed him by now. He pretended he was unaware of their eyes on him as he leaned against one of the dock's pylons and gazed out across the river. If he crossed his arms just so, maybe no one would see him cut the rope that tethered one of the rowboats.

Cut them all loose, Andriun had said. Zaide glanced down the dock, then turned to look down at the dog as she sniffed around a post and began to meander off.

"Where do you think you're going?" he asked, though as long as she moved in the right direction, he didn't care. She gave him an excuse to crouch beside the next boat and cut it from its moorings, too.

He made it all the way to the fourth before someone realized what he'd done.

It was also at that moment he realized a fatal flaw in Andriun's description of what should happen.

The boats were floating away, but in the wrong direction.

Someone shouted at him. He didn't understand the words, but anger sounded the same in every language. Zaide bit back an oath and hurried to the fifth boat. Of course the one they were after was the farthest away; he considered skipping the fifth and heading straight for it. The point was supposed to be disguising which vessel they wanted. There would be no hiding anything now.

"Just gotta come up with a better distraction than runaway boats," he muttered to himself.

Well, they wouldn't think him a thief if they thought him mad. Instead of abandoning the fifth boat, he went straight for it and gestured wildly with his knife. "The river! The river's going the wrong way!" He could only pray Andriun had ended up somewhere close enough to hear him.

The men who ran toward him didn't seem to understand. Fishermen, he thought; none of them had the bearing of soldiers.

Zaide pointed at the boat with his knife. "The water is wrong!" He snagged the blade under the rope and hauled upward to cut it.

At that moment, the water shifted. The runaway boats slowed and drifted sideways, and the boat he'd just cut loose began to move, pushing against the river's natural current.

The men skidded to a halt, the one in the front throwing his arms wide to keep his fellows at bay.

That had certainly worked. Zaide went for the last boat, and it lurched before he got close and strained against its rope. He cut it loose and repeated his warning. "The water is wrong!"

Whether or not they understood him, it didn't matter. They had eyes.

So did the others who had begun to gather.

Maker's mercy, he hadn't figured out what came after the distraction. He glanced at the half-dozen boats as they meandered upriver instead of down and gritted his teeth. They were already too far away from the dock for him to try to leap onto any of them.

He started at a jog, following the boats down the river and scrambling for the next idea. Or was he following them up the river? He growled at himself and darted between people, desperate to keep pace with the drifting watercraft.

The dog barked a warning, but it came too late. His eyes were on the water, and he slammed into an armored goborrin's breastplate.

CHAPTER TWENTY-SIX

PANIC SURGED through Zaide's veins as he stumbled backwards and his eyes shot up to his adversary's face.

The goborrin was a good foot taller than him, its blunt, piggish snout shining with saliva. It stared down at him with hard black eyes, and he shrank away out of reflex.

It's not your enemy, he told himself before he could take more than a step back. *Not here*. His hand itched for his sword and he struggled to be still.

The monster huffed as a handful more stepped out from behind it. Its fat jowls rippled strangely as it relayed commands in harsh, guttural words. The sound made gooseflesh break out across Zaide's arms. He'd seen so many, knew they had to communicate, but he'd never realized they *spoke*.

He reeled backwards a few more steps and put out a hand in front of Daisy's face to stop her barking. She stopped, but whined, shifting anxiously behind his spread fingers.

His retreat wasn't enough to deter the goborrin in front of him. It closed the distance between them with a single step and snagged him by the coat to drag him closer. His boots skimmed the ground.

It snarled something he thought was a question, but he

understood none of it, and his eyes fixated on the strings of spittle that stretched between the monster's peg-like teeth. The monster gave him a shake and repeated the phrase.

Zaide's eyes widened and he found himself shaking his head.

The goborrin snorted in displeasure.

"I don't speak Torec," Zaide said, unsure why he bothered. He didn't even know if that was what the monster spoke. What were the odds it might understand him?

Its eyes glinted and it curled its powerful fist harder in the front of his coat, drawing the leather so tight it choked him. Then the goborrin lifted him until his toes scarcely brushed the dock beneath his feet.

By his legs, Daisy howled.

Zaide wheezed and clawed at the creature's arm. It seized his hood, shoved it back, and wrenched his head hard to the side.

It dropped him and turned to bark a new order, still in words Zaide could not comprehend, but the other goborrins fanned out around him and shooed away the bystanders. The monsters turned their backs to him, as if he didn't matter, and he blinked in confusion.

The dog nosed at his hands and whimpered and he smoothed a palm over her head as he began to back away.

The goborrins did not look at him again. Instead, they pointed at the drifting boats and herded people into order.

Strange as the opportunity was, Zaide wasn't going to waste it, and he turned to run. The boat they needed had drifted farther than the rest, and he rushed to catch up with it. It passed beyond the edge of the village before he did.

Just when he'd determined he had no idea how he was supposed to make it onto the vessel, water rose from the river and coiled around his ankle like a snake. He stifled a shout as it dragged him off his feet and hauled him into the air, sending unwelcome recollections of the monster in the lake racing through his head.

The tendril swung him over the river and dropped him onto

the boat's deck before it burst, pouring water over his head.

Andriun was at his side in an instant. The Shaman gripped him by the shoulders and gave him an aggressive shake. "What have you done?"

Zaide's head rocked and he groaned as he tried to stabilize himself. "I got your boat, what do you think?"

His friend scowled, his eyes dark. "What have you told them? Why did they help you?"

"What are you talking about?" Zaide seized Andriun by the wrists and worked hard to free himself from that iron grip.

"The goborrins," the Shaman snarled. "They ordered the people to let you take a boat. Why?"

They'd done what? Zaide stared back, dumbfounded. "You understood them?" And they'd helped him?

Andriun's face grew hard, but before he could say anything else, a mournful yip from the shore stole his attention. He made a sound of exasperation as he stood, and another rope of water rose from the river to seize Daisy and haul her to the boat. She yelped in distress as he moved her and she landed with her tail tucked and legs trembling. "Nothing smells worse than a wet dog," he muttered as he stripped the water from her coat with his magic and left her fluffy again.

"Not even goborrins?" Zaide asked in a weak effort to inject a bit of humor.

The Shaman snorted. "You smell like goborrin."

"That's what happens when one manhandles you." Zaide brushed a hand over the front of his coat, as if he could get rid of the memory of the thing hauling him off his feet. Being that close to one of the creatures and not drawing his sword had been an unpleasant experience, and it made him itch just to think of what could have happened if it hadn't let him go.

His hand drifted to his ear. Once again, that had been what changed things. What made the monster let him go. He shook his head and let his hand fall. "I was going to try to start a fight or something to buy you enough time to get to the boat before that thing got me. You said they told them to let me take it? Did they say anything else?"

"No. Not that I heard, at least." Andriun glanced toward the shore, but there was nothing to see yet. The girls were to meet them farther upstream, where they could draw the boat close to shore and safely load their things.

Had Zaide known they could have simply strolled into town and asked for a boat, it would have been easier. "If they let me go, it meant they were all right with me leaving." And that they were willing to aid his escape. They were miles from Toren, though. How could the goborrins here already know to let him loose, when the people in the same city as their leader hadn't yet known he'd been to see Gadranus? He rubbed his eyes.

Andriun cast him a suspicious frown. "They have every reason to seize you, knowing you are the Bladebearer. Is there perhaps more about your confrontation you might wish to share?"

Zaide had remained tight-lipped about most of the visit for a reason. All that really mattered was that he'd been given the Shadowsliver and the message for Lark, which he would deliver when the time was right. The rest... He shook his head. "He could have killed me then if he wanted me dead. I guess this just reinforces how badly he doesn't want that."

"But you are the one person who can stop him." Andriun paused to shift the water beneath them, changing its direction to compensate for a bend in the river ahead. "There is no reason for him to want you alive, or for his armies to aid you in survival."

"He wants me alive so he can die," Zaide said, and he marveled at how strange the concept was. "He knows I'm going to kill him. That's why he wants the Spectrum Blade at its full power. Why he gave me that prism back."

The Shaman stared at him for a long time before he gave his head a shake and muttered something in his own language, thick with disbelief.

"Yeah," Zaide agreed glumly. "I'll try to explain it better

when I can." After he spoke with Lark. After he searched the royal library for clues as to how much of what had been said was true.

Andriun did not ask any more questions and focused on sailing, instead.

Some time later, tiny figures appeared at the river's edge. One merely stood, but the other hopped in place and waved arms overhead. She would have been recognizable even without the bold splash of her red hair against the bland backdrop of the landscape.

"There they are," Zaide said, though he was sure Andriun had already seen. "How do we get them on the boat? Are you going to lift them, too?"

"I will ground the boat and we will have to wade the shallows in order to load our things." Andriun eyed the door to the little vessel's interior with doubt. They hadn't taken the time to make sure there was space for cargo, or for people.

Zaide took the hint. "I'll make sure we can stow everything safely." In the future, they'd try to travel more lean. Their provisions had dwindled some, but the Oracle had not guided their preparation or packing, and they'd ended up carrying far more than necessary.

Then again, it probably would have been the right amount of food for a trip made by foot. With the way her visions showed possibilities, the Oracle had not likely predicted they would end up stealing a boat. Or, borrowing, he corrected himself as he slipped below deck. Aside from a jumble of fishing gear, the space was empty, though he doubted more than two people would sleep comfortably inside. There were no hammocks or cots, just cushioned benches. He settled on the floor and worked at untangling things so they could be put away and make space.

He hadn't made much progress before the boat lurched and groaned, then tilted at a strange angle. He crammed the last of the netting into a bin beneath a seat and scrambled for the door to help.

The first bag thrown almost hit his head.

"Watch out," Andriun warned, too late to make any difference.

"Thanks." Zaide slid to one side and raised an arm overhead to let Lark and Tula know where he was. To his dismay, the next bag appeared to be aimed at him, for it hit him squarely in the side of the head and almost knocked him down.

"Bullseye!" Tula cheered.

"Would it not have to hit his face to be a bullseye?" Andriun caught the next one and tossed it to the deck, neatly avoiding injury.

Zaide grunted in displeasure and shot Tula a glare.

"Oh, well, I can try that next." She pulled her shoulder back, ready to pitch, then stopped and thought better of it. "Actually, no. That bag was just clothing. I don't know what this is, it's heavy."

"Would you just throw it here and get on?" He opened his arms, ready to catch. The girls stood knee-deep in the river beside the boat, and Lark did not appear to be happy.

The princess tossed her bags to him instead, one at a time, giving ample opportunity for him to throw them through the door at his side. Daisy jumped and snapped at each bag as it arced toward him, all without catching a single one.

When the last bag came, Lark sloshed toward the boat and reached for its side. Zaide leaned over the edge to offer his hand, instead. She said nothing, but grasped him around the wrist and let him help her climb.

Andriun bent to help Tula, too. "Take them inside and help them dry off. I need to focus on lifting us back into the deep part of the water."

Zaide snorted. "You'll dry off the dog, but not the princess?"

"The princess does not smell bad when she is wet."

Tula ticked a finger. "That's a good point." Still, she made a face as she shook her wet and muddy legs, then sat to pry off her boots and dump out the water they still held.

Lark emptied hers without comment and padded past Zaide to dip below deck.

He followed, and the boat began to tip before she found her seat. The princess flailed in an effort to regain her balance, and he caught her arm to hold her steady. "Easy. Hopefully the rest of the ride will be smoother."

"It had better be. The last thing I want is another bout of motion sickness. I don't suppose you have any of that mint left?" The look Lark gave him was so pitiful, he could have laughed.

Because he valued his well-being, he didn't. "A bit, but not enough to get us back to Amrochan. Here, sit down. I'll find you something to change into." All the bags looked the same, but he knelt the moment he had the princess seated and began the search for clean, dry clothing.

Lark took a bag, too, but instead of drawing fresh clothing from it, she removed the crystals. "Give me the Spectrum Blade."

Zaide hesitated. "I don't think it's the right time for that."

"What you think hardly matters. If we're going to be stuck in here, I'm going to make good use of the time. Give me the blade." She sat the crystals on her lap and held out her hand.

He wanted to refuse. They'd no more than boarded, and the boat still rocked and swayed as Andriun moved it back into the water. Now was surely not the best time, but would it hurt to do as she said? It wasn't as if he'd need the sword while they were sailing.

His fingers found soft fabric and he pulled a pair of trousers from the bag. He didn't know whose they were, but they'd do well enough while she dried off. "Put on these, first."

Lark pursed her lips, but took them. "Not with you here. Leave the sword. And then leave me in privacy."

The order was so abrasive, it made his hackles rise. He smoothed a hand down the back of his neck, then reached for his belt. "Of course, Your Highness." Acquiescing left a bad taste in the back of his throat, but what else could he do? He'd said he was her Bladebearer, that he held it in her stead. It wouldn't do to refuse her orders now.

She lifted her chin as he removed the blade and handed her the scabbard, her face so haughty that he couldn't bear to look at her another moment. Hadn't she just accepted his help onto the boat? The way she tilted back and forth between cooperation and a concentrated effort to annoy him was going to drive him mad.

He made it back to the little boat's deck and shut the door before a growl of frustration escaped his throat.

"Settled?" Andriun asked. He stood at the boat's nose and gazed at the water without looking back. The vessel had stabilized in the river, but it appeared steering it—and keeping it in motion—would require concentration.

"I guess. She got the stones out the moment she sat down." Zaide didn't know where to stand; Tula leaned off the back of the boat doing who knew what, the rest of her bags abandoned by the door that led below.

The Shaman glanced back long enough to squint over his shoulder. "Stones?"

"The Sunshard and the Shadow... thing. Sliver." Zaide craned his neck to look for the dog. He found her walking circles around the boat's perimeter, sniffing at everything there was to be smelled. That would keep her busy for a bit, then.

"Ah. I will wish her the best of luck, then. Perhaps our time sailing will give her more ideas. Nothing births creativity quite like boredom." Andriun almost smiled, but it ended as more of a grimace. "I will not be able to assist in thinking. I will keep us moving for as long as I am able, but when I grow weary, I will need to halt somehow so I may rest."

And so they didn't lose progress. Zaide nodded, though his friend's back was turned and he would not see. "I'll look for an anchor so we'll be ready for that."

"Good. Please see that the others do not disrupt my concentration."

Zaide wouldn't make promises there. He studied the bags on the deck and decided they were of little consequence at the moment. Lark would want privacy to change into dry clothing, and then she'd begin her own work and would prefer peace. That left him with Tula, so he shuffled his way to the back of the boat. It wasn't particularly large or long, and the sails had not been raised, so he could see easily from one end to the other. He brushed a hand against the mast to help keep his balance. Or, he assumed it was part of the mast. For all the time he'd spent on ships, he still knew painfully little about them.

"There are some weird fish down there," Tula said as he approached.

"How'd you know I was coming?" He moved close enough to peer over the edge, but he didn't see any fish.

She sat upright. "I heard your boots. You're stomping, so you're mad about something."

"I am not," he protested, though he didn't know which statement he was protesting to. He hadn't thought he was stomping. He was relatively sure he wasn't mad.

Tula shrugged and turned to sit properly. He hadn't noticed until that moment that a bench spanned the back of the boat. Somewhere to sit and fish, perhaps. He settled beside her and watched as she stuck her legs out long and twisted her ankles to touch her toes together.

For a while, they were quiet, both of them listening to the water lapping against the boat's hull and the strange, gurgling swish that came from Andriun's reversal of the current. The dog circled the deck twice before she settled in front of them.

Zaide leaned back against the rail. "What are you going to do now?"

"I don't know. Wait for us to make landfall, I guess. Andriun asked me to keep my fire to myself while we're on the boat, so my magic doesn't distract him." She didn't quite kick her feet, but she raised them one at a time and let her heels drop back to the deck with a clunk.

"Speaking of magic," he murmured as he reached for his pocket. "You can sense magic things, right?"

"You mean like the artifacts? I guess so."

"I mean—I guess I mean that." Zaide knew it was rare for objects to be imbued with magic, but there were other ways to lay power on things. Charms or traps, things connected to items, rather than set within the items themselves. He hadn't removed the little wooden box with the earrings from his pocket since he'd accepted them, and while he suspected the others would have noticed if he'd returned with some new traces of magic on his person, it was better to be safe. He withdrew the box now and held it out. "Do you feel any magic on these?"

Tula perked up. "Ooh, what's this?" She plucked it from his fingertips and turned it every which way, examining every side of the container before she cracked it open. "Are these a present for someone? Are these for Dasienna?" The suggestive way she drew out the last vowel of the princess's name made him cringe.

Zaide shook his head, but stayed careful not to overreact, lest she make something out of his response that wasn't there. "No, they're for me."

"For you?" Now she sounded surprised. She peered at him through narrowed eyes, then leaned closer.

He sat still to bear her scrutiny without response.

Eventually, she sat back. "Hmm. Not your best purchase, these are the go-through kind, not the ones with screws on the back so they clamp on." She snapped the box shut and tossed it back to him.

Zaide caught it, but fumbled, and the box clattered to the deck. "But is there any magic stuck to them?"

"Nope." She spread her arms along the boat's railing and leaned back against it. "They're ordinary as can be. Why do you ask?"

"Just curious." Which was likely to make her ask more questions. "I don't really trust the people here. Even the vendors."

Tula nodded in agreement. "Yeah, I didn't have time to do any shopping, but I'd be suspicious of them, too. They looked at me funny."

There were probably reasons for that, but Zaide kept his mouth shut. It was strange enough to see a Jadoran woman so far from the desert, but her attitude made her unforgettable. He leaned forward to retrieve the box from the floor. "You know, you're pretty different from what I expected when I met you."

"Really?" She straightened, and if she'd been a dog, he could picture her ears straight upright, betraying curiosity. "How do you mean?"

"You were really serious and sedate when we first walked into the library. Kind of stuffy. You're actually not like that at all." Zaide cracked open the box to make sure both earrings were still in the padding, then returned it to his pocket.

"Oh. Well, I was working. The senior librarians expect a certain level of responsibility from the apprentices they leave to close the library in the evening. So, it wouldn't have been responsible for me to be too excited about having guests." A sparkle lit in her green eyes. They were an odd color, compared to the rest of her; he'd never noticed before now, but from what he recalled, most Jadorans had dark eyes.

They were all odd, he supposed. A Jadoran with strange eyes, a Desheni without a tail, a broken-born missing half an ear. Only Lark's imperfection remained hidden, as a Paragon without any power.

He tucked in his chin. "Yeah, that makes sense. The Elder expected us to behave a certain way in his library, too."

"I think librarians get stuffy if they stay in there with the books for too long. It makes them not fun. That's why I prefer being on the archaeology and research side of things. I get to be out here, doing this." She waved a hand to the open sky. "Not that riding a boat is very interesting."

Zaide agreed. They moved at a decent speed, but if Andriun's predictions about the river's length were right, they'd be on the boat for days. Better than walking, but with everything they had to think and worry about, sitting still would likely drive him mad.

Before that thought could settle too deeply, he stood.

Tula lifted and dropped her feet again. "Hey, Zaide?"

He glanced back.

"What made you want jewelry, anyway?"

"A tradition I heard about. It seemed like I should... well, it's something to do in memory of my father, anyway." Though now, he wasn't sure his father was worth remembering. He still had the little book, too, and that was a question for someone else. "Why did you think it was for the princess?"

"Because her birthday's coming soon. I thought maybe you were being nice. Silly me, right?" She scrunched up her nose and stuck out her tongue, though the grin she shared right after made it clear she was teasing.

"Is it? I didn't know." There were a lot of things he still didn't know about the princess, secrets he hadn't pried out from under that thick shell she kept around the most tender parts of herself.

Tula shrugged. "Well, you've got until the equinox if you want to get her something."

His brow furrowed. "She was born on the equinox?"

"Yep. Apparently, in Amrochan, that's considered bad luck. She's not very superstitious, but I think she worries about that a little bit." She stared at her boots for a moment, then thunked them both to the wooden deck. "Anyway, she likes flowers, so even if you don't do anything else, get her a flower or something, okay? I think she'd appreciate it. Especially if it came from you."

Zaide caught his lower lip between his teeth as he frowned. "Thanks. I'll consider that." He meant it sincerely, but the oddity of the situation stuck in his head.

There was nowhere to go to hide with his thoughts, but he headed for the front of the vessel, where he would at least gain some distance from the risk of more probing questions.

CHAPTER TWENTY-SEVEN

"I HAVE TAKEN us as far as I can for today," Andriun announced, long after the sun had set and stars emerged overhead.

Zaide glanced skyward. A thin sliver of a crescent moon hung against the deep blue velvet of the night, and for just a moment he was struck by how far from everything they'd gone. "The boat's not equipped with an anchor. You'll need to strand us in the shallows, I think."

The Desheni grunted in displeasure. If they were stopping, it meant he'd grown weary, and using more magic was probably the least appealing suggestion that could have been made. He rubbed the back of his neck with one webbed hand and examined both sides of the river. "Travel would be easier with a good wind. If I had the sails and the water to work together, we would move much faster, but the wind blows the wrong direction today."

Zaide had never thought to question why the sails stayed down. "Why don't we use the Hymnflute?" He still carried the songbook, as he was still copying it into a new volume to compensate for the water damage his various accidents had caused. He hadn't encountered a song that would let him order the direction of the wind yet, but he had no doubt there would be one.

Andriun turned to stare at him, dumbfounded. "How have I forgotten we carry the power to do such things? I must be more tired than I believed."

The artifacts had slipped Zaide's mind more than once, and he'd been the one to retrieve them from their hiding places. He couldn't blame the Shaman for failing to think of it. "We'll figure that out tomorrow. The rest of us can take turns with the Hymnflute while you handle the water."

"Yes, and I suspect I will grow very tired of the melody before this trip is done." Andriun chose a place at the edge of the river and lifted his hands. The water in the river rose along with them and carried the boat into the shallows, where its hull sank into the mud and stuck.

The moment the boat was still, Andriun gave a long sigh. He stepped down from the front of the boat—the prow? The bow? Zaide still didn't know—and dusted his webbed hands together. "How are the others?"

"Still on the boat, I assume." Zaide hadn't seen Lark or Tula for some time. The Magister had gone to join the princess hours before, and the dog had gone with her. He expected all three of them were nestled in a pile of bedding below deck, sound asleep. Judging by the stars, it was near midnight now. "Hungry? I dragged a bag out here earlier in case you needed anything."

"Ravenous. Magic does not look like much, but it is difficult work." Andriun strode over to join Zaide in sitting on the deck, and Zaide passed him a leaf-wrapped parcel of food.

Most of what had been packed for them was uniquely Nimultan food, and the preserved island fruits and smoked fish were a welcome reprieve from the salty provisions the journey from Amrochan had provided. Zaide took a packet of dried fruit for himself and savored the sweet and sour tang of the colorful slices.

"Magic looks like a lot to me," he said between bites. "I can't do any of it, remember? I'd have as much luck standing in front of a door and telling it to open."

"I do not think any of us would have luck with that." Andriun eyed the fish in his parcel with an appreciative grin. He touched a finger to his lips and then raised it to the sky with a murmur of words in his own tongue.

Zaide cocked his head. "What does that mean?"

"Thank you, Maker, for the fish." As if to prove his appreciation, the Shaman crammed a whole piece into his mouth at once.

"Does that count as cannibalism?" Zaide asked with a smirk.

Andriun shrugged and chewed, unbothered.

They ate half their food before Zaide spoke again. "Is it hard, speaking that many languages?"

"Sometimes. It is easy for me to forget words, or to confuse them. This is part of why I choose to speak slowly and clearly. Not only because of how muddy the words become when they run together." Andriun had explained his disdain for linguistic choices such as contractions before, so that came as no surprise.

"What made you decide to study Torec while we were in Nimultis?" Zaide hoped his purpose in asking wasn't too obvious, then chided himself for the thought. Of course it wasn't; nobody knew about the book he carried.

Andriun shrugged. "It seemed as if it would be useful. And it was one of the books the Oracle had at her disposal. I already knew some words and sounds. Expanding on them was not hard. As I have said, the language is very similar to what we speak now. Why, do you wish to learn?"

Zaide didn't know. It would be useful, he admitted, but he was wary of immersing himself too quickly. The reality of his lineage struck him as a mire, a sucking pit he could easily become trapped within. As it was, he already hovered, uncertain, between two traditions. He hadn't finished his carving for his Kolmari coming of age. But he hadn't pierced his ears, either. The two had no bearing on each other, yet he felt torn between them and whether the two pieces of himself could be reconciled.

"I don't think you know enough to be able to teach me, yet," he said. "But I wanted to ask if you could help me with something. Translating something. Just a little."

Andriun paused with a piece of fish halfway into his mouth. "Hmm?"

"Hang on. There's a lantern in that bag." They'd need light, if Zaide was going to have him read anything. He dug it out and then scoured the rest of the bag before he found something to light it with. Desheni-made lanterns were better, he'd decided, though the fact they were susceptible to other magic overpowering them made them less practical for a party like theirs. He doubted a Desheni lantern would work at all in the presence of two Paragons and all the artifacts they carried.

Three Paragons, he corrected himself as he sat the lantern on the deck between himself and the Shaman. Whether or not Lark had gained control of what power she was supposed to have, she was still the Paragon of Light. That secret was a heavy burden, but he bore it gladly.

He produced the worn leather-bound book he'd been given and held it out for Andriun to see. "Do you think you can read some of this? It doesn't have to be a lot. Maybe a few pages here and there, just to..." He trailed off. To what? He didn't know. Prove Gadranus had been telling the truth? Catch him in a lie? Learn more secrets of his heritage and the family he'd lost? Zaide no longer knew what his goal was, but he extended the book, all the same.

"You are fortunate," Andriun said as he wiped his hand on his trousers. "I read Torec much better than I understand it spoken, since I learned from the Oracle's book. What is this for?"

"I don't know," Zaide admitted. "I guess I hoped you could tell me." Knowing what it said could be irrelevant, but the unknown made his backbone itch.

"Well, I suppose we shall find out soon, eh? Let us see." The Shaman opened the tiny volume and held its pages spread as he tilted the words toward the light. "Ah, it is handwritten. The Torec language uses the same alphabet as the Amrochan common tongue. I believe they may be from the same root, which is why the grammatical structure is so alike."

Zaide fought back exasperation. "All right, but what does it say?"

"Give me a moment. This is not a word that... Oh, it is a name, I believe. Ah-zah-la...le..."

"Azalea?" Zaide guessed. Already, his stomach grew uneasy, making him regret his fruit.

"Ah, so it is. Perhaps you have learned some Torec on our travels already?" Andriun grinned, then cleared his throat. "'Azalea has asked me to forsake this campaign, but I cannot refuse. We are set to depart for the front lines in two weeks. The army sends word of snow in the north, but the forests here are warm, making this the best time to push forward.' It is a soldier's journal, then."

Zaide nodded. He'd already known that. "Keep going."

"'Gadranus has ordered a push unlike any other, and this time, I will lead.' Ah, so it is one of his officers? This is... What is this for?"

An unfamiliar pain welled in Zaide's chest, a sense of betrayal he'd never known possible. "Just keep going. Please."

"'The Rise will not wait, but the birth of our first child grows near. I fear she'll never forgive me if I miss it, but we finally agreed that a son will be—'" Andriun stopped short, his brows drawn with concern. "How long have you had this?"

"Say it," Zaide almost hissed.

His friend's face crumpled with pity, but he turned his eyes back to the book. "'A son will be named Zaide.'"

Everything Zaide had feared spilled out of his mind and memory, splitting his heart until he thought the pieces could never again be made whole. He curled forward over his crossed legs and gripped his head with both hands.

Andriun folded the book closed and gripped it tight. "This does not change anything," he said softly. "This is the history of lives that were not your own."

"How can it not?" Zaide almost choked. He'd spent his whole life yearning to live up to the shadow of a man who'd instead been touched by the very force they now opposed. "He was a military commander, Andriun. On the other side. He never wanted to take refuge in Kolmar. Until I happened, he never had any intention of turning against—"

"Until you happened," Andriun cut in. "Which means something changed. People can change their minds, Zaide. They can change sides, they can learn new ways. And even if he had not, that does not change you."

"But they're right!" Zaide flattened a hand against his chest. "Everyone who's ever doubted me because of what I am was *right*. Tula's guess wasn't even that far off. I'm the enemy's son."

"So am I," the Shaman said.

Zaide grew still.

"I am my father's son, and my father fell on the other side of this divide." Andriun's tone softened as he went on. "But I do not have to be him, and neither do you. You can do better. Be better. You are not only a son of the broken-born, you are the Bladebearer. Your father's name is his own, Zaide. You do not have to wear it like a shroud on your sense of self."

"I don't know how to take it off." It felt like confessing weakness. Admitting defeat. "My mother was so proud of him. I wanted to be just like him."

"Why can you not be?" Andriun asked. "Be the parts that made your mother proud, then. Be the skilled soldier who rose through the ranks. Be the strong leader who takes command in a war. Be the man your mother painted in your mind."

Zaide shook his head. He wanted to be, yet all those things were tangled with the knowledge of his father's role he now had. His shoulders hunched and he stared at the book in Andriun's hands. The words on the page were unfamiliar, promising more knowledge, more secrets, more things to tear him apart.

Yet something else rose to the surface as he sat and wallowed, a single, simple confirmation that perhaps some of what his mother taught him was true. He latched onto it, onto the words of his enemy, a clear beacon of hope he'd somehow lost beneath the torrent of fear and feeling. "Gadranus killed him."

The Shaman faltered. "Perhaps do not be like him in that."

Zaide didn't think it was supposed to be funny. He still gave a single, soft laugh.

A heavy lull fell before Andriun stifled a sigh. "Look, Zaide. All I am saying is, we cannot know what circumstances led to this. What we do know is that you were raised in Kolmar, away from all this." He waved a hand at the sky, at the endless stars in the clear night above them. "These people did not choose their emperor. They were conquered. Your father served, but so do many others, and at the end of the day, your mother still fled that life with you in her arms."

To shield him from death, because Gadranus walked with knowledge the Oracle had given him. Zaide hadn't shared that part of the story with anyone. He didn't think he would.

But the Oracle had said something else, too. She'd called his father a good man. Implied he was noble. Even if he hadn't been, Andriun was still right. His mother had chosen a new life, and with that, she had proven herself virtuous.

Every step of the way, Gadranus had chosen himself.

His parents had chosen *him*.

Zaide sucked in a deep breath and let it out hard.

"That is a good sound," Andriun murmured. "You are seeing sense now?"

He would have seen it sooner if he'd been able to put his head on straight and think things through, but fear did strange things. Zaide mustered a smile and lifted his head, then froze. "I'm seeing something."

In the distance, a long line of orange lights moved across the landscape.

CHAPTER TWENTY-EIGHT

A VIOLENT HAMMERING on the door jarred Lark wide awake. She kicked off the blankets as Daisy took to barking, but the door was open by the time she found her feet.

"We need the artifacts," Andriun announced.

Zaide shoved past him and stumbled over the bags piled in the middle of the floor, but instead of the artifacts, he sought the Spectrum Blade and took it from where it leaned against the wall.

"What's going on?" She scarcely took a step before the Shaman slid in and began searching the pile for the artifacts.

Zaide didn't wait for them to be found. Instead, he went right back up to the deck, strapping the sword to his side on the way.

"Soldiers coming. Headed straight this way. I do not believe it to be coincidence." Andriun tossed aside several bags before Lark found the one he was looking for and shoved it into his hands.

Tula groaned but pushed herself from her berth. "How many? Do I get to torch them?"

"We do not know. We will not stay to find out." The Shaman snatched the Captured Spring from the bag first. He splashed its remedy into his mouth and swallowed fast. It was a potent curative, but its ability to help with things as simple as fatigue made it invaluable. He did not use its power lightly, and that mouthful he took was enough to make her uneasy.

He took the Hymnflute next, but instead of absconding with it, he thrust it toward her. "Who knows how to use the sails?"

"Aren't you our captain?" Lark asked doubtfully, though she took the artifact and held it close.

The sour twist of his mouth said otherwise.

"I think I saw something about it in a book one time," Tula said as she stumbled toward the door. She'd pulled on her billowy Jadoran coat over the top of her cold weather gear, and it looked so much like a dressing gown that Lark had to stifle her amusement.

"That will have to do. Hurry. Tula will draw the sails. I will draw the water, and you must fill the sails with wind to propel us faster." Andriun was halfway out the door before he finished the instructions.

"Wait a minute," Lark protested. "I don't know how to—"

"Then you will have to learn very fast." He ducked outside and was gone.

Lark swallowed hard.

She shouldn't feel sorry for herself in this. It was something she could do, something that didn't require the power she couldn't awaken. All she had to do was figure out notes that would push their tiny ship forward, against the flow of the river. Her fingers tightened on the pipes, letting awareness of their magic flow through her as she hurried outside.

The boat lurched so hard that she fell, scraping her knees against the steps that went down below. She bit her tongue to keep from shouting and crawled up the rest of the way.

A long line of torches snaked across the landscape. A pulse of drumbeats flowed with it. A false drumbird's call; orders for the goborrins that marched toward them.

"I thought they let you go free?" Lark asked.

Zaide spun to look at her, puzzled. He hadn't relayed that

part of the story directly; Tula had gathered it, somehow or another, then brought it into the boat's tiny hold to share.

Or maybe he thought she meant something else.

She raised an eyebrow at him before Andriun snapped his fingers at her.

"Wind!" the Shaman barked.

She hadn't realized he could snap his fingers, what with the webbing of his hands.

Any other time, she might have grown angry at being commanded about. With the apparent army headed their way, her sensibilities mattered less.

Tula and Zaide both hauled ropes to raise the sails, and the Magister made quick work of tying knots. Something else she'd picked up from books, it seemed.

Lark stared up at the sails and raised the Hymnflute to her lips. She knew the melody for the barrier by heart, but the other times she'd used the artifact to summon wind, it had simply been a matter of shrieking whatever notes she could. But that had always given a wild torrent; she needed something focused now.

"Southward," she told herself as she moved to the back of the boat. She needed to blow them southward, and she didn't know how.

The first few experimental notes did nothing and Lark grimaced. What would a song to command the wind sound like?

Zaide paced the length of the boat over and over again, a mess of restless energy. He tripped over the dog twice as she tried to follow him, and he muttered something unpleasant as he caught her by the scruff and steered her back to the door to lock her away below deck. Lark almost asked that he bring the songbook out, but the door slammed shut before she could.

"Uh, not to sound alarmist," Tula called, "but what are those?"

Lark spun to see dozens of tiny lights arcing through the sky and her heart sank.

Zaide was on her in an instant, forcing her down to the deck, shielding her with his body as the volley rained down on their boat.

Arrows thudded into the deck and tore through the sail, leaving tiny, burning holes behind.

Tula waved both arms, smothering the flames with her magic before they could spread.

Lark put the Hymnflute to her lips and blew a single hard note.

A hard wind spun toward the east, slammed into the sail and dragged them sideways.

"Wrong direction!" Andriun snapped. The boat rotated in the water, caught between his artificial current and the natural one, and he leaned forward over the bow as he tried to correct it.

"Third pipe," Zaide said. He twisted back to look at the army, but remained where he was, kneeling above her. The arrows had missed him, though several landed close. He jerked them from the wooden planks and threw them overboard.

Lark moved to the third pipe and tried again. The note she blew was long and clear, and a strong, steady wind pushed in to fill the sails and drive them south.

He clapped a hand to her shoulder in approval and stood. "Tula, see if you can amplify the fire on the next volley they send."

"Amplify it?" Andriun exclaimed. "You'll burn down our boat!"

"With the Paragon of Water on board?" Zaide scoffed. "It'll incinerate the arrows before they land."

Tula turned to face the approaching army and widened her stance. "I've got it."

Lark prayed she did.

The boat rocked as Andriun corrected the water beneath it, then it surged forward with such speed that the wind whipped her hair against her face. It caught on the Hymnflute and she dared not try to fix it, holding the single note that stirred the wind for as long as she could.

The wind tapered the moment she stopped to draw breath, and she tried to keep it short. She wouldn't be able to propel them that way for more than a few minutes, but all they had to do was outrun that army. At this pace, it wouldn't be long.

"Arrows," Zaide called.

Tula stepped forward and raised her arms, and the tiny flames erupted into massive fireballs as they streaked through the night.

One by one, they flickered out and died, every single one of them falling short of the river.

"Perfect." Zaide paced to the front to check on Andriun, then returned to the back to crouch at Lark's side.

She blew until her chest ached with emptiness and the moment the wind faltered with her failing breath, he seized the Hymnflute from her hand and played the same long note.

He gave her a moment to catch her breath, and she was ready as soon as he reached the end of his.

Back and forth they went, passing the Hymnflute between them as the boat continued to gain speed. It soared across the water as Tula took down another round of arrows. The torches were already shrinking away behind them.

"I do not think they believed they would reach us," Andriun announced when the lights were all but gone. "Otherwise, why would they fire on us with arrows?"

"More importantly, since when do goborrins carry bows? Have we seen that before?" Zaide glanced between the rest of them, searching for an answer before his turn to play came.

Lark had seen so much at this point, she could hardly recall what was new. "We're in the Shattered Lands. The rules are different here."

"More ahead!" Tula bounded to the other side of the boat and pointed at a new cluster of torches on the hills.

Maker's mercy, what if they were all along the river? Lark

swallowed her dread and gripped the Hymnflute with one hand as she kept the wind going.

More arrows flew from that direction and Tula fed the flames, scorching the arrows to dust long before they ever landed. "We can't keep that up for long," the Magister said. "They'll figure it out and start firing them plain."

And the arrows would blend into the night. Lark met Zaide's eyes with the unspoken question of what they were to do.

He nodded in acknowledgement and signaled for her to blow for as long as she could. "Tula, get over here. Help me with this. Lark, get the Captured Spring from Andriun. Get its barrier up around us."

Relief washed over her and she nodded back. The moment she reached the end of her breath, she released the Hymnflute into his hands and sprang to her feet. How many seconds did she have before the next attack?

"Andriun!" she called.

"I heard." He already had the vial in hand, and he turned to press it into her palm as soon as he could reach.

She gripped it tight and paced backwards. They'd always relied on the Hymnflute's barrier. She hadn't used the Captured Spring to create one since they'd left the temple in Kolmar, but it had been intuitive before. Just an extension of her will, a desire for safety expressed through her contact with the vial. She leaned into that now, willing the spring to protect them. Light streaked from the artifact and pushed outward in a circle, encompassing their boat—and her friends—with a softly glowing barrier.

The next volley of arrows took flight a moment later. They struck the barrier like rain, but neither flame nor arrowhead pierced the shield.

Andriun tilted his head back to watch as they left little more than ripples on its luminescent surface. He shook his head and said something, though what language it was in, Lark could no longer guess.

Zaide and Tula traded the Hymnflute back and forth between themselves, keeping the boat rushing ahead, and in their newfound safety, they had a moment to relax.

The lights faded behind them and their vessel carried on, gliding along the glassy black water. The single note of the Hymnflute droned in her ears, and Lark did her best to remain focused on the barrier until she was certain no more lights peppered the landscape around them. Only when she was positive the hills were empty did she let the barrier fall.

The moment she did, Tula let the Hymnflute's wind fade.

Zaide flopped backwards onto the deck, breathing hard. "That takes a lot more out of you than you'd think."

"You are clearly not a musician," Andriun remarked mildly. "Imagine having music for only a fraction of a festival or ball."

"You're welcome to take a turn, next time," Zaide said between breaths.

The Shaman spread his hands, helpless. "If you think you would be better with controlling the water, then I shall be happy to trade places." Then he turned back to his task, his eyes focused on the horizon as the water continued to carry them onward.

Lark held the Captured Spring in both hands. "I don't think it will be safe to halt tonight. Andriun, when you tire, please let us know. The three of us can take turns with the Hymnflute while you rest."

Tula heaved a sigh and looked up at the sails. "The problem with that is none of us know how to steer. His water is doing everything right now."

"Our ship has no choice but to go where I command," Andriun joked. That he referred to it as a ship when it was scarcely twenty feet long was perhaps the most ridiculous part of it.

Zaide waved a hand, but remained flat on his back. "We'll figure it out."

"Then I will take you up on that, in time. For now, we will

continue as we were, taking advantage of as much speed as we can." The Shaman pointed at the Hymnflute in Tula's hands, then centered his finger on Lark. "Will you take the first turn, Your Highness?"

She took the artifact from the Magister's hand without comment and made herself comfortable before she began.

With the renewed wind, they sped down the serpentine river without any sign of torches or goborrins, or even so much as a drumbird call.

Hours slipped by in the still night and for a fleeting moment, Lark thought they might be safe.

Then the first blush of morning light touched the skies, and out of the dark loomed the dark shape of a war galley, filling the river from edge to edge.

CHAPTER TWENTY-NINE

"Stop the wind," Lark cried. She did not see if it was Tula or Zaide who held the Hymnflute when she shoved it down and ended the note.

Andriun released his command of water at the same time. The boat slowed, but momentum carried them farther forward. "Maker's mercy, we will never make it past that ship."

A vision of the warship spearing their smaller craft with a harpoon and dragging it closer raked across Lark's mind, drawing forth a shudder. "Grab what you can. We must get onto dry land." She darted below deck as she gave the order and squeaked when opening the door let the dog free. She'd forgotten the beast was in there.

Tula crowded in behind her to snatch a single bag from her berth, one she'd used for a pillow. Zaide was close behind her, but he stopped in the doorway.

Lark threw him a bag and hoped it was one that would be useful.

A hard, heavy thud made the boat vibrate beneath their feet.

"Drums," Andriun called in after them. A moment later, the boat creaked and canted sideways.

"Perfect," Lark breathed. She slid the bag of artifacts up her shoulder and ran for the door.

Tula darted out first, but Zaide stayed long enough to help Lark up the steps. Had he seen her fall earlier? Her cheeks heated with shame at the very thought.

The boat had pitched against the river bank, leaving a narrow gap of water between the deck's railing and the shore. Lights emerged across the war galley that loomed above them, but Lark dared not look more than once. She didn't want to see how many goborrins there were, didn't want to know what they were up against. She slid down to the railing and leaped the gap to land hard on the dirt bank.

Zaide went right behind her. Tula landed less gracefully and tumbled to the dirt.

"Up," Zaide breathed as he caught the Magister's arm and hauled her to her feet. Daisy landed beside them and circled the pair, nosing Tula's side as if to help her up.

More lights flooded the deck of the massive ship above and a beam shot down from above, directed by flames in a mirrored bowl.

Andriun joined them. "Go," he urged, herding them forward with spread arms.

The beam rotated and fell upon them. Fear leaped into Lark's throat and she started to cover her head, as if that might spare them. *Foolish girl*, she snarled at herself as she redirected her hands to the Captured Spring hung around her neck. Her fingers just closed on it, ready to summon the barrier, when the cry went up.

"Hold!" someone shouted, the voice distinctly human. "The princess!"

Lark's heart skipped.

More voices went up, relaying the information. Drums started again, relaying a new message across the water.

She turned to look up at the ship, squinting past the light until she could just make out the vessel.

Theirs. That warship was *theirs*. She could have laughed.

Zaide didn't share her sense of relief. He pressed close and his hand moved from the hilt of the Spectrum Blade to that of his Jadoran knife. "What do you want to do?" His voice was low, reserved for her ears alone, and she had no doubt he would have drawn his blade to fight every man on that ship if she asked it.

"Our goal is to reach Amrochan," she said. "If we can gain passage on one of my father's ships to cross Lake Sian, it's an opportunity we should embrace." She remained where she was, facing the light, hoping she looked as regal and commanding as she tried to be.

Men in armor rushed to lower ladders down the side of the ship. An officer was the first to reach the ground and he jogged toward them. She expected questions, or even an announcement they would be taking them prisoner, but the man dropped to one knee before her instead.

"Thank the Maker you're all right," he rasped. "The news out of the west has been nothing but bad. How in the blazes did you end up in the lake's tail?"

Her brows climbed. They'd made it as far as the tail? No wonder the current worked against them. She'd never realized the fat channel that spilled east from Lake Sian turned north outside Amroch's border. They were farther from Amrochan than she'd realized. "We came from the north. We hoped to locate and slay Gadranus within his own territory, but the mission did not go as planned. We must return to Amrochan with all haste. There's an army moving toward the river that runs between Yithel and Chithal. My father must be warned."

"Blasted beasts," the man breathed. "My ship has orders to keep this channel blocked. Gadranus may hold the southern field, but we still hold the lake."

A remarkable advantage, considering how many rivers laced the countryside, all connected to Lake Sian. If the fields west of Amrochan were lost and things became grim, Gadranus would be hard pressed to prevent them from fleeing across the lake.

"Has he tried bringing warships?" She thought of the vessels they'd managed to sink in Ganede. The tail was the only one of the lake's rivers wide and deep enough for such ships—and one of only two waterways that connected to the sea. If both were obstructed, there would be no way for their enemy to reach Amrochan by ship.

"A few," the man said with a grimace. "Transport vessels, mainly. We've sunk as many as we can, but the king felt plugging up the lake was the best way to defend for now. We can't get you to Amrochan ourselves, but Admiral Warinal himself has been running supplies for us while he fortifies the lake's defenses. We've already drummed word of your arrival. He'll be on his way."

Lark struggled to keep her thoughts from showing on her face. Of all the officers in her father's armies, she found the admiral one of the least palatable. As far as escorts went, though, there were few better suited to ensuring her safety. "Good. Please notify Admiral Warinal of my need for urgent transportation. Have your men retrieve the rest of my supplies from our ship." She glanced toward the rest of the soldiers as they gathered. "We shall board and wait with you until the admiral arrives."

"Yes, Your Highness." The kneeling officer touched a finger to his brow in a show of respect, then stood to spread the order.

Lark made for the ladder without direction. She doubted Warinal would be agreeable, but his ships were fleet and he would treat her circumstance with importance. Many of her father's men were stubborn and disagreeable with her, for all that she would someday command them, but they prized the safety of the Allied Kingdoms above all else.

Zaide hurried ahead to hold the rope ladder steady for her. "What do you need me to do?"

"Stay close," she whispered. "I'll let you know if I need you to threaten any surly old men."

He gave her such a sober stare that she felt obligated to crack a smile, so that he might know she was joking. Perhaps it was a poor time for levity, but while they were surrounded by her father's men, she took the distinct sense her companions were her only true allies and part of her regretted the necessity that she always be so cold.

He answered with a hesitant smile of his own and gripped the ladder tight while she climbed.

Lark started her ascent to the deck, but her mind was already racing ahead. The warship's presence was both a reassurance and a concern, given all the threats Amrochan faced, but it was the first blessing after a long chain of events that had not gone well, and she would accept a single stroke of good fortune with gratitude.

Even if it meant working with the admiral.

A scant few hours after the summons went out, a new ship sailed into view.

"That'll be the admiral," one of the men aboard the massive warship explained when he caught Zaide watching.

Most of the group had stayed on deck, though Andriun had retired as soon as they settled in to wait for their new escort. The Shaman was beyond exhausted, and the Captured Spring was all but depleted after the night they'd had. The remedy had been all that kept him going, but without him, they would not have reached their destination so fast.

The rest of them had sorted through their things, narrowing their luggage to one large bag each. They wouldn't need food or other supplies anymore. Personal effects and the clothing they wished to keep were all that stayed. Zaide stowed his father's journal and the box with the earrings alongside the rest of his belongings. Everything else was left behind.

The transition from one ship to the other was unremarkable. Tula roused the Shaman and the two of them settled on the new vessel to sleep, while Lark went straight into the admiral's private cabin to discuss what they'd done and what came next. The captain of the warship hadn't seemed intimidated by trouble coming from the Shattered Lands, but the moment Lark relayed the information to Admiral Warinal, the old man's face had grown hard and he'd spirited her away without giving Zaide a chance to follow. And so Zaide was left alone on the deck, too restless to sleep but too weary to assist the sailors as they shoved off, so he found somewhere out of the way and leaned against the railing while the admiral's crew began their launch.

There would be a lot for Lark to explain. The knowledge the goborrins that attacked them had likely been sent to attack the ship wedged in the river instead of being sent to capture them brought a sliver of relief, but the thought of Gadranus getting his own warships into Lake Sian's waters left him chilled. Amrochan could hold off almost anything, as long as they held the water and could bring in supplies from elsewhere, but a city surrounded was a city starved.

Eventually, it became clear Lark's conversation with the admiral would take longer than anticipated. Zaide gave up waiting, found his berth below deck, and settled in to sleep with his dog curled close at his side.

Lark woke him several hours later.

"I need the blade," she said without preamble.

He blinked groggily at her as he sat up. "Are you trying the shard things again?"

"It's the only way to make progress." She crossed her arms and it struck him as more sulky than defensive.

"I think getting back to Amrochan counts as making progress." He rubbed his eye with the heel of his palm. "What did the admiral say?"

"Give me the sword," Lark insisted.

Zaide was disinclined to cooperate. He still wore its belt, so the only way she could take it from him was to draw it from its sheath or wait for him to remove it. From the way she glanced at its hilt, he guessed she was still hesitant to try and touch it. "Talk to me, first. I didn't get to hear anything you talked about. Why didn't the admiral want me there with you?"

The princess set her jaw and contemplated her answer for a long time before she gave it. "He doesn't like you."

He could have rolled his eyes. "He would get along great with Vorkaris. Did he give you a reason?"

"He doesn't think we need you," she said with a small, indifferent shrug. "He doesn't believe you're the Bladebearer."

Zaide twisted his arm out of the way and looked down at the sword by his side. "Is he senile?"

"Just spend some time practicing with it where he can see tomorrow. That should correct any doubts."

He could do that easily enough. "What did he think about our plan to stop the Rise?"

"That we're fools." Her face remained serene, but that had to have stung to hear.

"Aren't you Amrochan's expert on it, though?" He asked that more cautiously. After everything they'd seen, she had to know more about it than anyone but the Oracle.

Again, she shrugged. "As close to an expert as someone with access to the royal library can be, I suppose."

He weighed that against the proposition Gadranus had made, then pushed himself up. "Do you have somewhere private to work? I'll come help you set up."

Lark stiffened and he was sure she would deny his help, but even as her jaw tightened, she turned to lead the way. "I've been given a small room to myself. I'll show you, in case any of you need something before we arrive in Amrochan, but I expect to be allowed to work in peace."

"Of course, Your Highness." Zaide struggled to keep from sounding antagonistic. Why did she have to make everything so difficult? It was as if she was determined to put their relationship under every strain possible. He hardly knew whether they *had* a relationship. For all that he considered Lark a friend, she didn't seem to consider him at all.

He motioned for the dog to stay put, then followed the princess through the narrow ship to the tiny room she had to call her own. It was better than the shared sleeping space the rest of them had been given, but far from luxurious. The admiral's ship had been built for speed, not comfort, and it sliced through the lake's waters at a pace that rivaled what their stolen boat had achieved with both the Hymnflute's wind and Andriun's water magic bending things in their favor.

Once they stepped inside, he unfastened his belt and removed the sword and its scabbard from his side. "Where do you want it?"

"Lay it on the bed." She gestured vaguely toward a padded bench that hardly resembled a bed, while she retrieved her bag and removed the two crystals from it. The other artifacts gleamed inside and he stared at them until she shut them out of sight.

Zaide drew the Spectrum Blade and placed it lengthwise in the center of the bed. "You know, we haven't had a moment alone since before we made it to Toren."

The princess froze, her wary posture reminding him of a woodland animal ready to flee.

Perhaps that had come out wrong. He tried to appear nonchalant. "I've wanted to discuss the meeting I had with Gadranus, but I didn't feel like the things he said were anyone's business but yours. I didn't want to worry anyone by requesting a moment to speak with you alone."

Concern etched hard lines into her face. "So you just didn't say anything?"

"Nothing we discussed was urgent," he replied with a soothing gesture. "I just wanted to ask about some of the things he told me. Things about the Rise I'd never heard. Whether they're true or not doesn't change anything, we still need to kill him. I just wanted to know how much time he spent lying."

That soothed her nerves. Her concern cooled and she sat on the edge of her bed. "I'm sure he's a master of deception by now. I wouldn't count on much being truthful."

"He said he gave your father a chance to settle things between them and end the war." He had no desire to waste her time trying to be diplomatic in his wording, but he wanted to know how much she was willing to reveal, herself.

Lark bit her lower lip and nodded. Somehow, he hadn't expected her to be forthcoming. Not after hiding who the Bladebearer was meant to be. "I suppose you could call it that. I was told he approached my father before I was born. He made the strangest proposal. He wanted my father to surrender and grant him rulership over the Allied Kingdoms. In return, he would let my father slay him with the Spectrum Blade after he was crowned."

"Do you know why?" He already knew how that offer had ended. The fact Sendassian had never believed the sword was real meant it had been an impossible suggestion, anyway.

"Some sort of bizarre power play? I haven't a clue. I don't know what his game was, but I don't believe for a moment that he would have faced death willingly after seizing power over Amroch." She traced the facets of the Sunshard with a fingertip.

"That was what he told me, too." Zaide chose his words with care. If he said anything wrong, he'd risk setting her off again. All he really wanted was a chance to make sure Lark knew he had nothing to hide. If showing her brought knowledge on whether or not Gadranus had been honest with him, that was a bonus, and nothing more. "He said he wants to make you the same offer. In case you take control of Amroch." He winced as he added the latter part and was grateful her eyes weren't on him. They both knew she would take the crown. Lark feared he was the one in danger, but they'd seen the same eclipse. It heralded the death of a king, not the son of some long-dead broken-born commander.

Her fingers grew still. "He told you this?"

"He asked me to tell you. I didn't know if what he said about your father was true, though. I didn't want to say anything until I knew." As he spoke, his mouth went dry. Had she grown any more still, he might have thought she'd become a statue.

"My father was right to refuse him," she said softly.

"I never suggested he wasn't. But he told me that... if you cooperated, that this would be the last Rise." His heart beat faster as he said it. He didn't even want to entertain the possibility the man had told him the truth, but what if he had? What if it was? The explanation of the curse of rebirth hung heavy in Zaide's thoughts and he swallowed hard.

Lark scoffed. "How would surrender end the Rise? How would that do anything but betray my people? I would never surrender. We'll defeat him, and we'll do it the way it's always been done." Her hands tightened on the crystals and she drew them closer together. The Sunshard brightened in response, while the Shadowsliver grew darker.

"He explained his curse," Zaide said. "How it works. How it's supposed to end. I need to know if it's true."

"You can't possibly be entertaining this suggestion."

"I'm not," he protested. "I just want to know—"

Her head snapped up and the glare she shot him was nothing short of vicious. "How dare you question me? Question my father? He is our enemy! How can you so easily forget what he's done?"

"I haven't!" He hated to shout. She flinched the moment he did and it churned guilt within him. He lowered his voice and went on. "All I said was that I want to know if it's true or not. If it's what's necessary to end all this. No matter what, I know I can kill him. If I do it now, he'll be reborn immediately. If I do it after we restore the blade, then we get a hundred years." He spread a hand toward the sword on her bed.

She looked at it begrudgingly.

"The Oracle was the one who said we had a chance to make this the last Rise, and he gave me a reason why that could be.

We're the ones who get to decide if the risk is worth it, but to do that, we have to know what's true." Zaide ran a hand through his hair and tried to breathe deep, hoping in vain that it might settle the hammering of his heart. This was precisely why he'd feared to speak with her in front of the others. It was not going well at all.

The two crystals in Lark's hands clinked together, but nothing came of it. "And if it is true? What would you say then? Would you call me a fool for refusing? Would you try to change my mind?" Her eyes darkened. "Or would you try to force the crown off my head by yourself?"

He stared at her in disbelief. "You think I would do that?"

Lark stared back, then turned and sat the two crystals atop the blade.

Her silence cut worse than any of the bitter things she'd ever said.

"All right." Zaide drew back a step and for the first time, he understood why she put such thick barriers around her heart. "Good luck restoring the blade, then."

He retreated from her quarters, leaving the Spectrum Blade in her hands.

He would not interfere. Not now, and not in the end.

CHAPTER THIRTY

LARK DID NOT KNOW how Zaide managed to avoid her on such a tiny ship, but she did not speak with him again. She caught glimpses of him, now and then, but always from a distance so they never had to interact. Good, she told herself; it was better that way. The better she was at keeping everyone at arm's length, the better everything would end.

A haze filled the sky long before Amrochan came into view. The city was no different from what she recalled, but the harbor was busier, and despite the urgency of her return holding precedence over everything else that came and went from the docks, they were forced to wait purely for room to be made. She watched the thick plumes of smoke that rose from the fields beyond the city walls as space was made for the admiral's speedy little ship.

It smelled foul. A thick, tarry smoke that reeked of rot and death. How was it Gadranus and his armies brought such things when within his own lands, Toren had been so peaceful?

Admiral Warinal made an appearance at the helm when it came time to dock and Lark posted herself close by his side. Her presence was an honor, one the admiral should have been proud to receive, yet she took the distinct notion he saw her as an unwelcome burden.

"I will escort you to King Sendassian myself," the admiral said as men on the docks scrambled to tie up their ship and prepare for them to disembark. "Since you have no guards of your own."

She almost corrected him. Zaide had been the only bodyguard she needed, but it wouldn't seem that way, what with how hard he worked to stay out of her sight. Instead, she nodded. "The Paragons are free to visit any part of the palace. They will likely need access to the royal library, for the sake of our continuing mission."

"And the broken-born?" he asked dryly.

Lark's eyes narrowed. "He is my Bladebearer. The same applies to him. He is not to be shut out from anything, and considering his role in this war, you should be eager to help him." Yet he had never come to retrieve the Spectrum Blade from her quarters. She didn't know if she should expect him to seek it now, or if she'd be carrying it into the palace, herself. The thought was tantalizing, but what good did it do if she couldn't even draw the blade from its sheath?

Warinal looked down at her with a clear shadow of disdain in his eyes. "I will see that he is escorted into the palace as well, but my eagerness is not yet at your command, Your Highness."

"Let's hope it never is." She forced the most cordial smile she could muster and slipped away as the gangplank dropped into place and sailors and dockhands lined up to empty the ship. She returned to her tiny room on her own, her things already gathered but her bags left behind.

The Spectrum Blade still lay on her bed.

Lark stared at it for a time before she collected its scabbard from where it had been left. The leather was stiff, but not rigid, and some careful maneuvering allowed her to return the blade to its sheath without ever touching the metal. It was better that Zaide hadn't taken it, she decided. She would meet with her father, but her efforts to unlock the potential of the Sunshard and Shadowsliver would resume as soon as pleasantries were over.

If there were any pleasantries to be had.

She slung her bag over her shoulder and returned to the deck.

She dreaded how her father would respond to her return. When he'd commissioned a ship to take her to Jadora, she had assumed it was out of a desire to send her somewhere safe. Away from the fighting, away from the war, away from the smoke-blotted skies and the stench that came with violence and death.

Instead, he'd sent it after her, somewhere no one would suspect what he'd done. She still didn't know how Vorkaris had uncovered the information, but she hadn't asked and she still didn't want the answer. There would have been an investigation, following the old Magister's death. She assumed there had been magic involved. Real magic, something the old Magister didn't have, but she'd sensed in the fellow they'd met. Something charm oriented, she'd suspected. Goodness knew he hadn't had enough personality to make him interesting, but he'd borne a certain magnetism that made him endearing.

If only she had learned how to utilize that sort of power, herself.

The moment the thought rolled through her head, she hated herself for it. She shouldn't need to charm her father with magic to make him care about her. He was her father. She should have meant the world.

Lark kept her head high as Admiral Warinal led her from the boat. She didn't see the others, but he reassured her he'd left instructions for them to be taken to the palace and made presentable.

She, on the other hand, would be taken straight to the king.

After all that travel, she had to look a fright. Her hands went to her hair, but her ponytail was still tight. There was little else she could do to straighten her appearance. A bath would have to come later. A handful of guards joined their entourage and they swept into the palace grounds.

The palace struck her as different. The rhythmic click of her boots against the stone was the same, the path through the palace the same, but it was as if the entire place sat crouched and waiting. She supposed that was accurate. The city was an animal hunkered down on the water's edge, fighting off a force that was sure to overwhelm it. Not for the first time, she thought of the army they'd passed on their way to Toren and how they would change the war.

But now something new touched her, and she hated that she even considered what Zaide had shared.

Toren had been peaceful. There had been children in the streets. Amrochan's people cowered inside their stone buildings, instead.

She gave her head a shake. No; it was the coward's way out. She knew nothing of what life beneath that man might be, and there was no reason to believe anything he promised was truth.

They marched through the palace without any regard for her troubled thoughts. The chamber where audience seekers waited was empty, as her father's throne would be. He'd be up in his council chamber, working through strategy and arguing with officers and noblemen who thought they knew best. That was where the admiral led her, and when Warinal let himself in without knocking, she was not surprised.

Sendassian glanced up from the table, where maps lay with dozens of cast metal markers atop them. He straightened when he saw her.

"Forgive my intrusion, Your Majesty," Warinal said with just enough of a bow to be proper. "Her Highness, your daughter, insisted I bring her to you with all haste."

Lark stepped forward. "I come with news regarding an army that approaches from the north."

"The north is held secure at the river," Sendassian replied. No greeting. No welcome. Just business, as usual.

She raised her chin. "They've built a bridge."

The other men at the council table looked between themselves, as if unsure what to make of the news.

Sendassian pinned her with a hard stare. "Where is your proof?"

It was not the challenge she'd expected. She'd anticipated being told she didn't belong there; that he might acknowledge her claim at all had not seemed possible. She struggled to find words for a moment, then strode across the room to claim a handful of unused markers from the edge of the map. "You'll be seeing refugees from Yithel within the next few days, as they make it down the river. They may have already arrived, and you just don't know it yet."

Her father said nothing, but his eyes stayed on her, the heaviest burden she had yet to bear.

Lark paced around the table so she stood at the north side of the map. This one showed more of the Shattered Lands than the one they'd obtained during their travels, but it fell far short of Toren. "The army crosses the river here." She deposited the pig-shaped markers that depicted the enemy's army near where she estimated the bridge had been. As she placed them, the shape of the pewter pieces struck her as boorish. Their own forces bore noble shapes, or the emblems they'd chosen to represent themselves. Everything that portrayed Gadranus was a mere pig, a filthy beast. "Their arrival will double the number of goborrins we saw when Vorkaris razed their army, a few weeks back."

A low murmur rose among the attending councilors.

"The flaming beast outside the walls?" one asked.

Lark turned his way. General Jobe was a level-headed man, and far more amicable than Admiral Warinal. She nodded. "The legendary Magister who once presided over Jadora. He has awoken from a long slumber to protect the city for the duration of the Rise."

"I've received no word of this," Sendassian said.

"Jadora has been undergoing a great amount of upheaval in the last few weeks, what with being infiltrated by Gadranus's forces and the death of the Magister you had imposed." She faced her father with her shoulders square and her back straight.

He remained silent for a long time.

General Jobe was the first to clear his throat. "It sounds as if your daughter may be in need of debriefing. Shall we reconvene at another time, Your Majesty?"

"Yes," Sendassian agreed. "We shall take a brief respite and resume in an hour. You are all dismissed."

The officers and nobles that ringed the table bowed and retreated. Lark watched their exit from the corner of her eye, but she waited to speak until the last man was gone. "I notice the women of your cabinet are absent."

Her father returned his attention to the map. He rounded the table to pick up a piece from the illustrated plateau that was Jadora. "Assigned to other things. Preparation for the potential of evacuation. Many of them are mothers. They know best what families will need during emergency relocation."

"Is Amrochan so close to falling?" She hadn't seen the other side of the city, where goborrins still pummeled the walls in spite of the dragon's aid.

"Amrochan has the defenses and resources to withstand nine more months of warfare. But as things are now, we cannot hope to push them back." Sendassian took a marker from the map. It resembled a man, though Lark hadn't gotten a good look at it. He curled his fingers around it as he removed it from play. His false Magister, perhaps.

Her heart fluttered with nerves. "Did you know he meant to kill me?"

He did not react. No surprise, but no anger, either. He returned to his place at the center of the great map, where he could stare at the markers that covered Amrochan. "The safety of Amroch must always be my priority. You know that."

She always had, yet some tiny sliver of her had hoped she

was considered part of what must be protected. "And what does that have to do with your false Magister?"

"Someday, you will understand the gravity of the choices a ruler must make. For now, it seems you and I simply do not share a vision." He gathered more markers from the edge of the map. Ships. One by one, he pushed them to the river that ran north from Lake Sian, toward Yithel. "Whether or not these forces are sent to engage this supposed incoming army will depend on the veracity of your claims. How have you gathered intelligence regarding the state of things in the north, if you were meant to be on the western coast?"

The suggestion it was some falsehood made her bristle, but she was used to the needling of politics. "We learned of the enemy king's location and planned a mission in hopes it would allow for assassination. We were ultimately unable to confront the target, but we collected information about the incoming army and the capital city from which he is operating before we used the river to escape." Lark didn't even flinch as she stretched the truth.

"You know where the capital is?" Now she had his interest. His mouth tightened, then he collected more of the pig-shaped markers, along with shapes like fortresses and castles, and pushed them into her hands. "Mark what you recall."

"Of course." She paced around the table until she reached the side that was all but blank. "Retrieve me a pen or a piece of graphite, and I'll provide information about the landscape, as well. Then we can discuss the situation in Jadora and Ganede." The more she could focus on numbers, terrain, and the western part of Amroch, the more she could distract him from their trip to the Shattered Lands. The less her father knew about that venture and its actual purpose, the better, though part of her itched with curiosity.

How much of what Zaide relayed had been true?

How much had her father kept from her?

Regret flowed over her in waves, tormenting her as she

placed the first markers to depict Toren and described the city's layout.

In the moment, on the ship, she had chosen her father's side. Now, as she skirted the truth in her recollection of the trip and thought of all Zaide had done to help, she knew she had chosen wrong.

CHAPTER THIRTY-ONE

DREAD HUNG on Zaide's shoulders like a mantle as he watched Lark disappear into the city. He lingered on the docks for longer than he had to, letting the milling porters and soldiers and whoever else flow around him. Daisy shifted uneasily beside him, nosing his fingers to beg for scratches.

"Are you coming?" Andriun asked. The two Paragons stood not far ahead, surrounded by an escort of their own.

Zaide hesitated. Part of him thought he should. Lark would be facing her father, and he didn't want her to have to do it alone. Yet he hadn't figured out how to breach the distance between them, and when she had disembarked, it had been with the Spectrum Blade at her side. What use was he, now that the sword bore no power?

He shook his head. "My family is here. I think I should go see how they're doing. I'll meet up with the rest of you at the palace before long."

Andriun shrugged. "Suit yourself."

"See you later," Tula chimed at the same time.

Zaide tried to smile as he waved them off, but he couldn't force it. His hand tried to settle on the Spectrum Blade's hilt when he lowered it, but the sword wasn't there, and he curled his fingers to a fist instead. Until the blade's power was restored, she didn't need him, and he suspected it was better if he gave her the freedom to seek him when it happened. If it never did, then his presence would only serve as a reminder of how close they'd come to ending things.

If he'd been slower in Ganede, the trip to Toren would have been so different. If the sword hadn't been depleted, if he'd just waited for Vorkaris to sink the ships and land to relay what he'd learned, everything would have gone better.

Except the sword was the only reason they'd gone to Nimultis, why they'd sought the Oracle in the first place. Would they have learned where Gadranus was if not for her? Would he have depleted the blade's magic along the way? He rubbed his temples and made himself walk with the dog trotting along at his side.

Zaide barely remembered the way through the streets, but they were emptier than they had been. He watched the forlorn faces of strangers as they went about their business, if it could be called that—he saw no vendor's carts or market stalls anywhere, just tired people moving from place to place. Now and then, stray soldiers hustled by with folded messages in hand, or fresh squads marched toward the gates to report for duty.

Everything about the city and its people struck him as weary, beaten down, a sharp contrast to the quiet, comfortable bustle they'd seen in Toren. Even Yithel had been more lively, when they'd pushed through the city on their way to the Shattered Lands.

The district where the Kolmari had settled was quiet, too, though he saw a few familiar faces. Former neighbors and family friends sat outside their homes, working at whatever menial tasks kept things going. A few glanced his way and smiled and he did his best to respond in kind. No one sat outside the place his foster parents had claimed, so he drew a breath and knocked.

It was strange to feel like an outsider to what should have been his home, too. But maybe it wouldn't have been—if not for the task that had pulled him from Kolmar, he would have stayed longer, but the razing of the forest still would have happened. If he hadn't become the Bladebearer, that probably would have driven him to the garrison, and at this point, who knew if he would even be alive?

The door opened, but it was not his foster parents who answered.

His mouth dropped open. "Resia!"

"Zaide?" She all but flung herself forward to wrap him in a hug. "How did you get here? Are you all right? Maker's mercy, your hair is so long now!" She brushed white locks from his face and beamed up at him.

He caught her by the shoulders and held her back. "What are you doing here? How did *you* get here? The forest was full of goborrins, it—"

"King Sendassian sent a ship for us," she cut in before he could finish. One after the other, she plucked his hands from her shoulders. "And yes, that means all of us. Murk and Aren are with the city's defenses."

"But *why* are you here? Why would the king call for you?" He was more troubled than excited by her presence, despite how happy he was to see her. Beside his legs, Daisy turned circles until he put a hand on her head to stop her.

Resia eyed the dog with curiosity as she caught Zaide's arm and pulled him into the house, but she did not so much as blink when Daisy followed. "There's a lot to explain."

"Is that Zaide?" Sarma's voice asked from the next room over. She hustled into the main living space and gasped. "It is you! Oh, by all that's good and right, I never thought I'd have all my children home again!"

"I missed you, too, Sarma," Zaide said before his foster mother swept him into an embrace.

Resia's smile faltered. "The Vale magic placed over Kolmar remains, but the king has declared the forest a lost cause. Father suggested I be called back to aid morale among the Kolmari, and also so I can help defend them if the worst happens here and we need to evacuate. They'll be safe back home, but only if someone can get them there."

"Is it that bad?" Zaide draped an arm around Sarma's shoulders and patiently endured the way she straightened his clothes.

"Not yet, but..." Resia trailed off and shrugged. "The city is holding, but the soldiers are losing morale. They had their spirits lifted a little a week or two ago, when that dragon decimated the goborrin forces in the field, but just a few days later, so many reinforcements arrived that it was like nothing had ever happened."

"You were already here when Vorkaris torched the battlefield?" He should have guessed. It had not been that long, and if she was supposed to be preparing for evacuation, that decision would have been made before it looked like they had help.

She raised her brows. "Vorkaris? I thought that—"

"Magister Vorkaris is a dragon," he explained before she could finish, knowing she'd heard the name before in her studies. "He shares his power with a person, and that person acts as Paragon of Fire. It, ah... It's complicated." He wrinkled his nose as Sarma smoothed and rearranged his hair.

"You're a mess," his foster mother said. "How long are you here? Please say you'll let me cut this mess before you go gallivanting off on some new adventure."

He caught her hands and made her lower them. "Yes, ma'am." It was probably wise to have it shortened before he joined the rest of Amrochan's soldiers on the battlefield. He could think of nowhere else he belonged, at this point. Sitting around and waiting for the Spectrum Blade was a waste of time, and it wasn't as if he was any real necessity. If he fell on the field outside Amrochan, the blade would just choose someone new, and the fight would go on without him. It was a disheartening thought, all in all. He'd hoped for better.

Sarma motioned to the dog by his feet. "Who's this, then?"

"Daisy," Zaide said. "She's my dog."

"Yes, we noticed." Resia caught his arm and tugged him farther into the house. She motioned for him to sit at the table. "So you met the Paragon of Fire? You were able to restore the Spectrum Blade's power?"

Zaide grimaced. Of course that was what she would ask, right after he'd already made himself glum thinking about it.

"No. I mean, yes. It—Maker's mercy, where do I start?" It had been so long since he'd had a chance to speak with her. "I did meet her. The Paragon of Fire, I mean. And the Paragon of Water. You might get to meet them, they're at the palace now."

"I would love to have the chance." She beamed at him as she shuffled over to the fireplace to fetch the steaming kettle. "What about the sword, though? If you're traveling with both of them, that means you were able to fix everything, right?"

He dropped into a chair with a sigh and leaned heavily against the table's edge while Daisy shuffled under it to lay by his feet. "No. I made it worse, instead."

"Well I find that hard to believe," Sarma said. She fetched a cup from a shelf on the wall and reached for a jar of colorful herbs mixed with tea.

"Tula and Andriun restored their part of its power, but I messed things up. I did something wrong, and I used up all the light. It can't seal anything right now." He raised a hand and then let it fall, some sort of helpless half-shrug. "We got some kind of crystal imbued with light power from the Oracle in Nimultis, and I got a purple one with shadow magic in it from Gadranus when I went to see him, but—"

His foster mother dropped the jar and it clattered against the hearth.

Resia stared at him, her mouth open.

"It's not broken," Sarma said quickly. "Silly me. I'll get it, hold on."

Zaide's hair stood on end as his sister stared at him. "What?"

She lowered the warm kettle to the table. "What do you mean, when you went to see him?"

"I think it's obvious enough what he meant, your question is just what led to it." Sarma tousled Resia's hair before she opened the jar and scooped herbs into the cup. She filled it from the kettle and pushed it across the table. "There, steep that a few minutes. Are you hungry? I'll get you something to eat."

"I'm fine. I ate on the ship." Zaide gladly accepted the warm cup, though, and wrapped both his hands around it.

Resia carried the kettle back to the hearth, but not without casting a puzzled look over her shoulder. "What ship?"

"Admiral Warinal brought us back from the tail end of Lake Sian. I thought about you while we were sailing, actually. I wished we could stop in Kolmar and say hello. I guess there wouldn't have been any point, huh?" He tried to smile, but an odd sense of nervousness brimmed in him.

"And why were you at the tail end of Lake Sian, exactly?" She retrieved her own cup, but chose a different mix of herbs to put in it. Their mother shuffled out of the room, and in her absence, the question felt heavier.

"Came down from the Shattered Lands after... well, you already heard that part." Zaide stared into his cup, studying the mix of herbs that floated on top. Sarma would expect him to drink those along with the tea. She'd always promised they offered valuable benefits to his health. Back home, he'd always secretly scooped them out. He lifted the cup to take a sip, mindful not to let any of the floating leaves and petals beyond his lips.

Resia settled across the table from him, and for a moment, the house was silent. Even the dog beneath the table did not make a sound.

"Where is everyone?" The stillness made him self-conscious and he kept his voice low.

"Busy." She gave a sad shrug and turned her cup between her hands. "Even the little ones are kept busy. Given tasks they can help with around the city. Father is helping in the armory, I believe. All the Kolmari children are doing things like tending chickens and running errands about the city. The only reason Mother and I are here is because I've been tasked with preparing to take the Kolmari back to the forest, so I'm drawing lists and charts and she's helping me."

"I guess we should have helped them get back right after we fixed things in the forest, huh?" The garrison had been full of goborrins then, but things outside Amrochan hadn't been so bad, and the front lines had not moved. He ran his thumb against the edge of his cup. "I'm sorry I haven't been so helpful."

"What are you talking about? You're helping the princess, aren't you?"

He shrugged. "She's unhappy with me."

Resia leaned against the table. "Because of the sword?"

"Because of things Gadranus told me, I think. Before he agreed to help with the sword." Zaide rubbed the back of his neck. "He asked me to give her a message. I did, and she didn't like it. I think she assumed I was siding with him."

Her lip curled, though whether it was bewilderment or disgust that twisted her face, he didn't know. "Why would you do that? And why would he help you? He knows you're planning to kill him, right?"

Questions he would soon grow tired of trying to answer, he suspected. "That is a little bit longer of a story."

Sarma hurried back with a brush and a pair of shears in her hands. "Well, you've got a moment, so you should go ahead and tell it while I get you cleaned up. When all's said and done, you can help us figure out the best path to take back through the woods, since you've gone every which way out there."

Zaide tried not to grimace. "You're going to do that right now?"

"If you're supposed to be aiding the princess, you'll be going to the palace, and no son of mine is appearing before the king looking like an unshorn sheep. Sit still." His foster mother posted herself behind him and laid the shears on the table while she attacked his mane with the brush.

He gave the softest snort and pushed his cup farther away. "Let's start with a map of Kolmar. I think I'll feel better knowing I can help with one thing without ruining it."

"Suit yourself," Resia said, though she turned to gather papers from wherever she'd left them with a small smile on her face. "Since almost everything was destroyed in the fire, I think it would be best if we shifted some of the rebuilding closer to the temple. That will be our new headquarters. We'll have everyone help clean it up, and we'll do what we can to prepare the place to be more defensible, not that I expect anything will make it past the new barrier." She spread her notes and maps across the table as she launched into explaining her plans.

Zaide sat perfectly still as Resia spoke and the soft snick of his foster mother's shears started at the back of his head. He'd have her cut it shorter, this time, so it would stay out of his eyes. It wouldn't be long before he had a sword in his hands again, and if he was lucky, he'd be part of the team escorting the Kolmari home.

CHAPTER THIRTY-TWO

"HELLO?" Zaide knocked on the wooden doorframe as he peered into the armory. There were only a handful of men inside, their backs turned to the door, and they reminded him of bugraks with the way they looked over their shoulders while still hunched over their work.

One of them looked twice, then sat upright. "Zaide!" Verlin put aside his work and all but leaped from his chair.

"Resia said you were over here." Zaide met his foster father with a hug.

"Yes, and will be until late. Look at you." Verlin held him at arm's length and gave him a quick inspection. "Maker's mercy, I think you've gotten taller. I would've thought you'd be done growing by now."

Zaide grinned. "I'm still a kid for what, two days? I think I'm allowed to grow until then."

"So you are. You've filled out a bit, too. You look stronger. And I see Sarma's already gotten her hands on you, you're too clean for a boy just in from wherever it is you've been." Verlin slapped his shoulder and motioned for him to join the men around the wide work table. Odd tools and boxes of hardware lay all across its wooden surface, alongside bits and pieces of leather. Straps and pieces of armor, mostly, though a few quivers and slings for weapons lay about, too.

"She said I looked like an unshorn sheep." Zaide took an empty seat and grabbed the first thing in front of him. A gauntlet with new straps, but missing buckles. He leaned forward to tip a few boxes and find them.

One of the men at the table barked a laugh. "This one of yours, then, Verlin?"

"My oldest," Verlin said. "Resia was a winter baby, though she wasn't far behind. This one's Zaide. A good boy. We're grateful every day that the Elder trusted us to raise him."

Zaide listened to the note of pride in his foster father's voice. He'd always claimed him, but had never spoken of him quite that way before—at least, not where Zaide could hear. *My oldest.* It was true, he was a little older than his foster sister of the same age, but the way his foster father said it without an ounce of hesitation put a warm sense of comfort in Zaide's chest.

He needed that, he realized as he retrieved an awl from halfway across the table and started the holes needed to sew the buckle to the unfinished strap. That sense of welcome, of belonging. To be reminded he was still Kolmari, no matter what other pieces of himself he'd found.

"Well, I see he's got your work ethic," another man remarked. "Right to it without a word. You got practice doing leather working, boy?"

"A little. I spent some time in the forge. Portran—Portly, I mean," Zaide corrected himself, recalling the friendly smith's military nickname, "helped me make a scabbard."

"Is that so?" The fellow leaned back to look at him. "Where is it, then? I'd like to see what sort of handiwork Portly's teaching, these days."

Verlin looked, too, and a faint crease of worry etched the space between his brows. "I see your knife, but where...?" He didn't take the question any further. Allowing Zaide the chance to hide his role, perhaps.

He didn't feel he had anything to hide. "With the princess. The blade is what's used to forge the seal that ends the Rise. She's... preparing it, for the end of things."

"Maker's mercy," one of the others breathed. "So it's true, then? The rumor Her Highness was sent to gather what was needed to end this war?"

It was the first Zaide had heard of it. It was also so far off the mark, he wasn't sure how to respond. In the end, he just nodded. Whether or not she'd been sent, that was what they had done. "The Paragon of Fire and Paragon of Water came back with us to join the fight. I don't know what all Her Highness has to do, but when things come to a head..." His breath didn't feel like enough to fill his lungs, but he made himself nod again, reinforcing what he'd said.

"We'll end it," Verlin finished for him. "You hear that? If Her Highness is back with the leaders of Jadora and Desheni, it means we're close!"

"Hear, hear," someone said, and thumped a fist on the table.

Zaide smiled, but it was short lived. He worked a few stitches into place before he spoke again. "Resia said she wants the Kolmari to head for the temple before the final confrontation."

"She does," Verlin said with a single nod. "But that doesn't have to include you. Her Highness needs you here."

"Maybe." Zaide realized how defeated he sounded a moment after the grumble escaped him. He made himself offer enough of a smile to diffuse it. "Lark was—I mean, the Spectrum Blade was meant for Princess Dasienna. I've carried it this far for her, but it's gotten more receptive to her over time. She may not need me anymore, and if that's the case, I... I'd like to join whatever part of the army is supposed to help escort the Kolmari back home."

His foster father smiled, though a hint of sadness pinched the corners of his eyes. "We'd be happy to have you. There's no telling what might happen after we set out, but I'm sure we'd all rest a little easier knowing we had you nearby with a sword in your hand."

Zaide didn't doubt it, but he thought he caught the slightest note of uncertainty. It didn't bother him; he was uncertain, too. For all that he longed for the peace he'd known, he'd accepted there was no going back. He didn't have a home to go back to, and even if he had, he wouldn't have returned the same person. Returning to Kolmar would be difficult. A fraught journey with no rest at the end. Resia could maintain the barrier for as long as her magic remained strong and the temple did not fall, but the world would still change around them. Peace would not be had until Gadranus fell and his forces were pushed back—a task that had begun to look more and more impossible.

The front lines had moved over years. Centuries, even, creeping outward across the known world until all but the Allied Kingdoms fell within their enemy's grasp. In the gaps and lulls between each Rise, Amroch's people pushed back, but they'd never reclaimed enough territory to make a difference. The Elder's maps, the ones that had shown only a sliver of the Shattered Lands, had dated back to before the previous Rise. Even that land had never been recovered. What hope was there to truly reclaim Kolmar when Gadranus was dead?

"I'm hearing lots of gabbing and not a lot of working," barked a man at the door.

Zaide turned at the familiar voice and smiled when he saw the smith.

Portran chuckled at the sight. "Ah, that would do it. Found your way back, did you, lad? Well, good timing. I've got something for you."

"For me?" Zaide couldn't hide his surprise.

The smith nodded and deposited an armful of boxes on the table. One tipped over, spilling spools of sinew between the men's projects. "Finish what you're working on. Then come see me in my workshop." He sat a few spools upright, then left the rest as he ambled through the wide door to the forge. He bore a more pronounced limp than Zaide recalled from his last visit, but the siege had worn down everyone.

"Make friends everywhere you go, don't you, boy?" Verlin asked with a small laugh.

Zaide put his head down and focused on finishing the buckle. "Call it a talent, I guess." At first, he wasn't sure he agreed, but thoughts of all the people he'd encountered and all the friendly conversations he'd had sprang to mind. Maybe there was some truth in it, after all.

The moment he had the stitches tied off, he put away the project and made his way to the forge. Portran sat at his work table, sorting a variety of new chisels onto their rack.

"I would have expected you'd make your own tools," Zaide said with a half smile. "Since you're a blacksmith and all."

"I can. Sometimes I do. But I'm best with weapons and armor, and when everyone's in a hurry, it's best to stick with your own specialty." Portran offered a toothy grin as he put the last one away. "The war keeps all of us on our toes, but I've found a few minutes to myself here and there. Just enough time to let me finish this."

The smith grunted as he leaned forward to take something wrapped in burlap from a shelf beside the table. He hooked a finger, beckoning for Zaide to come closer.

"What is it?" Zaide asked as he crept near.

Portran held it out with both hands. "Have a look. See what you think."

Zaide took the long object and peeled back its wrappings. They fell away and his breath caught. Inside lay the most magnificent scabbard he'd ever seen, tooled with silver filigree and lacquered a pale blue that shone with an iridescent sheen.

"I copied down the measurements after you left," the smith said with a touch of pride. "So it should be a perfect fit. A blade like that needs a better home than plain leather."

"It's incredible." Zaide ran his fingers over the metal and

tilted it so the lacquer shimmered in the light. "All these details... How did you do this?"

"Carved in wax and cast in silver. I make jewelry for my wife, sometimes. Or, I did, back when there wasn't all this to keep me busy." Portran waved a hand in a loose circle, indicating the forge and the armory next door. "Keep it waxed and it won't tarnish."

"Thank you." Zaide should have said that part sooner.

"You're welcome, lad. I hope it serves you well."

He gripped it tight. "It will. The blade is at the palace right now, but I'll try it as soon as..." He trailed off and stared at the scabbard. As soon as what? He'd just been discussing heading for Kolmar and leaving the blade behind.

A playful spark lit the big smith's gaze. "Lost your privileges, have you?"

"No," Zaide protested. "I left the sword with her because she needed it. It's just that she's... She's mad at me, that's all."

Portran made a thoughtful sound and reached for some unfamiliar tool on the wall. "Well, did you do it on purpose?"

Zaide blinked. "Do what?"

"Whatever made her angry."

"Of course not. I didn't think she'd react that way."

The smith grunted. "Well then you apologize for upsetting her, because you didn't mean to. Hiding in the forge won't fix anything, lad. But an apology might. And sometimes, a little gift may help." That glint came back and a smirk twisted the man's mouth behind his beard.

Zaide drew a finger across the shaped silver at the scabbard's top. "A gift, huh." He lifted his head and considered that as he stared at the glowing embers left in the forge's furnace.

Tula had mentioned flowers, but he didn't know what kind would be appropriate, nor did he have any idea where to get them while the city was under siege. Not that flowers seemed impressive when she had the royal gardens to provide as many as she wanted.

How would he pay for something, anyway? Zaide kept tracing the same shapes with his fingertip. He didn't have any money. The whole expedition had been paid for by Lark. That left making something, and what skills did he have there?

Portran said nothing else, just finished putting away whatever it was he'd purchased elsewhere. Then he stood with a groan and went to stoke the fires in his furnace.

Zaide turned in a slow circle, examining the workshop around him. It was warm, comfortable, and it was strange how he already had fond memories of the place. His eyes snagged on a bucket full of wood scraps, and he paused. "Could I...?"

"Whatever you need, lad," the smith replied mildly, not seeming to mind that the question was unfinished. "So long as all the tools are back in their places before you leave."

Which gave him the rest of the afternoon to come up with something. Zaide rewrapped the scabbard in his hands and left it on the work table, then crouched to inspect the wood. The bellows whooshed behind him, bringing the fire back to life, and heat washed over his back.

"Just remember it's the thought that matters most," Portran added.

"Yeah, and it's a good thing," Zaide said as he drew a pleasantly reddish scrap of wood from the bucket and turned it between his hands. His craftsmanship was so inexperienced, the thought was all she'd likely recognize. Still, it was something, and as he moved to the table to find a charcoal pencil and draw a rough design, he hoped the intention and effort would be worth enough.

CHAPTER THIRTY-THREE

LARK WAS SO ENGROSSED with the books spread before her that she didn't realize someone had cleared their throat to get her attention until the noise came a second time. She blinked and lifted her head, flustered. Andriun greeted her with a nervous smile.

"Yes?" she prompted when he didn't speak.

"Oh, you did not hear me at all? Forgive me, Your Highness." He pressed a hand over his heart and gave a gentle bow. "I asked if I could borrow the Captured Spring."

"Oh. Of course." She'd collected all the artifacts back into her bag after they'd boarded Admiral Warinal's ship, and while she never let them out of her presence, it was easier to forget the bag at her side when it was nestled into the voluminous skirt of her dress. Amrochan fashion was atrocious, she decided as she worked the strap back and swung the bag forward so she could dig through it.

She found the vial at the bottom of the bag, nestled between the two crystals she was studying, and passed it to him without a second glance.

"Thank you, Your Highness." Andriun bowed again, always

respectful, then hurried out of the royal library to leave her to her studies.

Lark rubbed her forehead with two fingers and tried to find her place on the open page before her.

Almost as soon as she'd given her father the information he demanded, she'd gone to the library and set to work. She'd scarcely slept since their arrival, and her father had not asked to speak with her again. It mattered little, she supposed; she'd provided intelligence for the war and while he had not tried to reassure her that he'd never intended her death, he had not tried to have her killed since her arrival. Within a palace he controlled, such a task would have been easy.

Perhaps she was useful to him yet.

She worked her way down the rest of the page and turned to the next before she lifted her head, the library's silence an uncomfortable pressure on her ears.

Andriun had asked for the Captured Spring. For *healing*. And she had not even asked why.

Lark all but leaped from her chair and slammed it in against the table. She gripped her skirt tight in both hands to lift it out of the way as she hustled out the door.

"The Desheni Shaman," she said the moment the guard in the hallway turned to her in surprise. "Where did he go?"

The man pointed, and Lark stormed off that way with a knot of dread growing in her belly. She did not run, but part of her desperately wanted to. Had there been an accident? A turn in the battle that persisted outside the palace walls? The smoke in the sky scented the air even in the palace, a perpetual reminder of what they faced and how little she'd discovered to combat it.

Dozens of books lay spread across her table in the library, and not a single one had offered clues as to how she was meant to utilize the strange crystals she possessed. She'd demanded the library staff aid her in research, and that the palace staff search her late mother's belongings for any books, journals, or notes that might provide clues, but neither group had turned up anything of value.

The lack of progress was enough to make her sick.

What would she do if it was already too late?

Familiar voices rose ahead and she followed them to the guest quarters assigned to the Paragon of Water. The door stood partway open, but she stopped outside with a nervous flutter in her belly. If he'd gone to his room, how urgent could it be?

"I thought you said the ice would help?" That was Zaide's voice; not one she wanted to hear.

"I assumed that it would. Hold still." And that one was Andriun. He sounded irritated, rather than concerned, and Lark's hands tightened in the fabric of her skirt while she tried to decide if that was worse than what she'd feared.

"I am holding still. Just do it."

"You are not holding still. It will not be even. There, do not move."

The order was followed with a sharp inhale and a sound of distress.

"Perfect."

Lark shoved her way into the room just in time to see Zaide raise the Captured Spring to his lips. Andriun turned in surprise, a bloody cloth in his hand, and both young men froze.

"What in the world are you doing?" Lark demanded. Her eyes darted from Andriun's cloth to Zaide's startled face, then to his shorter hair, and finally to his reddened ears and the bluish-silver rings in their swelling lobes.

"It is the autumnal equinox," Andriun said, as if that explained anything at all.

Zaide capped the spring and glanced away. His shoulders curled forward, as if that could hide the way he oozed guilt.

She stormed forward and snatched the Captured Spring from his hand. Half of her wanted to shake it in front of his nose, but she gripped it tight and forced her hand down to her side instead. "This is a precious resource! How dare you waste it on something so frivolous? So useless?" She turned her glare to Andriun. "And you. You're supposed to be the Paragon and a leader of your people. You should certainly know better!"

"It was only a drop," Andriun protested.

"A drop that could save the life of a man out there!" Lark jabbed a finger toward the west, where goborrins seethed beyond the walls in numbers she didn't want to fathom. The thought alone put tears in her eyes.

The Shaman put out a hand. "Your Highness—" he started, but she shook her head and drew back.

She didn't want to hear the excuses. She stormed to the hallway as she yanked the Captured Spring's chain down over her head, her full skirt tangling around her ankles and slowing her down. The walls felt close, constricting, and it made her chest grow tight. She made it to one of the palace's many balconies before the tears escaped, spilling her frustration down her face.

There was no relief or freedom to be found outside, not with the smoggy yellow cast that colored the sky and blotted out the sun. Lark strode to the balustrade anyway and closed her eyes as she leaned against it.

The sounds of the city had changed. Before all this, before she'd run off with the foolish notion she could do anything to change what waited ahead, Amrochan had hummed with business, conversation, and laughter. Now, all she heard was the ringing of a blacksmith's hammer somewhere on the palace grounds, and farther off, voices calling orders. The noise of battle was distant, but sometimes carried, screams and battle cries both adrift on the wind.

What she wouldn't have given to hear the sounds of life again.

In the still, the soft tap of hesitant bootsteps reached her ears.

She did not look, and her visitor did not leave.

Lark didn't want to speak to him. She knew it was him; who else would it have been? No one else tried so persistently to be near her when she fought so hard to keep everyone away. The knowledge made her heart ache. He was steadfast, dependable. Always there, even when she tried to make sure he wasn't. Why couldn't he simply leave her be?

Eventually, when she never acknowledged his presence, he strode closer. She forced herself to open her eyes, though she stared at the sky instead of turning to face him. It was more yellow than it had been earlier. Perhaps it was the afternoon light that bounced off the smoke, giving it a dirty glow.

"I had a reason," Zaide said when he stopped again, now only a few paces behind her. "I won't pretend it was a good one, but it wasn't completely frivolous."

Lark continued to stare at the sky. Her fingers twitched against the balustrade and she fought to keep from touching the Captured Spring around her neck.

He went on when she didn't reply. "I said I wanted to do it, Andriun offered to help. I said I was hesitant to do anything that might need time to heal. I've asked to join the army, officially, and I'll probably be on the battlefield in the next few days. Until the Kolmari are ready to go home, anyway. There'll be dirt, blood... not a good environment for self-inflicted wounds."

"A good reason not to do it at all," she said sharply.

"I know. That was what I said." He crept forward until he stood beside her and laced his hands together before he rested them on the rail. "But Andriun insisted I should, and suggested we could use the spring to heal it immediately. The Desheni are big on rituals, apparently. He didn't think I should have to miss out just because I might have to fight tomorrow."

Lark shook her head. "You can't fight with the army. I still need you." Still needed his hand, at least, to wield the blade she couldn't touch again. She'd tried more than once since their arrival, and each time her hand had drawn near, she'd felt the charge of refusal ready to spark against her fingers. She had not dared try to grasp it after that, and to be rejected again after she'd handled it once hurt worse than when the blade refused her in the chamber underneath Kolmar's temple.

"Then I'm yours," he replied without hesitation. He was looking at her when she turned her head, a simple, earnest determination in his piercing eyes.

Her heart ached so badly, she thought she might choke. "Are you?"

"For as long as you need me. No matter what." He shifted, and for a moment, she thought he meant to touch her hand.

She pulled back before he could. Fear and frustration tangled up within her and she found herself curling her hands to fists. "I wish you'd leave."

It was so contrary to everything she'd just said, she couldn't blame him when his face crumpled with confusion.

"I said I'd stick with you until this was over," he said slowly, as if trying to piece together what he'd done wrong. He'd be puzzled a long time. He'd done nothing, and that made her heart hurt so much worse. "If you want me to go with the Kolmari, then—"

"Then go," Lark snapped. "I wish you'd just stay out of the way. Just leave. Get away from all this, away from this war—"

"Away from you?" His eyes softened and she didn't know if it was sadness or pity.

She took another step back. "Yes."

Zaide studied her for a long time, deep creases of worry drawn between his brows. She wanted nothing more than to smooth them away with her fingertips. She held her arms ramrod straight at her sides instead. He studied that, too, the tension in her posture and what must have looked like fury on her face.

He lowered his eyes. "I don't think you mean that."

"Then take it as an order. Do not draw a sword in my father's name. Do not fight this war he should have ended. Just leave.

Leave with the Kolmari, whenever they go. Leave and never come back." Her voice cracked as she tried to look imperious, dashing any hope she might have had that he could take her seriously.

"I don't think you mean that, either," he said softly.

She tried to glare at him, but she didn't know how long she could without bringing on more tears.

Zaide leaned forward to rest his elbows on the stone balustrade and gaze out at the rest of the palace below. "I think the Oracle told you something that scared you, and you're still trying to fix it. I know none of this has gone the way we planned, but it's not like the Oracle really knows anything, anyway."

An odd shiver coursed through her. "How can you say that?"

He gave the slightest shrug. "Gadranus already tried to kill me once. According to the Oracle, there was only one outcome where I'd survive. A million other possibilities, and all of them said I'd die. But I'm here, right?"

Lark remained still, though her limbs grew cold. "What are you talking about?"

A tiny smile drew at the corners of his mouth as he turned his head and touched his blunted ear. "Maybe she's wrong again."

She didn't know what to say. She'd asked him what had happened before; she'd asked more than once, if she recalled. He'd said he didn't know. Yet he'd learned this, somehow—she could only guess from the Oracle herself—and he'd shared none of it since their time in Nimultis. Not when she'd expressed her fears and not when he'd gone to see Gadranus. To see Gadranus *again*, she realized as she stared at his ear. Maker's mercy, he'd known.

And he'd still gone.

"If you need my help, you'll have it," Zaide said when all she did was gape at him. "But I need you to know you're really bad at giving instructions, so I'm just going to listen to the first thing you said and stay here. With you."

That was enough to bring back the tears and put a knot in her throat. "I can't lose you to him," she whispered.

"Considering everything I've been through since this spring, I don't think I'm that easy to kill." He grinned and moved a little closer.

This time, she didn't try to get away, and when he reached to take her into a hug, she didn't fight. Her arms slid around his middle and she buried her face in his chest as she sniffed hard.

"Look at you," she grumbled. "Fixing everything again, when all I ever do is cry. You must think me terribly weak."

Zaide shook his head. "I don't think crying makes you weak. It means you're frustrated. You have to let it out somehow, so you don't get overwhelmed."

"You never get overwhelmed." She couldn't help the twinge of bitterness that rose within her. He was always so steady, so determined.

He snorted a laugh. "I get overwhelmed all the time. I just don't handle it the same way. I go practice with a sword, or I try to... storm off and find somewhere to brood, according to Andriun. You just don't like to let me." Despite the accusation, he gave her a squeeze.

Lark shut her eyes as some of the tension leaked out of her. Odd, she thought, how she felt like a sponge. Filled with negativity he managed to wring out of her with a hug. She nestled into it. "Well, someone has to keep you under control."

A soft chuckle shook in his chest, not quite a rumble, but a sensation against her cheek that struck her as so profoundly safe that all she could do was marvel. She'd looked everywhere for that; she'd tried to forge it herself, had hunted across Amroch to try and recover it, had dared to hope she might find it in her father. Instead, it had come in the most unlikely place, wrapped in the arms of one of the first people to stand in her way.

"I'm sorry if I'm out of control today," he said, and she took the notion he was only half joking.

She pushed herself back and raised her head to inspect what

he'd done. "You said it was a tradition? I've never heard of the Kolmari having such a practice."

"It's not Kolmari. It's, ah... well, you can probably guess." His eyes darted away and his posture grew a shade more stiff. "I hope that doesn't bother you."

Did it? Should it? She hardly knew anymore. It had, once, but those fears now seemed so shallow. "No." She raised a hand to straighten out his hair, shorter than what she was used to seeing on him, yet still somehow a mess. "It's not as if you have any say in the manner of your birth. They look handsome on you."

Zaide's brows shot up.

Heat rushed into Lark's face and she stepped back, breaking contact as ruddy tones bloomed across her cheeks.

Ever diplomatic, he cleared his throat and reached for his pocket. "Speaking of birth, I almost forgot. This was the whole reason I came up here. I've been down in the city with the Kolmari, and helping in the armory when I can, but—" He stopped as he removed something, as if hesitant to finish the thought.

Lark frowned. "What does that have to do with birth?"

"Yours. I mean, today." He gestured to the sky, as if that answered the question.

Her expression softened with surprise. She hadn't told him. She almost opened her mouth to ask how he'd known, then shut it just as swiftly. Any other time, without a war raging outside the city walls, this would have been an important day. The future queen's coming of age; the day she'd be entrusted with her mother's crown and told to keep it until ruling was her right.

As things were, she didn't know if that rite of passage would take place at all.

While those dismal thoughts whirled through her head, he cleared his throat again and presented something atop his open hand. "It's probably not really fit for a princess, but I didn't have much time."

It was a simple, wooden two-pronged fork for her hair, its top carved into three blooming lilies.

Lark took it, careful not to let her fingertips brush his skin. "You made this?"

"To keep your hair out of the way when we're doing dangerous things. You tie it back, but it still gets in your way."

Princesses didn't receive such gifts. All her life, she'd been heaped with jewels and dresses, rare books and luxurious perfumes. This served a purpose. It was based on a need. It was simple, yet it was one of the most thoughtful gifts she'd ever received. Her hand curled around it.

"I'm sorry if I didn't do a very good job," he added in a hurry. "I'm still learning. I was supposed to be finishing that bird I was working on before—well, it doesn't really matter. I'll be a little late in finishing the bird, but at least I got one tradition in."

All of a sudden, a strange wash of dismay came over her. A tradition. A rite of passage. She squinted at his earrings and held up her empty hand, palm out. "Wait. You, too? Today?"

"Weird coincidence," he said with a nervous smile. "But from what Tula said, it means pretty different things between your ancestors and mine."

"But I don't have anything for you," she almost cried.

Zaide gave a soft laugh. "I don't need a gift from you. You're talking to me again, and honestly, that's enough."

She raised her head to look at him. The hair fork was warm in her hand, and its presence put an odd flutter in her chest.

How did he do it so easily? Reassure her that everything was all right? Know what she needed to hear? She swallowed hard and held tight to the precious gift he'd made for her as words she'd hated hearing prickled at the back of her mind.

If you have not told him, he does not know.

She'd worked so hard to keep him from knowing, yet as they stood that way, no more than an arm's reach apart, she had no doubt that she'd failed.

Yet there was certainty that came with voicing things, and now, she decided, she needed that.

To know she understood right.

To make herself heard.

To surrender a fight she'd lost long ago, and accept all the wondrous things accepting that loss might mean.

"Zaide," she started, the tightness in her throat threatening to keep the words from escaping. They were hard enough to push to the tip of her tongue without it. "There's something I've wanted to tell you."

Yes; that was it. She'd wanted it. Wanted this, more than anything she'd ever denied herself.

A flicker of concern crossed his face, but he remained stoic. "You can tell me anything."

She knew. If there was anyone to be trusted with her innermost thoughts and feelings, it was him.

She'd been foolish to reject that for so long.

The moment she drew a breath to speak, bugles blared across the city.

Zaide's head snapped toward the sound as sentries across Amrochan picked it up and relayed the single, braying warning note to the castle. The courtyard below their balcony burst to life with messengers running and officers shouting new orders.

He hissed something that was dangerously close to a curse and paced backwards. "The Kolmari. I have to go. I'll be back."

"Zaide—" She reached after him, tried to get him to stop, but he caught her fingers in his hand and gave them a squeeze.

"I'll be back," he promised with another squeeze. Then he pulled away and ran for the door, for the family that waited for him elsewhere in the city.

Lark clutched the hair fork to her chest as he disappeared, struggling to keep her fragile feelings from falling to pieces.

A guard popped onto the balcony almost the moment Zaide was gone. Relief splashed across his face the moment he saw her.

"Your Highness, you must come with me at once. Your father needs you in his council chambers. I'll explain along the way."

"Lead me," she said, though she needed no help finding her way and she needed no explanation.

The bugles were joined by bells throughout the palace, and the alarm could only mean one thing.

The northern army had arrived.

CHAPTER THIRTY-FOUR

Daisy was keening when Zaide made it home. He thrust the door open with every intention of calming her. Instead, the frenzy that greeted him made him want to howl, too.

Verlin cast him one regretful look on his way past the table, where Sarma piled foodstuffs into woven bark baskets. Women Zaide recognized from back home in Kolmar bustled through the house, helping pack necessities.

"I thought we'd have more time," Verlin said, as if to explain.

The last Zaide had known, Verlin had been in the armory. He was surprised his foster father had made it to the house before he did, but perhaps he shouldn't have been. It was a long way down from the balconies in the palace. Zaide slid forward to help wrap jars of preserves in whatever bits of clothing lay on the table and stuff them into the baskets. "Goborrins from the north?"

Verlin gave a stiff nod and continued into the back room, where the voices of his youngest foster siblings rose in a chorus of protests. Daisy went after him and added her voice to the complaints, too.

"Resia's gone to make sure everyone is packing," Sarma said.

"She's the one who sent us help. She'll be back before long, but we'll need help getting everyone to where they need to go."

"No one knows how long the king's ships will hold the lake." Verlin came back with an armful of blankets. They couldn't take everything, and much of what filled their temporary house was being piled off to one side by the other Kolmari women, but the necessities they were taking would be enough to fill a cart.

Zaide lowered his head. "I'll make sure all of you get on the boats with everything you need, but I can't go with you."

Sarma paused. "You're not going? I thought..."

He wouldn't let himself be swayed. "Dasienna still needs me."

"Then..." Verlin hesitated, but a spark of hope brightened his countenance. "The sword, is it...?"

Zaide sobered, but met his foster father's gaze. "It's not about the sword."

Understanding lit Verlin's eyes. At the same time, Sarma raised a hand to her mouth.

"I'm sorry," Zaide added. "I know I said I'd go with you, but I was the one who chose this. I have to see it through to the end."

"I thought she didn't want your help anymore?" his foster mother asked. "I thought you said—"

He shook his head before she could finish. "She said a lot of things. Contradicted herself a lot. But she still can't wield the sword, and I can."

The door swung open and Zaide turned, expecting to see Resia. Instead, a breathless man in armor stood there with his hand on the hilt of his sword. "The Kolmari Elder, where is she?"

Verlin stepped forward to meet him. "Gathering our people for evacuation. Why? What's happened?"

The man held out a hand to stop him. "The Paragons have been summoned to the palace. King Sendassian demands her presence at once."

Zaide stuffed one last jar into the basket before him. "I'll get her. We'll report straight to the palace."

The guard cast him a skeptical look, but he ignored it and pushed out into the street. He'd grown so used to that sort of reaction, it hardly meant anything anymore. He didn't expect every last soldier in Amrochan to know he was a personal guest of the princess—or her Bladebearer.

The rest of the tiny district that had been allocated to Kolmari refugees brimmed with activity, but even with all the people running between buildings and loading carts, it wasn't hard to spot his sister. She glided between houses with the grace of a swan on the water, a bubble of peace following her wherever she went.

He hated to be the one to disrupt it, but he'd volunteered and would not take it back now. He whistled for her attention and waved an arm overhead when he caught it.

Resia's equanimity faltered, but she caught herself as she slid through the crowd and had it restored by the time she greeted him. "I didn't expect to see you back from the palace so soon. Is everything all right?"

"Sendassian wants all the Paragons. I said I'd take you." He had no doubt he wasn't invited, but if nothing else, maybe he could try to help Lark with the Spectrum Blade. Or would she be in the meeting with her father? Did the king recognize her as one of them, even if her power still slumbered? He fought a frown and decided that was a problem for after their arrival.

She gave an exasperated sigh. "Right now? No one has even started for the docks yet."

"He'll probably kick me out of the castle at the first chance he gets. When that happens, I'll come right back down and make sure everyone gets to the boats." Zaide tried and failed to inject even an ounce of humor into his words. How could he? He already knew what Sendassian thought of him. Their first meeting had made that abundantly clear.

Worry pinched Resia's face. "Are you all right?"

He hadn't realized he'd lifted a hand to his throat until she spoke. "Fine. Just remembering the last time I had the misfortune of meeting with the king." He forced his hand down. "Let's go. If he wants the Paragons, it has to be important." Or dangerous. After everything he'd learned, the fact the king had called for the Paragons at all seemed like a mistake. How could he acknowledge their power while refusing the Spectrum Blade?

Or maybe that was why he summoned them now. Maybe something had changed. Zaide's eyes darted toward the palace that loomed over the rest of Amrochan, but its imposing towers revealed nothing.

Resia fluttered a hand, indication he should lead the way. She followed close at his side, but they hadn't gone far before she touched his arm. "Are you sure you're all right? You look concerned."

Maybe he was. "Do you think the Spectrum Blade can change its mind?"

Her head canted to one side as they walked. "I don't think it has a mind, does it?"

Zaide didn't know. The Oracle had mentioned its spirit, but he'd never been able to discern if she meant a soul, or merely power that bordered on sentience. It hadn't always felt like simple power; he'd sensed things in the blade now and then that gave a strong impression of a personality, but he couldn't bring himself to imagine the blade was alive.

Belatedly, he shook his head. "I mean, do you think it can decide I'm not the best person to carry it anymore? Do you think it could pick someone else while I'm alive?"

"I don't know," she said, and the simplicity of the answer brought him no comfort.

The guards at the castle gates recognized them—or him, at least—and waved them through in a rush. The courtyard teemed with soldiers in varying states of preparation, some fully armored and falling into formation, others looking like they'd just tumbled out of bed. All of them stepped aside to let Zaide and Resia by.

The moment they set foot through the palace doors, a

steward intercepted them. "Thank the Maker you've come, Lady Paragon."

Zaide had never devoted any thought to how the Paragons should be addressed, and whether or not that was correct, he did not know.

"I've heard King Sendassian requested my presence," Resia replied, diplomatic, though they both knew it had not been a request. "Where am I to find him?"

"He holds a meeting of council. I shall take you there at once." The steward beckoned with one hand as he started off down the hallway, but when Zaide followed, too, he paused. "Forgive me, the summons was only for the Paragon. She will not require a bodyguard within the palace."

Zaide opened his mouth to object, but Resia gave a snort and waved a hand.

"He's not my bodyguard. He's my brother. You see the resemblance, don't you?" Her dark eyes sparkled. It was something of a rude joke; she was such warm shades of tan and brown from head to foot, and he was paler than the white stone walls around them.

The steward's mouth took a sour twist.

"I'm Princess Dasienna's Bladebearer," Zaide added. "If I'm anyone's bodyguard, I'm hers."

That did nothing to improve the steward's disposition, but the man sighed and continued down the hall. "Then it shall be up to His Majesty whether or not you should attend."

He led them through a maze of hallways and staircases, and they remained silent the whole way. When they reached their destination, Zaide expected a war room full of counselors and military officers. Instead, the steward let them into a quiet room where the only people around a table full of maps were Andriun, Tula, Lark, and Sendassian himself.

Lark cast him a worried glance, which he answered with a smile he hoped was reassuring. He supposed it wasn't, for her mien only darkened.

That response left him hesitant. What had he done this time? He hadn't even been gone an hour, and already her attitude toward him had flipped from warm and welcoming to cold and disapproving. Maker's mercy, he would never understand what she wanted from him. He sobered and strode forward alongside Resia to take a place at the table—near to Lark, but not by her side.

"Paragon," Sendassian said, less a greeting than simply addressing her. His expression was as unfriendly as his tone. "You have heard the alarms."

"My people prepare to evacuate, Your Majesty. We thank you for the hospitality you have offered while the protective magic over Kolmar's forest was restored," Resia replied, her voice the coolest Zaide had ever heard. The Elder had been right to choose her as his favored apprentice and his replacement. Though had the Elder truly chosen her? Zaide had never considered before that it may not have been the old man's choice at all, but that of the power he commanded.

"A favor you may now repay." Sendassian tapped the outline of Amrochan on the map that covered the table in its entirety. "You will remain here while your people depart."

Zaide quirked an eyebrow. "Your Majesty will be providing additional soldiers for their escort, then?"

"If they cannot get themselves through their own forest, they hardly deserve assistance. Consider what I have at my doorstep." Sendassian gestured toward what Zaide assumed was west, where the goborrin armies clashed with Amrochan soldiers. Then his eyes narrowed. "What concern is it of yours?"

"Zaide was the previous Kolmari Elder's other apprentice, Father," Lark put in smoothly. "If you'll remember."

Were it not for the war, Zaide would have been offended to be forgotten so easily. Sendassian had his hands full, to say the least, and they'd hardly visited the palace between expeditions.

But Sendassian's eyes fell on him and for a moment, he suspected he had not been forgotten at all. There was a weight in that stare, a shrewd sort of observation, and he watched Zaide for far too long for it to be merely an effort to jog his memory.

"The Kolmari will have the guards promised the last time we spoke," the king said at last. He returned his attention to Resia. "I can spare no more than that, and you must remain here, with the other Paragons."

Andriun and Tula said nothing, but both were troubled. Something that had been said before his arrival, Zaide assumed.

Resia frowned, but the king gave her no time to respond. He moved a collection of pewter figurines across the map with one broad hand.

"I hesitate to call the new arrival reinforcements." Sendassian remained solemn as he arranged them. "The army that has arrived more than doubles the force we already faced. If you are truly the most powerful mages your people have to offer, your skills will be invaluable in defending the city. And for what comes next."

Zaide glanced to Lark, hoping he didn't need to ask for an explanation.

Resia asked, instead. "I apologize, Your Majesty, I must have missed something you already discussed. What would you require our magic for, beyond aiding Amrochan's defense?"

"Humoring my daughter," the king replied dryly.

Now Resia looked at Lark, too. The princess bowed her head, as if she wished she hadn't been involved.

It was unlike her. She'd always been willing to take charge, to put herself in the forefront of everything that happened and lead the way. Even when she didn't know where she was going. Had the timing not been so inappropriate, Zaide might have smiled at the recollection of Lark trying to lead them out of Kolmar, only to tumble down a slope and land in the mud.

None of that independence shone in her now. She was quiet, browbeaten, and she did not lift her eyes from the table when she spoke.

"Your power may be necessary, if we are to try and create a

seal." Worry shaded the princess's expression and she laced her hands together before her to squeeze her fingers tight. "The approaching army carries the enemy's standard. They are led by Gadranus himself."

"That's impossible," Zaide blurted. "He was in Toren not even a week ago, how could—"

"You speak out of turn," Sendassian all but bellowed.

Zaide flinched and lowered his eyes.

"But he's not wrong," Lark said as she leaned against the table, palms flat on the map. "I'm as confused as you are, Zaide. I told my father how we meant to kill him in his own capital. He was there and we saw him. I don't know how he could have arrived so swiftly, but there is no denying his presence."

The only reason *they* had reached Amrochan so swiftly was because they'd been able to take the river. To approach along with the army that crossed between Chithal and Yithel meant Gadranus could not have used the same method of travel. Zaide scanned the same section of the map over and over again, trying to determine how such a trip could be made. He found nothing.

Resia paced around the table to position herself beside the forest in the southeast. Her fingers trailed over the unremarkable depiction of Kolmar. "How do we know it's him and not a fragment, like the wraith we saw in the temple?"

Sendassian snorted at the suggestion. "The man my scouts have seen is flesh and blood."

"That fragment was anchored to an object," Lark added. "A piece of the seal that once held him there. I doubt there would be any such fragment on our northern fields."

"But can those pieces be used for a seal again?" Zaide lowered his voice, but there was no avoiding having the others hear him.

The princess gave a helpless shrug.

"Let me be clear," the king said as he tapped a finger against the table, "I do not care about your superstitions. But I will use any advantage I can find in slaying my enemy. He now leads these beasts against us, but he will not be easy to reach. My daughter believes that you, her Bladebearer, have the skill necessary to strike him down. Is that true?" He pinned Zaide with a hard stare.

"I guess I won't know that until one of us is dead," Zaide replied.

"Then you are no longer needed. Leave me to speak with the Paragons in peace." Sendassian waved a hand at not only him, but at Lark.

She bristled, but spun on her heel to leave, and Zaide trailed hesitantly behind her.

Would she be angry at him? Would she shut him out again? He never knew what to expect and they walked a short way down the hall before he spoke.

"I guess I should be glad he didn't immediately throw me out, huh?" He said it light-heartedly, though not jokingly.

Lark scoffed, either way. "He knows who you are. He knows your role. He can pretend he doesn't remember you, but he's well aware it will be your hand that ends things."

Would it? Zaide swallowed. "The sword—"

"It can still kill a man, with or without its power. At this point, that's the best we can hope for." She stopped and turned to face him with sadness shading her endlessly blue eyes. "We're out of time, Zaide."

He'd hoped for anything different, but in the end, he'd known this was coming. He strode closer and rested his hands on her shoulders, hoping the touch might offer the comfort his words couldn't. "I know."

There would be no seal, no freedom, and no end.

CHAPTER THIRTY-FIVE

THE SPECTRUM BLADE fit perfectly in the iridescent scabbard Zaide wore at his belt. He traced the silver patterns with a fingertip before he met the princess's eyes. She was solemn, but not in the frigid way she had been.

"I'll do what I can," he promised, and hated he couldn't swear to do more. He didn't know what waited out there in the field, or how hard it would be to reach their enemy. None of this had come together in a way that was ideal. He gripped the hilt of the sword and hated how cold it was against his skin, but it was solid when everything else felt like sand slipping through his fingers.

"I couldn't ask for anything else." Lark tried to smile, but the effort put a tension in her shoulders. "And it doesn't have to be you. I think the soldiers want it to be you. They want to know there's an end to all this. But anyone can strike him down. If they do..."

"Then I'll come back." He hoped he would. They hadn't looked to see what they were up against, but he already had a rough idea. Finding Gadranus would be enough of a challenge. Never mind reaching him. The only benefit Zaide could imagine was that without the sword restored to full power and no hope of a seal being made, Gadranus would not expect a fight to the death. The advantage brought no comfort.

Lark looked as if she wanted to say something else, but they stood outside the throne room in the waiting chamber filled with benches—the best place for him to wait, she'd claimed—and a steady stream of people flowed through the space. Messengers with their hands full. Groups of guards and their commanding officers. Nobles were in short supply, but Zaide suspected most of them were off planning how to escape the city. They wouldn't be alone. Half the city would be preparing for evacuation, though he no longer knew where they were supposed to go. The army had come from the north; there was no guarantee there was still a way up the river.

While they stood in silence, the Paragons reappeared. All three of them were troubled, but Tula was more somber than Zaide had ever seen her.

Resia broke away from the group to approach them first. "I have permission to oversee the departure of the Kolmari. I'm the only one whose magic isn't of an offensive nature, so I shouldn't be needed yet. I'll be back soon."

"I'll be on the field by then," Zaide said. All that remained was outfitting himself with armor, and he did not suspect that would take long.

"I figured." Resia normally bore such a graceful serenity. Now, she seemed small and nervous as she twisted her fingers and curtsied to the princess. "I've been instructed to join you, Your Highness, once I'm done seeing off my people."

"And I'll be grateful to have you." Lark inclined her head, but no more than that. It wasn't as if they were strangers; the two of them had met and gotten along well, but now there was nothing but cold formality between them.

Better than being shut out entirely, Zaide decided.

Resia curtsied again before she excused herself.

"We were not given directions," Andriun said when he and

Tula lingered. "We are just expected to make a difference, somehow."

"Go with Zaide," Lark said.

"Stay with Lark," Zaide said at the same time.

Both paused.

Andriun nodded, as if he'd expected that outcome. "We will split up. One of us with each."

"All right." Zaide would have preferred if all three of the Paragons were at the princess's side, but he'd take what he could get. "You stay here, then. Your magic is better suited to defense, I think. Tula's is better for offense, so she'll come with me."

Neither looked pleased with the arrangement, but they took their places without complaint.

Zaide offered his most reassuring smile as Tula posted herself at his side. "We've got to go, now. Wish us luck."

"Good luck," Andriun said.

"And be careful," Lark added.

Zaide nodded in agreement, then headed for the door. It felt good to have the Spectrum Blade at his side again, but its profound silence rasped against the edges of his nerves. Tula trotted along behind him, but she kept looking back over her shoulder. Eventually, a soft sound of disappointment escaped her throat.

"What?" He tried not to sound short; it wasn't her fault they were in this situation.

"She didn't give you any favors," the Magister said softly.

"Any what?"

"Favors. You know, like a handkerchief or something. A lady is supposed to give her knight a favor when he goes off to combat. He's got to bring it back to her, so it's like a promise he'll stay safe."

It was such a sweet, storybook notion that Zaide couldn't help but crack a smile. "You think I'm her knight?"

"Well, aren't you?" Tula frowned. "Being a Bladebearer has to be close to being a knight, right?"

"Sure," Zaide agreed, though he was only humoring her. Knights were nobles and he was nobody, but if it brought a friend an ounce of peace, he wouldn't be the one to discourage her.

The armory wasn't far off, and Zaide selected leather armor for himself while Tula simply found more form-fitting clothing to wear on the battlefield. It was the best choice she could make; her billowy Jadoran garments would be too cumbersome, but she had no experience wearing armor.

He buckled himself into his gear while she twisted her ponytail into a bun and pinned it at the back of her head. It made him think of Lark and the hair fork he'd given her earlier, but instead of lending him warmth, it put a knot of dread in his middle. It was a gift he'd meant to be useful, but oh, how he prayed she wouldn't need to use it.

"Ready?" he asked when he had the last strap fastened.

Tula pumped an arm. "Not in the slightest."

"That's what I thought. Let's go." Zaide wiggled his fingers in his glove to seat it better as he led the way from the armory. "First, the Kolmari. I told Resia I'd help get them to the docks." By now, the guards meant to escort them should be waiting. It would have been nice to find them assisting the Kolmari in leaving their homes, but he was not surprised when they arrived and found the first carts just beginning to roll. His family was among them, and Daisy ran circles around the carts and people's legs.

"Resia?" Verlin asked.

"Waiting at the docks before she's to meet with the princess. Tula and I are headed for the battlefield." Zaide gripped one of the hand poles on the front of the cart to help pull. The Kolmari did not keep beasts of burden, and with the crush of soldiers pushing through the city, they would have been a burden themselves, anyway. He glanced at the load and paused for the briefest instance when he saw his shield waiting on top.

He set his thoughts on the task of moving things and people and tried not to worry about the battle that was to come.

~

Zaide had not stayed to see the ship depart. Every moment spent idle was one he worried about his family, his choices, and everything that waited ahead. As long as he stayed in motion, he would stay on his feet. He'd left Daisy at a guard house by the gates and regretted that he hadn't sent her to Kolmar, but it would have to be good enough. The battlefield was no place for a dog.

It was no place for *him*.

He sucked in a breath as he braced for the gates to open. The smoky air clogged his lungs and made him choke, but there was no escaping it. He would pass through the gates with the next wave of soldiers, Tula close at his heels, and the haze of smoke would be nothing but a backdrop for the pain and bloodshed that was to come.

Officers had tried to push them into formation or shoo them out of the way. Zaide had refused, and the moment he'd unsheathed the Spectrum Blade enough for its iridescence to be seen, they left him alone. He didn't understand the tactics they were using, didn't know Sendassian's plans, but he knew he was not a part of either.

"When that gate opens, stay right with me," Zaide said. "We need to cut as straight a path to Gadranus as we can."

Tula posted herself right by his side. "I'll do my best."

"That's all I'm asking." He checked his shield on his right arm, wishing he'd taken the time to ensure its straps were still solid before he'd departed his family's home that morning. It was too late to do anything now. He gripped his sword—if it *was* his sword—and drew the blade.

The moment he held it ready, the first gate opened and the order came.

Zaide sprang forward with the surge of men that poured beyond the city's walls.

The men fell into formation and pushed forward with shields. Zaide guessed the goal and joined them, pushing forward in an arc three soldiers deep until they began to swallow groups of soldiers retreating with injured men. There were far more of them than he'd anticipated, and when the front line reached the oncoming goborrins, he was more than ready to strike.

All the hours of practice in Nimultis made the Spectrum Blade light in his hand and Zaide tore into the first monster with all the ferocity he could muster. He parried its axe with his shield and drove the sword in to let it bite, desperately wishing to feel some of its magic at work.

The blade cut deep and he felt nothing but the force of impact.

He tore it free and stared in dismay at the muddy brown of monster blood that marred the blade's surface. It couldn't even purify itself now. How was he ever supposed to succeed at this?

A pair of goborrins came at him as if singling him out and he sidestepped the corpse of the one he'd just killed on his way to meet them. Before they so much as came close, flames burst within their armor and swallowed them whole.

"Keep moving!" Tula shouted behind him.

He had to. He couldn't let himself be distracted. He was with the army, but he wasn't one of them, and when he leaped forward to break away from the arc, someone was fast to fill the gap.

Zaide scanned the battlefield for the enemy's standard, but the ugly ram's skull with the four-pointed star on its forehead was everywhere. He pushed onward, ducking past clusters of combat, and Tula's magic cleared the way.

"I don't see any broken-born!" Tula cried.

"He has black hair," he shouted over the din. A goborrin slipped past her fire and he cut through it with practiced ease.

They'd been hard to kill, once. Had his skill improved that much, or was the sword still his primary advantage?

"*Black* hair?" Tula repeated.

He should have explained what they were looking for sooner. He didn't have time to deal with her surprise.

Nor did he have time to grapple with the sheer size of the army they faced.

He'd seen the encampments outside Amrochan before, both on foot and on dragon back. Their numbers had been terrifying then. Now, they seemed insurmountable, with formations and camps of goborrins stretching on toward the horizon and farther than the eye could see. The army they'd seen had not been even a fraction of this. There was no way they'd all come from the north.

There was no way they were going to stop this, Zaide realized with a pang of dismay.

Even if Gadranus fell, even if he succeeded in stalling the man's efforts by forcing him to be reborn again, there was no hope to best that many monsters. The goborrins outside Amrochan were there to destroy, to shred the last threads of hope that strung the Allied Kingdoms together, and even the death of their king would not stop what had already been set in motion.

"But you still have to try," he told himself through gritted teeth as he ducked around a skirmish and ran farther into the enemy swarm. A lone soldier running across the battlefield wasn't noteworthy and most of the goborrins ignored him. Only now and then did one come at him with a weapon ready, and each time, Tula's fire obliterated them before he so much as raised his sword.

Just when he'd begun to wonder if he'd gone the wrong direction, the fleshy-pink sea of goborrins split to reveal a column of the monsters in polished armor, and in the middle of their procession rode a dark figure on a pale gray horse.

Of course he had a horse. Zaide set his jaw and posted

himself squarely in the column's path, his eyes fixed on Gadranus. He'd never fought anyone on horseback before and didn't want to hurt the animal, but what choices did he have? He readied his sword and braced for impact. "Cover me," he shouted. He didn't know where Tula was or if she heard him, but he had to trust she did.

The steel-armored goborrins saw him and raised their weapons.

He had no hope of facing them all, but he stood firm.

Flames erupted beneath the goborrins, sending up howls of surprise and pain. Spouts of fire pushed them back, forcing the column to split until there was nothing between Zaide and the man on the horse.

"I don't think that was cover, but I hope it helps," Tula called.

Zaide sprinted forward and before he reached the horse, fire sparked to life right in front of its face. The horse whinnied and spooked, and the moment it turned, a new pillar of flame burst from the ground. It reared and Zaide thought Gadranus might be unseated, but he pulled the reins hard and dragged the horse back around until he could meet Zaide's eye.

A tight, strained smile twisted his face. "There are more graceful ways to ask for parley, boy." His voice boomed over the roar of combat, louder even than the bellows of goborrins.

"Wasn't asking to talk," Zaide shouted back. He tilted his sword and wished there was sunlight to reflect off the blade.

Gadranus stared at it, all the same, calm and neutral. His gaze traveled toward the castle and back again. Then, at last, he swung off his horse's back. "This is not how we're destined to meet, Zaide. The time for this battle has not yet come."

"Then you shouldn't be afraid to fight me."

A deep, harsh laugh escaped the tall man's throat. "Bold words, boy. But I fear nothing." His hand curled around the hilt of the longsword at his side and the blade gave a long, slow hiss as he drew it from its sheath.

Zaide tensed and checked his footing, braced for the first

attack, but it did not come. Instead, Gadranus adjusted his grip on the two-handed sword and shifted sideways, circling slowly.

Flames rose around them, clearing the area of goborrins, giving them space to move. The heat washed over Zaide in waves. Sweat beaded on his forehead and trickled down his back, but he circled, too.

"Is that what you were dreaming of when you came to see me?" Gadranus smirked, but his pale eyes sharpened. "What you've carried with you since your father's death? A chance for vengeance? Justice?"

Words were a waste of breath. Zaide stayed focused on his footing, the distance between them, the angle of his enemy's blade.

But Gadranus did nothing. He circled endlessly, every step tight and controlled.

They could not circle forever.

Zaide lunged instead of taking another step to the side, driving the Spectrum Blade's point toward his adversary's chest.

Gadranus parried and the single note of the steel rang high and sweet before he swung into a practiced retaliation. His sword swept high on the first swing, then low, slicing for Zaide's head and legs in turn, but he was light on his feet and his leather armor suited him well, and neither blow connected. Zaide sprang backwards, slipping just beyond his enemy's reach before Gadranus twisted his wrist and brought his blade up into the empty space where Zaide had just been.

"You're good at reading your enemies," Gadranus conceded.

Instead of replying, Zaide leaped forward and brought the Spectrum Blade down in a hard overhead arc.

The taller man twisted his sword to intercept the strike and the steel gave a long, strident shriek before the blades came to a halt. His sword was darkened steel, nearly twice as long as the Spectrum Blade, yet as Zaide bore down on his smaller weapon, it dug into the edge of the longsword without so much as suffering a scratch.

Gadranus shifted until he was the one who pressed, and he loomed over Zaide like a shadow. "It still bears no light."

"Feel free to give it back," Zaide snarled through clenched teeth.

"It's not mine to give. Not when all the necessary power rests in your hands. I've done my part." Gadranus's eyes narrowed. "You've fallen short of yours."

Zaide spun back and brought his blade around for a hard strike. It bounced off his enemy's weapon, but the Spectrum Blade was light and he recovered swiftly, using the motion to launch a flurry of attacks.

Surprise touched his enemy's eyes. Gadranus stepped back as he parried blow after blow, then retreated another step. Fire rose higher at his back, begging Zaide to push him into it.

He gritted his teeth and thrust high. Gadranus swung to parry a moment too late, and the Spectrum Blade raked across his cheek. A sharp line of crimson bloomed in its wake, and Zaide leaped back, expecting retaliation.

Instead, Gadranus laughed and raised a hand to his face. "Impressive. You've gathered remarkable skill for a boy your age. Your father would be most proud of you. But I grow weary of playing." His expression darkened and he swiped the trickle of blood from his cheek.

Zaide leaped forward with a roar and drove the Spectrum Blade for his stomach.

The blade plunged straight through and Gadranus exploded in a burst of smoke.

Zaide stumbled at the lack of resistance, shock and panic twisting up inside him as the black plumes dissipated into nothing, so much like the wraith he'd fought before that he thought he'd be sick.

He'd been there. He'd been real. Zaide *knew* he'd been real. A ruby bead of blood decorated the Spectrum Blade's edge.

He spun in place, scanning the area behind him, expecting a strike from elsewhere.

The ring of fire that had surrounded them dropped and there was no smoke. No shadow. No sign of his opponent.

Zaide could have screamed. The field around him was empty and no matter which way he turned, there was nothing.

Tula sprinted forward, worry pinching her face. "What happened?" she cried.

"I don't know!" Zaide swiped his forehead with his forearm and turned around again. He opened his mouth to speak, but his eyes traveled past Tula and toward the castle as a deep sense of dread lodged itself in his guts.

Gadranus was gone, and there was only one place he could be headed.

CHAPTER THIRTY-SIX

ZAIDE RAN until he couldn't fight the smoke anymore. He slowed to a stop as the first coughs racked his body. He leaned forward to rest his hands against his thighs. He'd sheathed the Spectrum Blade to let him run faster, but his shield was still on his right arm, and leaning forward with it was awkward.

Tula gagged and choked, too. She waved a hand in front of her face and her nose crinkled. "Still can't control smoke," she wheezed.

He hadn't realized she'd tried. Had he been able to breathe, he might have tried to reassure her, but sucking in another lungful of air only made him start coughing again. Tears streamed down his face and his nose ran, and still he couldn't get a good breath. But the city walls were just ahead, and he could not let himself stop.

Step by step, he staggered to the gate. He fell against the portcullis and gripped it with both hands. "Open," he choked, the rest of the words catching in his throat. He hammered his chest with a fist, as if that might knock them loose.

"Battle's the other way," the gate guard on the other side snarled.

"No." Zaide coughed twice more before he sucked in enough

of a breath to speak with. "Gadranus is coming. Have to warn the princess."

"Of course he's coming. That's why you're out there!" The guard rolled his eyes broadly and trudged out of view.

Zaide gritted his teeth and slammed his hands against the iron bars, but the gate was so large it did nothing at all. He tilted his head back to scan the gate and the surrounding walls, but there was no other way back into the city. His hands tightened against the grille.

To his side, more hands gripped the bars. He turned his head to ask for help and froze. Beside him, goborrins looked back, their ugly faces split in some facsimile of a smile.

Shouts rose within the city as more goborrins seized the gate and heaved.

Panic twisted Zaide's stomach and he dug in his heels, pulling down as the monsters pushed up, but he was small beside them and harsh, squealing laughter tore from the beasts as the portcullis began to rise. He dragged down with everything he had, but there were dozens of the creatures, and his toes soon skimmed the earth. It shouldn't have risen at all. Weren't there locks meant to keep it from lifting?

His grip gave out and he fell from the bars, his boots kicking up dust when he landed.

Again, the goborrins shrieked with laughter, and a deep voice joined them from the other side of the gate.

Zaide's hand went for his sword before he even stood up.

"Your courage is by far your greatest strength," Gadranus remarked as he strolled out from the gate house.

That explained the locks. Zaide glared at him, dropped to his knees, and scrambled under the gate as the goborrins heaved it ever higher. He all but leaped back to his feet and the Spectrum Blade sang free of its sheath, but the man in black was already gone.

He scrambled around the corner to the gate house to find the locks, to reengage them so the gate would seize and the goborrins would be trapped outside. He skidded to a stop as someone else tried to swing through the door at the same time.

"Zaide!" Aren exclaimed.

"The gate," Zaide responded.

"Get to the castle," his friend said before he could offer to help. "I'll try to lock it, you go warn the king!"

Zaide nodded back and spun toward the palace, but he'd only gone a few steps before new warning bugles sounded, accompanied by the triumphant roars of monsters behind him.

Locking the gate would do nothing now.

Amrochan had been breached.

The parlor was so quiet, Lark heard the soft rustle of fabric each time she twisted her hands. It was such a tiny movement, it was a wonder that it stirred her skirts at all. Or maybe she was more restless than she realized, and it wasn't just her wringing her hands. She shifted her weight from one foot to the other, wishing there was something to see beyond the tall glass windows.

"Do you think we'll know? If it happens?" Somehow, she couldn't bring herself to say *when*. She believed in Zaide's abilities, wholly and unwaveringly, but she knew so little of their enemy. She didn't even know if Zaide would find him out there on the battlefield. So many leaders issued orders from sheltered tents, rather than the battlefield itself. What sort of leader was Gadranus, she wondered?

Andriun glanced toward the window and a distant look took his eyes. Was he thinking, or was he trying to sense something beyond the parlor's walls? A long, tense moment drew past before he returned his attention to the trident in his hands. "I do not know," he concluded. He ran a whetstone over the trident's tines, something Lark suspected was unnecessary, given its apparent magical nature, but she did not know for certain. Maybe it was worn down. Or maybe the action simply gave him some comfort, letting him believe he was doing something to be prepared.

Lark rubbed her knuckles and breathed. Worrying did nothing. She tried not to worry.

Yet the moment she told herself she wouldn't concern herself with the things happening outside the palace that she could not control, a streak of color in the courtyard below caught her eye. Green garments billowed behind a running figure as it crossed the empty courtyard, and the moment it vanished from sight, a sense of ill ease settled in the pit of her stomach.

"Something is wrong," Lark murmured as she pulled away from the window and hurried for the door. That had been Resia, and she had not come from the direction of the docks.

Andriun was on his feet and after her before she reached the hallway. He said nothing, but posted himself close at her heels with his trident in hand. He was normally so calm. That his stride matched the urgency of hers made her stomach go topsy-turvy.

They were not slow, but Resia still intercepted them in the hallway, her dark eyes wide with fright. "Goborrins," she gasped. "They're in the city!"

Now Lark's stomach churned instead of just rolling over. "Where? Have the guards sent you?"

The Elder shook her head hard enough to make her brown hair bounce about her pointed ears. "I saw them. In the streets. I came as fast as I could. The guards have already secured the palace gates."

Lark gave a stiff nod. "My father has returned to the throne. We must tell him, then we must find out the plans for evacuation of Amrochan." A few goborrins having made it past the city's defenses did not necessarily mean evacuation, but it was better to be prepared.

She marched the two Paragons back to the waiting room it seemed they'd only just departed from. It was just as empty as it had been the moment they'd seen Zaide off, and in the still, the doors that led to the throne room seemed more imposing than ever.

Lark had intended to knock, but one of the doors was already ajar, and the throne room silent on the other side. She thrust the door open wide and let herself in.

Her father sat on his throne, as she'd expected. Sendassian sat straight the moment he saw her, his frustration at the disruption palpable.

She ignored it. "The Kolmari Elder brings news," she announced. Normally, officers and soldiers would be clustered around her father's throne. At the very least, General Jobe and Admiral Warinal would be there, offering counsel and arguing with each other. Where had they gone, and why had her father been sitting there alone?

She gave her head a twitch. It didn't matter. The news did. "Goborrins have breached the city walls. The Elder has seen them in the streets herself." Thoughts of Jadora flashed through Lark's head as she spoke and she frowned. Had Elsanna's guardswomen ever determined how the goborrins got into the city? They'd assumed it was the tunnels, and that notion put an uncomfortable itch between her shoulder blades. What was stopping those monsters from breaching Amrochan the same way?

"Impossible," Sendassian snapped as the three of them drew near to the throne. "I've heard no alarms. No warnings. If Amrochan had been breached, a report would have reached my throne far sooner than some mage."

"Ah, but it's true," an unfamiliar voice put in from the doorway.

Lark spun in time to see the man in dark armor slip inside and close the door behind him. He offered a tight-lipped smile and pressed a gauntlet to his breastplate as he bowed his head just enough to be respectful. It was not the deference one offered a king, but a greeting one might expect from a friend.

Slowly, Sendassian rose from his throne. "I warned you never to set foot in my palace again."

"Yet here I am," Gadranus replied smugly.

A shiver rolled down Lark's spine and she stepped sideways, removing herself from the walkway and clearing the way between her father and the dark-haired man who strode toward him. The Paragons moved with her, though Andriun stood a step before her now, his trident held ready to strike.

Gadranus did not so much as look their way as he closed the distance between himself and the king. "I had hoped to make the announcement myself, but I suppose I can't be too offended that your daughter beat me to it." His smile grew tight again. "Amrochan's gates have been breached, although admittedly by few of your enemies. But you... You have the chance to ensure it stays that way, don't you?"

The simple suggestion of the offer that had once been made sent a wave of cold racing to the tips of Lark's ears. She backed farther away.

The last confrontation wasn't supposed to be like this. Fear poured through her, sharp and bitter, until her skin rose in gooseflesh and she trembled.

Was this it? The moment fate foretold? She thought of the eclipse, of the red sky that had all but blotted out her hope, of the shining blade that had restored the thinnest sliver.

The sword was not here. Neither was its bearer. Yet the man he'd gone to kill walked toward the throne. Fear tightened her throat until she couldn't breathe.

Sendassian's lip curled. "You dare ask again for an answer you've already received?"

"I would ask you to consider you are being given one last chance," Gadranus replied. "When last we met, I promised you time to think. The time has come, Sendassian. You may choose to bow to me or I can force you, but the outcome is the same. You will bow to me, and your crown will be mine."

"Not while I draw breath," the king snarled.

Gadranus chuckled softly. "As you wish." His hand closed on the hilt of the longsword at his side and the metal sang as it pulled free of its sheath.

The king, too, drew a blade.

Lark reached for her knives out of instinct. All her hands found was the full skirt of her ugly dress.

A hand grasped her arm and pulled it back, all the same, as if to prevent her from drawing a weapon. "We must go, now," Andriun breathed beside her ear.

"We can't leave him," she gasped back.

"We have to," Resia said at her other side. "Don't you see? You're next."

Lark knew she was. The same choice had already been posed to her once, secondhand, and her decision had already been made. She set her jaw and twirled toward the door. She needed her knives. She stood no chance unarmed. "My rooms. Upstairs."

Resia nodded and drew her toward the door while Andriun took up the rear.

They had almost reached the door when thick curls of black smoke swelled before them. "Going somewhere, Princess?" The voice came from everywhere and nowhere.

Lark's heart skipped and she spun back in time to see her father's sword pierce nothing but shadow. A low, harsh laugh rose around them as the smoke began to resolve into the outline of a man.

The doors banged open, scattering the shadow.

"Zaide!" Lark cried. She would have thrown her arms around him if Resia hadn't still been holding her.

He met her eye as he gasped for breath, but only for a second. The next instant, the Spectrum Blade was in his hand and he shoved his way past her and the Paragons. "Andriun, right," he managed between breaths.

The Paragon of Water broke away from Lark's side as the smoke collected anew in the center of the room and took shape again.

Zaide closed in from the left while Andriun moved in on him from the right, and her father descended from the throne with his sword ready.

"No spirit of fairness, I see," Gadranus said as his body solidified.

"Fairness would be you staying in one place instead of turning to smoke like a coward," Zaide fired back.

The complaint sparked an idea and Lark grabbed the bag of artifacts that still hung at her side.

"We should go now," Resia whispered.

"No. We can help them. We can stop this." The Hymnflute was at the top. If she could use its wind to disrupt his form whenever he turned to smoke...

"Take this as a lesson, then. In warfare, there is no fairness." Gadranus burst into smoke again. Before Lark could raise the Hymnflute to her lips, he materialized behind Zaide's back and dove in with a hard sweep of his sword.

Zaide heard it coming and ducked low. The sword passed over his head as he twirled and lunged in with the Spectrum Blade, but his adversary dissolved again and struck at Andriun a second later.

The Shaman snagged the blow with the fork of his trident and twisted hard to drive it downward.

Sendassian sprang forward with a stab toward the black-armored man's back, yet again, his form fell away in waves of smoke before contact could be made.

Blowing him in any direction wouldn't be helpful, Lark decided. What she needed to do was hold him in one place. Was it possible to project the Hymnflute's barrier out away from the artifact? She didn't know, but she raised the pipes and tried anyway. The sharp, clear notes stirred the air around them, but the shield that formed surrounded her and Resia, and no amount of variation pushed the barrier outward.

"What are you trying to do?" Resia asked at her side, ready to help.

Lark let the shield fall. "We have to trap him, hold him somehow."

The Elder nodded and snatched the Hymnflute from her hand. The melody she played was strange, different, and wind gusted from the edges of the throne room to rush toward Gadranus. It caught him mid-swing and dragged him back a step before the barrier formed.

Zaide lunged forward, fully expecting the Spectrum Blade to pierce the shield, the way it had when they'd been on the inside and he'd fought through the field of goborrins just beyond the city walls. Instead, it bounced back hard and he lost his footing.

Gadranus barked a laugh, but his sword struck the shield and bounced back, too. His amusement faded, replaced with a bitter sneer. "You can't hope to hold me in here forever."

In reply, Sendassian roared and brought his sword around in a hard sideways sweep.

Resia stalled the song just long enough for the shield to fall. The sword passed through its remnants and smashed against smoke again.

A howl of frustration went up from the king as Gadranus surged forward with a kick that took Sendassian in the stomach. He collapsed with a wheeze.

Andriun sprang in to intercept their adversary's sword the moment it forged itself from the shadows. He caught it mid-swing and rammed it into the floor beside the king.

"Lark, the artifacts!" Zaide shouted.

She almost asked what he meant. Then a memory of a fight too much like this sprang to the forefront of her mind, and she gasped as she dug the Molten Dagger from her bag. The Captured Spring still hung around her neck. Both glowed, awakened by some force she didn't understand. Their power had been enough to freeze the apparition of Gadranus they'd faced before. Would it work now?

Resia glanced at the other artifacts and nodded.

Lark raised the dagger overhead and willed it to work. Waves of heat fell over her and light streaked out from the dagger to strike Gadranus in the chest. He staggered back with a cry. Light shot from the Hymnflute next and her heart leaped.

They were doing it.

It was working.

She seized the Captured Spring in her other hand and willed its power to answer. Light swelled in the tiny vial at the same time the dagger's light faltered, and panic lanced to her core. She could only use one. Maker's mercy, where was Tula when she needed her? "Andriun!"

The Shaman's head snapped up and he shoved his trident hard. Instead of the tines twisting the blade out of his adversary's hand, the sword melted into shadow. Andriun spat a curse but leaped aside to come to the princess's aid.

Smoke curled around his ankle and sent him crashing to the floor instead.

"Lark!" Zaide shouted again. He stabbed, but Gadranus had his sword again, somehow, and deflected the blow.

She gritted her teeth and flung the dagger at the floor. It skated along the stone and spun to a stop near the Shaman as she seized the Captured Spring around her neck. Its light surged forward and struck Gadranus, even as a plume of smoke snapped the Molten Dagger out of Andriun's reach. The Shaman strained after it, but the shadow around his leg tightened and dragged him farther back.

Resia shrieked as another tendril of shadow tore her feet out from under her. She fell hard and it dragged her across the floor, leaving the Hymnflute behind.

Only the Captured Spring's light remained, and Gadranus was already rising.

At the same time, Gadranus twisted his sword, and the Captured Spring's light bounced off the blade.

Lark yelped as it struck her eyes. Dizziness exploded

between her temples and she staggered a step as the spring dropped on its chain and its light faded.

Zaide raised the Spectrum Blade for a downward strike while their opponent was distracted, but no more did his muscles tense to deal the blow than he froze.

"Now, Zaide!" Lark screamed. "Kill him now!" She couldn't see, a single, searing point of white blotting out her vision.

Yet Zaide did not move, as still as if made of stone. The blinding white in her vision blurred his features and she struggled to make him out. "Zaide!"

"Move!" Andriun shouted. He clawed at his leg, but the coil of darkness that held him would not let him free. "Go, Princess, run!"

Lark took a half step backwards, shaking her head.

Resia gasped and struggled against her own shadows, and one had twisted around Sendassian's body to hold him to the floor.

Slowly, Gadranus pushed himself to his feet, a low chuckle welling in his throat. "A valiant effort, Your Highness, but as you can see, I am not yet out of tricks."

Lark stumbled back another step before something cold as ice slithered up her leg. She shrieked, but it curled tight and locked her in place.

"I have not fought this long and come this close to be defeated now." Gadranus paced toward her, his sword still in his hand, shadows dripping like poison from its edge. "But I am not without mercy, so I give you one more chance, Princess. A chance to succeed where all others have failed."

A chill shook her whole body as he loomed over her, his eyes as cold and emotionless as stone. She tried to move, but her arms remained stuck at her sides as surely as if she'd been bound.

"Surrender," Gadranus said, the single word a command as smooth as silk. "Bow to me, recognize me as king, and all of this will be over."

"Never," Lark snapped.

His frigid blue eyes bored into her until she swore they could cut and a slow, mirthless smile drew at the corners of his mouth. He raised a hand and reached for her throat.

Had her legs been free, her knees would have collapsed beneath her.

But he did not touch her skin, did not wrap his fingers around her neck and try to choke the life out of her. Instead, he snared the chain of the Captured Spring and gave a single, sharp tug. The chain snapped and he weighed the vial in his hand. "I suspected you'd say that. Just remember, Princess. This..." He turned and gestured to the Paragons, her Bladebearer, and her father, all of them trapped in coils of shadow. "All of this is your choice, and there is no going back."

Lark's eyes widened as he raised the Captured Spring before her face and curled his gauntleted fingers against the tiny vial.

The tendrils of shadow that gripped her father coiled around his throat and dragged him up onto his knees, and her heartbeat roared in her ears.

Gadranus gave her a wicked grin as his hand tightened and the finest cracks split across the vial's surface. "Congratulations," he whispered. "Your Majesty."

The Captured Spring shattered as the shadows that held Zaide exploded, and the Spectrum Blade drove into the king's back.

Lightning lanced up Zaide's arms from the Spectrum Blade's hilt, tearing a scream from his throat as a sharp, soundless shriek filled Lark's head.

A long, agonized keening ripped free of her as visions of the eclipse's promise and the Oracle's threat laced her mind. She collapsed onto her knees as Gadranus cast the shattered pieces of the vial to the ground and shook the last traces of its remedy from his hand.

"Your choice," Gadranus repeated as he seized Zaide by the throat and dragged him backwards. The Spectrum Blade clattered to the floor and Zaide went limp the moment it left his grasp.

"No!" Lark screamed. She scrambled forward until she found her feet, then she ran. She leaped her father's crumpled form and seized the Spectrum Blade from the floor. The pain of a thousand needles shot up her arms and stole her breath, but she pulled back as if to swing at the monster ahead of her anyway.

Andriun's arm snared her around the waist and dragged her toward the door. "Go!" he shouted.

It took a moment to realize he wasn't speaking to her.

Resia swiped the Molten Dagger and the Hymnflute from the floor as she ran and a low, cruel laugh swelled behind them.

Lark gritted her teeth and fought, but Andriun was too strong. He swept her off her feet and slung her over his shoulder. It was all she could do to hold on to the Spectrum Blade as it tried to reject her touch, sizzling heat spiderwebbing up her arm in crooked patterns of light. She lifted her head in time to see Gadranus drop into her father's throne with Zaide's body limp at his feet, then tears flooded her eyes and she saw no more.

A sharp note pierced the air as Resia spun the Hymnflute's barrier around them. Shadows struck the barrier from every side, chasing them into the hall, but the Elder held fast as they retreated.

"We have to find Tula," Andriun shouted.

"Zaide," Lark wailed. His name rose in her chest and she heaved a sob as it escaped, but the Shaman did not release her, and her tears did not abate.

They reached the castle's main doors as they burst open and goborrins poured in, but the barrier held fast and the Paragons pushed through the swarm. Just beyond the palace gates, fireballs arced into the sky.

"There," Andriun said. "Hold fast, Your Highness. We will get to the ships. Then we will be free."

Lark watched as fireballs streaked past the walls to land in the middle of the goborrin hordes that flooded the palace—the only home she'd ever known. No matter how many rained down, it made no difference, and as she watched Amrochan's empty palace shrink away behind her, a new and painful truth settled among the shards of her breaking heart. Her father was gone and the crown was hers.

She lowered her head, set her jaw, and clung to the Spectrum Blade until her arm went numb.

She would never be free again.

GLOSSARY

Addare – (uh-dare) – An oasis city on the western coast of Amroch.

Amroch – (AM-roke) – The Allied Kingdoms ruled by King Sendassian. Originally a number of smaller kingdoms, unified as an empire for defense purposes.

Amrochan – (am-ROW-kan) – The capital city of Amroch.

Andriun – (AN-dree-un) – The Desheni Shaman's son.

Aren – A soldier stationed at the garrison outside Kolmar. Friend of Zaide and Resia.

Arkosh – A well-respected Master Librarian and one of Tula's mentors.

Athradan – The Desheni Shaman and the Paragon of Water. Leader of the Desheni people.

Beshnai – (besh-NIGH) – An isolated city on the northern coast of Amroch.

Broken-born – People born in the western kingdoms destroyed by Gadranus. Many seek refuge in Amroch, but face difficulty integrating due to their history in the war.

Bugrak – (BUG-rack) – Small, flat-faced and ugly gray creatures. Hunt in packs and use primitive weapons.

Captured Spring – One of the three artifacts. A vial that contains a self-replenishing healing tonic.

Chithal – (chee-thal) – A large port city and trade hub

Daisy – Zaide's dog.

Dasienna – (das-EE-en-uh) – The princess. King Sendassian's daughter.

Desheni – (duh-SHEN-nee) – A settlement named after the race of aquatic people who live there. The Desheni people bear blue-tinged skin, fin-like ears, webbed fingers, and gills on their necks.

Elder – Kolmar's chief overseer and most skilled mage. Zaide and Resia's mentor. Also known as the Paragon of Forest.

Elsanna – (el-san-nuh) – Chief of the Magister's guardswomen.

Estkel – (est-KELL) – A marshy city at the edge of the Ellean Sea.

Gadranus – (guh-DRA-nuss) – Breaker of the Shattered Lands, leader of the army that threatens to destroy Amroch. According to legend, he has been cursed to be reborn a thousand times as a punishment for his misdeeds.

Ganede – (gan-NEED) – Jadora's sister city. A port of trade on one of the peninsulas that frame the Ellean Sea.

Goborrin – (guh-BOR-rin) – Bipedal man-like monsters with pig-like faces and tusks. The smallest of the goborrins are the size of an adult man.

Ikan – A high-ranking Desheni hunter and a relative of Andriun.

Jadora – (jah-DOR-ah) – Ganede's sister city. Referred to as The Watcher. A fortress atop a desert plateau.

Kolmar – (coal-mar) – A small forest village in the southwestern region of Amroch.

Lark – The name Dasienna uses while traveling to protect her identity.

Magister – The leader of the fortress city of Jadora. Also known as the Paragon of Fire.

Molten Dagger – One of the three artifacts. An obsidian dagger that appears to have veins of magma trapped within it. Contains fire magic.

Moros – The warden of Jadora's prison and Elsanna's sweetheart.

Murk – A soldier from the garrison outside Kolmar.

Oroduna – The Oracle of Nimultis, blessed with visions of the future.

Paragons – Leaders entrusted with the protection of the three magic artifacts.

Parral – (puh-rawl) – A port city at the southernmost tip of Amroch.

Plain – A soldier from the garrison outside Kolmar.

Raddan – A lieutenant and medic in Amroch's army. Stationed at the garrison outside Kolmar.

Resia – (ree-see-uh) – Zaide's foster sister and the new Elder. Bears a strong magical bond with the forest and wields earth magic.

Salamander – Bipedal lizard-like creatures found in Jadora's caverns. They attack anyone they deem an intruder.

Sarma – Resia's mother and Zaide's foster mother.

Sast – A fortress outpost on an island in the Ellean sea. Unfriendly to visitors. Little is known about the city.

Sendassian – (sin-das-see-an) – King of Amroch.

Shaman – The leader of the Desheni. Entrusted with the protection of the Captured Spring.

Shattered Lands – The western kingdoms destroyed by Gadranus.

Spectrum Blade – The fourth artifact. A legendary weapon said to be the only thing that can strike down the cursed knight Gadranus.

Tinith – (ten-nith) – A marketplace large enough to be its own city.

Tula – (too-lah) – An apprentice librarian at the Great Library in Jadora. Fancies herself an archaeologist and adventurer.

Vale Hymnflute – One of the three artifacts. A set of wooden pan pipes that serves as anchor for Kolmar's Vale magic. It bears power over earth and wind.

Vale magic – A spiritual shield that lays over Kolmar's valley and protects the forest from evil.

Valla – (vah-lah) – A high-ranking Jadoran guardswoman. One of Elsanna's most trusted soldiers.

Verlin – Resia's father and Zaide's foster father.

Vorkaris – The Magister who sealed away the Molten Dagger. Also known as the Dragonster, according to Zaide.

Yithel – (yee-THEL) – A trade city along the river north of Amrochan.

Zaide – (zayd) – A broken-born refugee fostered in Kolmar after his mother's death. Accidentally involved in helping the princess recover the artifacts and saving Amroch.